Worldwide Praise for the Erotica
of STARbooks Press and John Patrick!

"'Barely Legal' is a great potpourri...
and the coverboy is gorgeous!"
- Ian Young, Torso magazine

"A huge collection of highly erotic, short and steamy one-
handed tales. Perfect bedtime reading, though you probably
won't get much sleep! Prepare to be shocked!
Highly recommended!"
- Vulcan magazine

And about our other books:

"'My Three Boys' is a new title in this hotter-than-hot series..."
- Walter Vatter, editor, A Different Light Review

"Tantalizing tales of porn stars, hustlers, and other
lost boys...John Patrick set the pace with 'Angel!'"
- The Weekly News, Miami

"...Some readers may find some of the scenes too explicit;
others will enjoy the sudden, graphic sensations each page brings.
Each of these romans á clef is written with sustained intensity.
'Angel' offers a strange, often poetic vision of sexual obsession.
I recommend it to you."
- Nouveau Midwest

"Self-absorbed, sexually-addicted bombshell Stacy flounced onto
the scene in 'Angel' and here he is again, engaged in further,
distinctly 'non-literary' adventures...lots of action!"
- Prinz Eisenherz Book Review, Germany

"God bless John Patrick for putting so many fine tales, including his
own, into these volumes. You consistently produce not only good
writing but good plots."
- N.S., California

DON'T ASK. DON'T TELL.
JUST ENJOY.

Barely LEGAL

A New Collection of
Erotic Tales
Edited By
JOHN PATRICK

Plus Two Complete Novels
The Young and the Flawless
And
The Boys of Paradise

STARbooks Press
Sarasota, FL

Books by John Patrick

Non-Fiction:
A Charmed Life: Vince Cobretti
Lowe Down: Tim Lowe
The Best of the Superstars 1990
The Best of the Superstars 1991
The Best of the Superstars 1992
The Best of the Superstars 1993
The Best of the Superstars 1994
The Best of the Superstars 1995
The Best of the Superstars 1996
The Best of the Superstars 1997
The Best of the Superstars 1998
The Best of the Superstars 1999
The Best of the Superstars 2000
The Best of the Superstars 2001
What Went Wrong?
When Boys Are Bad
& Sex Goes Wrong
Legends: The World's Sexiest
Men, Vols. 1 & 2
Legends (Third Edition)
Tarnished Angels (Ed.)

Fiction
Billy & David: A Deadly Minuet
The Bigger They Are...
The Younger They Are...
The Harder They Are...
Angel: The Complete Trilogy
Angel II: Stacy's Story
Angel: The Complete Quintet
A Natural Beauty (Editor)
The Kid (with Joe Leslie)
HUGE (Editor)
Strip: He Danced Alone

Fiction (Continued)
The Boys of Spring
Big Boys/Little Lies (Editor)
Boy Toy
Seduced (Editor)
Insatiable/Unforgettable (Editor)
Heartthrobs
Runaways/Kid Stuff (Editor)
Dangerous Boys/Rent Boys
(Editor)
Barely Legal (Editor)
Country Boys/City Boys (Editor)
My Three Boys (Editor)
Mad About the Boys (Editor)
Lover Boys (Editor)
In the BOY ZONE (Editor)
Boys of the Night (Editor)
Secret Passions (Editor)
Beautiful Boys (Editor)
Juniors (Editor)
Come Again (Editor)
Smooth 'N' Sassy (Editor)
Intimate Strangers (Editor)
Naughty By Nature (Editor)
Dreamboys (Editor)
Raw Recruits (Editor)
Play Hard, Score Big (Editor)
Sweet Temptations (Editor)
Pleasures of the Flesh (Editor)
Juniors 2 (Editor)
Fresh 'N' Frisky (Editor)
Taboo! (Editor)
Heatwave (Editor)
Boys on the Prowl (Editor)
Huge 2 (Editor)
Fever! (Editor)
Any Boy Can (Editor)
Virgins No More (Editor)

First Edition Published in the U.S. in April, 1995
Second Edition Published in the U.S. in July, 1995
Third Edition Published in the U.S. in December, 1995
Fourth Edition Published in the U.S. in May, 1996
Fifth Edition Published in the U.S. in January, 1997
Sixth Edition Published in the U.S. in January, 1998
Seventh Edition Published in U.S. in January, 1999
Eighth Edition Published in U.S. in July, 2001
Library of Congress Card Catalogue No. 95-068064
ISBN No. 1-877978-71-X

Contents

Editor's Note

Most of the stories appearing in this book take place prior to the years of The Plague; the editor and each of the authors represented herein advocate the practice of safe sex at all times.

And, because these stories trespass the boundaries of fiction and non-fiction, to respect the privacy of those involved, we've changed all of the names and other identifying details.

INTRODUCTION:
A CORRUPTION OF INNOCENCE

John Patrick

*"Do not lie down (have sex) with a man, as (if) a woman.
It is idol worship."*
- Leviticus 17:22

What constitutes a minor in the United States does not constitute a minor in most of Europe or the rest of the world. What in this country could fetch somebody a 15-year term in the slammer would provoke only a wink from another observing adult in Denmark, Sweden, and Holland, where the age of consent is as low as 14.

"Today," STARbooks contributor and Philadelphia-based columnist Thom Nickels observes, "most teenagers (say 16 or over) are anything *but* innocent. They have already been what the Religious Right would call 'corrupted' by their peers, by TV, films, or life in the city, or life in general. Many talk openly of screwing their lovers and a good portion still experiment with drugs. In other words, they have run the gamut."

Nickels says his "corruption" began early on: "When I was ten, my brother and I were 'experimented' on by a female baby-sitter who lingered too long in our bedroom after she put us to bed. I can still see her now: her enormous beehive hairdo; her passion for rock 'n' roll; and her laughter as she asked us to do all sorts of 'tricks' with our immature penises, all the while rapidly smacking her gum.

"Of course, at the time, I sensed she was being 'bad.' But since she spent most of her time laughing about what she was doing, the activity seemed like 'playing doctor' – only with a half-grownup. But the fact is, I would have died rather than tell my mother or father on her (you just didn't mention the world 'penis' in the '50s). And besides, it would have been mildly hypocritical: I knew what we kids were doing in the woodshed, or out in the fields, so why tattle only on her?

"When I was in the ninth grade, studying to be an altar boy, our classes were conducted by Ted, a vigorous-looking seminarian who drove around in a large white convertible. He always struck me as a bit too worldly for the priesthood because he would laugh and crack jokes like a teenager. He tended to a clique of boys whom he would take on long car rides and then deposit by the basketball nets during recess (the nuns, I think, thought he was taking the boys on 'sacred missions').

"I was not included in these forays. I thought then that I had been excluded because I didn't like girls and knew why I didn't. But years later I discovered the truth: Ted was making it with roughly half my classmates - all the boys whom the nuns thought of as shining examples and understudy saints. Even I thought of these boys as goody-two-shoes.

"Everyone will concede that children need protection from sexually exploitative adults. Even the sexually liberated ancient Greeks passed laws protecting the rights of children, and homosexual and heterosexual violators were punished with equal fervor. Perhaps, however, we need to be a little more realistic in our determination of what constitutes a minor.

"I do not think it is outrageous to suggest that the age be lowered to 16. But in a society where we still have trouble dealing with the sexual rights of consenting adults, this idea is a long shot. How can society acknowledge that many minors are really adults when so many adults continue to act like children?"

Our childish, modern day hate-mongers such as Pat Robertson, Pat Buchanan, Jesse Helms, Newt Gingrich and their ilk are merely following a grand tradition. The ancient Jews, in fact, mirrored the views of today's Religious Right, convinced that if a heterosexual was near a homosexual, the latter's sexual preference and affectional proclivity would somehow either rub off or infect the heterosexual by means of direct or indirect contact. The Jews taught (in Leviticus 20:13) that "if a man lie down with another man, both of them have committed idol worship and they shall be most assuredly put to death." However, this line is more in keeping with the Jewish fear of the rape of men by other men, which was quite common in the ancient world, according to historian Arthur Frederick Ide in his

book, *Gomorrah and the Rise of Homophobia.* Ide states, "When captives were taken by conquering armies they singled out the virile and young men and forcibly raped them – usually in full view of the public – so as to humiliate them and demonstrate their own superiority over the vanquished."

By the time the Romans ruled the world, however, homosexuality was well accepted in most quarters because homosexuals were proud of their own sex and identified with the basic mannerisms, interests, and respects of their gender. They often considered themselves bisexual: Julius Caesar, for instance, was known as "every woman's husband and every man's wife." And Emperor Hadrian, who was exclusively gay, was universally admired for his great love for Antonius. When the youth died, Hadrian had his lover deified. But the glories of Roman could not last. "Phobia as a social force develops in times of political and social vacuum," Ide remarks. "Phobia develops at times when 'deviant behavior' seems most acute, even though such 'deviant behavior' has no natural boundaries or time limits. The behavior is 'deviant' because it goes outside of the common concensus of what 'should be,' rather than an appreciation and understanding of 'what is.' When this occurs, the deviance draws attention to itself since it is outside of that which the society anticipates, expects or desires."

But once the rules of society as defined by the "vocal minority/majority" are broken, those in power join together and gain a coterie or following to express their outrage at the offense, bear witness against the offender, and then punish the offender as if the punishment would also erase, or stop the behavior.

Ide asserts, "Deviance is not inherent in any particular act or expression; rather it is a property conferred upon that objectionable behavior by the people who come into direct or indirect contact with it. And the deviance is dependent solely upon the mood of the community, for what might be considered normal at one time may be considered abnormal – actually socially unacceptable – at another, and what may be considered abnormal/socially unacceptable at one time may be deemed normal and desirable at another. Although most societies historically have feared 'deviant' behavior, assuming that the behavior is in fact or principle harmful to the group

life, seldom is socially unacceptable/unexpected/undesirable behavior actually harmful to anyone or anything – unless the behavior was criminal (such as murder or arson) rather than an lifestyle expression. Most 'social deviants' are individuals whose activities have moved outside the parameters of the community, especially the margins of society defined at a time of economic, social, political or familial collapse. It is at that time that the 'deviant individual' is considered a social vagrant who will not blend into the surrounding community and environment as determined by those in power, especially if those who are in power can claim that they derive their authority from a god or gods."

Such was the case during the fall of the Roman Empire. As Christians moved in to replace the pagans, sexual pleasure became regarded as evil and sexual deviation from the principles of procreation were damned as being against God. Ide says, "No longer was the imperial house interested in protecting the magnificence of diversity, nor the freedom of the people, instead it meant to be lord over all things including the body and souls of those who swore allegiance to its power.

"To stifle dissent, to erode the free thought of humans, a scapegoat had to be found – a scapegoat which could be accused of bringing down the empire and making it weak, ineffective, overtaxing, and unresponsive. Since many of the senate members were homosexual, and since homosexuals were found in high positions within the government, they were the most logical choice – a visible minority which did not have a collective strength or identity to protect itself from the ravishment of the march of tyranny and bigotry. Many of those who feared persecution quickly joined the ranks of the persecutors, hoping that by attacking their compatriots in affectional expression and sexual proclivity, they would be tolerated and left alone. But the Roman rulers were not about to allow any deviance from what they considered the norm, although they heartily accepted the incriminations, litigations, and persecution of homosexuals by other homosexuals." (Shows you how little things have changed!)

Male prostitution was immediately taxed. After the third century, laws were passed to outlaw even *active* homosexuality. Ide says, "No longer was only passive homosexuality illegal;

the law specifically attacked men who turn to homosexuality for the eroticism – not to find love, implying that homosexuals engage in sex for the sake of immediate pleasure rather than as a talisman in a sustaining love relationship: 'when love is sought and not found.'" A Roman citizen now could lose up to one-half of his estate if he was passively engaged with another male. Passivity was not restricted to the sexual act – but now included transvestism or cross-dressing in the garments of the opposite gender. Homosexual marriages, which previously had been legal, were outlawed in 342. "But for a while," Ide reveals, "this law was ignored and defied. The imperial objection to homosexual marriages was generated by a fear of a dwindling population and what a smaller population meant in terms of manpower to prosecute war, arm defense, and sustain military preparedness. Uniquely the main objection to homosexuality, in the wording of the law, was to a man acting or appearing in the manner of a woman – remarkably on the order of legendary laws that condemned passive homosexuality since it allegedly degraded manhood or took from the man the image and birthright of manhood."

But while the law was aimed at *passive* homosexuals it was really a punishment for *active* homosexuals *(stupratores puerorum*, or the 'corrupters of boys' – or *active* pederasts). "At best one could see the law as being aimed those who ignored it anyway," Ide says. "Furthermore, this 'law' is actually only a part of a longer piece of legislation in which it is specified that the persons guilty of the offense named in the laws are to be dragged out of the brothels in which they work – therefore, the law is against prostitution and not against homosexuality."

That male prostitutes were legislated against is not surprising because Rome was traditionally against the selling of a Roman body for sex. They believed the seller was not only selling the birthright of the body but also Rome itself; Rome was to forever be free. Ide says, "The 'corruption' implied by the law's comment against the 'corrupter of boys' is nonsense since the 'boys' in the case of prostitution would be going voluntarily to the prostitute and thus by intent were already 'corrupt.' Seldom, too, is there any record of a male prostitute being active in sex, but rather numerous accounts exist detailing the passive nature and 'disposition' of the male prostitute who

offered the anal orifice to the 'pushings' of an active client."

Homosexuals continued to exist, Ide confirms, but lived in terror: "Like the early Christians, the homosexual community went underground. While many had defended the persecuted Christians earlier, now they were persecuted by the once-persecuted. Their blood would mingle with the Christians – their numbers decimated wrongfully, their cries for the right to live and contribute to the commonweal being ignored and shouted down by the same men and women who had demanded their right to choose their own life style, belief, and practice. But whereas the early Christians had men and women write down their trials and tribulations – the *passiones* – the homosexuals did not, and many of their works in prose and poetry, which today exist only by inference and passing comment, were burned along with the authors' freedom on the pyre of bigotry."

Despite efforts of the Religious Right to censor our words and images out of existence, we are still able to write down our trials and tribulations, to say nothing of our fantasies and most joyous past experiences – sexual and otherwise. So let us enjoy while we can - even if it is, in some cases, *barely* legal.

TELLING FATHER

Petronius

"When I was in Asia," Eumolpus began, "on work connected with the administration of finance there, I was billeted in a private house in Pergamum. My stay there was a delightful one. Not only were my accommodations both comfortable and civilized, but my host's son was a boy of extraordinary beauty. Under the circumstances, my strategy as you may have guessed, was to become the boy's lover without in any way arousing the father's suspicions. So whenever the conversation at dinner happened to touch on pederasty, I affected to be so scandalised and protested so vigorously that my modesty was offended even by the mere mention of such things, that everyone, and especially the boy's mother, took me to be a philosophical saint. In no time at all, on the pretext of keeping possible seducers from setting foot in the house, I was soon chaperoning the boy on his way to the gymnasium, supervising his studies, and acting as his adviser and moral tutor.

"One day, as it happened, we were taking our rest in the dining room, since a public holiday had cut short our studies and the fatigue that comes from too much merry-making had left us too tired even to climb upstairs to bed. With a trembling voice I made my prayer to Venus: 'O goddess,' I whispered, 'if I can kiss this sleeping boy without his noticing it, tomorrow I will present him with a pair of doves.' Tempted by the price I put on my pleasure, the little impostor started to snore away. For my part, I crept close to him and stole several kisses. Pleased with this auspicious beginning, I rose early the next morning and brought back a pair of doves to the waiting boy and so fulfilled my vow.

"The following night the same opportunity presented itself, but this time I made a slight change in the form of my vow. 'O goddess,' I whispered, 'if I can caress this boy's body with a free hand, tomorrow I will bring him a pair of the finest fighting-cocks in the world. But he must not feel anything at all.' At this the boy quickly snuggled closer, half-afraid, I think,

that I might fall asleep before I touched him. I swiftly relieved him of his fears and with roving hands took my pleasure of his whole body, all but the supreme bliss. The following morning, to his delight, I brought him back the gift I had promised.

"Once again on the third night, I seized my chance. By this time the boy barely pretended to be asleep, and I rose and whispered in his ear: 'O immortal gods, if I may take from this sleeping boy the perfect pleasure of my dreams, I will bring him tomorrow a splendid Macedonian stallion. But on one condition only: he must not feel a thing.' Never did the boy sleep more soundly. Filling my hands with his milk-white skin, I bound my lips to his, and with one supreme effort, fulfilled my every dream. The next morning he sat eagerly waiting for me in his room. As you can perhaps imagine, it is one thing to buy doves and fighting-cocks, but quite another to buy a stallion. Besides, I was apprehensive that the sheer size of such a gift might make my generosity suspect. So I strolled about for a few hours and then came back, giving the boy nothing more than a kiss. Bewildered, he looked about everywhere, then threw his arms around my neck and said. 'Please, sir, where's the stallion?'

"This breach of my word, of course, shut the door against me, but it was not long before I had my way with him again. In fact, several days later, another festival gave me my opportunity once more. As soon as I heard his father snoring away, I begged the boy to make it up with me, or rather, to let me make love to him; in short, I used all those arguments which only a frustrated lover knows how to use. He was still angry, however, and to all my pleas he said nothing but, 'Go back to sleep or I'll tell my father.' But there is no refusal so final that a determined lover cannot somehow get around it. So, quite ignoring his refrain about waking his father, I slipped into bed beside him, and after a brief and none too convincing resistance on his part, I had my way with him.

"Apparently this high-handed treatment did not in the least displease him. True he reproached me for breaking my word and told me that he had suffered from the jeers of his friends to whom he had boasted of my generosity, but then he said: 'Just to show you I'm not like you, you can do it again if you want.' So we made it up, and after enjoying myself a second

time at his own invitation, I fell off into a deep sleep. But the boy with all the passive ardour of his age, was still dissatisfied even with my double proof of affection, and in a short while he prodded me awake, whispering, 'Don't you want to do it again?' The offer was by no means unwelcome and I accepted with pleasure. Finally after a great deal of panting and sweating, I managed to oblige him and immediately dropped off to sleep, completely exhausted. In less than an hour he was pinching me again: 'Why don't we do it some more?' he asked. I was furious at being constantly reawakened and angrily turned his own words against him. 'Go back to sleep,' I cried, 'or I'll tell your father.'"

–From "The Satyricon" by Petronius (d. AD 69). A courtier of the Emperor Nero - Tacitus suggested indeed that for a while he was the Emperor's "arbiter of taste" - Petronius committed suicide, and the note he left detailed the Emperor's vices. Our thanks to William Arrowsmith, University of Michigan Press.

THE BACK ROOM

John Patrick

My young friend Terry, when he isn't tending to his studies at the local art college, tends my video store so that I might break away for a few blessed hours at the beach or cruising the park.

One day in early autumn I returned from one of my sojourns to find Terry breathless with the news: little Joey had come into the shop brandishing his driver's license, informing Terry he had indeed turned 18 and now wanted entry to "the back room" where the adult videos are displayed.

Terry agreed but I know there was a look of sadness in his eyes because, to Terry, Joey would always be 16 and attempting to sneak into the back room when Terry would be busy with other customers.

"Okay, help yourself," Terry had told him with a shrug.

Joey beamed and scampered off behind the curtain.

Minutes passed in silence before Terry got the courage to invade the back room. There stood Joey, surveying the gay tapes.

"What do you suggest?" Joey asked.

Knowing Terry, I presume there was much stuttering and stammering, much dropping of empty tape boxes, fumbling with this rack and that.

Joey, Terry said, dismissed all of his suggestions. This was understandable to me because I know what Terry likes - anything with boys who look like they might have a problem proving they are 18.

Joey had a mind of his own; he reached high on the shelf and took down "Daddy Hunt."

Terry said he was crestfallen. I can believe it. Terry is many things but "Daddy" he isn't. Appearing much younger than his years, he looks barely old enough to be in the back room himself.

As Joey was paying for his rental, he asked where I was. Terry told him I was "out."

"Joey says you don't like him," Terry told me when I

returned.

"It's true, I don't. He's a little sneak." I had to extricate young Joey from the back room a couple of times in the past few months. In fact, I had barred him from the place altogether.

"You can't blame him for being curious."

"No, I suppose not. It just got to be tiresome."

"But he has such a cute little butt."

"He is also jailbait."

"*Was* jailbait. The driver's license was real."

"And now I suppose we'll never be rid of him."

"We should all have such problems."

"What do you mean?"

"He's checked out 'Daddy Hunt,' for chrissakes, not 'The Young and the Hung.'"

"In other words, I'm just his type."

"You said it, I didn't."

My rental policy is three nights for $3. Joey kept "Daddy Hunt" for a week. During that time, I saw him pass by the store, peer in the window, and then move on. He never knew when I was going to take time off and Terry would be there. I gathered the little brat was really afraid of me.

On the fourth day of Joey's overdue status, he peered in the window and saw Terry. What Joey didn't know was that I had just returned and was in the bathroom. Joey entered the shop and timidly approached the desk. He waited until Terry had stepped away to get some tapes for another customer, then dropped the plastic box on the counter and swiftly made his way to the back room. I saw all this from the back, as I was leaving the john. I stood at the entrance to the back room until Terry finished waiting on the customer and the three of us were alone in the shop.

"Joey," I said, "come out here. Now."

Shamefaced, the kid slowly appeared. I stood there, my hands on my hips, staring at him. "You're four days overdue."

His Bambi-eyes were sad. "I know. I - "

"You can't rent anything more until you pay for the overtime."

"I'll pay, just let me pick out something else." Sheepishly, he scurried back into the back room.

"I don't like your sneaking in and dropping the box and

running back here. You had no intention of paying."

"I'd have charged him -" Terry butted in.

I turned to Terry and winked. "I should hope so. Sneaky little bastard!" I threw up my hands and went back to the storage room.

A few minutes later, Joey was at the counter with two empty tape boxes in his hand. I was busy behind the stacks putting tapes away so he didn't see me but when I saw him, I darted out.

"Joey, how many times do I have to tell you, leave the boxes on the rack, just come out and tell us what titles you want."

"I'm sorry, I forgot."

"I banned you from this place once, I can do it again. I don't care what age you are."

"I know. I'm sorry." He picked up the boxes and returned to the back room.

I was shaking my head but I was also chuckling.

Terry smiled, then called back to Joey, "I saw the titles. I'll get them. You just come back to the counter after you've put them away."

"Where you found them – " I added sternly.

Terry waited on him: "Two tapes for three days for five dollars and a dollar a day overtime on the last one makes it nine dollars," Terry said.

Joey handed him a ten dollar bill, Terry gave him the change. "Wouldn't you like a bag?"

"Yeah," Joey said, giving Terry the plastic boxes.

At that moment, I was coming out of the storage room and saw Joey pick up the bag, stop, turn, notice me, and then make a dash for the door.

"And don't be late," I hollered.

"I won't," came the weak reply before the door swooshed behind him.

But, sure enough, a week went by before Joey showed. It was Monday night and he was pounding on the front door five minutes after I had closed at midnight.

Unlocking the door, I said, "Can't you read?"

"I - "

I pointed to the sign. "I'm closed."

I pointed to another sign. "And if I'm closed, use the slot,

like it says."

"But these are overdue."

"Of course they are. They *always* are, aren't they?"

"I - "

"Stop! There is no excuse, Joey. None whatsoever." I flung the door open. "Well, come in."

After he had entered the store, I locked the door then followed him to the first row of videos. I stopped and stood watching him as he walked ahead of me to the counter. It was an unseasonably warm night, and he was wearing nothing but ragged denim cut-offs. He was, I had to admit, glorious. His long dirty blond hair badly needed a cutting, hanging down past his shoulders, but his smooth back was deeply tanned and seemed to be pointing the way to the most luscious buns I had seen in years. Terry was right about that ass and thinking how Terry had coveted it made it even more inviting to me.

Joey dropped his bag on the counter and stood there, tapping his bare foot impatiently as he slowly extracted a roll of bills from his back pocket. I went behind the counter and picked up the tape boxes. "Neither of these tapes is rewound. You did that the last time. We must have these rewound or there'll be an extra charge – one dollar per tape." I slammed one of the cassettes into the rewinder and hit the button.

As the machine whirred, Joey handed me a five dollar bill.

"What's this?"

"For the overtime."

"It's a dollar a day per tape, Joey. Per tape. You owe me five more dollars and a dollar each for the rewind."

"But then I won't be able to rent another tape. I wanted to get 'Daddy Hunt 2.'"

"That's out anyway. Just pay me what you owe me and never darken my door again."

"Oh, please – " he begged, his impossibly long eyelashes fluttering.

"Please what?"

"Don't throw me out again. Everybody's always throwing me out. Even my father threw me out."

I stared at him. He was absolutely divine when he was pleading. All of the smart-ass drained from him and he turned into an angel. Or at least that's the way I saw it that night.

"Tell you what. You help me close up tonight and I'll let you have something better than 'Daddy Hunt 2' - free."

"What do I have to do?"

"Just empty the trash into the dumpster outside and clean up the lavatory a bit. Then sweep the aisles. I'll lock away the cash."

"Okay," he said.

I showed him precisely what to do and returned to the front counter. I counted my change and locked everything up. When I returned to the storage room, Joey wasn't there but I could hear water running into the lavatory. I opened the door and there he was scrubbing the wash basin with a filthy rag.

"Why don't you try this sponge and some cleanser," I said, going to the little cabinet and opening the door.

"Oh, you didn't tell me where anything was - "

"I thought you could figure it out."

In the tight confines of the lavatory, I deliberately pressed against his slender body, pushing him back against the basin.

He smiled, looked up into my eyes and, as he cupped my groin, he said, "Well, I know where *most* things are - "

I grinned. I couldn't help it. He was adorable. I wanted to kiss him but instead I asked, "Now that you've found it, what are you going to do about it?"

His answer was swift in coming. He sat down on the toilet and began yanking my zipper down. He unbuckled my belt and pulled my pants apart. His mouth went to the bulge in my briefs. I moved closer to him, got into position. I was going to enjoy this more than anything I had done in years. Fucking Joey's face had suddenly become the most important thing in my life.

"You like that?" I asked as I shook my cock up and down.

"Yeah," he muttered, dry-mouthed, wide-eyed, "I like it a lot."

"Well, come on," I coaxed, "show me how much you like it."

He stared at my cock for a moment, not sure where to start first. I jerked it in his face and he took in his hand. He licked it, stuck the tip of his tongue on it, then enveloped the entire crown with his lips.

"Yeah," I said.

He let out a low moan, then started to swirl his tongue around the head, washing it with his spit, eventually taking a couple inches of the shaft into his mouth.

My hips began a subtle, thrusting movement and he relaxed his jaw, letting me slide the hard-on in and out. The kid was good. *Damn* good. He had done this before and I saw no sense in rushing it. I gently stabbed his mouth as I reached down and rubbed my hand over his chest, cupping one pec, finding the nipple, twisting it until it was hard.

He groaned as I ran my hands over his firm, hairless chest. I started teasing both nipples, rolling them between my thumb and forefinger, increasing the pressure till he was squirming on the toilet seat, his head bobbing up and down on my prick.

I brought my hands to his shoulders and humped my hips harder now, my hairy balls slapping against his chin, slamming the cock all the way down. He gagged, withdrew it, but I jammed it back in again.

His hands dropped to his shorts and he unzipped them, pulled them apart and let his own erection loose.

I reached down and caressed it while I continued to face-fuck him. I could feel it was not a big dick but a nice one and I wanted to see it.

"Get up," I barked.

His lips still on my cock, he raised himself to a crouch and his little denim shorts fell to the floor.

I stepped back and, as he stood up, his cock jutted out, tall and proud. I took it fully in my hand and began stroking it. His hand went to my cock and we stood there for a few moments playing with each other. I ran my finger up and down his crack, stopping every now and then to spit on it. Before long, my finger was slipping inside him and he began pushing back onto it. Soon my entire finger was all the way in. He kept stroking my cock as his head fell to my chest. He kissed one pec and then the other, finally sucking on my nipples.

Nothing would do, I had to fuck him. I spun him around and he bent over, presenting the finest piece of ass I'd ever seen. I ran my hand over the down-covered cheeks. He leaned forward, hugging the toilet tank.

"This won't hurt if you relax."

"I know," he murmured, jacking his cock.

He knew? This kid had a surprise every minute. I got a lubed condom from the medicine cabinet and slid it over my cock. My cockhead popped inside Joey easily. Still I stopped a moment to let him adjust. I was fairly certain he'd never had a cock as big as this one but you never know with kids nowadays. He pushed back and three inches of the wide shaft sank into him. I leaned down, pressing my chest against the boy's back and began humping my hips. As I got a strong, steady fuck rhythm going, he started bucking his hips underneath me. I reached under and began twisting his tits, which got him thrashing wildly and his head hit the wall.

"You'll never bring videos in late again, will you, Joey?" I kept pumping and pumping.

"No, no," he groaned, turning his head. "Never again."

I couldn't help it: with his lips so close I had to kiss him as I sent one final thrust deep into him, shooting my load into the condom.

Frantically, Joey jacked his dick, and I hugged his torso, egging him on: "Yeah, yeah, come for me, Joey," when suddenly I heard the bolt click and the back door swish open.

"Jack! Hey, Jack, you okay?"

It was Terry, the only person I trust with a key to my store.

Joey froze. I pulled out of him and turned to face Terry who was now standing in the doorway of the lavatory.

"Oh shit," he muttered.

"No, no shit. Cum, Terry, cum. Gallons of it!"

His eyes were glued on Joey's incomparable ass. "I'm sorry. I was driving by and saw your car was still here. I was afraid something had happened."

"Well, something *did* happen, as you can see. In fact, it's *still* happening. Joey was just in the process of shooting his wad."

Terry appeared to be bewildered at this new state of affairs. Our friendship had never extended to overt sex. Now he was confronted by the sight of me peeling a sperm-filled condom off my dick and Joey bending over wanting in the worst way to come.

I decided to make it easy for Terry. "It'd go a lot easier for Joey if you'd take my place at the helm." And, with that, I stepped aside. Terry was still not convinced he wanted to

engage in sexual relations before my eyes but Joey made up his mind for him: "Yeah, Terry, stick it to me."

Chuckling, I patted the obvious bulge in Terry's chinos and left them alone, but only for a few moments. After getting a Coke from the refrigerator in the store room, I stood in the doorway of the lavatory watching as Terry slid a condom over his cock and begin shoving it into the hole I had just vacated. I was impressed by Terry's equipment: it was of respectable length and quite wide. Joey was impressed as well, thrashing about as it slid in like a knife through butter. Watching Terry realize a long-held dream got me so excited, I took a long swallow of Coke and entered the lavatory, squeezing in between the wall and the bowl, and flopped my newly-aroused cock in Joey's face. He went ballistic now, jerking off while being fucked simultaneously in the mouth and ass. Whining, he shot blast after blast of spunk onto the toilet tank, but he kept right on sucking my dick as Terry went wild over his ass, fucking him for a good five minutes

A night like that, I was sure, had never happened to Joey before. On the other hand, maybe it had, but whatever he'd done in the past it was just a prelude to the many nights (and some slow afternoons) he spent in the lavatory of Express Video. As you might imagine, Joey never had to pay for any videos he wanted to see and he never had to worry about late charges again. Of course, he didn't seem all that interested in watching videos anymore, but when he did, he was so horny I often had to call Terry in to assist me. It was the least I could do.

HOT LOAD

John Patrick

"It's big." Johnny stared at the idling Peterbilt and the driver, nicknamed Pete after his truck. Johnny'd seen big trucks, sure, but this was the first time he'd ever stood next to one, ready to take a ride. He'd also seen big men before, but none as big as Pete, and he was ready to take a ride on Pete's cock, if he'd let him. Chances were good, though. He'd only known Pete for a few minutes and now he was about to climb into the cab and ride off into the sunset with him.

"Well, pretty boy," Pete said, breathing warmly on his neck, "I'll bring you home safe and sound. Just put your foot right there and reach for that bar and swing yourself up into the seat."

Soon Johnny was resting in the hydraulic passenger seat.

"What do you think of it?" Pete asked, flashing a big grin.

Johnny looked down at Pete's crotch and smiled. "It's big."

Pete went right on grinning as he fiddled with the CB, trying to clear the static from nearby motors. Johnny held his hands over his ears.

"Soon as we get on the interstate we'll be fine," Pete said, shifting out of neutral.

Johnny noticed Pete's tight jeans were faded across the thighs from the sun coming through the windshield and his lizard skin cowboy boots gleamed from a coat of polish applied during a layover the day before.

"A good boy and a good dog are always ready to go for a ride," Pete said as they roared onto the interstate. Johnny could feel his eyes glancing his way. "Let me know if you need anything."

"Okay," Johnny said, staring at the highway ahead of them. The yellow lines were mesmerizing and the cars they passed looked so small; Johnny'd never looked down on motorists before. The famous Sunshine State tourist traps slipped by, a kaleidoscope of tackiness, as Pete drove at a steady, efficient 70 mph. They flew past the Disney World exit and Johnny felt his stomach churn. He remembered the time his mother took him

there. What a wonderful day they had. It was the only place she ever took him, except maybe to the movies. He was beginning to feel homesick already. Johnny had always made a joke about running away, but actually doing it was something else again.

They stopped for supper outside Ocala.

"Order anything you like," Pete told the boy. He ordered chicken-fried steak, baked potato, tossed salad with blue cheese, and headed for the john.

"I'll have the same," Johnny told the waitress.

Pete came out of the restroom with his sandy blond hair slicked back and a big grin on his face. He said the truck would be fueled by the time they were done with their food.

Pete cut into his steak. "So how do you like being on the road?"

"Fine so far," Johnny said. He finished his Mountain Dew and asked for more. Riding had made him thirsty.

Pete's eyes were clear, calm, kind. He smelled faintly of toothpaste and soap. He seemed like a nice man to Johnny. They had struck up a conversation at the Stuckey's just off the interstate near Fort Myers. Pete had seen Johnny's duffel bag sitting next to his stool at the counter and had asked him where he was headed.

"Home," Johnny answered matter-of-factly.

"Oh, you just visitin', are you?"

"Yeah, a friend of mine brought me down here, to see the sights and all, but he up and left me." Johnny shook his head. "It's a long story."

"Damn shame when you can't trust your friends," Pete had said.

They ate in silence for awhile, then, talking around mouthfuls of food, Pete said, "I hope we can drop this load early."

Johnny thought again of Pete's abundant crotch and nodded. "Yeah, I hope so too." He didn't want to appear too eager; maybe Pete wasn't gay after all, just friendly. Still, he'd heard stories about truckers who took their fun where they could find it. He'd never had a trucker and he figured it was about time.

"Take a nap," Pete suggested when they got back to the truck and he saw Johnny was yawning.

"Okay," Johnny said, moving over to the doghouse. Looking out, Johnny saw the big rigs owned the night. They barreled past one another like giants in a race. With the vehicle's swaying movement, he soon fell fast asleep, only to be awakened to the clashing of gears. Pete was backing the truck up to a loading dock between an idling Mack and a silent Kenworth.

"Keep it warm for me, pretty boy," he said.

The cab began to sway as the forklifts unloaded the trailer behind them and when the unloading was finished, Pete turned in his paperwork and they were back on the road. Pete steered smoothly onto a dark, silent street in Gainesville.

"You want something to eat?" he asked. "I have to make a call."

"Yeah," Johnny said. He was always at least a little bit hungry. Besides he was uncomfortable; the truck rode rough without a load.

They stopped near the interstate. Johnny found the restroom while Pete looked for the phones.

As Johnny came out of the john, he heard Pete on the phone, shouting to make himself heard over the video games by the bank of phones. "You know I love you, honey bunch. Don't I call every damn chance I get? Give the kids a big kiss for me."

Johnny grinned as he walked over to the counter and ordered a piece of apple pie with ice cream. He'd always wanted to be with a married man. Now he was with a married trucker with little kids! He smiled broadly as the waitress brought him his pie.

Soon Pete was sliding down on the stool next to him. "Well, you'll be back home before morning. You did say you were goin' to Tallahassee, right?"

"Well, no, not exactly."

"I coulda sworn that's what you said."

"No. Truth is, I'm runnin' away from home. I really don't care where I go as long as it's not back to Fort Myers."

Pete's eyes were wide. "You mean I got a hot load on my hands?"

Johnny chuckled. "Yeah, I guess."

Pete asked the waitress for a cup of coffee and he sat quietly drinking it, deep in thought. Finally, when he saw Johnny had

finished his pie, he said, "Well, when a man's got a hot load, best thing he can do is move it fast. Let's go."

Once outside, Pete pulled the rig around to the back of the truck stop. "You know, I think we oughta get some shut-eye and think this thing through in the the morning."

"Okay," Johnny said.

Pete told Johnny to wait in the truck while he registered at the motel office.

The room was sparse but adequate. There were two double beds, plenty of towels, a TV, and a Gideon bible on the table between the beds.

Pete went straight to the bathroom, began taking a shower. Johnny sat on the edge of the bed fiddling with the remote control to the TV. Old movies, news headlines, religious programs, the weather. He settled on the horror movie, flipped off his sneakers and lay back on the bed, propping his head up with the pillows.

Pete came out of the bathroom with a towel wrapped around his waist. He was drying his hair with another towel. "What's on?" he asked, staring at the TV.

"I think it's 'The Bride of Frankenstein.'"

"I thought you were sleepy."

"This'll put me to sleep."

"You gonna sleep in those clothes?" Pete asked, dropping down on the edge of the other bed.

"No, I guess not."

"Bathroom's all yours."

"Thanks," Johnny said, lifting himself from the bed. He walked slowly toward the bathroom, his eyes on the screen. "This is a good part," he said. Standing in front of the TV.

"Then get outta the way," Pete said, grabbing him and pushing him aside. But his meaty hands didn't leave Johnny's shoulders; they held him tightly and Pete breathed on his neck.

Johnny squirmed. "My neck hurts, from sleeping in that doghouse."

"Oh? You want me to rub it for you?"

Johnny gulped. "Yeah, that'd be nice."

Pete began kneading Johnny's neck and shoulders.

"Oh, that feels so good," the boy sighed.

"It'd feel better if you'd take this damn shirt off."

Johnny was quick to comply. He already had an erection and now dangled the shirt in front of it.

As the massage continued Johnny dropped his shirt to the floor and brought his hands back, running his fingers along his thigh, groping Pete's crotch. His heart began to pound as he realized how well-hung Pete was, measuring the long, thick cock throbbing under the towel.

"You like that, don't you?" Pete said, turning Johnny around, "Why don't you take a real good look?"

Johnny did what he was told, lifting the towel away, revealing the biggest penis he had ever seen. He held it in his hand, watching it twitch and swell even larger.

"Play with it," Pete growled, spreading his legs wide. Turned on by the older man's new coarseness, Johnny stroked the thick, vein-gnarled shaft. "You know what I wanna to do with that big dick?"

When Johnny shook his head, Pete chuckled. "Well, I wanna pull those pants down around your knees, and put it up your little butt. Then fuck you till you howl for mercy. You'd like that, wouldn't you?"

"Yes," Johnny breathed, his voice barely a whisper.

"What?" he asked, bringing his hand to Johnny's face, caressing his cheek.

"Yes," Johnny said, louder now.

Pete crammed a finger into the boy's mouth, and he sucked on it greedily, treating it as if it was his hard cock.

"Oh, but first you want to suck it, is that it?"

Johnny nodded and dropped to his knees between Pete's outstretched thighs. The cock knob was ruddy, fat, helmet-shaped. Johnny probed the salty slit with his tongue, savoring the taste of the stud. Then he took him deep in his throat. Pete leaned over him, massaged his ass through the fabric of his jeans.

Pete was hung long and thick and the slight curve of the shaft allowed it to slip easily down Johnny's hungry throat. Johnny lunged forward, swallowing him till Pete's balls bounced against his chin, then slowly pulled back. His lips were tight and his tongue moved slowly all along the tender underbelly of the cock.

Johnny swirled his mouth over it, not really sure of what to

do with it. Pete grabbed the back of his neck and showed the boy what he wanted. He slowly fed the cock into Johnny's mouth, a little at a time, telling him to take it slow and easy when the boy took too much at once. Finally Johnny developed a good rhythm and Pete howled, "Hey, you've done this before," as he leaned back onto the mattress and watched Johnny go at it feverishly. "Damned if you haven't. Here I thought you was a virgin boy."

After a few minutes, Pete said, "And you've probably been fucked before, too, eh?"

Johnny nodded and, letting the cock pop out of his mouth, he said, "But it wasn't as big as this."

"Some little squirt at school, eh?"

Johnny nodded.

"Well, then you're ready for a man-sized piece of meat, ain't ya?"

Johnny had to admit he'd been ready for *this* meat when he first saw the bulge in Pete's jeans at Stuckey's.

Johnny took one last suck, swallowing convulsively, tightening his throat along the shaft of the cock, then he stood up and unbuckled his pants. As he slipped them off, Pete's appraising eyes lingered on the slender, nearly hairless body, the respectable six-inch, cut prick jutting up high in the air from a small patch of pubic hair. Pete made room on the bed for Johnny and took him into his arms as he climbed on. He tweaked the boy's nipples and tenderly ran his hands up and down the firm young torso.

"You're a pretty boy all right," he said, his hands coming to rest on the asscheeks. He lifted up so that Johnny could lie on his stomach.

Soon Johnny felt Pete's sweaty hands being replaced by his lips on his ass, his tongue occasionally plunging in. Johnny shivered and groaned when Pete's finger was inserted. As Pete kissed his neck and fingered his hole, Johnny's hard cock was rubbing against the sheet.

"You want my cock up there?"

"Please. Yes, please," Johnny begged, his big brown eyes flashing.

"Okay, pretty boy." Pete positioned the knob of his cock against the throbbing hole, grabbed both cheeks and slowly

inserted it. Johnny squirmed. Pete took it slow, not letting up the pressure until their balls banged together and his enormous prick was in to the hilt.

Johnny had never felt anything quite like the sensation of Pete's big dick pumping in and out of his body.

"Keep squeezin' it," Pete growled, smacking his butt with his open palm several times as he pounded rhythmically. After awhile, he rolled Johnny over and slipped his big hands under the boy's arms and pulled him up against him, holding his head in his hands.

He pressed the head of his cock into the hole and hunched his hips forward. At first, only the head and a couple of inches of the shaft were in Johnny. Finally, his thrusts became more powerful, driving inch after inch of the thick shaft up into the boy's ass until it was again all the way in. Then he slipped his arms around Johnny and sat up, pulling the boy along with him. He leaned back, bracing his hands on the bed behind him. "Now you fuck it," he moaned, his eyelids fluttering as Johnny clenched his ass ring down tight around the base of the prick. Johnny crouched over him, gripped his shoulders tight, and began to gyrate his hips.

Johnny looked into the mirror to watch Pete pistoning in and out of his hole as he bounced up and down on it, impaling him. He jacked off in this position, sending glistening white droplets flying. Then he lifted himself away from the cock, wanting to take it on his knees.

Pete got behind him and Johnny reached down and guided the monster dick into his ass. He rubbed his back against Pete's torso as the older man's arms encircled his chest and he started to fuck him.

Pete pushed Johnny down and, pressing his face against the boy's neck, his breath was soon coming in labored snorts. "Oh, shit!" he cried, hips pounding, eyelashes fluttering as he began shooting bursts of cum deep into the boy's quivering ass. When he finished, he collapsed on top of Johnny and held him tight. Johnny fell asleep with Pete's glorious cock still deep in his ass.

In the morning, when Pete came from the bathroom, a towel wrapped around his waist, he saw Johnny, dressed in a clean pair of powder blue shorts and a Mickey Mouse T-shirt, a

souvenir of his trip to Disney World, perched on the edge of the bed ready to go to breakfast.

"God, you're pretty this morning," Pete said, pushing him back onto the sagging mattress.

Johnny moaned softly as Pete began playing with his curving pecs and, in just seconds, his pointy nipples were trying to poke holes in his T-shirt. A quick glance told Pete that the bulge in Johnny's crotch was beginning to swell up nicely as well.

Johnny responded immediately to the tit play, and in less than two minutes Pete had his T-shirt pushed up under his armpits. With one hand cupping and fondling his smooth chest, Pete used his free hand to unzip the boy's fly and open it wide. Johnny's cock rose up tall and proud through the open gap. Ignoring it, Pete forced his hand down between his thighs. Curving his fingers under Johnny's balls, he found the still-moist asshole and eased two fingers right in. Johnny got wide-eyed at this quick action, and he groaned as the speed of the finger-fucking increased. He looked startled when Pete abruptly pulled his fingers out and took off his tennis shoes and tugged his shorts off over his feet and threw them into the corner.

"I thought we were going to eat breakfast," Johnny said.

"Breakfast can wait."

Johnny whimpered when he felt Pete's naked body pressing him onto his back.

Pete's hands cupped Johnny's wondrous buttocks, lifting his body off the mattress slightly, squeezing and fondling the lush mounds. Pete's cock nudged into the crack, his hardness separating the trembling buttocks with ease. He plowed into him with one steady slide. To torment him a little, he drew out again until just the enormous head was captured by the boy's tight ass ring. He held myself motionless, waiting for Johnny to thrust his hips to get more of the cock back inside.

"Oh," Johnny sighed, humping up against Pete.

When all ten inches were lodged inside Johnny, Pete began to pump. Johnny turned his head and Pete could see his grimacing face as he writhed beneath him, moaning as he plunged his cock steadily in and out.

After awhile, Pete got on his back with Johnny on top.

Johnny straddled him and began riding Pete's prick wildly. With a steady rhythm, his ass kept rising and falling, working the full length of the cock up and down. Soon he was squealing, then gasping, coming with a mighty spurt, splattering Pete's chest, squeezing Pete's cock so tight that Pete came himself, without much cum but with much relief.

Johnny stayed in the saddle and, rubbing his cum into Pete's skin, he asked, "Can we have breakfast now?"

. . .

At breakfast, Pete listened patiently as Johnny told him all about his troubles at school and at home with his mother. Johnny was too pretty to be a boy, Pete decided, and it didn't help matters that he liked art, music and books more than football, and his mother was hardly ever there, having to work two jobs to support them since his father died when he was five. It was a tough life. Pete had heard similar litanies of woes before but no one had told it quite so heart-wrenchingly as Johnny. Pete had gotten so he wouldn't bother with hitchers, especially ones over twenty-five. They could be downright dangerous. He'd begun to prefer the young runaways but even then, most of them were just too much trouble. Still, he got horny and he kept telling himself he was being faithful to his wife by fucking only boys on the road. Besides, they appreciated it more than the waitresses at the truck stops. The gay guys really got off on his muscular six foot-four frame and when they saw his dick, well, there was no stopping them.

Now Pete had a deal for Johnny. He told him if he went back home, returned to school, he'd stop in Fort Myers every time he passed through and they'd spend a few hours together. "I know that's not much of a reward for finishing school but – "

"It's big enough for me."

Pete was pleased Johnny had seen the light. He had two girls and his wife had lost the boy she was carrying. He could never have a son and Johnny brought out the daddy in him. Besides, if Johnny agreed to go home, Pete wouldn't have to go out of his way to take him to Tallahassee, which he was fully prepared to do, and could probably pick up a load in Ocala to take back to Miami. Yeah, Pete thought, the day was starting

out pretty good.

Pete grinned and suggested, "Why don't we go back to the room for a few minutes before we shove off?"

Johnny's eyes sparkled and he said, "Sounds good to me."

Back in the room, Pete was again aiming his prick at Johnny's butthole, amazed at how easily it slid in, how the boy practically sucked him inside.

Pete sat back on his heels. He always liked to watch his meat slide in and out of a cunt or butthole. Now the contrast of his leathery dark skin against the lily white of Johnny's buns was thrilling him beyond belief.

"You've been a bad boy, haven't you, lying to me like that."

Slap! Pete whacked his ass. *Slap! Slap!* He whacked it some more.

"Oh, yeah, spank me. I've been a bad boy. I deserve it."

Soon Johnny's butt was rosy red and Pete could see his fingerprints where he'd bruised the skin. He got up on his haunches like an animal and began fucking the boy wildly.

Johnny started bucking underneath him. His butt muscles clamped around Pete's cock. Pete was sweating profusely, breathing hard. Johnny's back glistened as Pete's sweat dripped onto it. Suddenly, close to coming, Pete stopped. He rolled Johnny over and fucked him with his legs flailing in the air.

With his ankles riding on Pete's shoulders, Johnny moaned, "Oh, God," as Pete hovered over him and buried his cock balls-deep up Johnny's spasming anus. Pete firmly gripped a buttock in each hand, slowly raising and lowering the boy's butt while he smoothly worked the full length of his cock in and out of his ass. Soon Pete could feel the intense contractions of the boy's ass around his cock and soon Johnny was having another orgasm, jerking away as Pete plunged into him again, coming himself, this time no more than a dribble, then reluctantly slid it out.

They slept until noon and Johnny was groggy with sleep when Pete pulled him up on all fours in the middle of the messy bed. He held the boy's hips in a tight grip while his cock entered again and began slamming against the jiggling ass cheeks. Johnny's ass was soon rotating and Pete wrapped his arm around his throat, resting his hand on his opposite

shoulder. Pete could feel Johnny swallow hard as the inside of his arm pulled the boy more upright. Johnny's heels pressed against Pete's big buttocks, as Pete's hand moved slowly up his back and then down again. Pete smiled and pressed his lips against the back of the boy's neck as the boy began quivering in agony as the fucking continued. Pete looked down to see Johnny's cock was hard and he was stroking it feverishly. Johnny wiggled around on the cock as he came again, to the pleasure of an astonished Pete. The older man had never been with anyone who could take him so repeatedly. Johnny could, he decided, take everything he had to offer and perhaps even more.

As much as Pete wanted to keep the boy with him the entire day, he knew their idyll had to come to an end. By the time they reached Fort Myers, the sun was setting and they stopped for supper. Before getting out of the cab, Johnny brought his hands to Pete's crotch and started kneading it. Pete cleared his throat and moved the truck to the far end of the parking lot. There, as it turned dark, Johnny gave him a blowjob that he would not soon forget. Johnny started by taking hold of the big penis, pumping it slowly with a tight grip of his fingers. Then he took his balls in his hand, rolled them inside the sack with his fingers. Johnny rubbed his nose in Pete's crotch, inhaling the rich, musky smell of him. Pete pushed his penis inside Johnny's mouth and began rocking back and forth, ramming Johnny's face with a steady rhythm. After a few moments, he rested, wanting to prolong it. Johnny worked his tongue back and forth on the erect cock, licked the pre-cum from the head, sucked it, drawing it out, twisting it with his mouth. When he took it deep, Pete moaned, his thighs opening and closing in ecstasy. In another moment he exploded, crying out as his eyes rolled up in his head. He started squirting into Johnny's mouth. Johnny's cheeks bulged as he tried to force Pete back, a gob of semen spurting out from one corner of his lips as the pressure became too great. He continued gulping, his mouth pulling at the cock until it was completely drained. When at last the cock left Johnny's mouth it was limp and wet. Nobody had sucked Pete like that in years. Johnny laid his head on Pete's thigh and idly toyed with the penis. Pete ran his fingers through Johnny's tousled brown hair and, with the other hand, he hugged the

boy to him.

Pete brought the rig to a halt on U.S. 41 about two blocks from Johnny's house. "Always take good advice," Pete said, pressing his hand against Johnny's back and pushing him out of the cab.

"I will. Thanks for the ride."

Pete reached over to touch him on the cheek. "Catch you on the flip flop."

"Ten-four," Johnny said, grinning.

Pete sat in the truck watching the boy trudge wearily down the street, illuminated by the headlights. When the boy was finally out of sight, Pete smiled. "Ten-four, little buddy," he said, and smacked his lips.

HE ONLY SMILED ONCE

John Patrick

*"got this photograph
keep it wherever I live*

*at spring street I was alone
. . . and was not privileged*

*except for a single smile
that I won't give back"*
— *from "Photograph" by Brian Daldorph*

Once. A single afternoon. Yet the memory of it is with me always. Many a dull or sleepless night I have pulled the events of that afternoon out to comfort myself. I have used it so often it has come to seem like a story I'd read somewhere, not something that had really happened to me. But it did. And it always makes me smile.

But he only smiled once. And that wasn't until the last day he worked at the house next door. My neighbors, the Hamiltons, were in London for the month of June and their young nephew, Bart, had been staying there, fixing everything that needed to be fixed. There was a lot to be done and he seemed to do it at night; the house was always ablaze with lights and I could hear pounding occasionally. The days he reserved for swimming in the pool and getting a tan while he read.

I often found myself inventing things to do outside so that I could get another look at the tightly-muscled youth. He was barely of legal age and it was obvious he'd been working on his body since he was a child, improving upon nature. But nature had been exceedingly generous to him if the basket he showed was any indication, creating a sight impossible to ignore.

But Bart ignored me for the most part. He would occasionally

nod if he happened to notice me, but never with a smile.

That last day he was to be there he must have been celebrating because he was playing rock music so loud it was rattling my windows. I couldn't concentrate on my work - and I had rewrites to do on a book that was due at my publisher in three days.

I went over to the property line and hollered, "Turn it down." I waited. Nothing happened. He obviously couldn't hear me. I went to the front door and rang the bell. Nothing. I pounded on the door. Nothing. I tried the knob. He had left the front door unlocked. I stepped into the house. I had only been in the place once, for a neighborhod open house when the Hamiltons moved in. I vaguely remembered the layout. It was an enormous house, twice as big as mine, with five bedrooms for all of their grandkids to stay in when they visited. I climbed up the circular staircase halfway and hollered again. Nothing.

I followed the music down the hall to the last bedroom before the master suite. The door was left slightly ajar. I knocked. "Hello!" I shouted. Nothing.

Being so adventurous was making me nervous as hell; I was sweating profusely. Bart hadn't turned on the air conditioning for a single day since he'd been there. The windows were always open. The bedroom was even warmer than the hallway. As I entered the bedroom, I saw steam coming from a partly-opened door, a door to a bathroom. "Hey!" I hollered over the din of the stereo which I now saw was on a bedside table. His tank top soaked with perspiration had been discarded on top of his cut-offs in a pile on the floor.

Suddenly he swung the bathroom door completely open. "Yeah?" he asked, holding a towel in front of him.

I blinked. Then I managed to say, "Would you mind turning that down?"

"What?"

I shrugged, walked over to the stereo and turned it down. "That," I said resolutely.

He shook his head and dropped the towel. "No, *this*."

This was incredible, I had to admit. It was semi-hard and about eight inches in length and it swayed tantalizingly to the left as he stepped closer to me.

"Isn't this what you've been wantin' since I came here?"

"How did you know?"

"I'm not blind, just cautious. I don't want any trouble with my Uncle Lloyd."

"Well, neither do I," I said, reaching out to take his cock in my hand. As I gazed at it, then began stroking it, he put his hands on my shoulders. At six-three, he was a good head taller than me. He pushed and I obediently dropped to my knees, his throbbing erection in my face. I gripped his silky thighs and began kissing the bulbous head of his cock. The more I kissed it, the longer and harder the cock became.

"Oh, suck that dick. I'm so horny I could die."

I had every intention of making up for lost time, and obviously so did he. He pushed me back against the bed and stood over me, fucking my mouth. I held on to his smooth ass as he rammed the hard cock into me. I closed my eyes and just let his power sweep over me. He planted his palms on the bed and began doing push-ups over my face. I unzipped my shorts and took out my cock and began stroking it. I had dreamed of this moment for so long, I couldn't hold back any longer. As I came, he pumped even harder and I couldn't remember having a more exciting orgasm.

But he hadn't come and he wasn't through with me. After I came down from my high, he backed off and told me to stand. He proceeded to pull my shorts off and then pushed me onto the bed. He rolled me over and the mauling he gave my ass was exquisite, occasionally spitting into the crack as he parted the cheeks.

"You have a nice ass. I bet you love to get fucked."

"Not ordinarily," I admitted.

"I knew it," he said, lifting me up so that he had full access to my puckering hole.

"Do you have a rubber?" I asked plaintively.

He stepped over to the bureau, opened the drawer and produced a Magnum in a gold-foil packet. It would have to have been a Magnum, I thought.

Cupping his buttocks with my hands, using only my mouth and my tongue, I put the condom on the tip of Bart's penis. With the soft wet skin of my lips, I slowly began to unroll the condom down the length of the huge erection. When it was halfway on, I stopped and used my tongue to tickle the

uncovered part, to dart and tease and forage into his hair and about his balls. Then I sucked and pulled on the covered part. All the while my hands were moving, probing, touching, caressing. He moaned and began running his fingers through my hair.

Slowly I began again to roll the condom on the rest of the way, backing up now and then to tease and suck the tip of him. When I finally had the condom all the way on, he was flushed and breathing hard. For a moment I had nearly the full length of him in my mouth; I gave him a smooth, tight suck at the back of my throat before he pulled out.

As he climbed on the bed, I rolled over again. He took some grease and worked his finger in my asshole. Satisfied it was ready, he lifted me up and aimed his cock at the target. His deadly earnestness about everything applied to his fucking as well. His need left no room for an easy entry. He lunged forward and slammed into me to the hilt, pushing me flat onto the mattress.

"Oh God," I groaned, and kept groaning. He said nothing as he gave me the most mechanical, efficient, and, for me, thoroughly exhausting fuck I had ever had, pulling out until my assring grabbed at his cock and then ramming it back into me again. Soon his breathing became ragged and I felt the cock swell. After a few moments, I could feel his spasms and I lifted my ass to meet the final thrusts. With my ass in the air, I began jerking myself and he left his cock in me until I had come, my jism spurting up onto the pillows.

As he pulled out of my ass, I collapsed on the bed. Climbing off the bed, he made a hasty retreat to the bathroom.

I heard the shower running again and when it was turned off, I began tugging on my shorts. As he was coming out of the bathroom, I said, "I must take your picture. Nothing scandalous, just a face shot. Okay?"

He was toweling off and his cock was semi-flaccid. "I don't photograph well."

"Oh, you do. It just depends on who's snapping the picture."

I raced back to the house and got my camera. When I arrived back at the Hamiltons, he was standing in the foyer dressed

only in his black bikini. I held up the Polaroid, snapped. "You didn't smile."

He shook his head. "I don't smile a helluva lot."

"So I've noticed. But try, just for my little picture. Think of something that makes you happy."

"Well, I kinda like what we did." His eyes sparkled. "Now that I think about it, I feel like smiling."

"Then do."

And he did. I snapped another picture. At last I had a picture of the smile I'd been waiting a month for.

"Now I have one and you have one." I held out the unsmiling photo.

"I don't want one."

"Okay. Then I have one with a smile and one without."

"Are you done?" he asked, impatience in his tone.

"Yes."

"Then why don't you come back upstairs?" He was rubbing the bulge in his bikini. "Just thinking about fucking that hot ass of yours has got me horny again."

I smiled and, wonder of wonders, he was smiling too.

BOYS IN SEARCH OF SOMETHING TO DO

Thom Nickels

Prologue

What does not fade: the memory of two encounters during the otherwise dull summer of 1976. These experiences occurred when I lived in Germantown, a sizeable neighborhood within Philadelphia city limits. Its claim to fame is the historic Battle of Germantown. In this battle, the Father of our Country lead a victorious battle over the British. Strikingly beautiful in the '20s, '30s and '40s with a surplus of Victorian mansions and cobblestone roads, Germantown today is a hodgepodge of housing projects and dilapidated houses. Many of the magnificent houses have fallen into ruin; the few that remain intact are a testament to the work of preservationists.

Germantown's reputation as a mecca for gay and lesbian couples is well deserved. Its location near the Wissahickon creek (where Edgar Allen Poe used to pilot a raft) is conducive to domesticity and monogamous relationships. In the '70s, cruising in Germantown used to occur at the YMCA, or along the main shopping drag. Hunky men could also be spotted in various neighborhood bars which once catered exclusively to German and Irish types.

In those days, I sometimes went to the Chelten Lounge, a bar located about fifteen blocks from my apartment. I'd go to The Lounge whenever I was strapped for funds, or when I didn't feel like going downtown. Beer there was cheap (the most popular drinks were whisky and gin). The Lounge was mainly a black straight pickup joint (only opposite sex couples occupied the rank booths which reeked of ammonia), but even a transvestite could pop in for a draft beer or a glass of wine and feel comfortable.

Situated along trolley tracks on Germantown Avenue, the bar was a convenient place to visit when I'd take a trolley from downtown. (Legend has it that Walt Whitman met Peter Doyle while riding this trolley line.) Germantown in the '70s had a fair population of bored white men and boys in search of something to do. Since the area was mostly black, the white man's minority status made them easy prey for

dubious types, though more often than not the opposite was true: blacks tended to view Germantown whites as honorary brothers. White men also sought one another out and usually found any excuse to approach a stranger. This did wonders for cruising because it was common for guys to approach you in Germantown bars just because you shared the same skin color.

I.

One night at the Lounge, I saw a boy about 17 ask the bartender for a sixpack. He was about 5'10", and the kid's lean body, stark white skin and pale blond hair made me think of a cornstalk. He had one of those big noses that always seem indicative of potent sexuality and a zest for life. I pegged him as the quiet shy type, and felt he'd been in the bar before because the exchange between him and the bartender was robotic: the beer was paid for in a fast but tentative flash as if both wished to avoid the eye of undercover cops out to bust underage drinkers.

When the kid left, I gulped down my beer and followed him outside. I approached him at an intersection.

"You go there much?" I asked, walking up alongside him.

"Yeah. I'm not 21 but the bartender knows me. I buy there all the time." I thought I saw a gleam in his eye--something that told me that he might be a game boy.

"With all the drugs around here, underage drinking is child's play. Cops should hand out blue ribbons for kids who do beer instead of shooting up."

Under the light of a streetlamp, he looked younger than 17. I guessed him to be a boy who knew he was beautiful yet who was not in love with himself – unlike the downtown clones who went out of their way to look and act cool.

"Going anyplace special?"

"Back to the orphanage."

"Orphanage as in Charles Dickens?"

"Not that bad. It's run by the Brothers of St. Vincent dePaul."

"Oh, a Catholic place. Must be strict. At least Catholics like to drink. Protestant orphanage masters would execute you for having sixpacks around."

"Well," he confessed, "we're just a small house. I live with two roommates but one of the guys is gone for the summer. Our monitor lives on the first floor. He's Brother Andrew. He's okay. He lets us live our own life but we can't have visitors after 10 p.m. He's always drunk on weekends."

The kid flashed a devilish smile and I couldn't help but wonder if Brother Andrew ever had sex with him. I asked him his name.

"Nathan. Born in Conneciticut, a late Virgo with Libra rising. And a little drunk – I love my beer, yep."

"Beer lowers inhibitions. Bless relaxes, damn braces – that's what poet William Blake said. My name is Nicholas, journalist, man-about-town, part-time poet. I love my wine. I like slumming through Germantown after midnight. Good things happen after midnight."

"Ya? Good things like what?"

"Like meeting you. Like finding a twenty-dollar bill on this sidewalk two weeks ago. Like having adventures."

"When I get home I'm going to hog out with this sixpack. That's my adventure."

"Do you want to hog out alone or can I join you? Hanging out alone is boring and solitary – like a coffin in a grave!"

He didn't answer but walked fast in a direction he navigated. I sensed he wanted to invite me back but didn't want to say so yet. We made further small talk until at last we were in front of the small orphanage, an ordinary three-story rowhouse. When at last he invited me inside, he warned me to be careful not to wake up Brother Andrew. "It should be okay," he whispered, "he's probably drunk and sound asleep by now. He drinks Chivas Regal. That always does a number on him. Poor guy."

"Why 'poor guy?'"

"He's got no life. He's married to the church."

Once in the house, we snuck past the first floor living room where I caught a glimpse of Brother Andrew asleep on a large chair. The only light in the room came from a TV. The light revealed the face of a man in a deep alcoholic coma. Did he look like the kind of guy who'd seduce a cutie like Nathan? I couldn't be certain, though I tried to analyze the contour of his lips: did they have the ripe fatness of lips used to giving blowjobs, rimjobs or deep French kisses? Definitely not – they

were thin, venal lips, the lips of a heterosexual rake who'd probably be good at muff diving were he not in a gothic, sexless marriage. "He probably drinks because he's having a hard time with celibacy," I told myself. "Holy Mother Church is such a cold vagina."

I followed him to the cellar where there was a makeshift weight room. He was already a little tipsy so he felt uninhibited enough to strip off his shirt, lie down on a bench press and begin lifting. I sipped the beer he handed me and studied his superb arms. I also watched the muscles on his swimmer's chest tighten as he held the weights above his head. He talked the whole time, asking me if I had ever met the Worm Boy. He told me the Worm Boy was a kid who wanders the neighborhood eating live worms.

"You might like that as a journalist, Nicholas," he offered.

I told him I'd never met a Worm Boy, though I've walked the streets of Germantown often enough. I laughed and let the reference pass but promised myself to be on the lookout for unusual types in the future. A boy that ate worms tickled my fancy, though at this moment Nathan and only Nathan interested me.

A little later on, when Nathan asked me to spot him, I stood behind his head to make sure the weights did not crash down on his handsome face. The position was suggestive, a kind of rehearsal of what might occur once I geared myself up to make a move. Nathan's jeans were so tight I was able to see the protrusion of his cock, and imagined myself sucking it as he worked out.

As he lifted, he told me his parents divorced just before his father was killed in an automobile accident. After his father's death, he said his mother began to have mental problems. It wasn't long after this that she was declared unfit to care for a fifteen-year-old. That's when he was shipped off to the Brothers of Saint Vincent. He'd been at the orphanage for just a year and worked full time at a local McDonald's but he said he wanted to become a model.

"You shouldn't have a problem doing that," I said. "You're very good-looking."

After a while he suggested we go upstairs to his bedroom. Upstairs we went, past Brother Andrew and up another narrow

staircase to a large room at the end of the hall. "Andre sleeps in there," he said, pointing to a room facing the street. "He's away this weekend."

"Andre's your age?"

"Same – sixteen."

He showed me a few things in his room, including a photograph of his girlfriend. She lived out-of-state, which pleased me because she wouldn't always be there when he was horny.

The seduction cue came when he stretched out on the bed. He was on his back, his legs open in a wide "V", his eyes closed. This was the position I loved best – a sleeping boy, very passive, welcoming a frontal attack. I got on the bed and lay beside him, placing my hand on his stomach, then sliding it inside his shirt where I proceeded to rub his chest. His skin was very soft, the area around his rib cage taut from the weightlifting. His nipples formed small, erect towers, and his adequate meat now extended itself in full bloom, a handsome seven inches that I quickly uncovered by unbuckling his jeans.

This was a challenge because his jeans didn't slip off easily. I had his legs bent upward and had to prop his firm ass off the mattress so I could get them down around his ankles.

Unlacing his sneakers took some doing. Even then I had to lift each foot and wiggle the sneaker free. Pulling his jeans over his calves and feet was an easier operation.

For a while, I just gazed at him, this boy beauty found in the bowels of shanty Germantown. A boy who was open, trusting, and all mine; a boy whose erect cock invited a plunge with my tongue. Yes, I let my loving assault wet every one of his sweet orifices. I kissed his lips, explored the clean cavity of his ears, ran my tongue along the contour of his neck and adam's apple. I traced the outline of his jawbone and let it run rampant over his chin. I outlined his eyebrows, murmuring "Sweet boy," as I kissed him on the forehead, or the Hindu holy spot.

I planted my lips on each of his nipples, sucking in what I hoped would become a boy's milk. I wanted all parts of him flowing into me. Whether he feigned sleep or was actually out, I didn't care. True, he moaned and turned his head to the right or left, even tilting it back as he parted his lips. His cock had the creamy translucence most blond cocks have, its purple head

much bigger than the shaft.

In the quiet of the orphanage, as Brother Andrew slept in front of the TV that was now probably only horizontal lines, I went over his body again and again. I refused to believe he would not come as I tried different methods of sucking: first with my mouth, then in conjunction with my hand. I tried gripping his cock with both hands, sucking him fast and then slow. I tried zipping ahead on fast forward, a Chaplinesque motion that produced a slither of pre-cum but that's all. No big spurts. No gushing oil wells. No lush tidal pools. Once I pulled him to the edge of the bed so that his legs draped over the side. Then I knelt on the floor in-between his legs. In that position I sucked his hairless balls and shaft and began the Chaplinesque motion all over again.

I was drenched in sweat in no time. Nathan was out cold. Dogs in the neighborhood began to bark and there was the sound of someone breaking bottles in the street. I thought I saw sunlight filter through the curtains. I knew I had to hurry. Leaving the orphanage at sunrise would be risky: I didn't know whether fellow brothers would appear, or whether a nun, breakfast bell in hand, would ring in the new day.

Wanting to climax, I turned Nathan over, his limber body rolling obediently so that his marvelous butt became the centerpiece of the bed. I crouched on all fours, thinking how much I was emulating the behavior of the dogs. My tired tongue entered the boy's warm butt. I drew in large breaths and wet the cavity as the special aroma peculiar to teenage boys filled my world.

The sweet taste had one effect: it made me want to fuck. I positioned my body over his, my cock in rocket-launch mode. He let me enter, though he squirmed when I went deeper and as my thrusts became more mechanically precise. He contracted and arched his back, which caused me to slip out. For twenty minutes we wrestled like this. I finally thrusted between his thighs in the femoral position favored by the Greeks.

Afterwards, I wrote my name and address on numerous bits of paper and placed them all over his room. One note was rolled up like a cigarette and placed in his package of Marlboros. Another note went into his wallet, another in each of his bureau drawers, another in his shoes. Finally I thrust a

large note in his hand. "I know I'm overdoing it with all these notes," I wrote, "but I want to make sure you call me – 'Nothing succeeds like excess!'"

Brother Andrew was not in the living room when I went back downstairs. The television set was off. I guessed his bedroom was in the rear of the house, so I tiptoed out, being careful to muffle the sound of the door as it closed.

In the morning light, I could smell Nathan everywhere--on my fingers, my lips, the ends of my mustache. I knew I'd have to sleep half the day in order to make up for the sleep I lost. Still, boys like Nathan don't come along everyday, so it's best to drop everything when they do.

When I got home, my roommate was up with a cup of coffee. He was in one of his "I'm not speaking to you" moods because I'd stayed out all night. I don't know why he cared. We had already reached the end of our rope – too many arguments and people had come between us, and we no longer called ourselves lovers. We lived together because it was financially feasible and because we were used to one another. Sometimes he acted as if he wanted to salvage the wreck of our marriage. This usually surfaced when I announced that I was going out on the town, such as the night I met Nathan.

"You were out two nights ago," he'd say.

"Well, I'm going out again."

"I don't want you to bring anyone back. No sailors, no urchins, no teenage vagabonds. You're not waking me up at 2 a.m. with somebody you found on the street. I'm tired of these guys with stinky feet. I'll never forget that guy you dragged in here with feet stinking up the house. It took two days to get the smell out!"

"I'm quiet when I bring somebody back. Besides, you always check to see who it is I brought home. Then you comment on his beauty or tell me how awful he is. But I can't help it if people have stinky feet."

"Listen to what I tell you: If you bring somebody back I swear I'll kick them out on their ass," he said, meaning he'd make my life miserable for a couple days. He could never be rude to a stranger unless the stranger was rude to him or dangerous in some way. At home, he excelled at yelling, slamming doors, and he talked about me to friends. Sometimes

I deserved it because I went overboard in my behavior. Other times he just overreacted to anything that might be happening. He was never violent but he could be a psychological terror. He must have smelt Nathan on me because he looked at me as if catching the scent of something nice as soon as I walked in the apartment.

We had had threesomes in the past, so he was not immune to the pleasures of extra-marital sex – despite the fact that he said he was faithful to his current boyfriend in New York. I knew it was only a matter of time before he and this new boyfriend left me high and dry in shanty Germantown.

II.

I'd recently become a Buddhist, so one of the things I most enjoyed doing was taking meditative walks in the woods near our apartment. These jaunts helped me to see my life more clearly, to plan ahead, to learn to trust in myself. My favorite meditation spot was beneath an elm tree in a small clearing. Here I could sit undisturbed for an hour or more, chanting until I felt light-headed and giddy.

Chanting had its benefits. After a half hour I sometimes felt as if I was beginning to levitate. Times like this I had no feeling but seemed to be floating in mid-air. During such episodes there'd always comes a point when I'd panic and snap to. I didn't really want to rise above the trees but wished to stay grounded so I could meet the Worm Boy – if such a boy existed. Chanting also drew boys to me in most peculiar ways. It caused them to telephone me at odd hours, walk up to me in the street. The net effect of chanting seemed to give me this electric field some boys found irresistible.

One day I was chanting my chant of "Ho Some Boy To Me Shoo, Boom!" when I noticed an impish blond kid, thin, about 5'3", blazing a trail through the forest. He wore a plaid hunter's jacket, green trousers and black and white sneakers. His hair was cut straight across his head at about ear level (the proverbial kitchen bowl haircut), which called to mind the work of an incompetent parent.

He seemed to be searching the weeds as he tossed tree branches and rocks every which way. I sensed he saw me but

was playing dumb. He eventually sat down in a patch of tall grass, his blond hair making a kind of halo in the sun. I watched as he brought something up to his lips, nibbling on it as if it were a small ear of corn. He was oblivious to everything but what was in his hand. Occasionally he'd lean over and pick up something else and munch on it. Only once did I see him inspect what it was he was eating. Then he spat it out and threw the remainder away. This did not conclude his meal but prefaced a long reach to another part of the grass where he grabbed a handful of soil. From this he selected particles and put them in his mouth.

I was sure I had spotted the Worm Boy, for who else would pick from handfuls of soil and eat particles which dangled from his mouth?

I walked over to him. I'm sure he heard me coming but he did not look up. He continued to bury his head in his cupped hands. I walked beside him, waited until he had finished chewing, and said hello.

"Worms are good for you," he said.

I saw him pick up a long, slender worm, bite it in half and swallow it. The remaining half wiggled over his thumb and forefinger, almost escaping until he consumed that too.

"Aren't you afraid of disease?"

"Worms are protein. No disease."

He had the most curious, childlike face. Big blue eyes set above a squarish boxer's nose offset thick, sensual lips. His hair was the color of haystacks with sun-bleached streaks mingled here and there. He was oddly cute, this adolescent of indeterminable age. His voice had a scratchy quality though I could tell by the size of his feet and the length of his fingers that he felt the sway and power of a man's sexuality.

"I've never seen anybody eat worms before. How long have you been doing this?"

"All summer. I came to worms when my mom and dad went away. We didn't have food. I tried it and liked it. I like the way they feel going down. They are round and I like round things. I don't have to eat them now but I do because they are okay. There's nothing else to do. Want to try?"

He held up a fat, short worm he seemed to have hidden up the sleeve of his hunting jacket.

"I'll pass. Is that all you do is eat worms? What about snakes?"

"Can't find any. Too hard to chew. I like to walk. There's nothing to do around here. My mother lives with her boyfriend. He hates me. He's always yelling at her. He knows I eat worms and he beats me."

"Eating worms makes you feel better?"

"Always. You should try."

"I've seen you before, up near the big WAWA store. I saw you along the side of the road. People have seen you around the neighborhood eating worms. You're famous, did you know that?"

"They have good worms near WAWA. Big."

"Tell me what they taste like?"

"Sweet. Some you have to spit out because they are not right."

As I watched him run his hands over the grass I wondered if it would be wise to try and seduce him. But how was I going to get him to concentrate on his body instead of worms? The symbolic representation was there: the worm as small phallus, the eating of the phallus, etc. All I had to do was work the alchemy. To be seen sitting or walking along with one so young was another matter. Because I tend to worry too much anyway, I dismissed these fears as paranoia.

"Do you want to take a walk with me up past my house? It's down the road about a mile," he said.

The request jolted me. He was asking me to leave the isolation of the woods for the busy streets. I agreed because I sensed he had something besides another worm up his sleeve.

We walked along a stretch of highway, cars and trucks whizzing past at breakneck speed. Occasionally we passed another person on the road and I'd get the eye. No doubt these people had seen the Worm Boy before and now had to match him with one considerably older. Most knew that I was not his young father or an uncle because my nightly cruising of the Germantown neighborhood had given me a dubious reputation.

When we came to the top of a hill, he veered off to the right. We proceeded to walk down a long street when I spotted a cluster of split-level homes. The boy, who said his name was Pip, pointed to a split level home with closed shutters, a

basketball net and a blue car in the driveway.

"Here it is. Where I live."

I wondered what I was supposed to see. I imagined a crazy woman peeking out from behind the shutters, or even neighbors taking note. I still did not know how old the boy was, yet I was allowing myself to be led. Used to the trance-like results of certain meditations, I half-wondered if the boy's magic hadn't lulled me into a hypnotic sleepwalk.

"Where are we going?"

He said to a place where he found the best worms, a place by a big tree where no one would come. Images of pleasure intruded, though I considered turning back or remaining chaste should the unexpected happen. He looked *too* young. I didn't want to wind up in jail.

"How much longer?" I asked;

"Up here."

He was now leading the way through a field. I followed at close range and kept checking to see if we were being followed. We came to a small, densely wooded area. We went in about 50 yards, and came out at a meadow.

He sat down and I did the same. He became very quiet. I was sitting across from him trying to figure out what was going on. I decided to do nothing, thinking that maybe he just wanted me to sit on the grass with him. He didn't look for worms but stretched back, his trouser legs riding up and exposing his legs. His green trousers were so baggy it was impossible to gauge signs of a hardon. We just looked at one another and smiled.

Without warning, he came over to me, knelt between my legs and undid my zipper. He didn't look me in the eyes but kept his head down as he moved his hand around inside my crotch. This action was not preceded by any sort of foreplay so it left me quite numb.

I undid my belt buckle but he was adept at sliding my pants and briefs down around my knees. I leaned back and watched as he put his mouth on my cock. He could only get part of it in his mouth. He had the slow, cautious style of a novice but he knew what he was doing.

He had very thick lips for one so young, so I was able to bask in the warm, tight wet of his mouth – a feeling the less

fortunate worms might have felt for just an instant before their untimely deaths. His minimal sucking motions brought me to full arousal. As he worked on me, I studied his small boxer's nose and the way his hair fell over his forehead. His uniqueness excited me: my legs were literally shaking.

Watching him suck produced tingling sensations I've rarely felt with people my own age. I was forced to ask myself: was it *the forbidden* that something in me craved?

I came quickly. He did not withdraw but kept up his mechanical motions, a maneuver which sent other spasms into his young mouth.

When he was finished, he sat up against the trunk of a tree, a look of satisfaction on his face. Obviously he had done this before; obviously I had been seduced – willingly, of course, but under his direction. I wasted no time approaching him and undoing his zipper. This was what I really wanted, to see what he had and how he would spurt. His coming on to me so abruptly was a psychic violation of sorts, something I had to remedy by blowing him as soon as possible.

His cock was already hard, a sturdy five inches-plus, the full size of which would not be known for at least another year. It had the fat width of an eel, its mushroom head vigorously inflated. His yellow pubic hair had a soapy smell. I did not have him in my mouth for very long when he came in furious, thick jets.

I was glad that the worms had not contaminated his jism.

Shortly after he came, I became fearful that somebody had witnessed the interlude. I was also concerned that Pip would experience delayed guilt and announce that he'd been seduced by a local newspaperman. I pictured myself being arrested and dragged off to jail, my reputation (what was left of it) ruined forever. I had only one recourse: to get away from him as soon as possible. Handing him some spare change, I said, "Good luck with your parents and finding good worms." It was prudent of me to do this. He would have hung out with me all day if I allowed it. The quicker I disappeared, the faster he'd forget about me – and that was the way it had to be. I was glad that I did not tell him where I lived, and I hoped that the people who saw us together prior to our having sex would experience memory loss.

Once I was home, I took a bath and brooded about this strange boy whose smell was still on my body. A part of me regretted that I hadn't seen him nude or taken off his sneakers and fondled his feet. These thoughts disappeared once I realized that prolonged lovemaking would have only worried me more. *The Germantown Courier*, the paper I wrote for, was notorious for reporting stories of men being sentenced to jail for having sex with minors. My editor loved these types of stories and he often gave them bigger headlines than murders, drug busts and gang rapes. Sometimes he published photographs of the so-called molesters on the front page. Ironically, almost all the minors involved were street kids with a penchant for crime. The men who were arrested were just ordinary guys who went into the experience with the same attitude I adopted when I met Pip. This attitude assumed that the kid knew what he was doing, that he'd done it before with his peers but just wanted to try it with someone a little older.

The day after I met Pip, I got to work on my novella, a tale about a queer Mormon missionary. The novella was an exorcism of sorts: it enabled me to work through my own Mormon guilt concerning sex. I'd spend about two hours a day on the book, then headed for the *Courier* for a meeting with my editor, a sandy-haired WASPish blond in his 30s with child-bearing hips. Both his grandfather and father had been newspapermen, so he used the illustrious "III" after his name, a habit which annoyed me because it forced people to compare him, albeit unconsciously, to lines of popes and kings. He had a handsome face and big feet but his body and his condescending (Philadelphia blueblood) attitude left me cold.

Resting at home one night after a *Courier* assignment (about a demonstration in front of an X-rated movie house), I got a call from Nathan. He said he wanted to meet in a neighborhood schoolyard. The schoolyard he was talking about was an immense space with many swings and sandboxes; it also contained a soccer field and a tennis court. It had been dug up in parts, so there were huge mounds of dirt and grass covering a good portion of it. Although reporting on the demonstration had left me exhausted (evangelical Christians and anti-pornography folks sap your energy like psychic vampires), the sound of Nathan's voice gave me new life. I was also happy

that I had taken the time to leave him so many notes.

When I met him by the schoolyard entrance, I could see that his eyes were glazed but that he could still walk. He wore a pair of tight jeans, a yellow T-shirt, and a pair of square-tipped boots. Naturally, my heart raced as we walked past the swing sets, the see-saw and the Jungle Jim. Nathan went over to one of the dirt piles behind the tennis court.

He stretched out on his back, legs wide open and eyes half shut. Reeking of beer, the unpleasant smell was still a kid's intoxication and not a longtime drunk's jaded aroma. Bushes surrounded the mound so we had some privacy. The schoolyard was dotted with broken glass and graffiti which made wise local residents avoid it not only at night but at all hours of the day.

I ran my tongue along the top of his sneakers and over his freshly laundered jeans. At his crotch, I opened my mouth and aimed downward, pressing and releasing until his sizeable boner slanted at an angle. Since I had not seen him cum, I was determined that this session would bring him over the top.

Unzipping him was easy; sucking him proceeded in the smooth-as-silk manner as before, only now I was on the lookout for gangs of kids. Gangs were known to hang out in the schoolyard. In the past it was the sight of many crimes, especially heterosexual rape.

I had Nathan's jeans down to his ankles and his shirt over his chest. He was positioned sideways on the mound. The elements of nature excited me: the odors from his wet cock and the green earth made me very passionate. Soon the ground under his ass was soaked with my saliva. Try as I might, my tired mouth only brought him to the verge several times but could not get him to pop his cork.

We were interrupted twice. Once by a barking German Shepherd, then by a pack of ten-year-olds scampering across the tennis courts. I covered Nathan up at their passing, then continued to suck him with a vengeance once they disappeared.

Crouched between his legs for about two hours, I finally admitted to myself that the beer had quelled his juices, even though his dry boner stayed erect the entire time. I achieved satisfaction by sniffing his sneakers and orgasming on his thighs.

I left him on the mound because he was too drunk to wake up. Since I had a pen, I wrote him a note: "I tried to wake you but you were zonked out. I had to go – the sun was coming up."

On the way home, a police car kept popping into view. It would stay put until I came within a few feet of it, then take off. It did this a couple times before coming up behind me at cruising speed. The driver was about 25 with dark hair and a mustache. He was leaning towards the steering wheel so as to get a better view of me. I remembered my experience with Pip and was afraid. Now I had plundered a Catholic orphanage.

I held my head high because I knew I hadn't done anything wrong. I'd expanded and illuminated Pip's world; I brought peace and comfort to a troubled, parentless blond. Puritans of the world might condemn me, but I adhered to a higher law – the law of Gide, Cocteau, Genet, Rimbaud. This was also the law of French philosopher Michel Foucault, who favored lowering the age of consent to 13 and who insisted that children can and do seduce adults.

When I got home, my roommate scolded me for staying out all night. When I told him where I'd been he calmed down and soon I was on the bed massaging his balls. This was the only thing left of our once-passionate sex life.

"What'll it be this time?" I asked him. If he wanted a fantasy story to jerk off to, I was more than willing to comply – provided it kept the peace.

"Make it over barrels. I want three bald men. Have them on a ship. They're deck hands."

His type was big and beefy. He hated skinny boys with no brawn or muscle. I tried to convert him to my slither-limbed youths but he'd always wince and beg for hairy chests and bald heads as shiny as Mr. Clean's. His fantasy cocks had to be oversized, their balls obscenely proportioned or bulging. The longer and fuller the balls, the better.

I saw his desire as the common Tom of Finland cliche, but sometimes my own descriptions of these immense men strung over barrels or lingering in woodsheds turned me on. After years of describing their huge limbs, pronounced biceps and pumped up pecs, I saw a glimmer of sexiness – but only a glimmer.

One day, as I was walking to the Gum Shoo neighborhood Chinese restaurant, a girl not yet 14 screamed at me in the street. "You have sex with 12-year-old boys! Pervert! You should be locked up!"

Since she was with two young black boys, ages 9 or 10, I assumed she was babysitting. I'd seen her before, mostly hanging out with older black guys smoking reefer and drinking beer. I thought she was a slut because I often spotted her sitting on different doorsteps late at night. Once she had a beautiful blond boyfriend but she traded him in for a toothless drug pusher and gang leader. I never respected her after that.

I didn't know her name, though I was more than aware that her mouth was a cesspool for gossip even before her comment to me. I'd shiver at the sight of her oval, judgmental face and her long flat hair. When she walked with her mother, the sight of the two of them together was enough to make me avoid eye contact or walk to the other side of the street.

"Whoever told you such lies?" I answered. "Do you realize what you're saying?"

I couldn't let the accusation pass. His exact age was impossible to determine, but didn't Foucault say that the age of consent should be lowered to 13? That was enough for me. Besides, Pip had seduced me; he knew what he wanted and went for it. I knew what I wanted when I was his age.

She seemed shocked that I defended myself. I suppose she expected me to cower in a corner or plead for mercy. Never! She was the voice of the puritanical, repressed society!

"Don't deny it. You blow 12-year-old boys!"

"You should be shot. But before that, your mother should wash your mouth out with acid. Then she should be shot."

The little boys looked at me with bulging eyes. I cringed to think that they'd tell their friends or families and then the word would be all over the neighborhood. I didn't know how many people in the neighborhood heard the heated exchange. The slut knew everybody in the area, too – the garage men in the auto body shop, the greengrocers, the Gum Shoo Chinese people, the drug dealers, the other sluts.

"You better stay away from my brother!"

"What brother?" Then I remembered a chubby boy with thick glasses who sometimes rode his tricycle up and down

Queen Lane. "Say what?"

"You heard me, queer!"

"That butterball is a baby – get real. I'll get the Gay Liberation Front after you if you don't shut up. How would you like a demonstration in front of your house?"

Homophobes had this idea that queer groups were crazier than Islamic fundamentalists. She paled when I mentioned a demonstration. I attributed this to the fact that for months I'd been tacking queer activist posters all over the neighborhood. She knew I meant business.

When she walked away, I couldn't help but wonder what led to this heated exchange. Had Pip talked? Did she know Pip? Had she seen me walking with Pip as we searched for the worm colony?

For the next several days I agonized silently, not daring to tell my roommate why I was so depressed. I avoided Gum Shoo, but I couldn't avoid doing my laundry at Clean-O-Rama. I was so paranoid by this time I feared that anyone who looked twice at me knew about Pip. I was always on the lookout for odd glances or hushed whispers when passing people in the street.

Meditation helped to ease the burden. Soon I regained my old equilibrium and began walking to Gum Shoo with confidence. Even then, I heard a kid call me a child molester. Then a rock whizzed past my head. Since this occurred very close to my apartment, I began to fear for my future in the neighborhood.

The next day there were reports of a shooting near the projects. A girl, not yet 11, was killed while playing basketball. Then an eight-year-old girl was raped by an unemployed air-conditioning mechanic. For two or three days there were police cars everywhere. This helped to quell most rumors concerning me. I felt further removed from scandal when an infant was thrown from the roof of the projects.

By the time I heard from Nathan again, I was suffering from frayed nerves and needed the consolation of his blond thighs. I was going over the proofs of my Mormon novella when the phone rang and he greeted me with a slurred "Hi." My roommate had gone to New York to be with his boyfriend, and I had planned to go into the city but the call changed that.

Nathan was now saying that Brother Andrew was away for the weekend.

At the orphanage, I could see that he was having difficulty standing up. A dark-haired boy, Italian or black Irish, appeared at the top of the staircase. "This is Andre," Nathan managed, though I could hardly hear the introduction over a stereo's blasting of David Bowie songs. Andre watched as Nathan and I made our way upstairs.

Andre was very handsome with a lean football player's build. He helped Nathan into his room, a maneuver which made me notice his long, thick fingers, blue eyes and high cheekbones. Although he looked as strong as an ox, Andre had amazingly gentle movements and was soft-spoken when he talked to his friend.

Andre disappeared into his own bedroom, and I sat with Nathan on the edge of his bed. He was in a sort of coma, eyes focused in space, body wobbling. Suddenly I wondered what I was doing there. Nathan was drunker than I'd ever seen him and in a few minutes he would be completely comatose. Since dry boners were his specialty, I imagined another all-night session in which I failed to obtain his juices.

"You're pretty drunk. Way over the limit. Wow!"

He lurched forward, groping the air with his arms. "Andre!" he moaned. I kept him from stumbling into his bureau drawers, then supported him as he stood up. Andre appeared in only his briefs, taking his friend in his arms and guiding him towards the bathroom.

At the sight of the nearly nude Andre I was more than shocked. His body was more beautiful than Nathan's: his sculpted pecs, exquisite arms and washboard stomach conjured up every pretty boy stereotype. His crotch called to mind all the oral fantasies I'd ever given my roommate – but this was no burly man over a barrel but a boy in perfect form.

Andre helped Nathan into the bathroom. I followed, though I went no further than the bathroom door. Nathan collapsed by the toilet, moaning as he grabbed the seat in an attempt to pull himself up. As vomit poured out of him in every direction, I thought to myself that this was the only fluid I had ever seen leave his body. Andre knelt beside his friend, his muscles flexing as he kept repositioning himself.

Andre's legs opened in a wide "V" as he draped Nathan's head on the toilet's enamel ledge and held it at an angle facing the water. I also saw the edges of the boy's crotch hair as well as the thickness of his killer cock.

These images lost their brutal impact compared to the affection between the two boys. Andre was stroking Nathan's hair; Nathan, though very ill, seemed to be at peace with his head resting in his friend's arms.

I never saw Nathan again after that night. True, I had my cursory dry suck after Andre, good friend that he was, cleaned Nathan up and walked him back to bed. Alone with my loveboy, I followed my routine of panting and licking, of almost entering and useless (but fun) rear-end pumping.

This last night was also the most tense and least pleasurable of our meetings together. When Andre brought Nathan back to his room, I sensed that he wanted me to come to him when I was finished with his friend. After all, Andre left his bedroom door open. I also had the distinct impression that Nathan had told Andre about me and wanted him to share in the experience. So what stopped me? Visions of my accuser, the gossipy teenager who categorized me as a monster. I wanted to prove to my soul that what directed me was affection and love as much as lust and that, despite my huge sexual appetite, I was capable of some kind of loyalty. I also made a "pact" with the invisible forces that control life. It went like this: If I forego Andre, will you help the neighborhood forget Pip – and not send me to jail?

I never entered Andre's bedroom, but stayed with Nathan until I saw the first rays of morning.

And after that, nobody ever said anything to me about Pip, and my accuser moved away.

SHERIFF'S POSSE

Dirk Hannam

It was an extremely hot, dry afternoon in Central California. I was exploring the countryside and had driven up from the endless flatness of the San Joaquin Valley into the foothills west of the Sierra Nevadas. I came to a small town nestled in a little valley – a couple of false-fronted stores and a gaggle of old, ramshackle houses. Several had empty windows, obviously vacant, falling down. Certainly not a place one would want to call home. Although I suppose the twenty or so families that inhabited the place no doubt called it that. Maybe it represented something precious to them. Or perhaps it was some sort of a hell they couldn't escape.

Anyway, the afternoon was breathtakingly hot and my throat was dry. I stopped at the combined store and side-by-side beer parlor to get a drink. Not beer. I didn't feel in the mood to sit around all alone in a dim room guzzling beer. Instead I thought a bottle of cold orange juice would fix my thirst.

The store building was very old. Outside, its false front had been renewed. Consequently the old display cases, walls and ceiling inside were a surprise. There was no storekeeper in sight and no customer other than myself. The store had no air conditioning. It was even hotter within than the air on the roadway.

I looked around, found a glass-fronted refrigerator on the back wall and glanced in to see if there was bottled orange juice available. There was and, surprisingly, it was ice cold. I carried it to the old-fashioned counter where there was an antique cash register and waited for someone to come to take my money. In the meantime I started to gulp down the juice. Delicious! Just the answer to a hot day!

I finished the bottle and decided to drink another. I drank slower on the second one, waiting. There was still no clerk. I was all alone among the rather skimpy displays of groceries.

Finally I yelled: "Hey! Where is everyone?"

I heard a chair thump in the beer parlor half of the establishment and a young woman banged through a door into the store. She got behind the counter, rang up what I owed on

the cash register – I was surprised that it still worked – took my money, gave me change and promptly returned through the door to the beer hall. Not a word was exchanged between us.

Surprised at the indifference of my reception, I stepped outside onto the high stoop that ranged along the front of the building. I had my half-finished bottle of orange juice so, while I finished it, I sat on the railing that kept people from falling onto the road.

A young man who had evidently been hanging around nearby came up onto the stoop and spoke to me.

"Hi! Pretty hot today."

"Sure is."

"Where are you from?"

"Washington."

"State or District?"

"District."

"You one of them politicians?"

"No, I'm afraid not. I'm a stockbroker."

"A stockbroker! Boy, we don't see many of those in these parts.

"Is this your home town?" I asked.

"It was when I was a kid. I live in Los Angeles now. I'm just back on a visit. Actually a kind of reunion with six other guys who used to live here. We're going to have a party later in the day."

"I'll bet you were glad you escaped this town. There are a lot more opportunities for a person in L.A."

"Oh, I don't know. There are some advantages to living in the boondocks which aren't obvious."

"Name one."

"Friendships. The guys attending this reunion, for instance. We've known each other since kindergarten. In a little town with few kids, the ones there are become lifelong pals. The same close relationships just ain't going to happen in a big city. Maybe between two guys but not among six or eight buddies closely bonded in a one-for-all-and-all-for-one way."

I had drained the last of the orange juice and tossed the plastic bottle into a nearby trash can.

"Well, I guess I better be on my way. I want to see what the country is like higher up in the hills."

"Don't go just yet. I like talking to you. Stick around. It's just a suggestion but would you care to come to the reunion party I told you about? There's always tons of food and plenty to drink, soft and hard."

"That's kind of you but I don't know any of your friends and I'd be a stranger barging in. I better not."

"Hell, no, you'll be our honored guest. The party's not here in town. It's way up in the mountains in a sort of hidden valley. We, us guys, own it. It's really private. There's a little stream runs through it. It's beautiful. Change your mind and come along. We'll give you a good time. I promise you, it will be an unusual experience for you. Okay?"

He seemed like a nice friendly young man and he was eager to have me accept. I thought: "What the hell, this may be fun. I don't have anything better to do, just driving around."

"Okay, I accept. Thanks for the invitation. How do we get there?"

"Probably the best way is for you to follow me to the end of the road. Then we hike in."

He went off to his pickup truck parked by the side of the store and started off driving north into the higher hills. I followed in my car. There was no danger of losing him; there was just the one winding road going higher and higher and no other traffic whatever.

As I drove along I wondered what I would find at the hidden valley, or rather, who I would find. The young man I was following seemed like a really friendly, honest guy. He was tall and slim, graceful in movement, lithe. His face was quite good-looking in a farm-boy sort of way. He was wearing well-washed jeans, a blue work shirt, pointy-toed cowboy boots and a cream-colored, straw cowboy hat. His appearance went with the mountain town he sprang from but the way he talked and the words he used were far from backwoods speech.

We drove for perhaps ten miles going deeper and higher into the mountains. While the road was constantly twisting around curves, it was blacktop and easy to drive. We came at last to a sort of a summit and turned off onto a one lane dirt road. The cars raised clouds of dust. I held back to avoid breathing it in from the truck ahead.

Possibly four miles farther, most of it downhill, we came to

a grassy meadow, a flat place where the road ended. There were five horses tied there on ropes long enough to let them browse on the grass. My new friend parked his pickup to one side and I parked alongside.

"Well, we've arrived," he said when we had both stepped onto the ground, "We have to hike from here. It's only about a mile."

"Say, before we go any further," I asked, "What's your name?"

"Elmer. Elmer Jacobs. What's yours?"

"Leon Marcos."

"Hi, Leon."

"Hi, Elmer."

He picked a grocery bag out of his truck and led the way. The trail was narrow and uneven, downhill all the way. It would be a difficult trail for horses – which is probably why they were left tethered up above. The hills on either side were open meadows of wild grass dotted with scrub brush and with clumps of pines and oak trees here and there. The trees grew closer together as we went down. It seemed more than a mile and I was getting very hot and sweaty but eventually we reached the floor of a little valley. It was shaded by a grove of oaks, tall trees with many slim trunks towering overhead to form a dense canopy of leaves. The ground underneath was covered with short green grass, almost like a lawn. And there was indeed a mountain brook running through the place.

In the center of this glade three young men were standing and talking near a mound of smoking hot earth, evidently the top of a barbecue fire pit. Beyond them two more young men were arranging dishes, utensils and plates of food on a blanket laid out flat on the grass.

As we approached them, Elmer called out "Hi, men! I've brought the guest. Meet Leon."

He turned to me. "Leon, those three guys by the fire pit are Zed, Carl and Josh."

I smiled at them and sort of bobbed my head in acknowledgement.

They were all dressed like Elmer: jeans, shirt, straw cowboy hats. To my surprise the three of them took off their hats and swung them almost to the ground as they deeply bowed to me.

They were so like the Musketeers in the movie I was taken aback.

"The two over there fixing the table are Michael and Ezekiel."

They were on their knees beside the blanket. They didn't rise, merely took off their hats, placed them over their breasts and bowed their heads to me.

Then everyone called out: "Hi!" "Welcome!" "Nice to meet you!" or "Join the party!"

In spite of being momentarily nonplussed by their doffing of hats and bowing, I felt at ease and welcome in their company.

Elmer went off with his bag of groceries to help the men laying the picnic. I joined the three around the fire pit. I had hardly answered the usual California question: "Where are you from?" when another, about year older, came down the trail and into the valley.

"All right, men," he called, "I'm here. The party can start now." He noticed me. "Who's this?"

Elmer came up from the picnic spread.

"This is Leon. I've invited him to be the guest of honor today." He introduced the late arrival: "Leon, this is Aaron. He's the Sheriff of our gang."

"Sheriff? Really?"

"I'm not the official County Sheriff," Aaron said. "But my old man was back when we were kids in the third and fourth grade. In those days we had our own gang and all the kids liked my dad so we called ourselves the Sheriff's Posse. The seven of us that are left still call ourselves the Sheriff's Posse. Anyway, I want to welcome you." He turned to Elmer. "Thanks for bringing Leon. He looks just the man to be our honoree and the recipient of our covenant. See that he receives every courtesy. The Posse is in your debt."

I didn't understand the true significance of this exchange but it was nice to be so readily accepted by the leader of this group of handsome young males.

In a minute or two we sat down around the blanket "table." Zed and Josh used a battered old shovel to open the fire pit. Underneath the hot smoking earth was a giant, covered, earthen pot. When the cover was removed the whole valley was filled with the most mouth-watering aromas. Plates were

passed; on each was placed a small bird, cooked to perfection and smothered in spiced gravy.

"Game hens, Leon, cooked a la Sheriff's Posse. It's a specialty with us. Help yourself to salad, rolls and anything else you see. You'll need to build your reserves up for later this afternoon."

I wondered idly what he meant by rituals but in the presence of such delicious food it didn't seem important. Vegetables, salads, breads, desserts, all prepared in gourmet fashion, the meal was indeed a feast. For me it was made even more pleasant because of the extreme courtesy with which I was treated.

Aaron sat cross-legged at the head of the table, with me at his right and the other six seated around the edges of the blanket. Every serving dish was passed to me first; every word I spoke was listened to with attention. Yet there was no formality, the men were relaxed and comment was free and easy. Everyone at the table was young – close to my own age – and every one was strikingly handsome. As the meal progressed I became more and more aware of the sheer virility of the company. It called forth from me strong feelings of being a man among men, a male among males.

At the end of the meal, Aaron announced: "We will now go to the Hall of Ceremonies, for the rituals," He turned to me, "At this point, Leon, we all take our shoes and socks off and roll up our pants. We are going to cross the creek."

I did as he instructed. The men of the Posse did likewise.

"Come and stand by my side," said Aaron, "and Elmer, you stand on Leon's other side. We'll cross the creek together. There are a lot of small rocks on the bed of the creek, Leon, it makes walking across difficult. If you feel yourself slipping, grab Elmer or me."

Actually we crossed the stream without trouble. On the other side was the same grassy lawn. The whole company walked across it, over a low rise and down into a private glen.

"This is our Hall of Ceremonies, Leon. Notice our totem and the Mound of Sacrifice both dedicated to the god Priapus."

At one end of the glen a huge pine tree had been topped leaving a trunk about three feet across and thirty feet high still standing straight up. The bark had been removed so that the

wood was clean of limbs and naked. The top had been carved in the shape of a flaring, swollen glans, the head of a gigantic penis. It was a formidable, almost frightening phallic symbol, a domineering hardon, a cock to conjure with. At the foot of this giant erection and a little way in front of it was an altar-like hummock of earth covered with grass, about waist high, with steep sides.

"We are about to do you a very great honor, Leon, the highest it is in our power to grant. But first I must ask you: would you accept honorary membership in this Sheriff's Posse if it were offered to you?"

"Yes ...I think I would. What do I have to do?"

"We will come to that shortly. You should know that this Posse has been in existence for twenty-one years. Every year for the past ten we have enrolled a new honorary member. Each one has taken a leading part in the ceremony you are now about to participate in. You will be the eleventh such member.

"I see your totem, Aaron. Is this some kind of erotic observance like the ancient mysteries of Dionysus?"

"Yes, you might say that."

It suddenly occurred to me to ask: "Are all you men gay?"

"Yes, we are. I believe you are also. Is that not so?"

"Well...Yes...I am."

That seemed to be a signal. All the members of the Posse started taking off their shirts. Elmer unbuttoned mine and pulled it off my shoulders.

"Do you have a lover?" Aaron asked.

"Not at the moment. I have had in the past."

Another signal. The men unbuckled their belts and slipped off their pants. Elmer loosened my belt and pulled my pants off my hips and down to my feet. I kicked them away as I saw the other men do. Eight of us were now standing on the grass in front of the giant phallus in our underwear briefs. Looking around, I saw that the members all seemed well-endowed. Several were becoming aroused. I am not ashamed of my own equipment, but I wondered what was coming next. A circle jerk-off to orgasm was my guess. With eight fleshly fountains gushing male seed onto the grass.

"Were you ever fucked by your lovers?"

"No. Never. I was always top man. I fucked them."

"Is your rear entry virgin then?"

"Yes...I guess you could say that it is."

"Well, then, you are about to enjoy a new experience."

"What... what do you mean by that?" I was beginning to get uneasy with the direction these questions were taking.

"You are the designated neophyte of this gathering, Marcos. As such I request you take your place upon the Mound of Sacrifice. You will offer up your virgin anus to mighty Priapus."

The seven men pulled down their briefs, exposing their genitals. All were getting hard. The huge size of their organs appalled me.

"Hell no. What the fuck is this? What do you mean, 'offer up my ass to Priap's? Who the fuck is he? Some old myth. Forget it."

"He is the god of fertility, of stiff cocks and fucking. Surely you've heard of him."

"If I have you can be damned sure I'm not offering up any part of me as a sacrifice to some forgotten god. I've told you – forget it."

"Oh come now, Leon. Don't be difficult. We've wined you and dined you. We want to do you great honor, make you a member of our band. It's a necessity under those circumstances that you become physically and psychically one with the inner spirit of the group."

"I don't understand your fancy doubletalk, Aaron, but one thing is certain: *I will not stand still to being fucked by one of you guys* – Priapus or no Priapus."

While we were talking, Michael was going around collecting the pants, shirts, and underwear scattered on the grass and putting them away elsewhere, leaving us all stark naked.

"Leon, please. Don't make us take by force what should be offered as a free gift. Come now."

I suddenly became frightened. This was no longer a purely academic discussion. Aaron was talking in a calm and reasoned voice but his words were threatening violence. I started getting set to dash out of this place, naked or not. The six other members of this gay gang were quietly drawing closer to Aaron and me. I felt the first twinges of panic.

"Aaron, for god's sake! What are you saying? I don't want to

be your sacrificial lamb. I will not, *will not*, allow one of your crew to fuck me on that mound. Let that be an end to it. All you guys are gay; I'm gay. Let's just recognize we have a lot in common and let it go at that. Give me my clothes back and I'll clear out. With seven assholes and seven cocks among you, you don't need me."

"Leon, friend, you don't understand. It's now a matter of necessity. I can't let you just get dressed and walk out of here. There are seven cocks that have spent all afternoon in tingling anticipation of knowing you intimately. I won't disappoint them. You must permit us to offer your anal virginity to the god."

"Wh-a-a-a-t? You mean you want me to bend over for all *seven* of you? No way, man, no way! You must be mad!"

I suddenly saw my chance. I ducked and ran. Out of the glen. Across the lawn. Into and out of the creek. Past the empty fire-pit. Up the trail. I was stark naked. I didn't care. Without shoes my feet were being torn on the stones. I hardly felt it. All I wanted was to reach my car and get to hell away.

I almost made it. I was nearing the parking area, gasping for breath, when Elmer, Zed and Carl, all totally naked, stepped out into the trail ahead of me. They must have taken another, hidden track, some shorter way.

Elmer spoke: "You can stop running now, Leon, you'll never make it to your car. You're coming back with us. Aaron is waiting.

"Like hell I will. Get out of my way you cocksuckers, I'm leaving."

I dashed to the side but they were too quick for me. They grabbed me and stopped me cold.

We were all hot and slippery with sweat but the three of them kept their hold. Zed reached down, grabbed my genitals, and squeezed. The pain was excruciating. Out of necessity I ceased my resistance and he relaxed the pressure but still kept his hand in my crotch.

"Please, Elmer," I pleaded, "let me go. I never did you any harm. I thought you were being nice when you invited me here. I never thought I was going to be the victim of a gang rape. Please let me go."

"Leon, I'm sorry. We've gone too far for that. Now it's got to

be. We're all too excited. If you didn't refuse us and agreed willingly to take part in the ritual it would not be rape. You are the one who is making it so. Why can't you just be reasonable? Anyway we've got to get back to the Hall of Ceremonies; Aaron is waiting for us.

I tried to break away; we were so close to my car. Zed squeezed again. I screamed and gave in. They didn't exactly frog-march me back to the glen with the phallic totem but they kept tight hold of my body all the way.

Aaron was standing in the same place when we arrived at the glen.

"Ah, Leon, how nice of you to come back to us. I assume you are returning to make a willing offering to the god. Well, we will be as easy on you as we can. First we must secure you to the Sacrificial Mound. Take him over to it, men."

"I'll never forgive you for this, Aaron. Never. Please, I beg you, let me go. You can keep my clothes. Just let me get back to the car the way I am. You're going to kill me, man. Please. I've never had anything up my ass before. I'm a topman, not a bottom. Seven of you! Jesus, you'll assassinate me!"

"Take him to the mound, men, and secure him."

They dragged me over to the mound and forced me to lie face down on it, hips, belly and chest on top, legs spread-eagled down one side, arms down the other, head hanging. I hadn't noticed before but there were ring bolts imbedded in the ground at the foot of the mound, two on one side, two on the other. In no time my ankles were tied to one pair and my wrists to the other. I could feel the crease between my buttocks spread wide and the touch of air on my secret place.

I was rigid with fear. I twisted my head from side to side. I could see the members of the Posse stroking their cocks to get them stiff. Someone came up behind me and slid a handful of grease – shortening or possibly soft butter – along my open crack.

"Elmer," directed Aaron, "he's your guest, you initiate him.

Elmer came over to the mound and ran a hand gently across my shoulders, down my back, across my buns and down the inside of my thighs.

"Elmer, please don't do it to me! You're going to destroy me. For god's sake, man, don't do it to me. What if you were tied

down here?"

"Once, years ago, I was. Close your eyes, Leon. Relax your butt, you're too tense. I'll be as gentle as I can."

He moved behind me and stood between my legs.

"Members of the Sheriff's Posse," he sang out in a kind of chant, "witness that I, Elmer, am about to become one with Leon Marcos."

I felt him come closer to me. His cockhead touched my anus and pressed gently against it. I was powerless to resist although I tightened my muscles as much as I could. I was mentally devastated and couldn't hold back a sob of despair.

Elmer continued his chant. "Leon, I enter you with love and kindness. From this day forth you and I are one. LET IT BE SO!"

His cock pressed mightily against me. As he forced his way into me, he felt huge and the pain of his entry was agonizing. I screamed but he ignored me, pushing deeper and deeper. Finally he drew back a bit but then again pushed forward. Over and over he rammed into me until, with a gasp, he reached climax.

"I leave you now with love and affection and welcome you as a member of the Sheriff's Posse." He withdrew his softening cock and moved away from me.

"Ezekiel" It was Aaron's voice.

He stepped into place behind me. Again my body tensed with dread. I realized now that there was to be no repeal from this ordeal. I was truly being sacrificed to pure, blind lust. It was going to go on and on until the seventh cock had exhausted itself inside me.

"Members of the Sheriff's Posse," sang out Ezekiel, "witness that I, Ezekiel am about to become one with Leon."

Again there was the pressure of a stiff cock against my anus.

"Leon, I enter you with love and kindness. From this day forth you and I are one. LET IT BE SO!"

With a sharp lunge he was inside me, fucking me strongly and rapidly. Again I cried out with the pain. In less time than Elmer he reached climax.

"I leave you now with Jove and affection and welcome you as a member of the Sheriff's Posse."

"Zed." Aaron again.

"Members of the Sheriff's Posse witness that I, Zed, am about to become one with Leon."

By now my sphincter had been stretched so that Zed's cock slipped into me with no resistance. He went slower and took longer but at last I heard him chant:

"Michael."

I no longer had the strength to tense myself in resistance.

"Members of the Sheriff's Posse witness that I, Michael, am about to become one...

"I enter you with love and kindness..."

It no longer mattered; I only longed for the torment to end.

"I leave you now with love and affection ..."

"Carl."

"...Witness that I, Carl, am about to become one with Leon Marcos... I enter you with love and kindness..."

My backside was becoming numb from the thrusting of so many   swollen rams.

"...I leave you now with love...Josh."

"Oh god, how many is that?" I cried in despair. "I can't take any more! Please, no more. Let me go now!"

Josh, if it was he who stepped behind me, laid his hands on the back of my neck and gently massaged the taut muscles of my neck and shoulders. His tender fingers worked their way across my back, along my spine, down to my buttocks and over my thighs. Under his sympathetic touch I began to lose the tenseness in my body. Hope arose in me. I thought this might be the end, that, perhaps, he would forego his turn. But no:

"Members of the Sheriff's Posse, witness that I, Josh...I enter you..."

The act, the relentless invasion, was repeated. I no longer knew how many had used me. My head drooped. I was losing consciousness.

"...I leave you now..."

"I guess it's my turn!" Aaron.

At last, at last...

"Members of the Sheriff's Posse witness that I, Aaron, am about to become one with Leon Marcos."

I felt an enormous cockhead, far bigger than any of the others, forcing its way into my ravaged entryway.

"Leon, I enter you with love and kindness. From this day

forth you and I are one. LET IT BE SO!"

The huge glans stretched my flesh beyond anything before. I screamed again with the pain and began to sob uncontrollably. There was no let-up, no deliverance. The thrusting back and forth was unrelenting. Finally one strong forward lunge and I could feel the convulsions of his orgasm.

"I leave you now with love and affection and welcome you as a member of the Sheriff's Posse."

Surely now it must be over. There could be no further excuse to force another prick into my private place. I was exhausted and near to unconsciousness.

"Release him."

I felt the bonds being untied at my ankles and wrists. Four sets of hands lifted me off the mound and laid me down on a blanket or sleeping bag stretched on the ground nearby. My eyes were closed. I just wanted to lie there, alone, perhaps forever, to recover.

Some time passed. I must have dozed. It was getting dark when I became aware of Aaron's voice:

"We must leave you now, Leon. The rituals are over. You are now a full honorary member of the Sheriff's Posse. Call on any of us at any time if you need any kind of help. If you wish to rest further in the sleeping bag, please do so. You can drop it off at the store on your way back."

He was kneeling on the ground beside where I was lying. He leaned down and kissed me gently, full on the lips. One by one the other six men, all now fully dressed, took off their hats and kneeled down beside me. Each in turn leaned down and kissed me goodbye. I turned my head to watch them leave the valley and start up the trail, seven pairs of boots, seven sturdy, jean-clad butts, seven shirt-covered torsos, seven straw cowboy hats.

I was alone in the valley. I lay on the sleeping bag thinking. Somehow, against all reason, my resentment toward this company of young men was evaporating. How can you deal with men who overpower you, tie you down, and fuck you against your will while all the time protesting they do it with love? *And then gently kiss you goodbye as they leave?* I couldn't figure it out.

I stayed in the sleeping bag all night. The morning sun shining through the canopy of leaves overhead woke me up. I was extremely stiff and the muscles of my back and thighs were terribly sore. I didn't know how I fared behind and I dared not try to find out. I discovered my clothes neatly draped over the mound. On the ground beside it, arranged in a row, were six used condoms tied at the tops to retain their milky contents. Evidently that was one thing I didn't have to worry about.

There were crackers and cheese and hard-boiled eggs for my breakfast placed close by. And a bottle of orange juice. I got dressed, ate something, rolled up the bag and took it with me up to the car which was sitting all alone in the meadow.

When I dropped the sleeping bag off at the store in town there was an old man sitting on the stoop railing. I asked him if he knew of a group of young man who called themselves the Sheriff's Posse.

"You mean Aaron and Josh and Elmer and that bunch? Sure I know 'em. Saw 'em grow up from babies. You want to know about them go ask Emily Rostand. She used to teach 'em. She lives just down the road a piece. House all covered with scarlet trumpet vine. You go see her. She'll welcome the visit."

So I called on Miss Rostand. She was a very old lady but still spry and with all her wits about her. I asked about the Sheriff's Posse.

"Oh, those dear, dear boys. Such treasures, every one of them. I taught them from kindergarten to eighth grade, you know. We had only a very small school. Those boys, seven of them, were almost a tenth of our enrollment. It's wonderful how they have stayed friends all these years. Each of them making his mark in business or a profession but they still cling together. There seems to be a special bond between them. They come back to this town three or four times a year, always lively, always manly. It's funny they're all in their thirties yet not a one of them is married. Don't you think it is *cute* the way they have retained the name Sheriff's Posse? They named their club that when they were all young rapscallions, many years ago..."

We talked for over an hour. The men grown to the Sheriff's Posse from her class of eighth graders were handsome, well set up, and generously endowed, and, god knows, lusty and vigorous, but I never thought they were *cute*!

THE VIRGIN YOUTH
& THE PROMISE OF THE DRUMS

Lawrence Benjamin

The Learjet, silver, gold where the afternoon sun touched it with gilded fingers, slipped from between clouds and touched down softly. As it taxied, turning away from the common terminal towards the private airstrip, the steward, Marquis, wafted into the cabin. He moved soundlessly. The plane's lone passenger, a boy named Adam, looked up as he approached. Wordlessly, Marquis handed him a note.

As Adam unfolded the note, he stretched his long legs. He was tall for his age, lean, with pale skin so delicate it seemed translucent. His face was beautiful – the face of a pansexual angel: terra cotta lips; eyes green as new money, flecked with gold; long, pale hair, the color of candlelight, that fell over his shoulders like caressing fingers.

When Adam looked up, Marquis had disappeared like a wisp of smoke. He folded the note carefully and tucked it in a corner of the seat. The message had been brief, almost terse – as they always were: "Unable to meet you. Dad and I delayed in Cannes..." Was it Cannes? He couldn't remember. Not that it mattered. The cities always changed, but the message remained the same: His parents were delayed, detained by a last-minute invitation to some soiree where silver-haired men in tuxedos spun bejeweled women in designer gowns into the dawn on delicate slippered feet. They were all dancing and he was alone.

Almost sadly, Adam realized that theirs was a world he would never know. And what could they know of his dark desires? Adam pushed his parents from his thoughts and stepped out of the plane's hatch into the blistering tropical heat. In the air, a sound like the beating of an angel's wings – the faroff beating of drums.

On the tarmac, beside a battered Jeep, gunmetal grey beneath its coating of ash-colored dust, stood a shirtless native boy. He was dark, sleekly muscled beneath a coat of sweat, a sprinkling of dark curly hair like black pepper across his chest. As Adam

approached, the native boy asked, "Youse the bwoy Ah-Dam?"

Adam, smiling at the unusual emphasis on the second syllable of his name, nodded.

"Ize Dale. Ize to pick you up an' take you 'ome."

The road they drove over was unpaved and badly rutted. As Dale changed gear, muscles travelled beneath his ebony skin; sweat slid over his massive shoulders and danced between the great slabs of his chest that rose up from his flat belly like twin Matterhorns.

The island was not a large one; you could drive from one end to the other in just over an hour. To the south was a rain forest, lush with active life. To the north, high up in the hills were staunch forts – red battlements, black cannon, facing the blue sea. Rushing up to the edges of the road were fields of sugarcane. In the distance the sea, blue, aquamarine, jade could be seen. Here and there were great white plantation houses. Dale pointed out that each plantation, some dating back as far as 1832, had a name; each told its own story: Whim, Peter's Rest, Work and Rest, Princess.

At a crude handmade sign that read "Anna's Hope," Dale made a sharp right turn. This was it, Adam's home for his Easter vacation. The plantation, one of many properties around the world owned by Adam's father, was originally purchased by Adam's great-grandfather, who had sent his spinster daughter to the island to recover from an unfortunate liaison with a sailor – a wholly unsuitable young man – who had presumably drowned at sea. She had, one bright morning, walked into the Caribbean – to be with her sea-faring love, thought Adam, ever the romantic.

Dale swerved suddenly, to avoid a mahogany tree that had been struck by lightning and now lay across the road, spilling its magnificent blood onto the parched earth. Jarred out of his thoughts, Adam could barely make out the house up ahead. Covered by a fine webbing of bougainvillaea vines, it was a large two-story, whitewashed structure with weathered shutters. A short distance away, the Caribbean roiled. What had his great aunt found to hope for here? What would he find? Of all the places his father had sent him to "educate" him about the family businesses, this was the bottom of the barrel so far.

As the Jeep jolted to a halt, an imposing woman, skin like cinnamon, with the bearing of a queen, descended from the veranda that ran around three sides of the house. "Hello, Adam. Welcome to Anna's Hope. I am Fabiana, the caretaker," she said in crisp Americanized English that was without the slightest trace of an accent.

Adam took the hand she offered him; he was tempted to lean over and kiss it. He caught a glimpse of Dale leaning insolently against the Jeep, a smirk on his handsome face. Fabiana followed his gaze. "Of course, you've already met Dale, my son."

Her son?, Adam thought. This woman looked scarcely old enough to be anyone's mother, let alone the mother of this strapping hunk of chocolate boy-flesh. And yet, he could see a resemblance. There was something princely about Dale.

"Come," she said. "You must be starved. We eat supper early here. It's nearly done. Dale will see to your bags."

Dinner – served on a rear porch that overlooked the beach and which was set up as an outdoor dining room – was a curiously formal affair: delicate bone china, and heavy crystal goblets. The jalousie windows were thrown open to catch the breeze and Adam listened to the faint murmur of the sea; in the distance, a faint drumming whispered back. Dancing to the powerful rhythms, delicate flames, sapphire, gold, in the hurricane lamps.

"Power failure," Dale explained seeing Adam stare at the flame. "Sorry."

"No. It's nice," Adam said. He couldn't take his eyes off Dale, who slouched, shirtless, in a Chippendale chair, light from a turn-of-the-century gaslit chandelier kissing his perfect pecs with lingering affection.

Fabiana stepped onto the porch, carrying a large silver tray. "Sit up," she snapped, glancing at Dale. "And go put a shirt on...We have a guest."

"No, it's okay. Please," Adam said.

Dale jumped up from his chair, glaring at his mother.

"Sit back down," Fabiana said in a thin angry voice. "Let's eat."

"I ain't' hungry," Dale flung into the air before storming from the room.

Fabiana and Adam shared a somber meal, Dale's anger hanging in the air between them like a mist. Pleading jet-lag, Adam excused himself right after dinner and went to his room. The room had been his Aunt's and he could see the Caribbean stretch to the horizon. Is this where she had stood at night waiting for her lover's ghostly return from the watery depths?

There was a full moon that cast a hard blue light, making the white sand and the surf glow like phosphorus. A cloud passed in front of the moon, the light faded but Adam still saw Dale walking along the beach. Soon Dale was stripping off his shorts and running towards the water. The cloud passed: adoring light spilled its bounty over him. Dale's ass, high perfectly rounded globes, glowed like black marble. It was hot in the house and Adam longed to lay his face against those cool orbs.

At the water's edge, Dale stopped abruptly and turned towards the house; their eyes met in a look so precise, that Adam had to turn away, his pale cheeks burning crimson, as if someone had slapped him, twice, very hard across the face.

Adam lay on his back in the high four poster bed, swathed in mosquito netting. At the open windows, the delicate lace curtains shimmered, barely moving in the weak breeze. Behind his closed eyelids, the image of Dale, naked at the water's edge, danced seductively. Between his thighs, his rose-tinted sex stirred and lengthened, the head flushing a deep purplish-blue. He held it lightly in his left hand, ran his encircling hand along its length; it gave a little leap. How he longed to touch Dale like this. He wanted to part those magnificent asscheeks and run his tongue along the tight crevice as unknown and compelling as a dark corner. He would flick his tongue at the hole until it bloomed like a flower against his suckling lips. Dale would beg him not to stop. He would plunge his tongue deeper, deeper into the warm circle of darkness...

His orgasm exploded into the air, its fleecy whiteness falling onto the concavity of his belly, puddling in the hollow of his throat, running down his sides in pearlescent rivers, damning as spilled milk. The sight of Dale standing naked at the water's edge, held fast, Adam slept.

The next morning, Adam, anxious to make up for last night's apparent mis-step, arose early and skipping breakfast set off down the beach in search of Dale. He found him sanding the

small dock behind the boathouse. "Can I help?"

Dale did not look up. "This is wuk," he said dismissively. "Wha' you know 'bout wuk, bwoy?"

"Look, I just offered to help you," Adam snapped."And stop calling me 'bwoy'! My name is Adam."

Dale looked up sharply, eyes shrouded behind the curtain of his thick lashes. He smiled and Adam felt as if he had passed a test. "Take off you shirt, if you gon help."

Adam, smiling, pulled his shirt over his head and squatted beside him.

Hours later, muscles aching (Adam had never worked so hard in his life), Dale pronounced, "We's finish. You wuk good. Hard." Adam forgot his aching muscles and basked in the faint praise.

"Come," Dale said. "We's both sweaty an' dirty. Le's go swim and wash off." He stripped quickly and ran for the surf. With only the slightest hesitation, Adam stripped naked and ran after him.

"Mon, look at you!" Dale cried, "youse all bun up!"

Adam glanced down at himself. His chest and shoulders were an angry deep red. He had scarcely noticed the sunburn. "That's all right," he said, just now feeling the intense stinging pain.

"Does it hurt?"

"No," Adam started to lie, then thought better of it. "Well, yeah...a little."

"Come," Dale said leading him back to shore. "I got somet'ing for dat."

Dale broke the succulent leaf off a small plant. "This here we call 'simpa wybe.' You call it aloe vera. It'll make you feel betta." He laid his hands gently on Adam's burgundy shoulders, lightly caressing the cool oily liquid into his hot skin. Adam relaxed under his caressing fingers, feeling the stinging pain fade as the aloe vera did its job.

Adam's hands reached out blindly for Dale as Dale's erection swung into the air between them, a proud ebony bird in gentle determined flight. Dale, hands slick with aloe vera, reached out and stroked Adam's amber prick. Guiding it towards his own, Dale held it in one slippery hand while he held his own in the other. Dale carefully worked his foreskin over the purplish head

of Adam's prick. Dale moved his hand back and forth over their joined cocks, slowly at first, then faster. Dale reached down and cupped Adam's balls, heavy, red, low-slung like over-ripe fruit on a vine bursting with seed – his apricots, he called then, fingering their gold-red fuzz. Dale dropped to his knees and stuffed one then the other into his mouth. With his tongue, he pushed them gently out of his mouth and pulled Adam's swelling cock in his mouth, swallowing until the base bumped up against his lips. Once Adam was lodged deep in his throat, he swallowed several times working his prick over with just the muscles of his throat. When he felt Adam swelling he pulled back, drawing his tongue against the sensitive underside, tracing the bulging vein that he found there. Adam could stand no more; his balls seemed to tighten and swell; his orgasm erupted against Dale's lips, a geyser of molten opal that ran down his chin, speckled his chest.

Standing, Dale kissed him long and hard, his tongue restlessly searching the inside of his mouth. "Dere," he said, ending the kiss at last. "Dat's what you taste like." Adam frowned at the unfamiliar alkaline taste in his mouth.

"Now, you do me," Dale said.

Adam reached out and grasped the hard column of flesh, hot to the touch. It was longer than his own and thicker. "Put it in your mouth."

Adam stared at the cock in his hand, mesmerized by its size and bulk, shook his head no.

"Suck it, Ah-Dam!" Dale commanded. Gone from his voice was the playfulness of a moment ago, replaced by the hard edge of desire. Dale placed his hands on his shoulders, exerting just enough pressure to force him to his knees. Adam was surprised to feel the throbbing cock brush against his lips. Tentatively, he opened his mouth, jabbed at it with the tip of his tongue. He opened his mouth and a shiver of delight ran through him as the endless piece of meat slid in and back...back...stretching his mouth until he thought his jaw would crack. His monstrous cock deep, deep in Adam's throat, Dale shot wave after wave of liquid fire. A taste like the copper of new pennies in his mouth, Adam's second orgasm tumbled from his body.

Spent, they lay on the beach. Dale held him for a long time,

until Fabiana called them to lunch. They splashed the cum off each other in the salty water and, dressing quickly, ran to the house.

They ate – batter-dipped flying fish and ice-cold local beer in thick frosted mugs – in silence; glancing at each other, bursting into staccato laughter.

"What's that?" Adam asked of the frantic drumming that seemed to erect a solid wall of sound around the island.

"Dem's de drums of de obeahman callin dem god to earth."

"How do they do that?" Adam asked, intrigued by the fantasy.

"Dey speak to dem t'ru de rhythms of de drums." Dale cocked his head to the side, listened to the insistent music. "Dere promising dem food...an' drink...an' – "

" – and virgin youth?" Adam offered slyly.

"No! Dey have no use for vir-gins," Dale spat contemptuously. "Vir-gins ain' know nuttin."

"And you?" Adam baited.

"I ain no vir-gin," Dale answered turning black eyes like burning coals on him. "An' I will teach you ev'ryt'ing a vir-gin doan know."

Dale knelt behind Adam, spread his hands across his ass, whiter than the rest of him. He pressed a finger against his rose-pink virgin asshole. It puckered prettily at him, remained steadfastly closed to him. He pressed his finger against it, harder now; it opened like the new day at dawn. Adam squirmed slightly, adjusting his hips, facilitating the accelerating movement of Dale's thrusting fingers, now three.

"Now," Adam shouted. "Put it in now."

Adjusting his position, Dale, with one long swift movement, entered Adam. The sharp pain of penetration gave way almost immediately to a pure liquid joy. Adam reared back to capture fully every driving thrust. Adam became for Dale a mighty white steed on which they both rode to a brilliant satisfaction. They collapsed on the sheets, Dale still deep inside Adam. "Wow," Adam breathed. "Wow."

"Now, youse a vir-gin no longer. Now, you are ready for de gods!" Dale laughed.

Adam laughed, too, and curled into the fold of Dale's arms. When Dale woke him, it was dark. "I have to go in town," he

said. "You wan come?"

"No," Adam answered sleepily. "I think I'll go for a swim."

Dale kissed him tenderly, longingly. In a moment he was gone. Adam dressed and soon stood alone on the dark beach.

The drums were louder now, more insistent, tugging him to the water's edge. The sea turned over itself anxiously.

Suddenly, the beating of the drums ceased. Adam found himself abandoned on a receding wave of sound. The sea stilled, its surface an endless expanse of black glass. The drumming started again as abruptly as it had stopped. The sea which had moments before been quiescent, as still as the water in the bottom of a basin, raced towards the beach, as if it too had heard the promise of the drums.

He erupted out of this seething, boiling cauldron, clutching the night about his nakedness like a cape. He moved through the rioting sea with the easy sinuous grace of an eel. He was a handsome man, a powerful man. His body, well muscled and solid seemed to vibrate with suppressed energy, seemed to hold within itself all the fury of the sea, tightly reined. His rich dark skin flowed over rippling muscles like a river of molasses over a bed of great polished stones. His powerful upper body tapered to a narrow waist then swelled again into massive thighs, between which hung a great black phallus. His beryl eyes, which seemed to hold all the colors of dawn, searched the beach, found Adam, standing, naked, flaxen hair cascading over alabaster shoulders.

"I am Damballah."

"And I am Adam. I am thine from my mother's womb."

Adam stepped into his embrace and Damballah leaned down to kiss him. Laying him carefully on the sand, Damballah fitted Adam's slender legs over his own massive shoulders; with a single thrust, he entered the body promised him by the drums. He slipped gratefully into the tight hole that gripped him like a velvet fist. Damballah fucked him easily with short, hard thrusts, guided in his rhythms by Adam whose hands held his hard muscled ass, squeezing, forcing him in deeper and deeper. Their orgasms tore loose from them like twin white rivers sharing a singular source. The promise of the drums had been kept.

Dawn's lips kissed the cold shoulder of the night, leaving behind the greasy red imprint of a new day.

"I must go," Damballah said.

"Take me with you," Adam pleaded.

"But I am not of your world," Damballah said gently. "Nor you, of mine." Then he turned and plunged into the jade sea.

Damballah exploded out of the sea, a delicate froth of white surf covered his nakedness. "You must know that you can never come back to this, your world."

"I don't care, Adam shouted. "I would rather be with you in your world than without you in mine."

"Then come," Damballah said, offering his hand.

Adam walked slowly into the water. A thatch of pale hair floated for a moment on the sea's shimmering surface then disappeared as Damballah, the sea, embraced him.

BREAKING & ENTERING

Greg Bowden

I have never subscribed to the notion that working late impresses people with your dedication. I think, rather, that it impresses them with your inability to get the job done in the time allotted. Nevertheless, that Wednesday I worked late. Someone had messed up the shareholder lists and I was supposed to have a statistical analysis to the legal people Thursday morning. Since Jim, my lover, was out of town on a business trip I just had a burger sent in and worked straight through. I finished just after eleven, heaved a sigh of relief, put on my coat and headed home.

I had forgotten how deserted lower Manhattan is at that time of night; I had to walk ten or twelve blocks before I found a cab. It was well after midnight by the time I got home. The instant I stepped into the apartment I knew someone else was there. As the door closed behind me I froze, listening with all my being.

There: a sound like a drawer being opened very quietly. The sound seemed to come from the bedroom, at the end of the hall. What should I do? Run? Call the police? Yell? Piss in my pants?

Something drew me silently down the hall. What the hell was I doing? This was madness – possibly terminal madness. Still, I had to see who was in there, who was quietly going through the drawers in the bedroom. We do dumb things when we're scared out of our minds.

As I reached the half-closed bedroom door I caught a faint click and realized that it was ever so slightly darker than it had been. Whoever was in there had just switched off a tiny flashlight. I held my breath. He knew I was there in the hall. Oh my God, I wanted to scream, what do I do now? I couldn't go back to the front door and I couldn't just stand there in the hallway, waiting for him to come and get me.

I let my breath out as silently as I could and did another dumb thing: I slowly pushed the door open wider. I had to bite my lip to keep from gasping; there he was, just a shadow

against the dim light of the shaded window. By straining my eyes I could just make him out, hunched over the top dresser drawer; he must have been going through it when he heard me. Now he seemed to be frozen too, perhaps holding his breath like I was.

He made the first move.

"Put your hands behind your head and take three steps into the room," he growled in a horse voice. "And don't try to be a hero. Heroes do stupid things."

I did as he said, clasping my hands behind my head and advancing very slowly into the room. I sensed him turning from the bureau to face me although I doubted that he could see me any better than I could see him. He took care of that by switching on the bedside lamp and twisting the shade so the light was directly in my eyes.

"Stop. Right there. Now. Very slowly. Take your jacket off. Toss it on the bed. Over here. Slowly."

He picked up the jacket and went through the pockets. The flat little slap must have been my wallet although it sounded like it hit the dresser.

"Now the shirt. Toss it over, just like the jacket."

I don't know what came over me. "What about the tie? You want that too or do I take the shirt off under it?"

"Look, pal, you want to get through this thing or not? Keep up the lip and you won't. Now, the shirt."

I stripped off my tie and shirt, tossing them gently across the bed. The shirt was damp with sweat and although my hands were icy with fear I realized that the room was very warm. That practical little voice in the back of my head told me it was wasteful to leave the heat on when I went to work. Jesus, I was beginning to crack up. I was also beginning to get used to the light in my eyes and now I could see a little detail. He was not very tall and was stocky, like a football player. He seemed to be wearing a short, black mask which just covered his head and the upper part of his face. I could see that he had a bushy, dark mustache, kind of like Jim's, and he was dressed in a shapeless black sweater and tight black jeans.

"Shoes. Lift a leg and take off the shoe and sock. Let me hear 'em hit the floor, one by one. And hurry it up, will ya, pal?"

I almost lost my balance several times doing it but I got them off. Once I had dropped both shoes on the floor he made me kick them under the bed.

"You wearing a watch? Guy like you? Sure you are. Take it off and put it in your pants pocket. Then outta the pants and pass them over here, just like you been doing."

I danced around a bit but I managed to get my pants off. As I tossed them over the bed I wondered if he meant to take this all the way. Probably. Who's going to run naked down the street after a burglar?

I was right.

"Well, come on, pal. You can't be so dumb you don't know what's next. Strip 'em off and toss 'em over."

I pulled my shorts off and threw them on the bed. Now what?

"Well, isn't that pretty," he said, looking at me. He pulled something out of his back pocket and tossed it across to me. "You did so well in your strip act that now you get to put something on." It was leather but at first I couldn't figure out what it was. He laughed as the realization hit me; it was a black hood, just like the one he wore except that there were no eye-holes.

"Put it on, pal. Now."

He wasn't taking any chances. A naked and blindfolded man definitely wouldn't be in any condition to chase a burglar down the street!

"Now turn around," he growled. As I did so, I heard him move towards me. I thought he was heading for the door, leaving. Wrong again. Strong hands grasped the back of the hood and pulled it tighter against me. I heard a faint click and knew he had locked me into it.

"Now, let's see what we have here." I felt a light touch across my shoulders, almost a caress. The hands slipped down my back, finally coming to rest on the cheeks of my ass. For some insane reason I found his touch erotic and my cock begin to lengthen.

"Let's see the rest, pal. Turn around."

As I turned his hand brushed lightly across my pubic hair and I felt my cock start to lift. I couldn't help myself. I was naked, blindfolded and helpless with a madman's hands on the

base of my dick and what did I do? I started to get hard.

"Well, I see he likes it. And what a tool to like it with. Okay pal, let's get on with it." He shoved me and I fell backwards onto the bed. As I lay there I got a pretty good idea of what was going to happen and I began to shiver a little, this time not in fear! I heard sounds: shoes falling to the floor, sweater pulled off. When I heard the zipper my dick flexed and I reached down to feel its hardness lying against my belly.

My hand was slapped away. "Over your head, pal, put 'em over your head." I heard his pants hit the floor and felt the bed sag under his weight. "You want to play with a dick? I'll give you a dick to play with, one you won't forget," he growled. My breath was taken away as he sat heavily on my chest, pinning my arms under his knees. I felt a light touch across my cheek and down, over my lips.

My god, I thought, it's his cock. He's going to shove that thing into my mouth and make me suck him off.

He slapped me firmly on the cheek with it. "Open wide, pal. You're going to take this big, thick cock down your throat and give me a blow job to remember." His hand went to my neck. "And if you don't suck good I'll just cut off your air." He pressed down, making his point, making me gasp for breath. "Now do it. Suck!"

I felt the cock-head pressing on my lips, forcing itself into my mouth. I took a breath and opened my mouth wide, suddenly wanting to take that cock-head down my throat.

"That's it, pal. Take it. But slowly, slowly. We're in no hurry here, are we?" He chuckled and began to push his cock into my mouth, pausing, finally, when the head was just pressing against the back of my throat. It was a big cock and so thick it completely filled my mouth. I was afraid I was going to gag as he pressed the head harder and harder against the back of my throat; he must have sensed this because he shifted himself on my chest, allowing me to take a deep breath. As I did, that huge cock slipped down my throat until I felt his balls against my chin and my nose was buried in his pubic hair. He held me that way, pinned down with that huge cock forced all the way down my throat, until I thought I would pass out for lack of air.

He finally eased back, pulling his cock out until just the head remained inside my lips. "You're good," he chuckled. "You

sure know how to take a cock down that slick throat of yours. Now let's see what you can do with your tongue." He pushed his cock a little further into my mouth.

I ran my tongue along the shaft and up, over the head, pausing at a big piss slit. I found that he wasn't cut and that I could get my tongue under the skin, between it and the underside of the head. He seemed to like that and began to stroke his cock slowly in and out of my mouth, letting the pressure of my lips roll the foreskin over the head and then pull it back until it was all exposed to my roving tongue. It seemed to me that his breathing had become heavier.

"Let's try something a little different, shall we, pal?" He shifted, turning himself around on me. Of course I couldn't see anything and my arms were pinned to the bed by his legs but I knew immediately what he had in mind when his masculine, musky scent suddenly filled my nose. My God, he's going to sit on my face, I thought. I rolled my head back and forth, moaning, but he grabbed me and held my head in an iron grip until my lips were forced between his ass cheeks, pressed up against the hole.

"Steady, boy. You're doing fine. So far. Now let's have a little service to the ass. Come on, get that tongue working against that hole. I want you to slick up my ass until you can slide your tongue up there as easily as you slide it between your lips. That's it, force your spit up there. Push that tongue in just as far as you can." He took hold of my nipples with his strong fingers and began to squeeze and twist them. "Let's see if this gives you a bit more incentive," he growled.

My nipples have always been wired directly to my cock and I felt it grow even harder as he fingered them. Another moan escaped my throat and I knew he had me. As long as he worked on my tits I would do whatever he wanted of me. He knew it too. "Like that, do you?"

As I began to poke at his hole with my tongue he squirmed, lifting himself just a little to allow me more room to work my tongue over his hot asshole. He groaned as I began to poke at his hole, trying to open it, trying to force my tongue deep into him. I worked up some saliva and pushed it into him making his hole slick and wet, letting my tongue slide deeper and deeper into it. He rewarded me with a twist on both of my

nipples that made my dick flex up from my belly. I moaned and pushed my tongue deeper into his asshole.

After a bit he shifted position again, twisting his body around so that his cock was brushing my lips. "Suck it in, pal, all the way down your throat. Make it as slick as you made my asshole." I opened my mouth and he slowly pushed his cock in, not stopping until it was buried in my throat and his wiry hair was pressed up against my mustache. He waited a moment and then pulled back until the head was just comfortably in my mouth; then he pushed again, until his cock was back down my throat.

"Can't do too much of that, pal." He pulled his cock out of my mouth. "Better get to the real stuff. Turn it over, pal. On your belly. Now!"

His knees released my arms and his strong hands forced me to roll over under him. He slid down my body until he was straddling my buttocks and then he forced my legs apart. I could feel his dick pressing against my ass, seeking entrance.

"Take a deep breath, Pal, and let's get on with it," he growled, pushing harder against me. Somehow I couldn't seem to make myself open up enough to take that huge cock.

"Okay, boy. Remember, you asked for it." He slapped my ass. Hard. I gasped from the sting of his hand and his cock slipped into me. He pushed it home with one long thrust and fell across my back, hands under me searching for my tits; when he found them he began to roll the nipples between his fingers. He stroked his dick in my ass a couple of times, pushing it deeper into me.

"Now that's a dick, kid! That's a big dick you got up your ass and you're going to get fucked so's you know you been fucked."

He began with long strokes, almost pulling the head out of my ass and then quickly shoving the entire length back into me until I could feel it poking around somewhere up in my belly. He let go of my nipples and raised himself up, legs straddling my buttocks, hands on my back, and thrust that big dick harder and harder into me. Suddenly he yanked his dick all the way out and grabbed my shoulders.

"Over, boy. I want it from the front."

He forced me over, pushed my legs up against my chest and

drove that huge dick back into my ass, all in one motion. He grabbed my wrists and pinned me to the bed again. His strokes began to shorten but the shorter they got the harder he slammed into my ass and the more I knew I was about to blow my balls. Both of us were gasping for breath now, ready for the big moment. I knew it was time when he suddenly stopped, pulled back, slammed into me and held his breath. I could hear a sound way in the back of his throat, working its way up until it came out as a deep yell. I felt his dick swell in me and as the heat of his come hit my insides I fell over the edge and started shooting mine all over the both of us.

We lay for a while, his body covering mine, his breath hot on my cheek. When his dick finally began to soften he slipped out of me and got up from the bed without a word. I heard the sounds of clothing, then the squeak of a door.

"Don't ever forget," he whispered.

I heard the front door close.

I lay there for a few moments, pulling myself together. When I finally tried pulling at the hood it came off quite easily. There was a little lock on the clasp but it was locked open. I looked around the room. There were my coat and pants, hanging neatly on a hanger. My tie was draped over a door knob. Wallet, watch and keys in their accustomed place on the night stand. What the hell?

Then I heard a key in the front door followed by a cheery "Hello, hello" from my lover.

"You're supposed to be in Cleveland aren't you?" I called.

"Finished the job early. Thought up a surprise for you," he said, coming into the bedroom, pulling off a shapeless black sweater. "I knew you'd enjoy it."

His voice lowered to a growl. "After all, pal, I know what you like."

CHAINED

Bert McKenzie

The boy was hot, *really* hot, and just looking at him flamed my desires. After all, it was a boring job, filing those little cards in the catalog of the university library, and I had plenty of time to look around and enjoy the scenery. I was hired as a temp to help get the backlog of work caught up during the summer semester, and I didn't mind the extra money. Grad students can always use a little extra cash. But I never knew I would have such great fringe benefits.

Every day it was a parade of young college kids coming to do their research and assignments, usually dressed for the hot weather of July. Muscle shirts showed off bulging biceps and occasionally a hairy pit when someone reached up to scratch or stretch. Short cropped sweatshirts and sports jerseys gave tantalizing glimpses of tightly corded stomachs. Tight, tight shorts displayed long, powerful thighs curved by strong muscles and covered in a dusting of masculine hair. The same shorts often framed bulging baskets, filled with the promise of manhood at its prime.

But on this day I was watching one particular kid who came in with a group of his pals. He was by far the sexiest guy in the bunch, but it was obvious that he didn't fit in with the college crowd. His long shaggy hair, tattered cut-offs and stained t-shirt showed him to be a rough kid, not the polished preppies that generally attended this small university. Perhaps he was just hanging out with friends he had known in high school who went on to college. The group all seemed to enjoy his company, even though the rest of them were dressed much better and appeared a bit more upscale.

I knew I should stay focused on the moment. I was being paid to insert the cards into the correct spots alphabetically and that did require a small amount of concentration. But my eyes were drawn to this rough kid. I watched as he moved, following along behind his group. He had an easy, self-assured grace about him. In another setting it would almost appear cocky. As he passed by the card catalog there was a brief

moment of eye contact. He had crystal-clear blue eyes that were deep-set under his brow, adding to the primitive quality of his looks. I dropped my gaze almost instantly, not wanting him to know my desires.

He walked on by and my eyes followed him. His feet were covered by dirty sneakers that were ripped, showing two toes on his left foot. The long muscular legs rose up to meet inside the tattered denim, and I noticed a small but substantial rip where the left hip pocket had been torn away. As he moved I caught a flash of skin. The fact that he wasn't wearing underwear got me instantly hard.

The group went on upstairs to the lounge area, and I turned back to my work, trying to concentrate on the alphabetical arrangement of my duties. I leaned in close to the card catalog so no one else would see my erection and hoped it would go away soon. But as I continued to stash the cards, my mind kept playing the scene of him walking by like a film loop stuck in the replay mode. I kept zooming in on that rip in the ass of his cut offs. I only grew harder until I knew I had to do something.

I dropped the cards at the reference desk and told the librarian on duty I was taking a biology break, then quickly headed for the rest room on the second floor. Once inside I noticed that of the two stalls, one was already occupied. This was unfortunate because I wanted the privacy to quickly bring myself to a climax so I could return to work. I certainly didn't need an audience listening to my masturbation. But without a choice I entered the remaining stall, dropped my trousers and took a seat.

It was only then that I noticed my next door neighbor. The foot just to my right under the partition was wearing a torn sneaker with at least three toes showing. I leaned forward and saw a tattered pair of cut-offs around the ankles. As I watched the toes moved, and the person in the next booth slowly inched his foot closer to the partition, then tapped his foot as if to signal me. I was astounded and didn't know what to do. Again the foot inched my way and tapped. This time I took action and slid my own foot right up against it, letting the boy in the next stall know my interest. But he immediately pulled his foot back away, and I thought perhaps I misread his intentions or was too bold.

But only seconds later, two bare knees appeared on the floor under the partition, and the boy scooted forward until his own hard dick slid into view. It was about seven inches long and curved up toward the partition wall. As I watched, it throbbed and a voice whispered hoarsely, "Suck it."

I dropped to my knees on the tiled floor and took him in my mouth. As I bobbed my head up and down, he hunched further under the partition and began to make fucking motions with his hips. All too soon he came, filling my mouth with his youthful seed. Then just as quickly, he jerked back, pulling himself from me and out from under the metal partition. The tattered cut-offs disappeared, I heard a zip, and the door banged open as he walked out.

It took me no time at all to bring myself to an explosive climax, then I too walked out of the stall and into the empty rest room. I cleaned up and splashed cold water on my face to try and bring myself back to reality. Then, adjusting my clothes I turned to the door and left. Just outside the rest room door was a drinking fountain, and there by the fountain was my hot young street boy. He was leaning against the wall, keeping his eye on the bathroom door. He obviously wanted to see who had just sucked him off. When our eyes met, a slow kind of sneer spread across his face, making him appear slightly sinister, then he shifted his weight to his feet and walked back toward the lounge.

I felt a cold chill go through me when I saw that sneer. It was as if he was laughing to an inside joke. What was he planning? Would he go tell the librarian on duty that I made a pass at him? That I sucked his dick? Was he going to tell his friends? I was disconcerted by the situation, and quickly hurried back downstairs to return to my filing job. In about fifteen minutes I saw him again as he walked by, heading for the exit along. Again we made eye contact and again I received that strange sneer that held a touch of distaste. That was it. He wanted sex, but he despised me because I was just some fag who he used to get his dick sucked.

Depressed, I returned to my own life, filing the cards and later going home to my empty apartment. The gloomy feeling lasted the rest of the night. It was as if I had accepted his condemnation of me, even though I didn't really know how he

felt.

The next day I was back at my post, filing cards as usual when I felt someone looking at me. Glancing up, I saw him again. He was at the circulation desk and was filling out paperwork to obtain a temporary library card. It was something that residents of the town could do if they weren't students. That way they were entitled to check out books and material. He then turned and headed upstairs, but glanced over at me before disappearing into the stairwell. He reached down and adjusted his dick right there in the library, making sure he held my eyes all the while, then walked upstairs.

The message was unmistakable, and I quickly dropped what I was doing to take a break. I hurried up to the second floor bathroom and found him in the same stall as before. No sooner did I enter the stall next to him, than he dropped to his knees and slid himself under the partition. It was obvious he wanted me to suck him again, and I lost no time in doing so.

Once again it ended quickly, but this time, I grabbed some toilet paper and scribbled a hasty note, passing it under the wall before he left. His hand reached down and took it. I had written, "Meet me later?" He kept the note for a while then his hand appeared under the partition. He made writing motions then held it out. Understanding his meaning, I handed him my pen. I heard him scribble on the paper, then he reached down to return it to me. I opened it so see he had written "FAGOT" misspelling the word he obviously meant. As I sat there in stunned surprise I heard the doors bang. He had left, taking my pen with him.

What was with this guy? He didn't mind my sucking his dick, but then he called me a faggot. Well, I suppose it was true, but the hostility surprised me. I guess he was just some rough trade who liked to get sucked.

That afternoon before I got off work, I noticed the applications for temporary cards sitting on the circulation desk. No one was around, so I quickly glanced through them. There were only three, two women and a man. I found his name was Mike Steele and I quickly copied down his address.

That evening I found myself in a small apartment building on the east side of town not far from the university. I don't know what could possibly possess me to go there, but I felt drawn

like a moth to a flame, a very dangerous and possibly deadly flame. The halls were painted white, but there were plenty of scrapes, scratches and scuff marks to make them appear dingy. The floor was carpeted, but the carpet was ripped and stained. The whole building smelled like grease from frying food mixed with the tang of urine.

I came to the door of apartment three, Mike Steele's home. I don't know what I thought I would do. I had no intention of knocking. I didn't even want him to know I was there. I just had to see the place. I guess it gave me a superior feeling, knowing something about him. I was turning to leave when the door opened, and there he stood. He was dressed in a clean shirt, jeans and boots. The surprise on his face when he recognized me was almost comical. Before I could think of anything to say or do, he blurted out, "What the fuck are you doing here?"

I was too stunned to speak. I just stood there with my mouth hanging open. He stepped back and held the door wide. "Come on in," he invited. I did. I stepped into the tiny apartment. It was remarkably clean despite the stained carpet and dingy walls. The door opened into a living room/kitchenette. The only furnishing consisted of a broken down couch, a coffee table, and a black and white TV which was showing a car commercial with no sound.

"So why are you here, faggot?" he asked after closing the door. I turned to see him standing in front of it, his hands folded on his chest. I didn't know what to say. He smiled that sneer again and said, "Couldn't resist my cock? You come by for another taste?" I didn't know what else to do, so I nodded.

He laughed, a harsh barking sound. "Well, I was just going out to buy some beer. Why don't you sit down and wait. I'll be right back." Then he gestured to the couch, turned and left. I wanted to run. I had the perfect opportunity to get out of there, but for some reason I felt compelled to stay. I slowly sank down onto the couch, and looked at the coffee table. It was covered with magazines, a couple of issues of *Hot Rod*, and several back issues of *Playboy*.

I felt the need to piss, so I stood up and thought I'd find the bathroom. There was only one door, and I walked through it to find the bedroom. It held a dresser and a full-sized unmade

bed. Clothes were strewn about the room, shirts and jeans, shoes and socks, but I didn't see any underwear. Driven by a strange curiosity, I looked in the dresser drawers. They contained handkerchiefs, socks, sweaters, T-shirts and tank tops. But no shorts or briefs. I looked in the closet which held shirts and a couple of jackets, then I went into the bathroom. It was clean and neat. A medicine cabinet with shaving items, mouthwash and some aspirin, another cabinet with clean towels, and a clothes hamper. I opened the hamper and rummaged through the items, towels, jeans, socks, shirts, no undershorts. I guess he just didn't wear them.

I pissed, then returned through the bedroom when my eye was caught by the nightstand next to the bed. It held the one drawer I hadn't checked, so I stepped over and opened it. I reached in and pulled out a heavy bag of white powder, cocaine. Under it were a number of photos, mostly polaroids of naked men sucking and fucking. So, my straight friend did have a hidden side. The pictures were bent and the corners dog eared as if they had been frequently examined.

"Put that back," an angry voice said. I turned and saw Mike standing in the doorway. I quickly slipped the cocaine back in the drawer and closed it, then turned. He was standing next to me. "Nosy little faggot, aren't you? Had to suck my dick. Had to find out where I lived. Had to go snooping through my stuff. Well, you want this cock and you're gonna get it, but not right now. I've got friends coming over to make a purchase. You're gonna have to wait till they leave. And I don't want them to know you're here, so you're gonna hide in the closet."

"I better just go," I said as I stood up.

"I don't think so," he said, a cold edge to his voice. "And just to be sure, strip."

"What?"

"You heard me," he barked. "Get naked, now!" He whipped out a switchblade, clicking it open under my nose. "Or do you want me to show you my talent for cutting the balls off of faggots like you."

I slowly began to take my clothes off. I wondered how I could get the knife away from him. I figured once his friends were over, I could appeal to one of them for help. Just because they bought drugs didn't mean they weren't compassionate.

Soon I was totally naked, then without letting his eyes stray from me, he bent down and reached beneath the bed, the one place I hadn't looked. Mike pulled out an assortment of odd things, including handcuffs, and a rope. In seconds he had me cuffed and tied up, and shoved into his closet. "Now you sit there nice and quiet. When my friends leave, I'll untie you and let you out. Don't even think of making any noise, cause if you do I might have to hurt you. And don't expect any of my friends to help you out. They know better."

The closet door banged shut and I was alone with my thoughts. I couldn't believe I got into this situation. What a stupid thing to do to come to some stranger's apartment uninvited. Now I was beginning to get scared. What would he do when his friends left? Would he really release me? Would he kill me? I heard sounds from out in the apartment, voices and laughter.

I tried to reach the door, but was tied so tightly that I couldn't get my hands near the knob. A while later I heard the toilet flush and knew that someone must have just used the bathroom. Hoping that the talking in the living room would mask my voice from Mike, I called out. "Hey, help, someone!"

The closet was suddenly flooded with light. I blinked up to see some young man looking down at me in surprise. "Can you get me out of this?" I begged. "He's crazy. He pulled a knife on me and tied me up. Please help me."

"Tony," the young man called. "Can you come here a second?" In a moment, another man appeared in the doorway and looked down at me. I repeated my urgent plea for help and he shook his head in sympathy.

"Help me with him," he told the first man and the two of them reached down to lift me to my feet and pull me from the closet. I expected them to free me, but instead, they dropped me on the bed.

"What's going on, guys?" Mike asked, appearing in the doorway, then he dropped to stunned silence, realizing his friends had found me.

The one called Tony shook his head. "Mike, how many times do I have to tell you not to mistreat your pets." He slapped my rump and then all of them left the room.

I was lost. There was no help. I began to shout and call out.

"Somebody help me!" I screamed. Then suddenly the air was forced from my lungs. Mike had jumped on top of me. He reached down and stuffed a dirty sweat sock into my mouth, then tied it in place with a handkerchief.

"Listen, faggot. I'll deal with you later. Tony and Mitch are cool, and they convinced the others not to say anything. They don't care if I want to screw your ass. But you're gonna be good or I will use that knife. I've always wondered what it would be like to castrate a human."

The party broke up shortly. I felt the gag removed, then some of the cords were untied, but my hands were still cuffed. Then Mike undid the handcuffs and pulled me to a spread-eagle position, refastening the cuffs on my right wrist to the post of the headboard, and producing another set of handcuffs for my other wrist.

He then stood up and stepped to the side of the bed. Slowly he slipped off his shirt and then bent down to remove the boots. Next he unfastened his jeans and dropped them, revealing his naked body to me. Despite my perilous position I couldn't help but admire him. Other than a couple of amateur tattoos on his arms, he was in perfect condition. His chest was broad and well-muscled, with firm pecs and crowned by tiny erect nipples. His cock was beginning to rise from its position of rest over his generous balls.

"We'll begin with a little sucking just to get me good and hard," he said as he climbed onto the bed and straddled my naked torso. "And remember who's in charge here. You try anything funny, or so much as nick my cock with those teeth and you will be singing soprano for life." He dropped down over me and slid his lengthening shaft into my mouth. Grabbing my head by the ears he began to brutally fuck me, pistoning in and out of my mouth as he grunted and sweated above me.

Then to my surprise he pulled free before cumming. "Now I'm gonna try something a little different," he said and climbed off, only to move to the foot of the bed. He spread my legs apart and lifted them up to his shoulders. "I've never fucked a guy in the ass before. But I've heard it's pretty good. Don't disappoint me, faggot," Then he sank his cock between my asscheeks. Slowly it slid in, filling my guts. "Oh, Jesus," he

cried as he began to slowly pump in and out. "This really is good! Better than I ever expected it to feel. Jesus, this is tight. Better than any pussy I've ever had."

Mike picked up the pace and began fucking me hard. As he did so, his cock pushing against my prostate caused me to become aroused despite my fear. If I could only reach for my dick I could really enjoy the moment. But he had other plans. Suddenly, he shoved in to the hilt, smashing his pelvis into my ass and began to unload inside me. In a few moments, he began to come down from his orgasm.

Now was the moment I really worried about. He had his sex. He was finished with me. Would he kill me? Castrate me? I wasn't sure, but I was definitely scared. He reached down and picked up the knife, flicking it open with that wicked grin. I was shivering with fright when we were interrupted by a banging on the door.

"Mr. Steele," someone was shouting.

"You keep quiet, baby, and maybe I'll let you have another taste of my dick," he said and then quickly gagged me again.

Mike left the room and then I heard him arguing with someone at the front door. It was apparently the landlord who was angry because the rent hadn't been paid. He was insulted that Mike came to the door stark naked. He was furious about the noise from the party earlier. He threatened the police, and demanded money immediately or Mike was to hit the road.

I heard the door shut again and Mike returned. "Well, faggot, looks like I won't have time to let you enjoy my cock again. I've got to split before old man Warner gets back with the cops." He was stuffing clothes into a bag as he talked to me, moving about the room. He then bent down and picked up my underwear. "I've always wondered what these would feel like," he said, then slipped them on. He continued to dress, then stuffed the coke in his bag. Finally Mike took the polaroid photos from the night stand and scattered them on the bed around me, and said, "See ya."

I couldn't believe it. I was left chained to the bed, stark naked, gagged. And he left me. What was I to do? I could only hope that old man Warner returned soon with the police. They would surely release me. I could make up a story about being held against my wishes, which wasn't far from the truth.

Unfortunately, Warner was just bluffing. He didn't return until late afternoon of the next day. Then when he didn't get a response he used his pass key to enter the apartment. He found me, and undid the gag. But when I tried to explain, he just smiled. Replacing the gag, he began to take off his clothes.

THE PAPERBOY

Edward Bangor

Even with the money I got for my birthday, it bothered me I'd have to go without something in order to buy the new Saxon live album, *The Eagle Has Landed*. I suppose I could have borrowed the money from my parents, but Father had placed limits on my borrowing and insisted I repay not only promptly but with interest, in order, he said, to teach me the value of money. Obviously something would have to go, but what? I made a fateful decision: Instead of buying my favorite Heavy Metal magazine I would simply steal it.

By the time I got to the news agent it was fairly late on Thursday, the issue day for *Kerrang!* The shop itself was small but crammed to the rafters with one of every magazine imaginable. Every wall, including the one behind the counter, was shelved out in racks. Every square inch of the available floor space was similarly stacked, with barely enough room left for customers to pass from the front to the back. I calmly selected *Kerrang!* and leaned back against the shelves, as if to read through it.

Though I had been here before, Mr. Courtney, the owner, didn't know me which, of course, is why I'd picked his shop, far away from my usual hang-outs. And Mr. Courtney carried a line of nudist magazines. This I found was the only way I could get to see full color plates of naked men. Unfortunately most of the men depicted weren't attractive, being overweight, but there were often one or two hard-bodied teenagers whose swinging willies and balls fascinated me.

On each of the previous occasions I had popped into Mr. Courtney's to look at such things I needed protection over tell-tale lumps and stains appearing in, or on, my jeans. This involved wearing over-tight underpants under baggy trousers in case Mr. Courtney guessed my intent.

Little did I know, Mr. Courtney was just waiting his moment. And that moment had arrived. I suppose I can't really blame him. Looking back now at pictures of me from that period I can see the attraction and I'm not being overly modest

either. I was cute: Light brown, almost blond hair; blue eyes with just a hint of green; a small but sturdy figure and a full round, typically English face.

On that day, though, I had abandoned my regular little-boy-about-town look for something more suiting to my operation. Unfortunately this made me look like something of a teen terror. Since I didn't as yet have any of the stereotypical Heavy Metal attire, such as black leather or denim, yet, I had dug out the oldest clothes I could still get into: Old, faded and ripped jeans, slightly flared but not embarrassingly so, and an even older windbreaker, over a plain black T-shirt.

Several minutes passed, each one seeming like an hour, while I waited for just the right moment. Meanwhile, Mr. Courtney continued with his regular closing time business, counting up that day's unsold newspapers for returning to the distributors.

Finally the last customer left and we were alone. With the heavy-set, broad-chested man engrossed in his ledgers, I took my chance and folded my magazine into a half moon, ready to slip it inside my jacket when a ringing bell announced the door was opening and a head popped around it.

"Do you sell maps?" asked a woman motorist. The open door of her car, standing alone under the street lights, sent a wave of light classical music into the shop.

"No we don't, luv." Mr. Courtney walked down the remaining aisle towards the door. His rough voice betrayed his working class routes, so mismatched with the more polished surroundings I'd grown-up in, and in which his shop was located. "Try the Information Center down the street a bit, inside the Library. They're open late on Thursdays."

My eyes remained fixed on the back of Mr. Courtney's head as I slipped the magazine into the purposely left open zip of my jacket. A quick jiggle flattened it out and secured under the waist band of my jeans.

Just as Mr. Courtney closed the door, sounding the bell again, I pulled the jacket zip back up to my chest

Turning on his heels, Mr. Courtney looked right at me.

I shivered.

"All juvenile thieves should get a good whipping." Mr. Courtney spoke to me, carefully, with great, controlled,

purpose.

Unnerved, my mouth hung open.

Then I held my shaking hands out to show they were empty.

Mr. Courtney said nothing. His hands came up to turn mine over as if he was performing a finger nail inspection.

Then, looking me directly in the face again, he ran the zipper on my windbreaker until it parted, revealing the evidence tight against my shirt, held there by my jeans. The leering face of Steve Harris, Iron Maiden's bass player, was right over my navel, his multi-colored Lycra trousers hidden by my own, giving my crotch an oddly symmetrical appearance.

"I'll give you the money for it," I offered when my voice finally returned, knowing I didn't have it but just trying to buy some time.

"I don't need no money from yer, boy. I could report yer to the pigs and yer know what would 'appen then don't yer, my laddo? What would yer folks think of that then?"

I was trembling now. Sweat gushed from every pore in my body as my mind worked through all these terribly punishments I naively thought the police could impose. The lap spankings, over-a-chair canings, and strapped-down whippings, all ran through my mind with me bare-assed in each and every one. Then there was the violent rape I would be forced to endure in Borstal as part of the government's *Short, Sharp, Shock* plan. Of course my father would never allow anything like that to happen to me, even if I wouldn't have been overly upset.

"However," Mr. Courtney continued switching the sign on the shop door to *CLOSED*, pulling down the shade and snapping the deadbolt, locking us in, "I could do with some 'elp in the shop."

"I'll help you, Mister. Honest I will. I'll do *anything* for you," I nearly sang, sounding like Jack Wild from the *Oliver!* soundtrack album. "Anything you want me to. I'm strong, honest. Stronger than I look."

I flexed my right arm trying to crack a barely existing muscle which Mr. Courtney clearly felt through my coat. "I can see yer big, my laddo, but that ain't the sort of 'elp I meant. Yer see I could do with some relief and I don't mean in the shop, neither. Yer get me drift, boy?" His hand moved firmly up my

arm to my face, and gently stroked my cheek, then the soft dark fuzz sprouting on my upper lip.

I didn't understand at all. "I'll do any job you want me to," I repeated, parrot fashion.

"I thought yer would. Yer looks the type. Same as last time." His hand moved again down my neck to hook a thumb into the collar of my windbreaker and ease the jacket from my shoulders and down my arms.

Now I caught on to what was being asked of me. Just a second too late to catch my windbreaker as it passed over my hands. "Please, I don't do anything like that. Please," I begged remembering his name from the Off License plate over the front door, *Robert John Courtney. Licensed to sell intoxicating liquors, for consumption off the premises.* Judging by the smell of his breath, there'd been some recent consumption on the premises as well.

"Don't lie to me, my laddo." Mr. Courtney raised one eyebrow and winked the other. "I know yer type. I know what yer wants. I know what yer thinks abou' all the time."

My head dropped, shamed. "I've seen you in here staring at that *Health & Efficiency* and it ain't no woman what yer is looking at neither, is it boy? Tell the truth."

I said nothing. I couldn't. Something odd was happening on the inside of my jeans. I moved my hands into camouflage positions and hung my head.

"Oh *yes*, I know yer sort all right. I bet yer want ter do everything ter them, don't yer? Yer want them ter do it back ter yer an' all, don't yer? Why else would yer spend so much time staring at 'em - yer bein' such a big boy an' all. Big and strong like, is just what yer is. I bet yer done it with everyone in yer mind, ain't yer? Every bloke, anyhow."

I blushed.

Mr. Courtney raised my chin with the back of his hand until I was looking into his kindly face once more. This time he spoke both calmly and smoothly. "I could give yer a job if yer wants. Delivering papers, evenings only, mind."

"Please, Mr. Courtney." I sounded like a frightened mouse if a mouse could talk that is.

"You'd be me paperboy?"

"Please, Mr. Courtney."

"That's set then." Mr. Courtney smiled "But before, there's the little matter of yer stealing off me, then I need yer to 'elp me relax, and then we'll talk business."

He reached out. I backed into the shelves but he wasn't reaching for me, just the magazine. He grasped the top, his fingers covering the blood dripping letters but he didn't pull it free. Instead his other hand popped the button, and then the zip on my jeans until my magazine was free. Only then did he replace it on the shelves, in the wrong place.

"Please, Mr. Courtney," I repeated. I couldn't say anything else. It was as if my mind was frozen in time.

"Remember, I caught yer stealing from me shop, plus I gave yer a job. Yer owe me." Slowly he lifted my shirt, my arms raised by reflex to allow it to be removed. "A nice big boy!" he added as my jeans were eased down my legs, revealing my prick. It tried to rip through my underpants, tenting them, the head of my enlarged organ trapped painfully in the slitted opening, twisting it back on itself towards my furry balls.

"Please, Mr. Courtney," I said yet again, my little voice wobbling up and down its entire breaking range. Still I made no effort to stop him. My hands rested on his shoulders to keep my balance while my feet were raised and the denim was completely removed. My white trainers and black socks following them over to a pile beside the confectionery counter.

"A nice big paperboy who wants me to do it to 'im. Who would love for me to do it to 'im." Mr. Courtney seemed half asleep or dreaming and I was little better standing frozen to the spot as he stroked his fingertips gently across the front of my swollen underpants. Finding the longer of the two bulges within the plain white garment, he straightened it. He stretched it and caressed it until it throbbed out over my right hip. He held it in his fingers, as if feeling for the pulse that ripped through my being. His other hand eased the top down of my underpants, releasing my burgeoning prick for only as long as it took for my last piece of protection to be removed.

Then his hand clasped me tightly near the knob of my being and made the purple knob swell further, splitting the crown, as he directed it towards his mouth. Pressing the knob to his pale drawn lips he kissed it with great respect, like a priest would a cross. His tongue poked into the slit driving me to a near-

frenzy as he rimmed the head of my prick, then all around and down the shaft until it was ringing wet. Dribbles of saliva trickled back into my sparsely decorated pubis, tickling my marble-like balls before dripping to the floor.

Slowly he swallowed me. First the knob, then inch by inch the whole of my length. His breath was soft on my bum-fluff covered pubic thatch as he emptied his mouth and formed a seal around my root. I was in heaven. Then he stopped.

"Yer like that, my laddo?"

It took a while but eventually I stammered: "Thank you."

"Then yer'll love this."

Holding onto my hips with his wonderfully large, strong hands he turned me around to face the shelves, all the while gently caressing the tender swells of my bum. One hand slid around to my front, rubbing across my balls, then both hands working together as his clothed body covered my back. Then he held my wrists, one on either side. Something long, hard and thick covered in course cloth pressed into my nude buttocks as my arms were raised up to the top shelf.

Unable to resist, I wiggled my willing bum against him and heard him moan in my ear. Eagerly – scared of falling I guess – I grasped the edge of the second-to-top shelf. My fingers entwined in the elastic holding the girlie magazines and *Health & Efficiency*. Staring right down at my undressed, pale body were multiple images of a gorgeously hairy man, his genitals concealed by a banner headline proclaiming the magazine to be "The world's oldest naturist publication." Reading this I missed Mr. Courtney take up the copy of *Kerrang!* I had attempted to steal. One hand remained on my prick, gently tugging my foreskin back and forth over my crown, keeping me up on my toes. Then he slapped me.

"OUCH!" I yelled as the rolled-up magazine was slapped across my previously untouched rear.

"Hold still, yer little thief." The news agent growled in mock anger. "It's no more than yer deserve."

"Yes, Mr. Courtney." Well, it made a change from "Please," though I secretly added that word.

"My paperboys need to know how to be'ave."

"Yes, sir, Mr. Courtney."

I settled down after that. At last I'd found someone whom I

could respect. That was more than I could ever do for my father and his wishy-washy ideas on child-rearing. At least, I intended to settle down, but the feel of the magazine rapping across my ass near drove me crazy. It was better than anything I had previously imagined, and that was saying something, even in those early days.

After the first two I couldn't hold back any longer. I yelped and cried out, not in pain, you understand, but because of the pleasure of it all was just too much.

His big strong fingers covered in newsprint rapped around both my ballsac and prick making those the only parts of me which didn't move as I struggled against the elastic bonds which held my wrists. Sweat broke out all over my body, but mainly on my forehead, clinging to my long hair, clumping it into near dreadlocks. My virgin ass quickly blushed red, yet there was no pain, just an intense burning that was lighting my fire far quicker than any magazine ever had. And while I tossed and turned spread-eagled against those shelves the friction on my prick was tossing that in a different meaning.

Then, just as I was approaching the natural ending, it all stopped.

Mr. Courtney crouched down. He stroked my legs, then stroked the top of my thighs, opening them. I let him. I knew he'd never hurt me. One hand jammed itself up between my cheeks. I pushed my hips back to meet it. Fingers pushed at the back of my balls while the thumb pressed first around and then into my hole.

He penetrated me with all the ease of the broomstick handle section I had hidden in my bedside drawer. Without my conscious cooperation my sphincter automatically opened and let him in. With a groan that could have been heard clean across the street, Mr. Courtney gave me one great big, thumbs-up sign right up my bum.

Meanwhile, his other hand pushed my feet practically under the unit. My toes crunched up on the dusty skirting below the motoring magazines. I was so much on the edge of it all that I couldn't even realize what was going on let alone do anything about it. Not only that but I didn't notice Mr. Courtney reaching into the center isle for the small jar of baby cream, slip his braces off, take down his trousers and coat his news agent's

prick with the cream.

I began to come back down onto the planet with Mr. Courtney's attention taken so. I peered back over my shoulder and saw the largest prick I'd ever seen. Not that I'd seen that many, only the occasional glimpse in the school showers and that one time the captain of the upper sixth rugby team had been stripped by his teammates in the middle of the field as a leaving present. That teenager had been limp in the trouser contents department, but Mr. Courtney certainly wasn't. His prick roared up from the hairiest human body I'd ever seen. There's gorillas in zoos who have less hair than Mr. Courtney. They also had far smaller genitals. A good ten inches long and as near to three around as it was possible to judge. It was as frightening as it was intriguing. One thing was certain though. I wanted to see more of it.

However, I didn't get to see anything further for Mr. Courtney bent over and stuck his face right smack in the middle of my little ass. Right up between the cheeks, in fact. At least his tongue was. The slippery tip pushed right on past my, admittedly, limited defenses until it was inside me. Pushing and moving around inside me. I would never have guessed that kissing a boy's bottom could have been so wonderful, yet Mr. Courtney was obviously enjoying it as much as I was. When he started to jack me off as well I thought I was going to die.

"Please," I murmured my voice tracking up and down the register like a choirboy whose voice was breaking. It wasn't the only thing either. My prick, once a soft little tube of flesh, was now a pounding cricket bat of an erection, that sprung and bounced with every movement of my tense body.

"Yer love it don't yer?" Mr. Courtney said from my bottom, his breath hot, tickling my flesh. "I bet yer loves to get fucked an' all."

I never had been but I was hardly in a state to tell Mr. Courtney that and, anyway, I wasn't so sure I wanted to.

"Yermy little paperboy."

"Big."

"Yes, my *big* paperboy."

He stood. His arms closed around me. One stroked my chest, toying with my nipples like no one had ever done before. The other stimulated my asshole. A whole finger sliding into me

without the slightest hint of trouble. A second joined it. Together the two of them pushed and tweaked around opening me up for what was to come. At one point they brushed over what I now know as my prostate gland. Then, I just knew it made my eyes light up.

Mr. Courtney pressed his body close to mine. His hairy chest rough against my skin. His knees pushed against mine. Electricity snapped across the small divide hoisting up the smaller hairs which covered my bum.

I felt him get closer. Felt his body heat. Felt the course hair in which his groin was coated teasing my skin. Felt his fingers raising my nipples until they stood as proud as my prick, still slick with his spittle. But most of all I felt the young man's fingers as they moved around within me. Opening me wide, wide enough to receive him. To receive his gorgeous prick right up my arse. To touch me like a red hot poker. To drill me like a North Sea oil rig. Already it was pressed into me. His fingers guided its path, his knob stretching me wider then I had ever been stretched before. I gasped.

"Yer love it don't yer?"

Both his arms closed around my chest, then up around my shoulders and behind my head, his fingers interlaced as he pushed himself further and further into my asshole. Harder and harder he went at it, his hips rotating until he could get me to swallow his whole length. "I knew yer'd love it. Just knew it. Yer just like all the others I 'as in here. All my paperboys loves it! "

I didn't say much. Don't reckon I could, but I did look down. My own prick was as stiff as it had ever been, if not more so, twitching and pulsing with every movement. Every second or so Mr. Courtney pulled back with his hips and/or bent his knees, then rammed himself back home again, rammed himself so hard that his balls would slap up against mine. That was the only pain I felt. I decided that every schoolyard tale about the pain involved in getting your ass fucked was crap.

Then the great surge took control of me. For the first time since I had learned about wanking, putting two and two together from the schoolboy jokes and jibes, I was going to achieve the one thing I had never done before. I was going to spurt without having to touch my prick. I could feel it coming.

Feel it burn through my prick with the subtlety of an express train as it ripped from my split eyed prick and splattered all over those magazines, ruining them as my thin spunk dribbled down to pool on numerous shelves. Simultaneously my once-virgin sphincter clamped onto the intruder and milked his life blood right out of him.

Mr. Courtney screamed and hollered far more than I had ever done. He pounded against me as if he were a jack-hammer and I was the concrete he was trying to impregnate. His hands dropped from the back of my neck and fell, uselessly to our joined sides.

In the end, it was up to me to draw the manly sperms from their home and into my rectum. My sphincter working overtime on the shaft taking all Mr. Courtney could give me and then returning for more. As it did, my prick dribbled some sort of clear liquid and then shot a second, third, fourth time until the front of the motoring magazines crinkled under the damp I had newly created.

. . .

I worked for Mr. Courtney for nearly three years before the newly empowered child welfare office intervened. You see, what he'd said during the height of our passion was perfectly correct. All his paperboys, *did* love him, and it.

Unfortunately, Mr. Courtney was such a nice guy he just couldn't refuse any lad a job, even if some were under the lawful employment age and that's why they closed him down. No one ever mentioned the other things which went on in his shop after hours, or just why he needed so damn many paperboys. In fact he was so over-staffed it was a joke, all over town. You see, there was only one evening paper round but there was a total of six paperboys attached to it. We took it in turns. One would deliver the papers while the others...

DOES THIS MEAN I'M GAY?

Leo Cardini

"So what happened?" Kevin asked as soon as I walked into the bedroom. He was sprawled out on our unmade double bed with his Jockey shorts down to his ankles and his knees spread wide apart, giving him lots of freedom to play with his big, fat ten-incher. "Don't you ever give that thing a rest?" I asked, dropping my gym bag onto the foot of the bed and pulling out my sweaty workout clothes to find the grass I had stashed away below.

"Look who's talking! Besides, it sure beats this dumb TV movie." He was referring to whatever was on the second-hand, black-and-white TV we kept on the second-hand dresser that went so well with the second-hand everything else in our apartment. "You watch too much television."

"So what? You suck too much dick."

I'd just pulled my sweat-soaked jockstrap out of my gym bag. I gave in to the urge to throw it at him. Bingo. Right in the face. He reached up for it, pressed it against his nose, took a big sniff, and then threw it back at me, hitting me bull's eye on the forehead. "So listen, Antoinette..."

Actually, my name's Tony.

"... you gonna tell me what happened, or not?"

"What's to tell? We went to the Back Bay Health Club, like we planned, we worked out together, and then we came home." "Home," is Jamaica Plain - though everyone just calls it J.P. - which is actually part of Boston, but when you took the trolley from Back Bay, it's like you crossed the border into another country, and a poor-neighbor one at that. This was back in 1977, before it became "gentrified." Very family-oriented; mainly Italians (like me), Irish (like Kevin) and Poles. Everyone knew everyone else's business, and no one ever seemed to move out of the neighborhood, or for that matter, even leave it to go into Back Bay or the South End, which of course Kevin and I did all the time because that's where all the gay bars and discos are. You'd think we'd have moved - hell, we were both nineteen - but there we were, best friends for as

long as we could remember, living just a few blocks away from both our families. "And it took you six hours?"

I found the small baggie of grass and threw that at him, too, and then began rummaging through the top bureau drawer, with, "So listen, Red, where the fuck's the rolling papers?" He hates it when I call him "Red" because all through junior high and high school the other guys razzed him about his flaming red pubic hair. I think most of them actually did it just as an excuse to gawk at his dick. He might be six foot three, but even for his height it's a pretty big one, and you don't have to be gay to recognize he's hung like a horse. "Oh. Here they are."

I'd located some E-Z Widers behind our collection of cockrings, and tossed them over to him. He caught them and persisted with, "Now about you and Norm."

"You know, Kevin, your interest in what I did with Norm is downright...queer."

"It's not you I'm interested in."

This Norm Kevin was so curious about was Norm Pulaski. He's one of the guys we grew up with. Still lived with his family, just down the street from us. Well, Norm was one heart-throb of a guy. Not very bright, but handsome as hell; broad, smooth forehead, full, sensual lips, unbelievably white teeth, brown, puppy-dog eyes, and a thick mane of wavy, dark brown hair that he parted in the middle. And what a body! A little over six feet tall, and broad-chested, with muscles everywhere you looked. And the fairest, smoothest skin in the world. Not a single blemish on him anywhere. Believe me - I know. Oh, and his butt! I used to fantasize about him stripping down after gym class, wondering what it would be like to be the backstraps of his athletic supporter, stretching across those two firm asscheeks that pressed so tightly together like two evenly-matched opponents locked in battle. So are you surprised when I tell you he was one of our high school's football stars? But then after we graduated he became a mechanic in his father's garage, spending all his spare time hanging out with all the same dumb jocks he went around with in high school. Except he wasn't exactly like the rest of them - not as loud-mouthed or narrow-minded. I mean, we even got him smoking grass with us, which is how I got to suck his cock. Yeah, I really did! You see, four Saturdays back...but

that's another story.*

And yesterday afternoon, I got him to shove that big dick of his up my ass for a fucking I'll never forget. What happened was...well, that's another story, too.**

What I will tell you about yesterday, though, is that after he fucked me, he got to feeling kinda confused. I suppose it's one thing to let another guy suck you off when you're stoned for the first time in your life. But then when you have sex with him again just three weeks later - even if it's just shoving your cock up his ass and nothing else - well, you gotta start wondering about yourself, don't you think? And Norm did start wondering, which made him a little sad and upset. He even said to me, "Does this mean I'm gay?"

The way he said it broke my heart. You should've heard him. And all I could think to say was, "I don't know. Does it?" Actually, I wanted to hold him and tell him everything would be all right. That's when he brought up the Back Bay Health Club, which is where I go to work out, and which he knew from me was probably fifty percent gay. I invited him to join me today, and he accepted. He said, "Sure. It's a date."

Well, it wasn't exactly a date. But still, the idea that he would even call it one... Anyhow, so yesterday afternoon, when Kevin came home from work and I told him what had happened I could tell he was a little jealous. I mean, he was the one, not me, who really had the hots for Norm all through high school. But it worked out well for me because then Kevin fucked me, thrilled at the thought that he was sticking his cock where Norm's had been just a few hours earlier. So, all in all, yesterday I had one hell of an afternoon.

And if that wasn't enough for one weekend, well, today...

"Okay, Red. Here's what happened, but I want you to roll us a joint right now, and get us good and stoned while I tell you."

So there we are at the Back Bay Health Club just a little past noontime. And I'm thinking, whoever would've imagined just a couple of years ago that someday I'd be hanging out in a locker room with Norm, changing into gym clothes so we could work out together? You see, back in junior high I always tried to make myself as inconspicuous as possible in the locker room,

hoping to avoid the notice of Norm's jock buddies, while at the same time envying them their well-developed bodies, their crude banter, and the rough-house physical freedom they enjoyed with each other. Yes, there I'd be, a real chicken wing of a sissy, cautiously sneaking a peek whenever I though I could get away with it, all the time struggling to maintain some sort of control over my troublesome cock, which seemed to have a life of its own and delighted in springing erections on me at all the wrong moments. But times change. In high school, gym was no longer a requirement, and I certainly didn't bother signing up for it as an elective. That's when I started coming here. To be honest, I first joined up because I'd heard it was really gay. But then, when I saw what went on in the Jacuzzi and in the shower stalls, and the type of guys who got the most action, I really got into developing my body. By the time I was eighteen, I was one of those guys getting all the attention. Being as it's early Sunday afternoon, there's hardly anyone else here; just a few other die-hards like me who can manage to stay out late as hell on a Saturday night and still work out, even with just a few hours' sleep.

And a lot of guys wouldn't be caught dead here at this hour on a Sunday because it means either you didn't go out last night (uncool), or you did go out but didn't score (uncool and embarrassing), which is why you're here instead of brunching at Ken's Delicatessen with last night's trick for everyone to see. Ah, but the few who are here - well, you can tell they're all wondering "Who is that hunk hanging out with Angelo? Haven't seen him around." Oh, some of the regulars call me "Angelo." They used to call me "Michelangelo" and then it got shortened. He's this sculptor who did a statue of a kid named David. You know the one? Well, I look a lot like him. And it sure beats Antoinette, which is what they used to call me in junior high. "So how do you know who's straight and who's gay?" Norm whispers to me, glancing around while pulling on his jockstrap, scooping that huge, pale cock of his into its cotton and elastic pouch. It's clearly a jockstrap that's been worn many, many times – possibly one left over from high school – and it's really hard-pressed holding all of him in, sagging at the waist under the pressure of its contents. At first it strikes me that a question like that just goes to show how

dense Norm is. He might be one of the nicest, sweetest guys you'll ever meet, but brains aren't his strong point. Sometimes he even makes me look like an Einstein. But then I think, how do you really know?

Well, without trying to analyze it, I say, "When you catch someone looking you up and down - if he smiles at you, he's gay; if he frowns and looks away, he's straight."

"Oh."

"Ready?"

"Yeah. Let's go."

As I lead the way out of the locker room and onto the floor, he leans towards my ear and says, "So that guy down at the other end of the lockers from us – he's gay?"

"That guy" – muscles and good looks – if only Norm knew how many times I'd seen him deep in the Fens late at night sucking cock, stroking his own dick with one hand, while beckoning over his next selection with the other, he'd never have asked the question. "Yeah. And you should've seen how he was checking out your ass every time you bent over. Given half a chance, he'd have rimmed you right then and there."

"No kidding?" Norm says, beaming. "But you couldn't get away with anything like that in there, could you?"

I guess he really did like it yesterday when he let me stick my tongue up his ass. I forgot to mention that earlier. It was just before he fucked me. "It's been known to happen."

"Really? Wow."

Well, I begin leading him through my usual routine, which turns out to be a major ego trip since Norm can hardly keep up with me. Sure, the warm-up stretches are a cinch, though naturally I'm a little more flexible than he is. But then we move on to sit-ups. He can hardly do fifty to my hundred. And when we start lifting weights, he insists on using the same poundage as me, though you can tell he's really straining. Next we do bench presses. Norm's lying on the bench, legs spread apart, his jockstrap-constrained bulge of cock and balls conspicuously pressing up against his gym shorts. I stand behind him to spot. I can't force my mind away from the realization that my cock is so close to his mouth, separated only by the thin material of my gym shorts and my jockstrap. Why, just one quick tug would be all I'd need to liberate my dick so's to plop it right into his

mouth. Norm grips the barbell, lifts it off its support and successfully raises it. Then a second time, a third, a fourth. I keep count for him as I admire the complex play of his muscles. His chest heaves, his biceps and triceps bulge, and his butt and thighs strain to hold him in position. I savor the sight of the abundant hair in his armpits glistening with dampness, and I can just imagine the funky sweat accumulating below his balls, right at the base of his jockstrap pouch. Shit! I'm getting an erection! I glance down at my crotch. The soft bulge that's usually there has swollen to a hard, protruding lump that's a dead giveaway. Desperate for distraction, I concentrate on counting Norm's reps. He's reached eight. He's sweating and straining and giving it his all. I encourage him to go for nine. He grunts himself into it. Yes! And now ten. Come on, you can do it, Norm! And he does, letting out a loud, tortured exhalation as if he'd just had a mammoth orgasm. He sets the barbell down again, pauses a second, and then kicks himself into a sitting position. He's flushed and sweating. Breathing heavily, he stares down at the floor while he recuperates. I look down at my crotch again. My semi-erection's still visible. Let me tell you, a big dick has its disadvantages. Like when you don't want anyone to know you have a hard-on, there it is, blatant as a billboard. I look around to see if there's anyone's noticed, and I spot this guy across the room at one of the Universal machines. I'd been vaguely aware of his presence for the past few minutes, and sometimes it seemed to me like he was checking us out, but now he's just standing there, arms crossed over his chest. And he's staring right at Norm.

Well, he's such a breathtaking hunk, a little over six feet tall, with the rockhard, muscular development of an all-around athlete, that I forget all about my hard-on and check him out. He's irresistibly handsome; dark skin, high cheekbones and angular facial features like they'd been chiseled from a slab of granite. And the combination of an abundance of wavy black hair cut fairly short and combed back, startlingly thick eyebrows, black piercing eyes, and a Roman nose identifies him as paysanne. He's wearing a white, low-cut tank top with shoulder straps no wider than a shoelace, presenting his well-defined pecs to full advantage, and tight, red sweat pants pulled halfway up his calves, with a big indistinct bulge in his

crotch like a ballet dancer's. I've never seen him here before, but I know I recognize him from someplace, though I can't quite put my finger on exactly where. In my mind, I run through the catalogue of Boston's gay bars. No luck. Ah, maybe the Club Baths? No.

The Fens? No, that's not it either.

Possibly cruising the Esplanade, or standing at a urinal in the men's room behind the Hatch Memorial Shell? No, though I'd sure like to run into him there someday. Then I realize I'm staring at him as conspicuously as he's staring at Norm. He, too, looks like he's pre-occupied with trying to figure something out, as if he's not as much staring at Norm, as through him, into his own thoughts. Then I see it register loud and clear on his face that he'd found what he was searching for. He bursts into a wide smile, and strides over to us. "Jesus fucking Christ, if it isn't Norm Pulaski!" he says, slapping Norm on the shoulder. Norm looks up, startled, and instantly recognizes him.

"Mike! How the fuck are you?" he says jumping up and vigorously shaking his hand.

" Not bad, man. You?" Mike asks.

"Fine, fine. Oh, remember Tony?"

"No," Mike says doubtfully.

"Yes you do. Tony Bielli."

He takes my hand in a real bone-crusher of a grip and says, "You're Tony?" But I still don't recall who he is, which he picks up on, prompting me with, "Mike Franzi. Remember? Played football freshman year? Before my family moved to Malden?" Oh, yes, now I remember him. Awfully nice guy, I recall, though I didn't know him very well since he hung out with all the other jocks. Good-natured and always quick to laugh. Oh, and very physical with his pals. You know, throwing them playful punches, draping his arm around their shoulders and leaning into them to confide something obscene, and (my favorite) whacking them on the ass with the back of his hand. How I envied him all that uninhibited intimacy. "Yeah, I remember," I say. "Hi!"

"Jesus, you used to be so…"

He releases my hand and scans me up and down. Leaving the worst unspoken, he skips over to, "…but just look at you

now." Though as he says this, his eyes are glued to my crotch. Then he looks up into my eyes. He sees I've noticed him checking me out, and he gives me a quick, confidential wink. Well, he pulls Norm into the sphere of his attention again and we spend several minutes catching up on each other's lives. Mike relates how he's moved into Back Bay because, "after all, that's where the action is," and how he's a travel agent at the C.S. Travel Agency. "You know," he says by way of reference, "just down the street from Chaps." So it dawns on me not only is he assuming I'm gay, but that Norm is also. Of course, maybe Norm is, but damned if anyone knows. Especially Norm himself. "Listen," Mike says, "I gotta get back to my routine. Usually I'm only here on the week mornings, but..." So that explains why I'd never seen him here before. "...well, it's really not important. Anyhow, I'd better finish my routine, so I'll catch you guys later, okay?"

"Yeah, sure," Norm says.

Mike shakes our hands again, we all exchange see ya's, and he returns to his workout with, "Oh, and if you're interested, I usually hang out at the Ramrod Sunday afternoons."

When he's back on the other side of the floor, Norm asks, "What's the Ramrod?"

"A denim and leather bar. Over on Boylston Street just across from the Fens."

"You mean like Hell's Angels?"

"Norm, it's a gay bar."

"Mike's gay!"

"Wasn't it obvious?"

"Well, maybe to you, but...are you sure?"

"Yes, I'm sure."

We move over to one of the Universal machines and take turns working on our shoulders. But I notice Norm has this pre-occupied look on his face, like he's trying to figure something out. He finally says, "You mean to say there's a gay bar practically right next door to Fenway Park?"

"I didn't say Fenway Park. I said the Fens."

"Same difference."

"Not quite, although I guess both of them have a lot of men swinging their bats and playing with balls."

"Huh?"

"The Fens is where all the guys go cruising to have sex with each other in the bushes."

"Right in the bushes?"

"Yup. And on a warm Saturday night, after the bars close, there's a good five or six hundred guys in there, fucking and sucking to their heart's content." Norm's staring at me like he thinks I'm making this up.

"Really?"

"Honest to God."

And then, since he's so amazed, I can't resist adding, "Besides, there's not just one gay bar near Fenway Park. There's three: the Ramrod, the Twelve-Seventy, and the Lansdowne." "Boston has three gay bars?"

"No. It's probably more like fifteen."

"Go on!"

"No, really. Let's see. Besides those three there's the Shed, next to the Conservatory. There's Chaps and Styx behind the library, and Darts just down the street. Then there's 119 Merrimac, the Other Side, Jacques - but that's for women only - the Napoleon and Playland. And then in Cambridge..."

"How can there be so many gay bars?"

"How can there be so many gays? And I haven't even mentioned the Club Baths, or the South Station Cinema."

It's his turn to do a set. But before he does, he says, "It's like there's this whole other world in Boston and you don't even see it."

"That's because you're not looking for it."

"Yeah. Guess so. "

As he goes through his reps, I think of something a couple weeks back that proves the point. This was how me and Carlos, this Puerto Rican grease monkey with a ten-inch dick, had this really hot time in the men's room at Norm's father's garage. His dad's out on some towing job, Norm's busy pumping gas, and there I am, barely yards away, down on my knees with this huge fat dick in my mouth, having the time of my life. And no one ever noticed me slipping in and out of the men's room when Carlos was already there. Anyhow, soon we're done with our workout. We go back into the locker room and strip off our sweaty workout clothes. As I peel off my jockstrap, Norm amazes me by saying "You know, you really have a big dick.

It surprised me the first time I saw it because I thought..."
Here he stops with an embarrassed smile.

So I finish for him "...how can someone who used to be such a big sissy have such a great big dick?"

"Well, not exactly."

"Bullshit! That's precisely what you meant."

Then I say, "C'mon," as I spin my combination lock shut, "I'll show you around." Draping my towel around my neck, I give Norm a quick tour of the facilities, pointing out where the steam room, the Jacuzzi, the showers, and everything else is. Norm follows me, clutching his towel in front of his crotch, clearly not as comfortable as I am in parading around in the buff. Pity, considering how much he's got to show. Well, of course, we end up the Inhalation Room, the first stop on everyone's post-workout routine. Actually, it's hardly really a room, even though it does have a sign saying that's what it is. It's shaped like one of those six-sided figures - I forget what you call them since I was never good at geometry - sliced in half right down the middle. The long slice is all glass, with a door dead center, and the other three sides are bordered by one continuous bench built right into the blue and white tile wall. What makes it the Inhalation Room is the odor of eucalyptus they somehow pipe in. It's like Muzak for your lungs, except it's supposed to do wonders for you. Well, the odor's usually weak, sometimes non-existent, and I don't know if it really does do you any good, but most of the guys wouldn't miss a few minutes here before moving on to the other backroom facilities if their lives depended on it. You see, it has one great advantage. It looks out onto the locker room, giving you a completely unobstructed view of the central, dead end aisle of lockers. If you're lucky, you can catch yourself one real hunk of an exhibitionist pretending not to notice you while making a complete, mouth-watering production of changing into, or out of, his gym clothes. I'll tell you, some of these guys - well, Gypsy Rose Lee could've learned a thing or two from them. When we enter the room, we're the only two there. I seat myself facing the glass wall, as if it's a giant television screen, pull the towel from around my neck and set it down on the bench beside me. Norm seats himself next to me. He, too, places his towel on the bench. But he's clearly uncomfortable

sitting there in the nude. He leans forward, rests his forearms on his thighs, and begins to self-consciously study his toes, which he wiggles up and down and up and down. I, however, find my own toes less interesting than the bare-assed Steve Reeves lookalike out at the lockers with a towel draped around his neck who seems to be having difficulty with his combination lock. He keeps spinning the dial and yanking at the lock, as unsuccessful at opening it as he is successful in captivating my attention with the way his submarine sandwich of a cock flops around below his big bush of black pubic hair, responsive as a puppet on a string to his every movement. Oh, yeah. How could my toes ever complete with his dick?

Well, he finally succeeds in unlocking it. He pulls out a men's toiletry bag, re-secures the lock and struts down the aisle towards us, a breathtaking vision of pumped-up muscle and generously-endowed dick. At the end of the aisle, he turns in the direction of the showers, gracing me with one final eyeful as he lingers at the water fountain before disappearing around the corner. Almost immediately, Mike appears from around the same corner. He's looking behind him, presumably having passed by Mr. Reeves, as taken with him as I was. His towel's draped around his neck and he's yanking on his cock, a big, fat Italian-Stallion dick. Not unlike my own, I might add. He finally snaps his head forward and sees us through the glass wall. He releases his dick, revealing that he's cut, flashes us a "So there you are!" smile, and opens the door to join us. Norm turns embarrassed and covers his crotch with his towel, though his big bush of brown pubic hair spills over and you can just make out the base of his thick manroot. I see Mike's gaze zoom in on Norm's crotch. Then he seats himself opposite Norm, spreading his legs apart and gripping the edge of the bench with both hands, allowing his huge dick to flop over the edge of the bench. Leaning forward, he says, "Sure is quiet here on Sundays, isn't it?"

"Yeah," I weakly respond.

Norm just nods, his eyes fixed on Mike's dick. Then he looks up and his eyes meet Mike's. Embarrassed, he quickly redirects his gaze at the wall over Mike's right shoulder. "So..." Mike says, making a second stab at conversation, "...you two guys just friends, or what?" Norm looks over to me like he doesn't

know how to answer.

"Hell," I say, "We've been friends all our lives."

"Roommates, maybe?"

"Nah. Remember Kevin? Tall Irish guy with the red hair?"

"You mean Red? The one with the...uh...?"

He holds his hands out in front of him, palm facing palm about a foot and a half apart. "Yeah, that one. We're roommates."

"Just roommates?"

"Yeah. Well..."

But I leave it unfinished since I don't know what to say. The funny thing is, a lot of guys we meet in bars, especially older men in their thirties and forties, say Kevin and I are really lovers, except we don't realize it yet. Norm's silent, glancing back and forth between the two of us as he follows the conversation. "Hmh," Mike says. "Sorta like fuck buddies?"

"Yeah. Sorta."

"I always liked Red," he says by way of an afterthought.

I can just imagine why.

Mike plants his hands on his thighs and takes in a big, chest-expanding inhalation, thrusting his two hard nipples into lip-smacking prominence. He runs his hands up and down his chest a couple of times, exhales, and settles into a comfortable, open-legged position with his arm draped across the back of the bench. I take this opportunity to savor the sight of him. I mean, it's obvious he's showing off his body - and his equipment - so why not? Ah, so broad-shouldered and trim-waisted. I gaze at his chest – the prominent contours of his pecs a work of art – and then follow the ever-narrowing spread of short, black hairs that descend from between them across his rippled abdomen, passing below his tight navel into the full forest of his pubic bush. And such a fat dick dangling over the edge of the bench, with a thick, brown cockshaft networked with a riot of prominent blue veins, and crowned with a large, reddish-brown cockhead looking like it has a life of its own as it scans the floor below. His balls, nestled in a ballsac big as a baseball but furrowed and fuzzy, huddle in close confinement between his powerful legs. Then I look up at his face. He instantly turns towards me and our eyes meet. It's clear he knows I've been checking him out. Pleased, he just grins and slides assforward

a few inches more, forcing his legs further apart. His cock begins to stiffen, slowly rising up between his legs. Norm notices and out of embarrassment leans forward, resting his forearms on his thighs, losing himself once again in the deep, compelling contemplation of his toes. Mike's humungous cock is now sticking straight out in front of him, no small feat for such a fat, heavy-hanging log of a dick. I mean, all that gravity it has to fight against! And now it starts to ascend. Norm looks up, catches a glimpse of Mike's cock, and then hurriedly looks down at his toes again. He readjusts the drape of his towel over his crotch. Could he be possibly be hiding a hard-on of his own? Mike looks over at me, catching me admiring his huge member, which I now make no attempt to conceal. Fact is, I'm having a hard time resisting the urge to go down on him right then and there, regardless of who might see. But Mike distracts me with a "what gives?," scrunching up of his face as he nods towards Norm. I shrug my shoulders in response. "Well," he finally says, rising, presenting us with one final view of his huge dick. He grabs its, gives it a long, slow stroke and then shoves his towel in front of it so his hard-on gets as lost in its folds as is possible for such a big boner. "Guess it's time for me to hit the steam room. See ya."

"See ya," I say.

"Yeah, see ya," Norm mumbles after him as he goes through the door. "So," Norm says several seconds later, "did you notice he had an erection?"

"Notice! How could you miss it?"

"Yeah. Guess so."

"And was sure making a play for you."

"He was?"

"Well, both of us, actually."

"At the same time?"

"Maybe he wanted to have a threesome."

"A threesome? Jeez!"

And with that, he falls into his thoughts.

"So, listen," I say standing up, giving into the persistent, cock-tingling urge to check out what further adventures might lurk in the steam room, "I've had enough of this eucalyptus."

"Mind if I hang out here a little longer?"

"Go ahead."

"I'd sure like to try the Jacuzzi, too, maybe."

"Well, you know where it is. I'll be in the steam room. If you decide to join me, when you walk in, be careful you don't slip and break your neck. Someone's always unscrewing the light bulb in there."

"So screw it back in."

"Not on your life."

"Oh? Why?"

"Norm, figure it out."

Well, he thinks for a second and then goes "Ohh" with a roller-coaster inflection. "And that's where Mike is, huh?"

"Yeah," I say, flashing him a wide smile as I leave him to himself in the eucalyptus room. The bulb in the steam room is off, but there's enough light coming in through the translucent glass door that once I enter I can see the dark outline of someone sitting off to the right on the second bank of tiled rises. I approach a few steps through the misty semi-darkness. "Hiya Tony."

Yes, it's Mike. He pats the tiles on his right, inviting me to join him. As I step up beside him I notice he's seated so far forward that not only his cock, but also his balls hang down in front of him, tempting as forbidden fruit, ripe and ready for the having. "So where's Norm?"

"Still in the eucalyptus room. On the way to the Jacuzzi, I think."

"Oh," he says, sounding a little disappointed. "Well, I'm sure he'll make a lot of busy hands happy in there."

You see, I didn't tell Norm, but there's an awful lot of jackoff activity that goes on in the Jacuzzi. Everyone's always groping everyone else, jacking each other off like there's no tomorrow, which is why I hardly ever go in there. Not because I object to that sort of thing. It's just that I get so damn frustrated because I always end up wanting to go down on whoever I'm fooling around with. And believe me, what with the chlorine and the turbulence and trying to hold your breath, you simply can't give a good blowjob in a Jacuzzi.

"Actually," he continues, "I was kind of hoping that both of you would follow me in here."

"Listen, Mike, I gotta tell you something. This is Norm's first time here."

"So?"

"And he's not even sure he's gay."

"He's not?"

"That's right."

"Hmh. I just assumed since he's hanging around with you..." "Yeah, I know."

"No wonder he's so...tense.

He thinks about this for a moment. While he does, I notice his cock's getting hard again "Well," he finally says, giving my thigh a pat and then letting his hand rest there. "You just leave it to me. I have a knack for finding out about things like that. And jocks are my specialty. Especially jocks with big dicks."

"Yeah?"

"Yeah, but in the meantime..." he says, inching his hand across my inner thigh, "...speaking of big dicks." My cock twitches in response.

"Christ. You two guys have got me so fucking horny. I mean..." He leaves this unfinished as he stands up, turning towards me. His cock is fully hard again and he holds it up in front of my face, his cockhead barely inches from my mouth, looking like a ripe, shiny plum. "Well, I guess you can see what I mean!"

I wrap my hand around my own dick and go down on him. His cock's completely rockhard, with absolutely no give to it. He doesn't release it, which means I can only get the first five or six inches of it in my mouth before I reach the roadblock of his fist. So I suck on what's available - quite a mouthful in itself - until I dismount him to lick the swollen underside of his cockhead, working on it with slow, deliberate tongue strokes. "Oh!" he moans with every lick.

He leans forward and reaches for my own cock, which willingly I transfer into his grasp, and slow-strokes me as I go down on him again, pushing his hand away from his dick so I can deepthroat him with complete abandon. I feast on his huge member, sliding my lips up and down his outrageously thick, veiny shaft until he groans with the first signs of the advent of orgasm, which he interrupts by pulling his dick out of his mouth and stepping down onto the floor. With his hands bracing the edge of the tier on either side of my legs, he takes two steps back, positioning himself push-up style at a forty-five

degree angle. He slowly bends his elbows, lowering himself until he's close enough to wrap his lips around my cock. "Ahh!" I gasp.

His mouth is so warm and his tongue is so busy swirling all around my cockhead I feel like I'm melting. I watch as he continues to lower himself, admiring the graceful coordination of his muscles while he gradually takes more and more of me into his mouth. Soon, my cockhead's pressing against his throat. He pauses for a second and then he continues to go down on me. My cockhead slips into his throat and his nose presses against my abdomen. Still in push-up position, he slowly dismounts my aching rod and looks up at me with an irresistible, sex-crazed smile on his face. "Christ, you have such a fucking beautiful big dick, I could work on it all afternoon." And to prove the point, he lowers himself into another push-up, sliding down my cock and driving me crazy. After I don't know how many suckoff push-ups, his body begins to shake with the strain of it all, so I place my hands on his shoulders and gently push him up off my cock. "Here. Let me get up, Mike."

He stands up and steps back, his hyperactive dick twitching out of control. I lower my feet onto the floor and stand facing him.

He immediately sinks to his knees.

"Spread your legs apart a little more," he orders, staring at my cock. Even through the steamy mist I can see he's practically spellbound scrutinizing me from this angle. How well I understand, considering the countless times I've been in that same position. As my dick twitches repeatedly in front of his face, he leans forward and begins licking my balls with long, flat-tongue slurps. I grab my cock and slowly stroke it, my hairy ballsac rising and falling in response. Mike manages to suck my right nut into his mouth, swirling his tongue all around it as he applies his thumbs and forefingers to his nipples. Then he manages to maneuver the left one in. I continue jacking myself off, feeling the delicious, accommodating tug of Mike's mouth on my ballsac. I'm so wrapped up in the overwhelming pleasure of the moment that when the door suddenly opens I don't even care who might be there. "Tony?"

"Norm?"

Mike and I freeze where we are.

Norm steps in, clutching his towel. The door slowly shuts behind him. When he makes us out in the dim light, his mouth falls open. I see Mike glance up at Norm. I wonder how he feels having Norm catch him kneeling in front of another guy with his mouth full of ballsac. "I..." Norm stammers.

Mike thrusts his left hand out towards Norm's crotch, beckoning him to come closer. "I..," he repeats, unaware, I think, that his free hand grips his enormous cock and slowly tugs on his soft, pliable meat as he stands there indecisively. To encourage him, I extend my own free hand towards him.

And just when it looks like he's going to join us, the door opens again and in steps Mr. Reeves! Norm jumps out of his trance with, "I gotta take a shower!" And with that he makes a hasty exit, his heavy-hanging dick flopping around in front of him like a log crashing its way down a turbulent river. As the door slides shut behind him, Mike jumps up with, "Good idea! Me too! Listen, Tony, leave it to me. If there's one thing I know how to do, it's getting a little action going in the showers. Okay?"

"Uh...sure."

"Those guys in Malden sure taught me a trick or two that still come in handy. Just give me a few minutes and then join us." Mike exits making no attempt to conceal his rockhard, upstanding boner. So there I am, standing there with a hard-on in the presence of Mr. Reeves. "I hope I didn't ruin anything for you guys," he says seating himself several yards off.

"No. You see....well, it's a long story."

I sit down again. My hard-on sticks up between my legs, and Mr. Reeves looks over, stroking his own dick in appreciation as I ponder what a remarkable afternoon this has been, giving Mike what I estimate would be enough time for him to do whatever he does to get a little action going, and then I get up to leave the steam room. It's a pity to pass up an opportunity with Mr. Reeves, so I flash him a broad smile before I exit, just to keep future possibilities open. I hear Mike and Norm's voices over the splash of the showers, and follow the sound down the left aisle to the two furthermost stalls. As I approach, I see that Mike's stall door is open and he's talking to Norm, whose stall

is opposite his. Whatever he was just saying, Norm goes, "What?"

"For chrissakes, Norm, would you open that fucking stall door before I lose my voice! There's no one around..."

Norm opens his stall door. "...except for Tony. Hi, Tony."

"Hi," I say standing there in the aisle.

"So listen," Mike continues, winking at me, "I was just telling Norm about the time he was home with a sprained ankle when I stole Coach Dudley's jockstrap right out of his gym bag.

"Well, I'm prancing around the locker room in it, aping the way he was always reaching in and scratching himself, except I'm pretending what he's really doing is playing with himself. All the guys are hooting and hollering and imitating me, and before you know it, I've pulled off Coach Dudley's jockstrap, tossed it onto one of the benches, and I've got all of us standing around in a circle and stroking our dicks with the intent of depositing our big, wet loads on it before I return it to Coach Dudley's gym bag." Here Mike stands on the edge of the stall facing out at us, playing with his dick as he continues to reminisce. "I think most of the guys were as nervous as I was at first, because suppose Coach Dudley walked in on us. But as soon as we all had hard-ons, I don't think we cared anymore. And I was really getting off on the idea of shooting my cum all over Coach Dudley's jockstrap with all the other guys. And you know..." He's taking slower, more deliberate cockstrokes now.

"That was the first fucking time I ever realized that the way I felt about other guys wasn't just a phase or something. You see, when we started shooting our loads, I could tell that the other guys – except for Todd...remember him?" Norm and I nod yes, the two of us practically mesmerized by Mike's slow up-and-down application of his hand on his fat, ever-hardening dick. "Well, except for Todd, I realized all any of them cared about was how good it felt to shoot their loads and what a big joke they were playing on Coach Dudley. But for me it was different. Watching them stroke their cocks, I wanted to touch them so badly it kinda scared me. And when I happened to look up at Todd's face, I could just tell he felt the exact same way I did." Mike's cockstrokes have practically come to a halt. Norm's standing motionless in his stall, the shower water hitting him on the back. His cock is swollen, hanging down

heavily between his legs, and he's staring intently at Mike. "And the next day, Todd and I both just sort of 'happened' to be the last two guys in the locker room after gym practice. We've just come out of the shower and we go for our towels. Well, Todd steps right in front of me..." Mike turns off his shower and steps out of his stall, facing Norm. "He looks nervous as hell, and he reaches out, wraps his fingers around my dick, like this..." He grips Norm's cock.

"...takes a step forward..."

He steps into Norm's stall.

"...and..."

He gets down on his haunches and gobbles up Norm's big, fat dick. Norm's eyes widen with equal parts pleasure and amazement as he looks down and watches Mike devouring him. I can't resist joining in. I step into the stall and get down on my haunches next to Mike. Mouth full of cock, his eyes flash over at me, inviting me to share in his good fortune. He fumbles around in my crotch until he gets a good grip on my dick, which he begins to stroke. At the same time, he skillfully maneuvers Norm's cock over towards me, pressing Norm's cockhead against my lips and kissing me across the welcomed, juicy obstruction that it is. Mike slips his tongue under Norm's cockhead and I greet it with my own. We run our tongues up and down the underside of Norm's dick several times, and then concentrate on teasing his piss slit with the tips of our tongues. As we watch Norm's cock repeatedly jerk upwards, we hear him groan in grateful response. The next thing I know, Mike stands up again. Alone on my haunches, I work solo on Norm's cock, eagerly taking all of it into my mouth. I look up as best I can to see Mike and Norm vigorously kissing with a deep-drilling exchange of tongues. Mike pushes his cockhead over towards my mouth. I struggle to maneuver it in next to Norm's. I mean, they both have such big cocks, and to make matters even more difficult, Mike's hard-on sticks up, stiff as a soldier at attention, while Norm's hangs down like a diviner's rod relentlessly drawn to an underground bonanza of water. But some problems are better than others, and I willingly accept the task set before me. Though in no time my mouth feels stretched to its limit and my jaw begins to ache, I do manage to get them both in. Well, at least the first four or five inches of

each of them. Never before in my life have I had so much cock in my mouth at once. There they stand towering above me locked in a kiss as their cocks slip in and out of my mouth. They begin to run their hands across the nipple-capped contours of each other's chest. Shit, I could suck the two of them off like this forever. Eventually, Mike looks down at me and says, "Hey Tony, get up here." I dismount their cocks, massage my jaw and rise.

Mike immediately gets down on his knees.

"C'mon, Norm," he says, nodding up at him, "Get down here with me. I'm going to show you what good cocksucking like that's all about. To my surprise, Norm joins him with no hesitation.

Well, the two of them start lapping on my dick like there's no tomorrow. Mike's tongue is the more active one - he's clearly had lots of experience - and I see that Norm's watching and imitating, gradually broadening his own tentative licks into long, drawn-out slurps. I look down at them in amazement. Yes, there they are - two of my favorite high school jocks - licking my dick, playing with it like some special toy they like so much they're actually willing to share it! Mike suddenly deepthroats me and commences to work the length of my cock with long, slow suckstrokes. Norm looks on, keenly observant, until Mike dismounts me and uses his lips to push my cock over towards him. Without hesitating, Norm takes me in his mouth. He swallows more of me than he should, though, considering it's the first time he's ever done anything like this, and he gags. But he keeps my cock in his mouth and it doesn't take him many suckstrokes before he's working his lips up and down my shaft like an accomplished cocksucker. As Mike witnesses Norm sucking on my dick, he runs one hand up along the back of my leg, across my asscheek, and finally into my asscrack. He plays around with my butthole, and then slips in one shower-wet finger. Then a second. Moaning, I thrust out my ass to accommodate the entry of a third finger, which he skillfully does in no time. He stands up again. Norm abandons my cock and follows suit. Mike positions me spread-eagled against the shower wall under the nozzle. His fingers are still inside my butthole, driving me crazy. I twist my head around to him.

"Fuck me! Please!"

He loosens me up a little more, withdraws his fingers, and pulls my asscheeks wide apart with his big, strong hands. "Such a beautiful butt," he says half to himself as he admires my exposed hole. "Norm, get some soap from that dispenser." Norm complies, squirting out a handful of the liquid soap and smearing it against my butthole. "Now, work it in with your fingers."

The sensation of Norm's slippery, uncertain fingers poking around inside drive me crazy, sweetly spreading across my ballsac and down my cockshaft, like too much of a good thing. I tilt my head back and shake it from side to side with one "Oh!" after another, trying to toss off the excess pleasure. "Yeah, that's it, Norm. Get him nice and lubed up. Now put some of that soap on my cock." I twist my head around again so I can see what's going on behind me. Mike's standing there with his legs spread apart and his hands on his hips, looking down at his crotch as Norm spreads the soap all over his dick. It constantly twitches, jumping up out of Norm's hand until Norm finally manages to control it by grabbing Mike's ballsac with one hand and pulling it downwards, while wrapping his fist around Mike's shaft with the other, slowly stroking it, even after it's clearly all soaped up. "Put some more in Tony's butthole," Mike says urgently, sounding on the verge of shooting his load if Norm continues jacking him off. After Norm begins to massage a fresh load of soap up my ass, Mike reaches over to the dispenser himself. He takes a big gob of the stuff and reaches behind himself to work it into his own butthole. Then he reaches for more. With one hand, he continues to work the soap into him, and with the other he smears it on Norm's dick and then spreads it up and down with his fist wrapped around Norm's cockshaft. "Oh my God!" Norm goes when it sounds like Mike's got him close to coming. Mike lets go of him, repositions himself behind me and skillfully slips the first few inches of his cock into my hole. "Ahh!" I go as I surrender to the sweet feeling of him filling me up. He slowly slides another few inches in and then stops.

"Okay, Norm. Now you," he says.

"Me? He'll never be able to take the two of us."

"No. Stick your cock up my ass."

"Oh!"

Still, the thought of both of them inside me at the same time...

I twist my head around again and watch as Norm takes his cock and maneuvers it up Mike's ass. "Ah, shit!" Mike goes. "Slowly."

Norm places his hands on Mike's hips and carefully slides more of his dick up Mike's ass. "Yeah, that's it. Ahhh!" Mike says. "Now pull out of me about halfway."

"Like that?"

"Yeah."

Mike slowly rotates his hips. His cock slips in and out of me while he manages to ride Norm's dick. At first his progress is slow, strained and slightly irregular as he gets things coordinated. I find the way I can best move my own hips to receive his cockthrusts. I twist my head back again briefly and I can see from the way Norm's straining that he's working hard at establishing the rhythm he needs to slide his cock in and out of Mike's ass. "Yeah. That's it, guys," Mike says when we reach the point where the three of us are working together with clockwork precision. The little conversation there was between us comes to a stop. Soon the three of us are gasping and panting, absolutely unconcerned that anyone standing outside the stall would know exactly what was going on. After a while, Mike's cockstrokes quicken, growing more forceful, almost brutal, which I definitely like. I brace myself with my right forearm horizontal against the wall and press my forehead into it so I can reach down and stroke my own dick. I don't know how long we remain like this. The noisy splash of the shower against the side of the stall mingles with the sounds issuing from our throats and all the sensations of cockstroking and buttfucking until I feel like I'm drowning in a perfect moment where nothing else matters, nothing else exists, but this overwhelming, three-way orgasm. I feel Mike's grasp tighten on my hips. I can tell he's close to coming. Norm, too, since the way he's aahing sounds like he could blow open the stall door if he wanted it to. Mike holds me real hard, lets out a loud wail of an "Ohhh!" and gives his cock such a violent thrust up my ass I have to rally all my strength against it in order not to be crushed against the wall. I feel his warm cum spurt out inside

me as he repeatedly rams his cock up my ass like he has an endless supply of hot jism to discharge. Finally, spent of his king-size load, he comes to rest with his dick still up my ass. He wraps his right forearm around my chest and pulls my body tight against his. He grabs my cock out of my hand and jacks me off. I'm so horny I know I'm going to come in no time at all. Now that Mike's shot his load, Norm has the freedom he needs to control his own orgasm. I can feel him pounding in and out of Mike's ass through the aftershocks of Mike's body slamming against my own. I hear Norm's bass-baritone "Ohh!" as he shoots his load up Mike's ass. At the same time, Mike jacks the cum out of my own cock. The sweet sensations of discharge that electrify me are so strong and staggering that I buck with each new eruption of cum that splatters against the tile wall in front of me. To support me, Mike tightens his grip on my chest. I fling my head against his left shoulder, my legs shake, and I have to tense them in order to remain standing. As my cum slowly drips down the wall, like it was measuring our return to a normal state, we take our time recovering and gradually manage to disentangle. Mike re-directs the shower nozzle and the three of us quietly shower off, until Mike gets things going again by playfully sliding a soapy finger up into Norm's butthole. "Ah!" Norm says squirming with pleasure, "This should have happened to me ages ago."

"What," Mike asks playfully, "having someone stick a finger up your ass?"

"No. All of this!"

He takes our two dicks and holds them, one in each hand, like he was estimating their weight. Then, as soon as Mike withdraws his finger, Norm gets down on his haunches. He stares at our cocks like he's trying to decide which one to suck on first. But before he chooses, he looks up at us and says, "But the next time we do this..." (Ah! Notice who's the first to say anything about a next time!) "...let me try being the one in the middle, okay?"

"Sure thing, Norm," Mike says. Then, as he slides an arm around my waist and the two of us look down to see who Norm's going to take into his mouth first, Mike turns to whisper in my ear, "Told you jocks are my specialty." Afterwards, when we're putting on our clothes again, Mike

asks, "So you guys wanna join me over at the Ramrod?" Is Norm ready for a gay bar, let alone the Ramrod?

But Norm's dressed, as usual, in tight, faded Levis that caress his butt and crotch and a white tee shirt that's stretched so tautly across his body it looks like any sudden flex-muscle movement might cause it to explode in a mass of threads and tatters. Definitely a good look for the Ramrod. "I don't know," Norm says, hesitantly as he watches Mike – who's now dressed in a tank top and Levis, like myself – pull a pair of black, square-toed, cowboy boots out of his locker. "I sure wish you would," Mike urges. "I wouldn't want to give it away, but I think I've got a big surprise in store for you there."

"Oh?"

"Mike," I say, "if your surprise is what goes on in the men's room, maybe Norm's not ready for it."

"Why? What goes on there?" Norm asks.

"Guess," Mike teases. "I mean, a dimly lit toilet packed to capacity with hot, horny studs? But that's not what I'm thinking about. Just trust me, guys."

I hesitate to respond. But, to my amazement, Norm, who's been practically mesmerized by Mike's boots as he puts them on, turns to me and says, "Wanna?"

"If you do."

Mike now pulls a black leather vest out of his locker and begins to slip it on. Then he takes it off again and holds it out for Norm. "It'd probably fit you if you'd like to wear it."

"Yeah?" he asks, his eyes widening at the sight of it.

And then, slipping on the vest, he says to me, "Tony, I definitely think I wanna go."

"Wow!" Kevin exclaimed in stoned awe. "This is fucking good grass! I haven't been so high since...whenever. So what happened at the Ramrod?"

"Well, as you can imagine, Norm was the star of the day. You know, new boy in town looking like L'il Abner gone leather. And then that enormous dick of his snaking down his right leg, since Mike and I convinced him back at the Health Club to dispense with his briefs. "Anyhow, after we ordered a second round of beers, Mike looks out into the crowd and says, 'Great, and now for that surprise I promised you guys.'

"Then he yells across the room 'Hey! Todd! Steve! Over here!'"

"And who do you think should come over to us but Todd and good old Coach Dudley!

"Well, you can just guess how amazed we all were, and everything we had to talk about. Turns out Todd and Steve - that's Coach Dudley - are like really close fuck buddies. "Though once Steve heard we were roommates, he kept asking questions about you - how you were, what you were up to, and stuff like that. And when he wasn't quizzing me about you, he kept reminiscing, 'I don't think I ever saw a bigger dick on a kid his age.'

"Anyhow, after a while we all went over to the Fens to smoke some of Steve's grass. Same stuff as this. In fact, it was Steve's idea I get you good and stoned so's you can catch up with the rest of us."

"Oh?"

"Yeah. Because, baby, we've got company coming. That is soon as they pick up some more beer and score some poppers down in some dive Steve knows about in the Combat Zone!"

"Well, if that Coach Douglas thinks he can have his way with me..."

"Not to mention Todd, Mike and Norm."

"All of them?"

"All of them."

"Well, if they think they can have their way with me..."

He paused for the well-timed interruption of the doorbell ringing. And then I joined in for the inevitable, "...they're absolutely right!"

* See "Go Ahead and Touch It" in *Big Boys, Little Lies*, (STARbooks Press, 1993).

** See "Muscles" in *Insatiable/Unforgettable*, (STARbooks Press, 1994).

SOMEBODY

John Patrick

An ass like Johnny's shouldn't have been legal, Steve Parker decided. And then there was the rest of him: the perfect proportions, the flawless skin, the mischievous smile.

Oh, but that ass. Steve often wondered if the other students noticed him watching Johnny every day as he made his way to the same spot: back seat, middle row. Of course, *he* must have known. Just as Johnny passed Steve's desk, he'd dig his hands in his pockets, spreading the fabric tight for his walk to the back.

It was bad enough for Steve to watch him in his classroom and not being able to touch, but then Johnny began showing up during his office hours. *Orifice* hours, he began to think of them, because that's how he wanted to apply his talents on those days when Johnny scooted his chair up close to his. He was always the proper, respectful student, but most of the time his questions were pretty lame; Steve began to think he just wanted attention, and, like most beautiful people, couldn't resist watching the impact he had on others. Steve tried hard to maintain his polite-but-firm classroom persona, but it was rough. All he could think about was locking the door and grabbing that ass and...

But Steve was not amoral; he just lusted for Johnny in silence until one day just before the Thanksgiving holiday recess. Knowing Johnny would be coming in later that afternoon, Steve had been reviewing his file. The report saddened him. After Johnny was thrown out of every private school his mother, Rae Lawrence, a Tony-award-winning actress, put him in, it was decided public school was the place for her so-called incorrigible son. He would live with a housekeeper at their "cottage by the sea" and on holidays he would join his mother wherever she happened to be in the world. Of his father, nothing was mentioned.

There was a knock on the office door. Steve put down the report, stood and stretched, taking his time to let the boy in.

When he did, Johnny entered slowly and stood by Steve's desk, shifting from foot to foot.

"Yes, Johnny," Steve said, trying to keep his eyes on the latest progress report about Johnny when all he wanted to do was gaze at his crotch, which today was unusually well-packed in his chinos.

"There's something I want to show you," Johnny said.

They piled into the tight quarters of Steve's white Volvo. For a quarter-hour they journeyed up along the highway edging the sea that defines the island's landscape. Sometimes, while adjusting the clutch, Steve's hand brushed Johnny's knee, causing Steve to feel a sting of intense pleasure. They took a road that seemed somehow familiar, though many of the roads here look alike.

"I live up this way," the boy said, pointing to the left. Suddenly, Steve saw it: the sprawling whitewashed house was framed by a broad stretch of cloudless sky.

Inside, it was fashionably decorated, with white leather chairs and sofas soft as sponges. The mosaic floor was a sea of alternating swirls of blues and yellows. Steve thought a camera crew from *Architectural Digest* could have come right in and started snapping, but it all had a friendly, lived-in air.

The housekeeper, Nell, a small, grandmotherly-type, greeted them. Johnny introduced Steve as his "counselor," ordered by the school administration to get a report on his living conditions.

This was all coming as a shock to Steve; he swallowed hard and continued to glance about the immense living room.

"Is Johnny in trouble again?" Nell asked.

Steve blinked. "Oh, no, not exactly. It's just that – "

"It's just that I'm a transfer," Johnny interjected. "They do this with all the transfers."

Nell seemed to accept this feeble explanation. "Well, make yourself at home," she said. "I have to go to town to do some shopping. I was planning on going when I picked Johnny up at school but now here he is."

"Yeah, here I am," Johnny said, smirking. "Come on, Mr. Parker, I'll show you my room."

Johnny's room was a private suite overlooking the ocean. It

had the best views of any room in the house. He had every conceivable toy a boy his age could want, most of which looked unused. As soon as Johnny had closed the door and locked it, his impatient hands caressed Steve's crotch. Steve let him revel for a moment in the glory of his swelling, aroused by simply being in forbidden territory: *his* bedroom. Then Steve pulled away. "Whoa! What's going on?"

By now Steve was almost mindless with frustration. By sheer force of will, he kept his arms at his sides as Johnny came to him, pressing against him, warm and hard. Johnny hugged the older man and he hugged him back. Then Johnny kissed Steve. Suddenly generous, Steve relaxed and let the boy continue. As Steve's tongue slid across the boy's full lower lip, savoring the sweetness of him, his cock rose, pressing against Johnny's thighs. Johnny moaned softly, deep in his throat, and closed his eyes as Steve took over, kissing his neck, hearing his quiet breath, and his own, separate amid the crashes of the surf below them. What joy it was to Steve to feel the boy stirring sensuously into him, to imagine this always – two lost souls, cast up on this shore, finding home. He couldn't help himself. In that moment, he loved him madly, entirely.

"Take off your shirt," Johnny commanded.

Steve was stunned by his pleasure in being so direct. He did as he was told. Soon Johnny was covering his skin with kisses and tiny bites, his headful of uncontrollable blond curls adding to the sensation with their tickle. Soon he was unzipping Steve's pants. Steve's penis, dangling free, excited Johnny unbelievably. "Wow!" he cried as he dropped to his knees. Hands or lips, after awhile Steve didn't know which, worked him over; he knew only he was as soaked as a squashed fruit whose skin has burst in the heat. The permission the boy gave freed him to indulge in sensations he had only dreamed about.

Johnny pleaded, in muffled cries, that Steve come in his mouth. At that moment – why, Steve didn't know – he was reminded of his wife, Susan, of how she could never do this for him. And he thought how unfortunate it was that there was only one boy who had – until now. And how, maybe, finally, he was again allowing this for myself.

As Steve came, Johnny's hands were pressed tightly on his firm, hairy buns. The boy took all Steve had to give; it was the

most intense orgasm Steve ever had. Recovering, he reached down and tilted the boy's head. His cock, still spurting, flopped from the boy's mouth.

"Why?"

"You thought I didn't know?"

Steve shrugged. "I don't know how you could know."

Johnny smiled slightly. "How could I *not* know?"

Steve shook his head. "But I hadn't thought of this."

"But you *had* thought of it. From the first day, you've been thinking about it."

Steve raised his eyebrows at him. "But just this once. No more. This is wrong." He used a stern tone.

Johnny stood, slid his underpants down to the floor, bent at the waist and presented the older man with the lightly muscled expanse of his back, his magnificent ass, the sight of which gave Steve's cock a renewed twinge. Straightening and stepping out of the wad of fabric at his feet, Johnny became absolutely bare. He was so astonishingly beautiful that Steve suddenly felt his forehead relax, his worries dissolve. His temptation was to say that he wasn't himself, but he knew this was as true to himself as he'd ever been.

Johnny lay back on the bed, stretched himself lengthwise, putting his hands behind his head on the pillow. He provocatively raised one knee, and studied the ceiling. As he leaned closer to the boy, Steve's eyes consumed his every part. He fondled his nipples until they popped out in sharp, half-inch points. After sucking and flicking them around with his tongue, Steve worked them over with his thumbs and forefingers. Soon Johnny's stiff cock poked straight out. Steve's hand encircled the shaft and gently played with it. Although not unusually large, the cock was in perfect proportion with the rest of him and beautifully cut. Steve knelt between his thighs and started his tongue traveling up and down Johnny's vibrating cock, then worked over his balls with a gentle lapping motion. After a few minutes, he worked his way farther down between his legs, his hands firmly planted on the boy's buttocks.

"Show me your beautiful ass," Steve said, rolling Johnny over. Steve sighed; it was the most perfect ass God ever created. He spread his plump buttocks apart with his thumbs.

The boy's hole was tight and puckering while Steve gently blew against it, watching it tighten more.

Johnny groaned. Steve began to kiss and nibble on his firm buttocks, first one, then the other. Raising the ass higher, Johnny spread his thighs wider while Steve licked and kissed more urgently, causing the boy to shudder with delight. Steve stuck the tip of his tongue into the narrow, pink opening. Johnny started to protest, but he couldn't find the words. His cock immediately went rigid again when Steve's tongue moved around slowly, conscientiously exploring the sensitive rim.

Johnny began rocking his butt back and forth on Steve's spearing tongue, humping his ass more firmly up into his face. Steve's hands gripped the globes as the tip of his tongue tortured the clenched asshole, flicking around it with feathery strokes.

Soon Johnny was rolling his head from side to side, his asscheeks contracting with pleasure. Steve kept pulling it out and plunging it in, then swirling it around in the tight hole until he knew Johnny was ready. He brought his thick dick up against the frantically squirming butt. Nudging the mushroom head firmly between the writhing globes, he separated the asscheeks. He rubbed his erection smoothly back and forth over the fluttering hole, and the pucker opened like a delicate flower. With steady pressure, he managed to stuff most of his nine inches into the boy's willing hole.

As the boy whimpered beneath him, Steve leaned across his back and began kissing his neck, nibbling on his ear, caressing the back of his head while plunging his cock in and out of him.

The day had been clear and sunny but also windy and cool. While they made love, the light outside changed from a pale gold to a deep coppery tint. It was so dazzlingly beautiful in Johnny's room, in that bed, that Steve thought he had truly found paradise. Or maybe one thinks like that only if one is an unhappily married man. And a dedicated teacher. He'd heard remarks about certain of his colleagues who were thought to be lecherous, but he was never numbered among them. As an instructor of English, he considered himself sensitive to nuances of dialogue, and innuendo, and had gone out of his way to keep that kind of thing out of his remarks to his students. But with Johnny, although his interest was never verbalized, he

caught on. It taught Steve a lesson.

Now Steve came in another glorious rush. He rolled off of Johnny and stretched an arm across his warm back. He turned his face to his. "I hope I didn't hurt you," he panted.

"I love you," Johnny whispered

"Oh, you're just a boy," Steve chuckled.

"Yeah, but I know what I like," he said, groping Steve.

Steve turned away. "So do I."

Steve was seeing *somebody*, and Susan, somehow, with that intuition women have, sensed it. With the afternoon sunlight streaming through their living room windows, they had a quiet but definitely unpleasant chat. Marriage is so damned fragile and complicated, Steve thought.

"Steve," she said with her lips tightening, "I know these things happen. But I'm not just going to stand by. You make your choice. Either you're in or you're out."

Steve knew he had to stay in. He had his career to think about. They had two young girls. They agreed that he would cease seeing *somebody*. As of immediately. But, Steve knew, *somebody* would have some things to say about it.

Driving to school the next morning, Steve knew his situation was impossible. He knew the minute he saw Johnny he would desire the boy. His goal that day was to avoid him. But Johnny would not be denied. It was the last day of school before the Christmas recess. Their affair had been relentless for three weeks. They would take drives and Johnny would blow Steve; they would switch and Steve would suck the boy off. They invented the need for special tutoring sessions in Johnny's room that lasted three hours. He was playing with fire, but could not seem to stop himself.

They went for a drive. Johnny was not smiling. He announced he would be flying to London to be with his mother, who was performing on stage there in the West End, for Christmas. He asked Steve to take him to the airport. He managed to change his reservation so that there would be time for them to rent a motel room.

As desperately as he wanted to tell him it was over, that they would never do this again, Steve simply could not. Naked on

the bed in the dim light of the motel room, Johnny was intoxicating to Steve. He had never been with anyone so passionate, so inexhaustible. Or so beautiful.

After the initial, obligatory nervousness of being in a strange motel room, Steve surprised himself by managing erection after erection, fucking the boy repeatedly.

"Oh, God," Steve cried, entering the boy for the last time.

"Oh, Jeeezus," Johnny cried as Steve slid it in, began thrusting in and out of him.

"Oh, Johnny," Steve moaned, his body convulsing as he came inside the boy, as if it was the first time, now wanting it to last for eternity. Steve realizied this was it, he had done it, he truly had a lover – somebody he could not live without. He could no longer fight the pleasure coursing through his body.

They were speechless for a long time after the orgasm; Steve finally disengaged from Johnny, pulling his now limp and moist penis from the warmth of his ass. He kissed him on the lips with all the tenderness he could muster, even as he knew that neither gestures nor words could properly express what he had just experienced. The cover of the bed was rumpled, soaked with sweat and sperm; they had not even bothered pulling it down to uncover the sheets.

Steve got up, led the way to the shower. He soaped Johnny, his fingers lingering more than hygiene demanded in the gaping crack of his ass, caressing his erect cock with lather until it shone like a wet jewel. He realized he had been selfish: Johnny had not come a third time, or even a second time. He had come only when Steve was fucking him moments after they entered the room. Johnny rubbed Steve's back and manipulated himself into a position where he could enter the older man. Steve was astonished. The thought of this had never occurred to him. Still, he did not protest. Johnny's attack on Steve's ass was savage. It seemed as if he literally intended to impale Steve, tear him apart. His roommate at college, Roger, was the only one who had ever fucked Steve and Johnny was better than Roger ever thought of being. Johnny would thrust hard and slip part way out, then slam into him again with incredible force.

Steve lifted myself up to him and Johnny pressed his cock in all the way. His energetic pumping continued for several

minutes, Steve's moans growing more intense with each thrust, until Steve reached down and brought himself off. Hearing Steve's groans of ecstasy, Johnny rammed it into his lover for the final time, his orgasm filling him. Where did he learn this stuff? Steve asked himself. Paris? Rome? The kid was far more experienced than he and it showed. In that moment when the boy was finishing, furiously, pressing down on him, shoving his head under the shower, Steve only wished he could fuck that well.

On the way to the airport, Johnny's hand never left Steve's crotch. He began to cry. "Mother wants me to stay in London with her. She's signed on for an extended run. Maybe a year. It's what she's always wanted, for us to be together."

Steve was speechless. He pulled the car over to the side of the Interstate. Tears came to his eyes as well. He felt free at last to tell him: "I love you, Johnny. I'll miss you." He wiped a tear into the boy's smooth, rosy cheek.

"I'll miss you too, Steve. But I'll be back."

With Johnny in London, Steve was able to focus his attention on Susan. As her anger subsided, he began remembering what an attractive person he had married – blonde, tall, very thin and willowy. Suddenly he noticed what subtle taste she had in clothes, or perhaps she had bought some new outfits. Whatever, he decided what a pleasure she was to look at. It seemed as if his time with Johnny had revitalized his interest in Susan. And when he had sex with her, although he was thinking of Johnny, and only him, he was very good.

"Things are better, aren't they?" Steve asked her one evening when they were lingering at the table after dinner. The girls were in the basement watching television.

"They're not so bad," she said, turning her head towards the dining room window in a way that he knew meant she was thinking about it, that she would always think about it, wondering who the somebody was who had threatened her. Then she got up and walked around the table, stood behind him and ran her fingers along his shoulders. "In fact," she said, "it's really better than it's ever been."

NIGHT OUT

Edmund Miller

In it went. And out. And in and out. Once, twice, five times. Then it was over, and Tim relaxed with a sigh as he eased himself out of Larry (or was it Gary?) and flopped over on the bed, glad at the thought of being able to get a little sleep at last.

But Larry (or was it Barry?) was not ready to quit. "Is that all you're gonna do, sir?"

"Listen, kid, I'm tired. Couldn't we continue this discussion in the morning?" Tim slipped off his cock ring, yawned, and waited for oblivion.

But Larry or Barry or Gary was not to be put off so easily. With a little prodding from his partner—a stroke here, a lick there—Tim found that sleep did not weigh so heavily on him after all. He considered whether he was up to another scene.

The boy, when no longer able to close his hand around Tim's rousing cock, slipped his mouth over the head and went to work again in earnest. Looking down at Gary's curls bobbing against his hard abdomen, Tim decided he might just be up for one more go. But the boy was giving head with an enthusiasm perhaps too wild.

"Slower, kid," Tim said, slipping his fingers into the curls. Larry slowed down immediately. But he slowed down too much, of course. However, Tim had hold of his head by then and soon heard himself passing compliments like "That's it!" and "Ah! That feels good" and "Do that some more." He tried to reach for the cock ring again but only succeeded in knocking it off the night table and onto the floor with a clunk. "Fuck."

Harry was taking direction well. Tim began to think the kid might really be able to bring him off again, ring or no ring. And the kid certainly seemed to be enjoying his work. Perhaps to see how much, Tim reached up a bit and under, searching. He managed to find what he was looking for, hard and lean and taut, thrusting up into the dark. As Tim ran his fingertips up and down along the length of the sleek shaft, the boy's whole body began to quake. The cock leapt away from Tim's fingers.

The boy gasped, just for a moment interrupting the rhythm of his sucking. And within seconds Tim found himself messy with cum.

Not just on his hand, it seemed to be all over his chest, accumulating in pools. And here and there a lurking dampness insinuated itself into the sheets. Tim wanted to wash up. Or rather, since he was too tired to get up, he wanted to be able to reach a towel; he seemed to recall that there was one by the side of the bed someplace. He longed for that towel. Despite his own climax, however, the boy continued his cocksucking and was going at it with renewed abandon—with a vengeance, in fact. Tim wiped his hand on the sheet.

The boy was obviously in a frenzy to bring Tim off. He did not seem to be particularly daunted by the fact that his partner had come just a few minutes before. Tim considered whether this was a good moment for a news bulletin about the post-teen powers of renewal. Perhaps a diversion was in order. "Sit on it, Kid."

"Yes, Sir!" Barry or Cary jumped up with such enthusiasm that he knocked something off the motel night table—ice bucket? lubricant? Bible? Tim yawned and opened his eyes. As he did so, he felt the boy already back up on the bed and straddling him in what would have been a grotesque squat if he had not been so intent on his objective. With swift single-mindedness, the boy unfurled a pre-lubricated condom over Tim's cock. Hefting the fullness of the cock, which was still hanging in there with the firmness of rubber, the boy lowered his firm little bottom down onto it, taking his time about this last delicate manoeuvre. Then he started forcing himself down on the broad shaft of the cock. Down. Up some. Down a little more. Up a little. And down. Down. All the way down. When he was, in fact, all the way down, he began riding the shaft of Tim's cock, taking longer and longer strokes and moving with accelerating vigor until he was at last slapping his cute little bottom against Tim's hips with each thrust.

Then, as a particularly wild thrust slammed home, Tim awoke with a start, opened one eye, and (identifying what had disturbed his rest) reached out to put a hand on the kid's waist to slow his progress. As the kid got the idea, his own cock bounced up to full erection again, as Tim happened to notice

while giving some additional two-handed suggestions on prolonging an experience. Considering whether he should again let his fingers play along the smooth, taut surface of the cock swinging its long, affable length before him in such an inviting way, Tim thought, "Perhaps if I jerk him off, he'll fall asleep afterwards at last. Even a teenager can't come more than six times in two hours. Any pleasure pales at last."

Since his hands were busy holding the horses and since the long shaft was dangling right before his face, shimmering in the dimness, Tim leaned up a bit, slipping out as much cock as necessary to carry out this manoeuvre, and darted forward with a trick tongue that had been the talk of the town in his youth in Appleseed, Vermont, some years before (was it only six?). Scarcely did he have this magic instrument wrapped around the sleek cock than, much as he had expected, the boy came. Withdrawing from the boy's bottom with aplomb, Tim leaned forward a bit more to drink it all in: there was no point in getting the sheets any messier although the flow did seem to be going on at amazing length considering the fact that it was the kid's sixth go-round for the evening.

But, his first passion spent, Barry suddenly yanked his cock away. "What did you want to go and do that for? You paid for a bottom. I'm a bottom. I thought I was with a real man for a change!"

"Real men," Tim mumbled, yawning, "suck cock."

A little later he awoke with a start. Barry (or was it Gary?) was dressed and on his way back to the streets, slamming the door on his way out.

"Hey, what about your tip?" Tim called after him, squinting through half-open eyes. Rolling over, Tim made a mental note to get some rest next time before getting into a long scene.

WHERE THERE'S A WILL...

Sherwin Carlquist

In my class at high school in Los Angeles the '70s, the guys knew all about what gays did in Hollywood and where they did it. For instance, in the locker room of the boys' gym, Roger Modena, drying off after a shower, often teased Nick Alden, "Been down to Santa Monica Boulevard, Nickie-boy?" And Roger pulled his towel around his leg, demonstrating how a hustler would showcase what he had in his tight cutoffs. Yeah, you could see that on Santa Monica Boulevard, all right, everybody knew it. Other times, Roger tormented Nick by rolling up his T-shirt to expose the rippling muscles of his abdomen, or by leaving open two or more buttons of his fly while he acted out campy poses he thought looked gay, although no sensible hustler would think of trying them. Poor Nick. He really wasn't gay, although Roger and others thought he was. Nick had made the mistake of saying, because of his religious convictions, he'd decided he didn't want to date and he wanted to stay a virgin until he married. Of course nobody believed him, and Roger started the rumor that Nick's alleged virginity was just a cover for being queer.

Nobody at Hollywood High suspected I was gay. One day when I was in a stall sitting on the toilet, I heard Roger telling a friend, "Ever notice how Vince has lunch with that fat slut Stephanie all the time? She really must be giving it to him."

When I heard that, at first I resented anyone thinking I was hot for Stephanie, but I quickly realized that this rumor was keeping them from thinking the unthinkable. But I did feel a little guilty that I was safe while people thought Nick was a closeted gay and Stephanie was a hopeless slut, but in high school, it's a dog eat dog world, so what ever you can do to survive, you do. Besides, Nick belonged to a religion that thinks homosexuality is a horrible sin, so having him at the butt end of Roger's jokes was poetic justice as far I as was concerned.

But I wondered how my English teacher, Mr. Riskind, managed to survive. Somebody had stencilled his name and some flowers in lavender paint on the corkboard outside his

classroom, and it couldn't be removed, so it was like a notice to the whole school   he was gay. Maybe he knew that if the corkboard was replaced, the stencil boys would be back with more purple paint, and maybe he realized there was no way to get back into the closet once the door had been blown open.

After awhile, Roger's crude imitations of Santa Monica Boulevard hustlers got me thinking. Was there anything there for me? No, I didn't have any intention of going into the hustling business, although I thought I did have a decent body. It was just that if there were hustlers there, certainly there must be some guys just plain cruising each other, and I could stand some companionship. My folks didn't pay much attention to me – it was as though they had already done their job raising me, and when I reached adolescence they wanted to withdraw, thinking I was okay and they didn't need to tinker with my life. They didn't suspect I was gay; I deliberately misled them, saying I usually had lunch with Stephanie, and I didn't tell them that the lunch get-togethers were Stephanie's idea, not mine. Besides, my folks spent a lot of time at their jobs, and their business associates seemed to be more important to them than I was.

I had been waking up frequently with a persistent hard-on and it seemed to be a signal saying, "You have been given this penis for a purpose, isn't it time you did something about it?" Something other than jerking it until it creamed in my pajamas, that is. So I started to spend some time after school looking around Hollywood. My folks didn't get home until six, and supper was at 7, so they wouldn't find out about my explorations. And no, I didn't walk down Santa Monica Boulevard. That's what hustlers did, when they weren't sitting on a bench at a bus stop, never boarding any bus, of course. I did have to cross Santa Monica Boulevard now and then, it divides Hollywood in half, after all, but I always tried to look as though I was going somewhere. You could never tell when Roger Modena or somebody might be watching. And I didn't want any man stopping his car and trying to pick me up, thinking I was a hustler. It wasn't that I couldn't have used the money, it was that I wanted to do the choosing. And I really wasn't exactly sure how the hustling game worked.

I focused my attention on Escondido Way, a street paralleling

Santa Monica Boulevard, with some apartment houses, a church, a senior citizen center, a public library branch. I thought these were good places for cruising inconspicuously. I mean, if a guy sits down at one of the picnic tables in front of the senior citizen center with a lunch bag or something, is some old bouncer going to come out the door and make him leave? No, senior citizens are happy if anyone joins them. So I sat at one of the picnic tables with an open book that didn't get read very much because I kept looking up a lot to see who might be cruising.

I had nearly given up when a guy suddenly sat down at my table, and, after finding out my name was Vince, asked me to go to his apartment. He didn't even tell me his name, but of course I figured it out by seeing an electric bill on his coffee table. So what would have happened if he had told me his name was Percy Ticeman? Anyhow, Percy wasted no time in unzipping my fly and taking my dick out and sucking it. I suppose I should have enjoyed it, but there on the sofa were three longhair cats staring straight at me, and I started giggling and couldn't stop. I guess that was my way of saying I didn't want that blowjob – and after all, Percy hadn't asked me if I did want it. And his moustache tickled when my dick was all the way into his mouth. So I pulled out, zipped up my fly, waved goodbye and thought next time, no cats and no moustache. Better to stay at my picnic table in front of the senior citizens center until I saw a guy I really liked. But when I saw a guy whose looks I really liked, he circled around for a while as though he was looking for a table, and finally walked away. I snapped my book closed and followed him down Laurel Street. He had serious blue eyes and wavy brown hair, a nice plaid shirt and denims that showed he might have something in them, and I wanted to find out what that something was. I had almost caught up with him when he turned up the walk to an apartment building, and when he noticed me, I waved as though I knew him. I told him my name and said I wanted some information. He invited me in.

It turned out his name is Willard, but he wanted to be called Will, and when I told him I thought he looked great, he really loosened up and forgot about how dumb my approach was. He said he really liked looking at me, said how could anyone not

like looking at me, but he didn't think he was good enough for me. "Why not?" I asked, then told him exactly what I liked about his appearance, and, I admit it, I unbuttoned his shirt a little, I wanted to feel the hair in there, and one button kind of leads to another, you know. He must have thought I was a sex-crazed kid – I just wanted to let him know I was interested. While I was fingering the curly hair on his chest and touching one of his nipples, he told me he had been in the Navy, but that didn't prepare him for a civilian job, and so he came to Hollywood and took the first job he thought he could stay with – managing an apartment building.

Will pulled the bottom of my T-shirt out of my pants so he could run his hands over my hairless chest. I discovered I really liked the feeling of his rough fingers sliding over me.

"And in addition to thinking I wasn't attractive enough for you," Will said, "I thought you might be underage. Are you?"

"No."

"Well, then, what's your name?"

"Matthew Bates. And please, no puns on 'masturbates' – I hear enough of that. Maybe I wouldn't be so sensitive about that if I really liked masturbating, but for me, masturbating is a way of admitting I don't have a guy I can get it on with, and I don't like to admit that. And if you want to know the truth, I'm two months short of my 18th birthday, but please don't hold that against me. I think there are some gay guys in my high school, but if I messed around with one of them and the word got out, I'd be teased about it and probably the principal would hear about it and tell my parents, so I really wanted to find somebody outside of my high school to play with, and I was hoping that might be you. If you like me, you won't make me wait two months. I'm sure not going to tell."

Will pulled me into the bedroom, brushing his hand over my hair and mussing it. It was a neat little bedroom, with a view of some banana plants nobody could see through, but he pulled the blinds down anyway. I let him take the lead, so when he stripped down to his Y-front briefs, I did, too. When I finished tucking my socks into my shoes like Mom had told me to do, my face wasn't far from the crotch of his underwear, and I moved in even closer. I could feel his body moisture through the cotton and I could take in the scent – which seemed like a

mixture of the soap he had used to shower that morning and the light, musky sweat that had accumulated since then. I had never experienced that smell except when I had sniffed my fingers after playing with myself, but somehow Will's body scents seemed better than mine. I wanted to get lost in Will's scent.

He pulled me up into a standing position so he could slide my briefs down; he motioned for me to take them off, so I did. He patted my butt, which I thought might mean he just thought I had a good butt, but when he reached into the drawer of the night table by the bed, took out a tube of lubricant gel, and put it on the bed, I realized he had something else in mind. "First time?" Will asked.

"Yeah." Whatever guys do to show they have had some experience at this, I hadn't done it.

"I bet you wanna be fucked," he said, positioning me on the bed so I was lying on my side, my butt facing him. "Maybe sailors just take naturally to assfucking. I read that in earlier days in England, one of the reasons men went to sea was to fuck each other. They thought cocksucking was something you did if you only had a few minutes in a back alley somewhere, and might have to cover up fast if you heard someone coming along. Once a ship left shore, the authorities couldn't watch, and there was lots of time when watches were over to do some fucking – which does take time.

"Want to imagine we're on a ship?" he asked, lubricating a finger with the gel.

"Sure," I answered, "be my commanding officer."

His lubricated finger entered my hole. Will was like a good doctor: He told me what he was doing and why, how he was loosening me up. While he fingered my anus and massaged my rectum, he told me it would probably hurt a little at first, but that once I had been fucked a few times, that wouldn't happen much, and it would feel so good to me I'd really like it. I wasn't so sure, but I was willing to try. It was about twenty minutes before Will finished fingering me and slid his penis into me very slowly. He had shown me how his dick was cigar shaped, long and slender, a little thicker between base and tip. The head wasn't wide and helmet-shaped (like mine was), it was small and sort of pointed, and because his penis tapered, he

said, it would go in more easily. It was long enough, he said, so that he didn't slip out during fucking. The small size of his dickhead, he claimed, meant that he had to fuck longer than most guys to get to orgasm. He wouldn't go fast, he explained – and I felt him slide out and then in again very slowly – because then the friction is wearing and the next day it hurts. So he said he was going to go real slowly, and we both would probably like it better. This guy really knew what he was doing. He did accelerate when he was getting close to orgasm, and after he got there, he slid his lubricated fingers around my dick until I got off, too. It felt real good with him inside me, and his hands were cool on my sweaty body.

I wanted to stay for at least another hour, but Will asked me, "Don't you have some homework?"

I nodded and, hugging me, he said I might feel a few twinges of soreness "down there," but that was just the muscles getting used to spreading open. If I stayed away from fucking for a few days, they'd get tight again, and I didn't want that, did I? So in order to make fucking feel really good, he should do it to me regularly, even though it might be hard to find the time. So he made me promise to come back to see him the next day, and we made a date for 3:30, right after school.

"What about weekends?" I asked.

Will thought maybe I could sneak over on a weekend, perhaps telling my folks I had some errands to run.

"Okay. I think I can manage. They're just as occupied on weekends as on weekdays, and they don't seem to care what I do as long as my grades are good and I don't ask for money."

Besides being really good in taking the time to give me super assfuckings, Will seemed to like me a lot and I wanted him to have a really good time, too. Sometimes when I went over to see him after school, he was busy and didn't seem to have his mind on sex right away. When that happened, I took my clothes off, put my arms around him, and said something like, "I'd really like a good fucking this afternoon if you could manage it," and he always could. I found out if I got naked and sat in a chair or lay on the bed so my hole was visible, Will just couldn't stay soft for long. And there would be times when I'd come by after school and I'd be the one whose mind wasn't on sex. So he'd open his fly and let his dick flop out. There was

something magical about watching that cigar-shaped thing puff up. The deep pink dickhead was a sort of question, asking, "Don't you want me to fuck you, Vince?"

My answer was to get my clothes off as quickly as I could.

My last few monthsin high school seemed to fly by. It would have been nice to have known somebody gay at school I could tell about Will and me, but that would be asking for too much. My grades were better than ever, and nobody asked why. But by mid-March, I realized I hadn't been planning past graduation. Mom and Dad hadn't sat me down yet and asked me what I'd do after that – not a surprise, but sooner or later they would wonder. They had assumed maybe I'd be going to business school, but I hadn't applied to any and they hadn't asked if I had. It was vital to have a plan if my afternoons with Will were going to continue.

"Why don't you move in with me?" Will asked, but it sounded too simple at first. "You could tell your parents you're a trainee assistant manager at an apartment building as part of going into real estate or something. I can teach you some handyman skills or you could take some classes so they see you're learning stuff. As long as parents think you're learning something, they're not worried."

Will's ideas sounded plausible, but he didn't know my parents. Even if they didn't seem very interested in me, they could get awfully skeptical about stuff, like when a teller at a bank hands them money, they always count it and look at it as though maybe it's fake. I had to have some credible authority figure to back up Will's ideas. I didn't know any really credible authority figure, so I got desperate and decided Mr. Riskind would have to do. By this time I was sure he was gay; on sunny days he walked home after school, but when it was raining, a guy in a red sports car always picked him up. I decided to tell him about Will and me and how we wanted to stay together. I asked him to call to my parents and convince them that it was a good idea if I learned apartment management and handyman skills, and that I'd have to live at the building in order to do this. I would also be able to save up for tuition to business school. I wrote all of these things down on a sheet of paper I handed to Mr. Riskind so he wouldn't forget any of the points I wanted him to make. Whatever Mr.

Riskind said to my parents, they did let me move in with Will. It turned out Mom had been wanting my room at home so she could use it as a home office anyway.

Will fixed up a bed in the second bedroom in his manager's apartment so it would look to my parents as though I slept there, although, of course, I always sleep in his bed. I still invent new ways to get Will hard, even though I know if I didn't do anything, sooner or later he'd poke me. Like only this morning when we were waking up, I took his hand and put it between my buttocks, and sure enough, it was only a minute before his dick was sliding into me.

Oh, and Stephanie went on to law school, where she has probably found some other gay guy to have lunch with. Nick Olden is in a monastery, and, wouldn't you know, Mr. Riskind told me he saw Roger Modena in a gay bar in Hollywood a few times.

KEYBOARD STUD

Thomas C. Humphrey

I slowly fed him my twelve-inch man-tool until its bulbous head, broader than a beer can, bulged his cheeks and brushed against his tonsils. He pushed at my loins with both hands as if to free himself, but his eyes were begging, "More," so I shoved on past the obstruction and deep into his throat.

Milton leaned back from the keyboard and peered myopically at the screen through thick glasses that gave his soft, pink face a frog-like cast. As he whispered the words he had just written, his breath came in passionate gasps. "Oh, yes, oh god, yes!" It was exactly the tone he wanted. So rugged, so virile, so – manly. If it kept going this well, one of those skin magazines would certainly buy it. He already knew what pseudonym he would use: Rod Strange, a name in itself as evocative as the story. Just envisioning it below the title set up an exciting tingle so intense that he just had to massage the tight little mound in his crotch. Glancing at the clock, he knew that he had no time for such indulgence now. He had to shower and dress before the young stud who would provide further inspiration for his story arrived.

As he ran the blow dryer and teased his thinning hair forward to disguise his receding hairline, he inhaled the heady masculine aroma of Stetson and thought about the stud who was due any minute. He had sounded so macho over the phone that Milton just knew it would be an afternoon to remember. What was his name? Paul? No, no, no, that would never do! Paul was too weak, too fluid, too lacking in force. He would have to come up with something more aggressive and dominating. Brad! Yes, that was as direct as a punch to the solar plexus. Brad it would be. And for a last name – Steele. Brad Steele! Yes, that had it all, abrupt and powerful, more solid than mere muscle. And he could work out plays on words with both names. Delicious! He loved it when the creative energy was flowing!

He was momentarily nonplused when the chimes sounded early, before he had chosen his outfit. He stood hesitantly in his

bedroom for a few seconds and then daringly moved to answer the door in nothing but his burgundy silk robe. Silk was so sexy next to bare flesh.

Paul (Brad) stood arrogantly in the doorway, legs spread teasingly, a strategically placed hole in his tight, worn jeans forcing one's eyes to lock in and envision what lay coiled there, ready to spring forth at the slightest provocation. He was not – exactly – what Milton had expected. Just over six feet tall, he was pale and emaciated, despite solid bone structure. His unkempt strawberry blond hair fell from a wide center part and covered his ears; the reddish mop swept in an inverted "V" in the middle of his forehead just above practically nonexistent eyebrows and green, darkly circled eyes. His thin, lightly freckled face was marred by several pimples, and his thick, sensuous lips pouted boyishly. Milton suppressed any tinge of disappointment before it reached full consciousness. Brad was here, and the stud was his for an hour.

"Would you like a drink?" he asked, resisting an impulse to reach out and grasp the stud's biceps.

"Got some beer, man?" Paul grunted. He hoped so; he needed something in a hurry. The pinwheel he'd smoked on the way over had helped some, but the anxiety was building again. He could tell from the way his hands trembled and how he had to keep closing and unclosing them. What he really needed was to do a few lines. But that would have to wait until he was finished here.

His eyes swept the apartment appraisingly as he followed to the kitchen. The guy must have money. You sank up to your ankles in the carpet, and the place was filled with expensive-looking furniture and lots of junk sitting on the tables. The paintings were real. Maybe he would try to make the little faggot a regular and pry more bills out of him.

Milton handed him a St. Pauley Girl and debated for a second; what he would really like himself was a frozen daiquiri, but maybe the occasion demanded something more virile. He took another beer, closed the refrigerator, and reached for a tall Waterford crystal glass. Should he offer the stud one? No, he obviously was the type who would drink directly from the bottle.

In the living room, the stud collapsed at one end of the

curved leather sectional. Milton scurried to place a marble coaster on the highly polished table in front of him. These rugged types thought nothing of setting things directly on the table and leaving rings that were a real chore to remove. Sometimes they even propped their dirty, sneakered feet directly on the table.

Milton settled in the curve of the sofa where he had a clear view of the stud. He was careful to keep the robe together as he demurely crossed one leg all the way over the other. No sooner had he settled in than the stud reached for a crumpled Marlboro pack and a lighter. Milton had to hurry for a silver ashtray before he got ashes ground into the carpet. Then he withdrew a Gallois from the inlaid box on the table and lit it with the silver table lighter. He inhaled cautiously, then flicked non-existent ashes with his pudgy forefinger.

"Damn," Paul thought, "I ain't got but one more smoke, and from the smell of it, this guy's got some imported brand. I've got to sit here sippin' a fuckin' sissy beer and pretty soon bummin' fuckin' fag cigarettes. Just my fuckin' luck." He decided he'd better get things moving so he could hit the street and make his connection.

"You ready?"

"Oh, yes."

"You did say fifty, right?"

"Yes."

"And for nothin' but talk?"

"That's right. An hour of talk, and I tape it." Milton shivered with excitement as he set up the recorder and positioned the mike.

Talk suited Paul just fine today. It had stung pretty bad the last couple of times he'd pissed, and he noticed his jockeys were discolored. Just his fuckin' luck! Now he'd have to go to the clinic again and get a shot and lay off of booze while he took the pills. Another fuckin' hassle, like he didn't have enough of them already. He picked up some stupid little egg thing in a silver stand on the table and jiggled it nervously in his hand.

Milton practically fainted when he saw what the stud was doing. His ceramic egg from Tiffany's! He could just see it shattered into a million pieces on the table. He resisted an urge

to snatch it from the kid's hand, and then sighed audibly as he put it back in its stand.

Paul noticed the little fag's reaction, which made him curious. He might as well find out. "What the hell is that?" he asked.

"It's a very rare ceramic piece I bought a long time ago."

"Worth a lot of dough I'll bet," Paul said, careful to sound only mildly interested.

"Quite a lot. Now, I think we're ready." He returned to his place on the sofa.

"What d'ya wanna talk about?"

"Tell me about the best sex you ever had."

"With a chick or a guy?"

"A guy."

"Shit, I ain't so good talkin' about things like that, man." Sure he'd rather talk about a chick, but it wouldn't be about Jolene. He'd rode that pussy so much he was tired of it, sick of it, actually. But what the hell, the bitch paid the rent and kept beer in the fridge. Though she'd been muttering a whole lot lately about him not contributing, and about how everything he got went up his nose, like she didn't snort herself. Since the fifty he was getting from the fag would go for powder, he'd have to fuck her tonight to keep her happy. Thinking about it made his anxiety level rise another step. Lately, he was having trouble getting it up and keeping it up with her, and all he fuckin' needed was the bitch to accuse him of goin' impotent on her. And now, he'd have to use a rubber the next few times; if he gave her the clap, the bitch would kick his ass out into the street for sure. He hated goddamn rubbers. They seemed three inches thick, and killed so much feeling he had even more trouble than usual keeping it up.

"Just start talking; say whatever comes to mind," Milton encouraged as the silence lengthened. He just knew he could pull some hot material out of this stud.

"Ain't none of it ever seemed real special," Paul said. "I just go along with whatever the guy wants, depending on what he's paying, and keep on until I pop a nut."

"Which do you prefer, anal or oral?"

"Don't really matter, man." He wanted to say butt-fucking, because that way he could fake coming and be ready to score with somebody else right away, but he had this fag figured for

wanting it that way, and he wasn't in the mood to encourage it, though he could use some more bucks.

"Tell me about a good anal experience."

"Christ, I gotta tell him something," Paul thought, "and then I gotta grab the bucks and dip. No telling how long I'll take connecting with Germaine, or I might have to go all the way to Earle on 166th. I'll be climbing the fuckin' walls by then."

"The other night this guy wanted it real bad," he began. "We was both naked in his living room watching a gay flick, and he started asking me to do it...."

He lay with his muscular thighs spread, his ass raised in invitation. His eyes were glassy with desire, and he silently begged to have my massive cock in him. I rubbed the head against his pucker and teased until he put his plea into words: "Fuck me! Oh, please, fuck me!"

Milton's eyes zeroed in on Paul's crotch and he envisioned a massive piece of uncut meat waiting there for him. He could reach over and caress it and... But no, he just could not be so coarse; he would have to restrain himself and write about it later.

"So I bent him over the arm of the couch and humped him standing up," Paul continued. He spread his legs and slowly rubbed his crotch, giving the little fag a good show. He had him licking his lips already; maybe he'd cream in that sissy robe soon and get it over with so he could get the hell out and get rid of some of the pressure that was tensing his neck and shoulders already. If he didn't have the fuckin' clap, maybe he would let the fruit give him some head; that relaxed him sometimes. He could pick up some extra bucks, but if the guy saw the discharge, he couldn't come back again, and this could turn into something nice and steady.

As he talked on, Paul tried thinking about popping it to some chick and just made sure to say "him" when he thought "her." It wasn't Jolene he thought about; he needed something strange, like maybe that black chick down at the deli. She would be a good piece. But to be honest, he couldn't get terribly worked up even thinking about cramming her. Lately, he just hadn't especially wanted it, even if it was strange, instead of Jolene's tired old snatch. Maybe it was true you passed your prime after seventeen and didn't crave it so much

afterward. He'd much rather do a few lines and get that warm, good feeling all over and have all the tension and anxiety just melt away and life become fuckin' beautiful again.

"I kept popping it to him there on the arm of the couch until I got a nut, and then I went in and took a shower," he finished.

With one lunge, I sank my rigid love-saber to the hilt in his desiring fuck-hole and kept sheathing and unsheathing it until he trembled beneath me. My grenade-sized nuts tightened and exploded and I shot gallons of my steaming love-juice into that hot velvet-soft scabbard.

"Oh, god, I'll bet this stud's an indefatigable fuck machine," Milton thought, eying Paul's crotch to catch any stirring of excitement. Even though he saw none, he simply *had* to know what the tight jeans concealed. "Tell me about your tool," he said boldly.

"It's just a regular dick, man. Big enough, but nothin' special."

"How big?"

"Man, I don't know. Maybe eight inches," Paul lied.

"Uncut?" Milton held his breath.

"Cut."

"Thick and straight?"

"Naw, sorta thinnish and curved to the left."

"You ever take it up the ass yourself?" Milton asked, exciting himself with his crudity. His groin tingled as he waited for the answer.

"Hell, no, man. I don't get butt-fucked or give head or nothin'." He remembered when that was true, when he was fifteen, before he ran away from his hick hometown, Martinsburg, West Virginia, and hitched up Interstate 81 and over to Baltimore. He was just a dumb kid without any money who couldn't get a job. It didn't take long to find his way to the meatrack and to start craving weed and then powder, and to learn to do whatever it took to get it. Shit, there wasn't nothing he hadn't done, and wouldn't do again.

He started fingering himself while I pounded into him. The look in his eyes told me he wanted me to stroke it for him, but I wasn't into that. He was here to service me, any way I desired, and I disdained even to touch his puny pecker.

Paul kept feeding the little fag stories about getting his joint

copped on a public bus and packing this guy's ass in a taxi going across town. It seemed the clock on the wall across the room had stopped, and he got more and more fidgety and anxious the longer he talked. Finally, he had been there fifty minutes. All at once, he couldn't stand it any more.

"Man, I'd like to keep talking to you, but I gotta catch a bus back downtown," he said, standing up.

Milton was mildly disappointed, but it had been a very rewarding afternoon. He was eager to get back to the keyboard. "Well, if you really have to go," he said.

"First, I gotta piss," Paul said, moving toward the hall.

He didn't close the door, and Milton heard the heavy torrent streaming into the toilet.

He lay on the floor, eyes closed, and I straddled his body. I dangled my huge man-hose over him and let fly a heavy stream all over his chest and guided it up his neck, and into his face. He opened his mouth greedily to accept my offering.

After he flushed, Paul left the water running in the sink and eased into the bedroom. On the triple dresser was an ornate jewelry box. Nervously, he lifted the top and gazed at gold chains, tie pins, and cuff studs. What really caught his eye, though, was a gold-looking watch. He picked it up and read "Cartier" on the case. It looked like it hadn't come from any drugstore rack, so he dropped it into his pocket. Maybe he could hock it for twenty or twenty-five, enough for a little more powder. To hell with planning to see this little fag again.

As the water ran, Milton imagined this hot young stud living here with him, sharing his bed, and standing in the bathroom naked every morning shaving, with his huge man-cock roping down to rest on the edge of the sink.

"You got my money, man?" Paul broke his reverie.

"Oh, yes, certainly," Milton said, moving toward the bedroom.

Shit, I hope he don't notice the fuckin' watch gone, Paul worried. I'd hate to have to bust him one and run. Making sure the little fag couldn't see, he quickly grabbed the stupid egg and slipped it in his jacket. Then he waited by the front door so he could get his bucks and get the hell out.

After using him every way I could imagine and giving my fuck-pole as much pleasure as it could take in one afternoon, I

dressed and walked out, not saying a word, leaving him exhausted but desirous on the rumpled bed. He would remember it for a long time, I was sure, because when I pin them to the bed with my huge Steel Brad, they know they've had the fuck of their life.

Yes, he'd even managed to work in the play on words. He was damned good. The story completed, Milton leaned back and opened his silk robe. Using both hands, he rubbed and kneaded and pulled until he found well-earned release in the midst of a torrid love-bout with the kind of rugged stud he had never been – or known.

A FAMILY AFFAIR

Andrew Richardson

Even though it was my day off, I was excited when my dad asked me to return some tools to his friend Alan because I really fancied getting another look at Alan's adorable son Robbie. A sweet schoolboy, he had shoulder-length brown hair, lovely skin and a firm physique. Unlike his father, who had a short-cropped beard, Robbie's cheeks were smooth with soft, downy sideburns. He had become my fantasy: an untouchable hetero kid, naive yet secretly eager to see what other men's cocks are like. At least that's what I hoped he thought. I wanted to see naked his smooth and fleshy ass that always filled his jeans so tantalizingly. And I longed to see if the nice bulge at his crotch really heralded much larger and grander things.

At first I thought to delay my departure until Robbie would be home from school, but then I realized they were on half term and maybe the lovely creature was enjoying a lazy morning in. If he was half like me at that age, then he'd still be in bed having the fifth wank of the morning and breezing between the men's underwear section of the mail-order catalogue and having some horny dreams about friends at school, screen idols or an imaginary "Biggest Cock in the World" competition. If he was half like me, his bed sheets would be soggy with semen already and he'd have the big handle of a hairbrush rammed up his ass, feeling the bristles on his ass cheeks and wondering if that's how another man's pubes might feel. If he was really like me, his legs might be up in the air and he'd be tossing his cock and jerking the hairbrush around, then he'd reach his orgasm and let the next batch of his own cum spurt onto his face. As he'd lick his own cum off his face and gradually ease the dildo brush handle from his rectum, this would make him immediately horny again and he'd play with his soft cock a bit more until he could bear it to get hard again.

I set off and already began getting a hard-on in the car thinking about seeing Robbie again. As I travelled down the road, I rubbed my cock through my trousers. Knowing that the

journey wasn't long enough to have a full wank, I made do with just gently squeezing the head of my cock, imagining Robbie's lips clamped over it, his eyes gazing at another man's lengthy prick so close to his own face. I'd be waiting for him to tongue it and lick it long and hard.

My thoughts made the trip pass in seconds and before I knew it, I was pulling up along the drive to their cottage. I had a quick grope of my balls, full and heavy, and then I repositioned my cock to make its state of arousal less obvious. Fetching the bag from the back of the car, I locked up and wandered down the drive. Which was Robbie's bedroom window? Where might he be lying now? Gently having a wank with an array of gay mag's around him, gazing from cock to cock, wanting them all to appear like magic and spurt their own loads onto him.

My over-active mind had already invented the idea that Robbie would appear at the door in his dressing gown, obviously caught out in his attempt at a swift toss, with his chest showing and perhaps a bit of thigh. Then I'd walk in, drop the bag, and forcibly shove my hand under the top of his gown, pulling at an erect nipple and letting him gasp with shock. His cock would rise like a mad thing and it'd spring out the front of his gown letting my other hand clasp him hard and strong. I'd suck him off and then I'd fuck him right there. We'd shower together, he'd screw me in the shower and the rest of the day would be spent licking, rimming, kissing, panting and coming. God I wanted to fuck him so much. My cock was glued to my stomach and ached for his juicy ass hole.

As usual, I went to the back of the house. The front door was often locked since they had such a lovely back garden they invited guests to "rear entry" as it were, in order for them to admire the landscaping. Through the gate in the high fence, I glanced briefly at the large and clear pond, the shrubs and bushes, the apple tree and the high conifers which made the garden rather secluded and quite private. In the heat of the morning I was hardly surprised to find the back door open slightly to allow the summer air in.

Alan and his wife were such good family friends we rarely knocked on doors when we arrived. And today since the door was already open, I thought nothing about simply wandering

into their kitchen and hollering if anyone was there. Hey, maybe Robbie might just be in his underwear, waiting for me – just me – to tear his briefs off and offer him something better than another hand job. I might find him snoozing in an armchair, one leg cocked over the side with his balls slung out of the side of his briefs (he was fondling them before he dozed off). Just as I was about to shout my arrival though, something stopped me in my tracks and made me blush with uncertainty. Blood flooded into my head and it was as if it was all swirling in my eyes.

I hadn't seen anything yet, but the heavy grunting of sexual panting was unmistakable. Someone was having a shag in the dining room next to the kitchen, and by the sound of things, they were enjoying it. I hadn't listened for long before I'd decided to creep back outside and sneak a look through the window. Could it be the bearded Alan and his wife enjoying a bit of passion whilst their only son was out? Getting frisky after a leisurely breakfast and deciding to get right down to it? ("Never mind the dishes dear, they can wait.") Hell, could it actually be Robbie, getting his oats while his mom and dad were out, and quickly having phoned some hot date up to come round and they could "do it on the dining table?" One thing was certain, they were truly enjoying themselves and had totally forgotten about my visit this morning.

I stepped outside and made a note of my shadow, careful not to indicate to the happy twosome that someone might be watching them. Slowly, I edged along the wall towards the window and peered beyond the curtains to see what was happening. I nearly blurted out laughing at first when I glimpsed Alan's own hairy backside pumping away – his thighs ramming forward and his buttocks clenching tight – as he fucked his wife on the table. He was in very good shape too. Nice big shoulders and good looking ass cheeks which squeezed and parted as he fucked away. My cock was still solid.

But no, hang on, I thought. No, fucking hell, no. My God! Though I couldn't get a good look at the person laid out on the table, their legs lifted up being held with Alan's hands shoving them back, I could see that they were slightly hairy. Jesus Christ, Alan was shagging another bloke, right there in front of

my own eyes and in his own house on his own dining table. As he pulled his cock out, I swiftly glanced the sac of balls hanging down and the base of a thick cock, rising above the asshole Alan was inserting himself into. Lucky for me the wall was there to hold me up when I saw the person sprawled out on the table lift his head up and lean forward to kiss his father on the lips. Then Alan let rip and shoved his cock right into Robbie's anus again.

Good god! Alan was fucking his own son in his own house on his own dining table! Should I join in? I simply had to. But what might happen? I (Christ look at that humping ass shift up a gear). What if they don't want me there? (Robbie is tearing his hair out -- his own father is driving him wild with passion). What if a third person is just what they want though? (I could fuck Alan fucking Robbie). My prick is stiff. (Look at Alan's length slip in and out of Robbie's ass). Just to watch from inside the room, hear the panting, the cries of ecstasy. See Robbie fire his load out onto his father's pumping belly.

I went into auto-pilot and walked into the kitchen. Silently, I placed the tool bag (I had virtually forgotten about it) on the floor and fetched my own cock out of my trousers. It was bright red and each vein was quivering with astonishing power. Calmly and confidently, I masturbated as I walked into the room, and discovered that Alan was now kneeling on the floor licking Robbie's asshole and chewing on his ball sac. Robbie's cock was an enormous member of dynamic proportions. As my trousers fell to the floor, he was the first to look up and notice me. He hurled his head up.

"Fuck me Dad!" Robbie screamed as he sprang forward and his father's excruciatingly reddened face turned, already transformed in horror that they had been caught. It became almost quizzical when he saw it was me, and that I was busy with my own cock – now the only hard one in the room.

"Actually," I said calmly, "it looks pretty much as though he just was."

This broke a nervous smile out on Alan's face – my heart leapt when Robbie looked at me and winked.

"Can anyone join in or is this just a family affair?" I said to him.

Robbie certainly was ready to continue the session. He

couldn't keep his hands off his hefty cock and balls, unconsciously fondling himself up to a grand hard-on again. A startled Alan looked at me and gasped, "Aren't you supposed to return the tools tomorrow? You're a day early."

"Obviously I'm not. Now how about bending over and letting me have a bit of that hairy crack while I suck your son off?"

Alan grinned, and crouched wantonly under the table with his knees far apart. Robbie rested back on his elbows keeping his legs apart as I dropped my pants and followed his gaze to my hung testicles and rigid prick. Like me, he too was furiously erect. It was a spectacular sight: A grown man bending beneath a table, awaiting a firm prick to slice his pucker in two, and his own son, legs splayed, laid out on the table-top. I looked at Robbie's beautiful face, his broad shoulders, firm smooth chest and nipples, rapturous stomach, tree-trunk thighs. His member almost glowing in the heat of the sunlight through the window, and his balls sagging into the crack of his legs, hovering high enough for me just to see the underneath side of his ass cheeks starting.

I knelt down and rubbed my cock against the crack length of Alan, feeling his furred buns and tacky plum-like hole. Then I simply dived onto the cock of my dreams and chewed my way down Robbie's fantastic length – all the time teasing my own prick along Alan's buttocks. I parted the slit of Robbie's phallus and lashed the tip of my tongue over his dainty red clit. His eyes and pensively silent stare down at me told me all I needed to know – he was in heaven. As was I when I licked down the fat helmet, past his ripple of foreskin, down the tumescent shaft and into the sweet smell of his pubic hair. Robbie ran his hands through my hair as I performed on his cock, and he gently sighed when I got his prick past my throat and slipped it down my neck.

Alan soon became eager to feel my cock right up into his intestines as he was already parting his ass cheeks wide and gently stroking his own hole. When I motioned my prick over the hole, he grabbed my prick and hissed, "Fucking get that rod up there."

Robbie looked at me and grinned, then, without hesitation, I let Alan take the aim and I thrust my pelvis forward. Without

a problem, my cock slid right up to the hilt of his ready lubricated ass – I figured Robbie might have been fucking him earlier – and as I gasped over the prick in my face, Alan panted underneath the table, occasionally bucking his ass up in the air to ride my cock good and proper.

Alan had large testicles which swung heavy between his legs and as I writhed in and out of his asshole I could sense him fondling his own balls and grasping mine each time I rammed into his guts. My own hands were busy sliding over the supreme cock I had in my mouth, and with his son's penis so close, I wanted to get a good feel of Alan's member to compare. So, holding the tip of Robbie's luscious erection with my mouth, I released my vice grip on his shaft and got a good handful of the fleshy buttocks my cock was sailing in-between. With expert swiftness, Robbie held his own cock and guided it into the depths of my throat while I dug deep and got my hands under Alan to explore and masturbate him.

His prick was almost fastened to his belly with its rigidity. And boy I could feel it was quite an impressive size too. If this was the mold, then Robbie was certainly living up to expectations and, it seemed, might have a few more years growth left yet.

"Christ, how does anyone get that thing up them?" I asked with my lips around Robbie's dick.

"A lot of practice," Robbie answered, now cocking his left leg up slightly as I delved into the crevice of his thighs and buttocks. But by now I was really getting into his father's crack and working our fuck up into a thick and salty sweat. Alan's prick was slick with moisture which let my hand slip up and down over his impressive cockhead onto the raw nerves concentrated there. Alan was grunting away and split his legs further to allow my full thrust up his backside.

"Fuck me, fuck me, fuck me!" He was almost chanting with the rhythm. "Fuck me, fuck me, fuck me. Fuck my ass. Oh, fuck my ass. Feels good. Ooh, that feels good."

I was being ripped apart with passion. Big cock in my face, hungry ass slurping my own cock up. And I wanted to taste that hairy ass. I thought, Just, one, last, fuck, up, his, hole, and then I'd slip out of Alan and get my face between his furred cheeks for a while, offering his beautiful boy my ass to poke

while I fed my face. That was until Robbie cocked his left leg up enough for me to realize what he was really offering me. I let his member fall out of my mouth as he rolled over slightly and I saw the deep wonder of his wet and shimmering crack. A damp area on the table, where his ass had been, let Robbie slide over easily, guiding his cock over the edge of the table and placing his spunk moistened asshole to my face. So, I thought, they'd been at it for while before I arrived. Already, Robbie had dumped a load into his dad, and now, before my very eyes, was Alan's own cock lube seeping out of Robbie's crinkled but fleshy sphincter. I got my mouth into that cum-coated hole as quickly as I could, and sucked on his ringer like a vampire drawing blood out of his last victim before sunlight.

My cock in an ass, then my face in an ass, tongue deeply parting Robbie's hole, drawing the cum from depths of him. Robbie was swiftly jacking his cock and pressing his balls onto my chin hard. I abandoned his father's cock in order to peel Robbie's buttocks far apart and get a good entrance to the glorious hole. It was purple and oval, and slightly wrinkled until I feathered it with my tongue and Robbie relaxed to force an appetising bulge and allow me oral / anal delight I'd never had before. We were a trio in bliss. I had become part of a new family, a special, secret family.

Bringing himself to an explosive climax, Robbie's arm was furiously blasting away over his raw prick. Likewise, his father enjoyed tossing himself off as I filled his ass and tore his son's apart with my tongue.

The room was sweltering and sweat gathered along my pubes and as I fucked him, adding to the lubrication of Alan's hole. Perspiration glistened on Robbie's broad, smooth back. His shoulders shimmered as the muscles in his arms bulged – his right hand maintaining a splendid grip on his prick.

As sunlight blazed through the windows, Robbie pursed his lips, his asshole clenched tight, and he strained his neck upward.

"Oh, oh, oh," he cried, his elbow nearly hitting me in the face.

Streams of cum blasted out of his cock, onto the carpet, onto the underside of the table, and all over his father's hair. I was so enraptured by the exquisite appearance on his face that I

hadn't noticed the man I was fucking had also shot his load and was enjoying the sensation of my hard cock still ripping his rectum to pieces. My erection was livid and I pumped faster – building up to the final seconds before coming. My cockhead was rubbing harder and harder against the soft flesh of Alan's back passage. Licking Robbie's hole still, I climaxed and shot my entire load of spunk up into Alan's backside, shooting the full amount deep into his guts. The only bit of cum on the outside of Alan's ass was the drop that drained from the tip of my prick as I gently drew my rod out of him.

My cock was deliciously drained and began to go slack after releasing it's load. But within seconds, Robbie had knelt down next to me, and while he began rubbing my soft length, he leaned forward to his father's rectum in order to slurp my load and determined to start all over again.

THE BOY TRAP

Peter Z. Pan

"Well, there's a devil in the angel,
And I'm in trouble again.
Well, there's a devil in the angel,
And I'm in need of a prayer."
 – Bad 4 Good

PROLOGUE

As long as I could remember, I guess I always knew I was a little different from other boys. And it confused the hell out of me, too. I mean, imagine a six-year-old boy watching "Flipper" on TV and popping a boner at the sight of Luke Halpin – Flipper's cute little blond friend – in those wet, tight cut-offs.

Yes, I was a fickle youth. As a matter of fact, at fifteen I was still pretty fickle. But I had graduated from Luke Halpin to...Shaun Cassidy. Wow, what a babe! And because I collected every magazine with his picture on the cover, my closet was filled with stacks of *Tiger Beat* and *Teen Beat*. And I used to put up the magazine posters on my bedroom walls. I think that's when my mother first started suspecting that her only son was queer. I mean, most ten-year-old boys put up posters of football teams, sports cars, and even the U.S.S. Enterprise. Aside from Shaun's big brother David, my walls were plastered with Donny, Jimmy, and the rest of the Osmond Brothers.

Anyway, the moment of truth had finally come. After seeing "Ode To Billy Joe" a dozen times – and fooling around with my best friend Vinny Bonaducci – I'd finally come to the realization that I was homosexual. And unlike Billy Joe McAllister, I wasn't jumping off no Tallahatchee Bridge.

While I accepted the fact I was *different*, I wasn't ready to admit I was really *gay*. My Uncle Bruce was gay and I'd seen firsthand how cruel people can be. My father, for instance, called him a faggot every chance he got. They were brothers and they hadn't talked to each other for as long as I could

remember. Now I was going to walk into his den and tell him his only son, his only child, his namesake, was a member of the same church as his black-sheep brother whom we never talked about. I was sure he was going to have a massive coronary.

I just hoped Father wouldn't call me a faggot to my face. It wasn't like it was going to ruin our relationship or anything. We were strangers really, and we avoided each other every chance we got. I'd always sensed that he was disappointed in me. And that always pissed me off, too. I mean, I was a straight-"A" student. My room was anal-retentively neat. And in that day and age I'd never been to the principal's office, let alone jail. Yet he was disappointed in me because I wasn't some dumb-ass sports fanatic like he was. He played college football and I think that kind of warps your mind a little. And the fact that I wanted to be an interior decorator didn't exactly help situations any. Wait till he found out I fooled around with his hunting buddy's son.

Well, I didn't mean to. It just happened. We were in his room after school looking at his collection of girlie magazines and...well, one thing led to another...one hand led to another...one lip led to another...and pretty soon Vinny looked like The Lone Ranger riding Silver. It was quite dramatic really. Two days later, I was still glowing.

Unfortunately, the experience wasn't mutual. Vinny's Catholic guilt hit him half a second after he shot the sheriff. He started saying we were both going straight to hell for being queens. He'd been shaving his palms twice a day for the last four years, but yet he was going to hell for doing it with me *once*. Then he had the nerve to accuse me of seducing him. He was the one who stuck his tongue in my mouth all the way to my tonsils. Anyway, he didn't know how he was going to bring himself to break this news to Father O'Brien at his next confession. After being one of the good Father's altar boys for a year, I assured him that Father O'Brien would more than understand...and probably even identify with him. That's when he threw me out.

I wasn't worried at all about my mother. You know what they say: the mother always knows. She'd probably cry. Then I'd cry. Then we'd both cry and embrace. It would be a

Hallmark moment. I wished the rest of the world would be as open-minded as my mother. But I knew it wasn't. I knew it wouldn't be easy being gay. Hell, it's never easy being different. People who didn't even know me would call me names and hate me just because I happen to like men instead of women...no other reason. Macho guys with one foot in the closet would be repulsed by me because I remind them of a part of themselves they can't accept. *Girls who live in glass closets shouldn't toss pebbles.* Preachers would sentence me to eternal damnation just because some book of ancient mythology says that it's a sin to be what I am; the same book, by the way, that's caused most of the wars in this world.

But I couldn't live a lie. I couldn't be like one of those limp-wristed actors who went on Merv Griffin's show and sat there lying through their bonded teeth about all the women they'd had. I had to be honest with myself, and everyone else. That meant I had to tell my father.

As I left my bedroom and began a slow walk downstairs to where my father sat drinking a beer and watching baseball on TV, I couldn't help feeling like The Beaver about to tell Mr. Cleaver he and Wally were butt-buddies. Well, *my* Ward took it a lot worse than I thought he would. He began calling me every ugly name he could think of, and when he started beating me, my mother tried to intervene, but he began smacking her around too. At the end of it, he told me to get the fuck out of his house.

I.

It was my third night on the streets when I first met Robin, the beautiful serpent whose apples were succulent yet had many strings attached to their core. Hungry and desperate, I was dumpster-diving outside the grocery store. My little suburban world had collapsed and I just wanted to die.

Robin strutted out of the market in what looked like a Catholic school uniform. She was just barely carrying two giant bags of groceries, so when she looked up and caught me gaping at her, she called to me for assistance.

"Boy," she said, "could you please help?"

But it was too late. She'd dropped one of the bags, its

contents spilling all over the parking lot. As I helped her put all the food back into the bag, I couldn't help ogling her divine figure, her shapely breasts, the way her long blonde hair got in her pretty face when she bent down to pick up something. I had never before lusted for a girl and for a brief moment I was excited at the prospect: maybe I was straight after all and could soon go back home.

"Boy, I'll pay you five dollars if you help me carry my bags home," she said, blowing a wisp of curl off her face to reveal beauteous eyes of hazel: seductive eyes that could have enticed me into doing almost anything.

I said yes so fast that it brought a smile to her adolescent face. Five bucks: a hardy dinner and breakfast at Mickey D's!

We walked four blocks down Biscayne Boulevard to her house. The bags were really heavy and I was too hungry and sunstruck to try to make small talk. But she was very inquisitive and somehow managed to get my life story out of me. Except for the part about my sexual orientation of course.

I was a bit suspicious when we stopped in front of an old warehouse and she told me that was where she lived. However, I was too fatigued to question anything. She opened the warehouse door and we stepped into a disheveled office of sorts. The lights were dim, yet I could see the walls were plastered with photographs of naked little boys sporting erections.

"What is this place?" I asked her rather bemused.

"We make porno here," Robin said bluntly.

"Starring cute youngsters like you," said a hoarse, deep voice from behind me. "Good job, Robin."

I turned around to find a fat man who resembled Jerry Garcia from the Grateful Dead. He was dressed all in leather and was pointing a gun at me. Quite overwhelmed, I dropped the grocery bags and came dangerously close to passing out. A hand then reached into my back pocket and removed my wallet. It was Robin.

"I don't have any money," I blurted out as tears filled my green eyes.

Robin found my student I.D. card. "His name is Tommy Syms and he's just the right age," she said, handing the card to the man.

erection had disappeared up his petite ass. The kid did this flowingly as if he'd done it a million times before. He then began to move up and down on my cock, riding me while he furiously masturbated.

My body spasmed as I shot my load into the depths of the kid's ass. I felt the warmth as my seed trickled down his creamy buttocks onto my scrotum. Shayne began to quiver himself, obviously experiencing a dry orgasm. He then fell on the bed beside me and pulled his butt cheeks apart. My jism was still oozing from his crack, so the fat man zoomed in on it with the camera and ordered Robin, who was more than willing, to lap it up with his tongue.

But that was not the climax of our little flick. No, the fat man had more in store for his new star. He called out the name Secretariat. In the distance an enormous black man wearing only a leather mask emerged from the darkness. His gargantuan cock led the way, a cock that was as long and fat as my forearm. I felt hands on my body then, rolling me over on my stomach. That's when I was struck by a scary revelation. I was about to be raped! And while Vinny's modest cock felt great up my butt, this monster was going to tear me apart.

I think Robin saw the fear in my eyes because he mercifully asked the fat man, whom he called Dale, to inject me with heroin once more. Dale produced the syringe from a nearby table and decided to shoot us all up. Within seconds that euphoric warmth again rippled through my young body. It was the answer to all my problems. For the first time in a long while I was happy. I had achieved a perfect state of nirvana and I never wanted to come down. I was an insatiable sexual creature who yearned to have that black cock inside me to quench the fire that burned in my loins. I welcomed the pain, I welcomed the blood, I welcomed the degradation. I was living for that moment in time and it felt fucking great!

Secretariat plunged his horse cock into me with one hard thrust. And before I lost consciousness, for one brief shining moment, I thought I saw the face of God.

"Wake up, kid!" barked a man's voice.

Before I could open my eyes I could feel my body was underwater. I was quite disoriented. My head was throbbing

with pain and my ass felt like a colony of fire ants had invaded it. Slowly I remembered the motor-skills that worked my eyelids. The part of me that hoped it had all just been a bad dream was greatly disappointed when my eyes focused on Dale. He was sitting on the edge of the bathtub, shaking me. I was *in* the bathtub submerged in bubbles.

"What the fuck...?!" I managed to get out.

"Calm down, kid," he said. "It's all over...for now." He then shocked me by throwing a fifty dollar bill into the tub. "That's your fee. And there's a lot more where that came from."

"What do you want from me?" I inquired while snatching the bill and clutching it tightly in my right hand.

"Your soul," he quipped. "And you're going to hand it to me on a silver platter."

I began to get up.

"Sit down, motherfucker!" he snarled, then pushed me down with all his might. "Let's get something straight, kid! From now on, you work for me! And you will do everything I tell you to do! You will appear in my movies; you will let me and my friends fuck you; and you will wipe the shit from my ass with your tongue if I tell you to do it. And if you don't, I'll blackmail your ass. I went through your wallet, Tommy Syms. I know where your parents live: 146 Southwest 9th Avenue. I know where you go to school: Citrus Grove Junior High. If you betray me, I'll mail your family and friends pictures of you being butt-fucked by a big, black nigger. Not to mention all the stuff we made you do after you passed out. They're all gonna know that you're a queer, cocksucking faggot!"

One thing I've always had is a bad temper. He was pissing me off and I grew weary of the whole charade. It was time I took control.

"Are you finished?" I asked flippantly. "Because if you are finished with your idle threats, I think you'll be interested in what I have to say."

Dale was taken aback; he carefully eyeballed me for a moment, either studying me or trying to intimidate me. An amused look then took over his plump face. "Is that so?" said he.

"I'm sure those threats are very effective with all the scared

little kids you bring here and exploit," I said, now sounding exceedingly cocky for a boy in my dire predicament. "But now that I have my wits about me, I'm afraid I'm a little too smart to fall for that bullshit. First of all, it's obvious that the beautiful Robin and her, or should I say *his*, helpless grocery store scam is the bait you use to lure kids here. Then you rape them and blackmail them to work for you. Second, let's say you were stupid enough to send those incriminating photos to my family and friends. I don't give a shit. You see, I have no use for those people anymore. They're out of my life and, frankly, I don't care what the fuck they think of me. You can tell them I'm a transvestite necrophile if you want. But we all know that you're not going to tell or mail anyone anything. Because, third, you're guilty of the abduction and rape of a minor, and producing child pornography. The authorities would find you and throw your fat ass in jail so fast that it'll make your head spin. Especially if the victim, namely me, is ready and willing to testify against you."

Dale studied my face once more. For a moment he looked like he might grab my neck and drown me. "You think you got it all figured out, huh, hotshot?"

"I know I do," I assured him, not backing down. "And if the money's right, I know I can be an asset to your operation."

Dale was genuinely intrigued by now, if not blown away. "Go on," he said.

"You see, I'm not one of those straight boys you have to force to suck cock, I'm queer and I really enjoyed last night. I especially enjoyed the heroin. So you be good to me and I'll be good to you."

Dale stared at me coldly for what seemed an eternity. Then, between guffaws, he said, "Kid, you're a fucking trip! And I'll tell you something, I feel safer having you as a friend than as an enemy."

"Does that mean we have a deal?"

Dale stood and aimed his cock at the toilet, releasing a powerful jet-stream of piss. "Only if you accept my terms," he said, turning his cock on my face without breaking the urine flux. "All my slave boys have to take my golden showers." By then, he had drenched my bemused face. "I hereby christen you...Kid Porn!" said Dale, the Sleaze-Baptist with pride. He

then jumped into the piss-filled tub with me and kissed me on the mouth. Thus began an exceedingly dysfunctional family.

II.

Within weeks, I had *earned* the name Kid Porn by becoming Dale's right-hand boy. It wasn't before long that I was luring more chicken into the slaughterhouse than Robin – and with a much different approach. I would find kids on the streets and at bus stations who were just as hungry and desperate as I had been. Then I would befriend them, gaining their precious trust. After that, it was easy. I'd just fill their puerile heads with sweet stories of easy money and free drugs. Once they were in the fold, it was up to Dale to drug and blackmail them.

I wanted to feel guilty for my actions, yet I was so strung out on heroin all the time that my mind wouldn't entertain that emotion. Besides, in a way I felt that I was helping these unfortunates: I was putting money in their pockets so they wouldn't starve or have to live on the cruel street. At least they weren't out stealing or hustling on the boulevard. And aside from the initial shock and pain, nobody was really getting hurt, were they? At the time I didn't know that I was an expert at rationalizing.

I was making a small fortune too, with close to three hundred bucks in the bank. And even though I was self-destructive and out of control, I must confess that I was having the time of my life. The sex was great! The drugs were awesome! The power was intoxicating! My sexual freedom was liberating! It seemed like I had it made in the shade.

Then I met Gabriel and the world as I knew it got a lot more complicated – and *dangerous*.

I fell in love with Gabriel the moment I saw him emerge from the Greyhound bus. It was dusk and the setting sun's rays hit him like a spotlight, so there was this surreal radiance about him. An angel had somehow stepped off a Caravaggio painting and onto the Miami bus station. His divine wings had been clipped, but there was no doubt about it, this boy had descended from the heavens. Perhaps to save me. But could anyone?

I stood transfixed, watching him, studying him, devouring his young and tender form with my ravenous eyes. I had never before witnessed such natural splendor and I was overwhelmed. All my life I had been blind and this creature was the first glorious vision that my eyes beheld. That is the only way I could describe the emotions that deluged my mind at that moment.

The kid was a living, breathing paradox. He looked ragged but seductively alluring nonetheless. Long chestnut hair fell over his callow face in an unruly yet enticing way. He seemed innocent yet he was a very sexual animal, just oozing sensuality. His body was scrawny but he moved with a feline, almost elegant, poise. Yes, a paradox. He was clad in blue denim: an old jacket and worn-out jeans. A faded skull on his t-shirt was the perfect contrast to his delicate face: the high cheekbones, the pouty lips, the flawless olive skin.

My lithe young angel stopped to look around as he adjusted the timeworn knapsack strapped to his back. He seemed so lost and scared, unsure of his next move. It was sad how timid and alone this poor child appeared. Every fiber of my being wanted to take his fragile little body in my arms and protect him from the hawks that were always circling. But wasn't I a treacherous predator myself, a wolf in sheep's clothes, sent to infiltrate the unsuspecting flock and corrupt the virginal? Who was going to protect this child from *me*?

The boy looked in my direction. With a quick jerk of his head, he flipped the hair off his face like a flirtatious little girl and smiled at me. Our eyes meet for the first time, kissing and caressing like old lovers. I could now see the lovely windows to his soul: they were baby blue.

Surely, bringing this prize to Dale would mean a big feather in my cap, not to mention a handsome finder's fee. But I just couldn't bring myself to do it. We would steal his innocence, then eat him up and spit him out. No, this boy deserved better. This boy deserved *much* better!

He began to walk towards me and I panicked. I couldn't give in to temptation! I had to be strong! I was determined that I wasn't going to ruin this boy's life. So I ran away from him before I changed my mind. I ran as fast as I could and never looked back.

Secretariat rammed his whopping shaft into the kid hard! I turned my head away when I noticed the cherry red blood streaming down the boy's milky white buttocks. That's when I saw Robin bringing the German Shepherd in. Within moments, the tied up little boy was on all fours on the floor being humped by the sexed-up pooch. I was overtaken by nausea and made a run for the toilet. As I knelt over the porcelain bowl emptying my guts, I knew that I couldn't take anymore. And I prayed to God for the strength to leave. Sadly, God didn't know who the hell I was anymore. Neither did I.

Morning came and I listened outside the bathroom door as Dale blackmailed my angel. The boy was frightened, crying. He begged Dale not to send those nasty photos to his family and friends in Rome, Wisconsin. Dale assured him that if he played his cards right, no harm would come to him.

"Just don't fuck with me!" he snapped at the boy as he stormed out of the bathroom, walking right into my naked body. "What the fuck are you doing, Kid? Eavesdropping?"

"I need to take a bath," I said quickly.

Dale shoved his index finger up my ass, then brought it to his mouth and sucked it. "You're right, you do need a bath." Having amused himself, he let out a hearty laugh and walked away.

I stepped into the bathroom, locking the door behind me. The boy was crying in a tub of bubbles.

"Are you okay?" I asked.

He looked up at me with an accusatory stare. If looks could kill, I would have been fatally castrated at that moment.

"Were you their scout?" he said brusquely. "Is that why you ran off so fast when you saw me – to tell 'em that fresh meat had just gotten off the bus?!"

The boy couldn't have wounded me more if he *had* castrated me. "No, you've got it all wrong."

Shaking his head, he said, "Whatever, man."

I tried to think of something meaningful to say. Something eloquent and sensitive. However, all I could come up with was: "How do you feel?"

"How the fuck do you think I feel?!" he snapped. "How would *you* feel if you had just been fucked by a dog?!" He

began to weep again.

Overcome by an overwhelming urge to comfort the boy, I got into the bathtub with him, taking him in my arms like a baby. Instead of resisting, his body went limp against me. He gave himself to me completely as he cried on my shoulder.

"I'm sorry," I whispered. "I'm so sorry."

The boy looked into my eyes. "Why are you in here with me?" he said coldly. "Is it your turn to fuck me now?"

"No. I would never force myself on you."

"I bet you say that to all the boys...before you rape 'em."

"I mean it. I'm so sorry that this happened to you."

"Then why did you let it happen?!"

The boy hurt me deeply with those words. I felt like a worthless coward.

"What the hell could I have done about it?" I asked, trying to justify my humiliating cravenness.

"A lot more than you did, I'm sure."

"I was high...I was sick..."

"Spare me, man."

I felt like a loser in this boy's eyes. I had failed him miserably, and now I had to somehow redeem myself.

"I can help you now, though," I whispered, for the walls had ears. "Dale was bullshitting about the blackmail. You can leave and never come back and *nothing* will happen to you. I promise."

"Oh yeah," he said, skeptically. "If that's true, and you know it's true, then why *are* you here?"

"Because...I have no other place to go."

"Now who's bullshitting who? You're not like the others, you're not evil, you don't belong here."

"I need the smack, okay!" I blurted out, surprising myself with my enlightening admission.

"What's that?"

"You know, H. Heroin."

"That explains everything. You're a junkie. And I thought those were just mosquito bites all over your arms."

"Now do you see why I can't leave?"

"Back in Wisconsin, I was kind of a junkie too. I was hooked on three meals a day, a big house with central air, and all the toys I could play with. And even though I was dependent on

my old man – the same way you're dependent on that Dale guy – I had to be strong enough to leave it all behind. And you have to be strong enough to do the same thing."

"Damn, you're smart for your age," I said, taken aback by his precocious insight.

He nodded. "In school they called me 'gifted' and separated me from the normal kids like a freak. They even put me in another school full of other freaks."

"Is that why you left home?"

"No," said the boy. He stood to show me his back. As the lather dissolved, I could see the black and blue marks beneath. "This is why," he said somberly, then fell into my arms once more.

"You're so beautiful," I said. "How could anyone do that to you?"

"Are you gay?"

"What makes you think that?"

"Oh, the way you looked at me at the bus station; the way you're looking at me now; your dick pressing into my stomach."

"I'm sorry."

"It's okay," he said, smiling for the first time. He then took hold of my hand and placed it on his budding erection. "I feel the same way."

I kissed him then – softly, delicately, lovingly – and he kissed me back, his wary tongue gingerly exploring my mouth.

"By the way, what's you're name?" I asked him between kisses.

"Gabriel," he said.

"The Angel Gabriel," I muttered, laughing at the irony.

"What's yours?"

"Tommy."

"Oh, Tommy, it feels so good in your arms. I wish you could hold me forever."

"And I'll never let anyone hurt you again, my Gabriel."

He kissed me and I kissed him back, deeply, with as much passion as I could muster. Everything about him was intoxicating: the taste of him, the smell of him, the touch of his fervid, silky skin. My senses were overcome by manic exhilaration. I was *high* on him! And it felt more intense than

any junk I could ever shoot up! Maybe I could be saved after all.

III.

Through the hazy mist I could see a comely boy walking through a field, when he came upon a herd of sheep. A cuddly lamb soon caught his eye and he dropped to his knees to pet the creature. He caressed the lamb gently and methodically at first. But suddenly he pulled out a knife and cut its tender throat. I screamed when I saw the boy's face. It was my face! And the decapitated lamb wasn't a sheep after all. It was a nude boy with wings. His head laid next to his dead body, glaring at me with an accusing face. I screamed again when I realized...it was Gabriel! He lugubriously whispered the words: "Yet each man kills the thing he loves."

A deafening blast of thunder rattled the bed. I woke up in a cold sweat. A tidal wave of relieve struck and enveloped me when I looked down to find Gabriel sleeping in my arms. He was alive! I kissed his forehead and began to weep.

With the warehouse all to ourselves, we had apparently slept the day away. The other boys were at school and it was Friday. Every Friday Dale flew up to New Orleans for the day to deliver a week's worth of kiddy porn to his superiors. I gazed over at the clock and was suddenly filled with dread. Four o'clock! Dale would soon be home! I had to get Gabriel out of there before he returned! How could we have been so careless to allow ourselves to fall asleep? "Carelessness had nothing to do with it," said a voice from deep within me. "You need your fix and you're too much of a pathetic, cowardly wretch to split before daddy gets home with the goodies!"

Lightning struck outside with a blinding furor as the door suddenly swung open. A towering figure loomed from the darkness and approached the bed.

"Rise and shine!" he roared. "Daddy's home!" Dale grabbed my head and violated my mouth with his slimy tongue.

With Gabriel still soundly sleeping, Dale had me follow him to the office. Once there, he peeled off his wet clothes and set them to dry by the air vent.

"It's pouring outside!" he grumbled, then sat behind his desk

buck naked, his fat hanging everywhere.

"How was your trip?" I inquired, pretending to care.

"Very productive," he said, with a maniacal smile. "They're very pleased with my work. That's why they're trusting me to organize their new venture. It seems the market is gettin' saturated with stuff from Europe. There's no money in it anymore. So we're gonna start makin' snuff films."

"What are snuff films?"

"Same old shit, except for one thing: During the climax the boy dies in a violent, bloody massacre."

"Like a horror movie."

"Yeah, I guess you could call it that," said Dale. He stood and commenced opening the safe over his desk.

"Cool. My favorite movie last year was 'Halloween.' They showed the making of it on TV and I learned how to make fake blood out of..." 66! Bingo! He had been careless yet again and I finally had the last number to the combination.

"No, you don't understand," he said, taking a small bag of heroin out of the safe. "We use *real* blood. We use a *real* knife. We *really* kill the boy."

A chill ran down my spine; the son-of-a-bitch was serious! All I could do was just sit there and stare at him with a benumbed face.

"Of course, we're going to need some new blood," he continued, unfazed. "I've grown quite close to you boys and I wouldn't dream of slaughtering you. But that new boy sleeping in there is perfect. So innocent, so pretty. He's going to be our first star. And you're the lucky bastard who's gonna get to slash his pretty little throat."

Yet each man kills the thing he loves.

I jumped to my feet. "Over my dead body!" I screamed.

"Oh, that can be arranged, Kid. But it won't come to that. You'll do it all right." He waved the heroin in my face. "And this is the only motivation you'll need." He glanced at his watch. "It's getting to be about that time again, ain't it? Time for your fix, junkie."

"You're fucking insane!" I cried. "I wouldn't kill Gabriel for all the junk in the world!" I picked up the phone. "I'm calling the cops!"

That's when he took his gun out of the safe. "Big mistake,

Kid," he said, pointing the .44 at my head. "You know, I'm very disappointed in you. You're my favorite, my protege, my apprentice. I thought you had more backbone in you."

I dropped the phone when I heard him cock the pistol. Satan had me by the balls.

It was to be a closed set. Dale left a note on the door for the other boys. It read, "Away for the weekend. No trespassing!" But I doubted if anyone would even stop by. There was a tropical storm warning for Miami/Ft. Lauderdale.

I wanted to make it as easy on Gabriel as possible, so I pleaded with Dale not to tell him about his unfortunate fate. Dale agreed. Not out of the goodness of his heart, he just wanted to see the surprised look on the boy's face when he felt the knife at his throat. We told him instead that this was the last film either of us ever had to do for Dale. Afterwards, we would be released from our commitment and sent on our way with a hundred bucks each. Gabriel resisted at first, but he finally gave in when he saw that I was in favor of it. The poor unsuspecting fool actually trusted me.

With the bright lights pointed at us and Dale at the camera, we began rolling. The first part of the film was routine enough. Gabriel and I sucked each off, then he ate out my ass. Dale wanted us to kiss, but I just couldn't bring myself to kiss the poor soul that I was about to betray. That's when Gabriel first started to suspect that something was terribly wrong.

Dale ordered the boy to roll over, then told me to mount him from behind. I was angry at myself for having an erection. And I was frightened. Some part of me was getting off on this whole depraved scene. Maybe I was a lot more like Dale than I wanted to admit to myself.

Gabriel took my cock up his ass with no trouble at all, Secretariat had seen to that the night before. After a good five minutes of steady humping, Dale ordered the boy to roll on his back for the "money shot."

I sat on Gabriel's chest, with a leg on each side of his head, my hard cock throbbing just inches away from his pink lips. He looked up at me with his big, sad eyes and that's when I realized what I had to do. After I took the boy's life, I was going to slash my wrists and take my own.

Dale directed me to give his face a good fucking, so I did just that. Moments later I experienced what I knew would be my last orgasm on this earth, shooting a hefty load all over the boy's face. Dale then stood over us with the camera and handed me the knife.

"It's time, Kid," he said in a foreboding tone.

The boy was dumbfounded. I could feel his small frame shaking beneath me.

Dale removed a syringe from the knapsack by his feet. "Come on, junkie," he said. "The sooner you do it, the sooner you get this."

I held the knife tightly in my shaking hand and brought it to Gabriel's throat.

"That's a good junkie," said Dale.

The room began to spin then. I was on some kind of macabre carousel. The only thing my eyes could focus upon was the needle oozing junk.

"Do it, junkie, do it!" Dale ordered.

My brain bade my hand to start carving. I could feel the blade pressing into the boy's neck.

That's when I heard him say, saying, "I love you, Tommy."

"No!" I wailed. "No!" I dropped the knife on the bed next to Gabriel's hand.

Dale tossed the syringe aside to remove his gun from the holster he wore around his naked waist. He put the barrel to my forehead with one hand and pointed the camera at it with the other.

"Pick up the knife and snuff him out, motherfucker!"

"No! You're gonna have to shoot me, you vile piece of shit!"

"With pleasure," he said dropping the camera, cocking the gun. "Good bye, Kid Porn."

I closed my eyes, bracing for severe pain, followed by forever darkness. Then I heard the loud bang! But I felt no pain. I opened my eyes to find Dale spasming with the entire length of the knife plunged into his gut and blood gushing everywhere. I seized the moment to knock the gun out of his hand. It went off when it hit the floor and I realized then that the previous bang had merely been thunder. Blood began to pour from Dale's mouth just as he toppled over us, driving the knife deeper into his bowels. Gabriel and I quickly got out from

under Dale's bloody body on the bed. I took Gabriel in my arms and kissed him lovingly on the lips.

"I don't know what came over me," the boy said, weeping. "I couldn't let him kill you. I just picked up the knife and shoved it into him as hard as I could."

"It's all right, my love," I assured him. "You did good. Now let's get outta here."

I had Gabriel take the incriminating film from the camera just in case we needed it in the future. Meanwhile, I opened the safe and was pleasantly surprised. The bastard had over ten thousand dollars in hundred dollar bills neatly stacked inside. I shoved all the cash into my bag along with all my personal belongings and told Gabriel to do the same.

After washing Dale's putrid blood from our bodies, we got dressed, got our bags together, and locked the warehouse door behind us. Yes, it was *all* behind us.

I took my angel's hand in mine and we ran out into the pouring rain.

"Where to?" he asked.

Laughing joyously, I said: "Everywhere, my love! Everywhere!"

MY FIRST COP

William Cozad

My first car was just an old bone-white Ford, but it was all mine. It ran like a top, too. Only problem was that the muffler was rusted and made noise, especially when I gunned the engine and laid rubber to show off. Part of the deal with my folks was that I'd maintain the car with the money I earned after school working in greasy spoon.

One night when I was driving home from work I heard a siren and noticed a whirling red light in my rearview mirror. Jeez, it was the cops. I was in trouble, probably because of the racket from my muffler.

I wheeled over to the curb and waited. In the mirror, I watched the cop get out of his squad car. It was Big John – I could tell by his size. He had a reputation in our small town for harassing teenaged drivers by pulling them over and checking them out.

When he came up to the driver's window he shined his flashlight on me.

"You got a license?"

"Yes indeed."

"Let me see it."

I handed him my opened wallet.

"Take it out of the holder."

I gave him my license.

He studied it carefully using his flashlight. While he read the information I focused my eyes on him. He was incredibly beefy, and he had a big nose, which made me think he had a huge dick, even if he needed a mirror to see it. His hat was fringed with black hair, and he had a thin mustache. His eyes were a beautiful green, like a cat's. I couldn't take my eyes off him.

I'd gone through some changes lately and had these funny feelings inside. I thought a lot about cocks – not just my own, not even those on the good-looking jocks in school. Nope, I thought about cocks on real men, macho men, men like Officer John – the fuzz, the heat, the pig.

"Uh, did I do something wrong, officer?"

"Your heap sounds like a goddam thrashing machine. Hole in the muffler I'd guess. Afraid I'm going to have to give you a ticket for excessive noise."

"Do you have to?"

"Enforcin' the law is my job."

"I've never had a ticket before. I just got the car. I was going to get another muffler when I got paid this weekend. My dad will get mad and ground me. Couldn't you let me off with a warning? I'll do anything you want."

Looking down, I focused on the gun on his hip and the bulge of his crotch. I licked my lips nervously. My mouth was dry and my hands felt clammy.

"You're a virgin, right?"

Blushing, I nodded.

"I mean, you've never been charged with a crime?"

"Nope."

"Okay, William – "

"Call me Billy, everybody does."

He gave me back my license and stared right into my baby blues.

"Get out of the car."

Suddenly I felt panicky. Maybe he was going to teach me a lesson, like stomp my ass.

I got out.

"Hands on the roof."

He frisked me right on the street with people driving by and gawking. He put his hands in the front pockets of my jeans and felt my jewels. I got a hard-on. It started to drool when he patted my butt and rubbed down my legs.

"Any weapons?"

"No."

"Call me *sir*. Show some respect for the law. You've got a choice. Go along with the program or I'll write that ticket. Up to you, Billy."

"Whatever you say, *sir*."

"Drive out to the woods. No funny stuff. I'll be right on your tail."

My asshole puckered with fear, I drove out of town, carefully watching my speed. When he signaled me with his lights I drove off the road to a secluded spot by a clump of trees.

Big John climbed into the passenger side of my car and sat down. I swear I could hear the springs creak.

"Shut off the engine."

I did as he said. Moonlight bathed the car.

"What are you going to do to me, *sir*?"

"It's what you're going to do to me, Billy."

"Please don't hurt me."

"You can trust me, I'm a cop."

"Yes, *sir*." I was shaking like a leaf.

"Show me that weapon."

"Ain't got a weapon."

"The friendly one in your pants, that big dick. Don't act dumb. I felt it, remember?"

I couldn't believe this was happening. Big John wanted to see *my* cock?

Ripping open my fly, I finally freed my erection from my shorts.

He smiled. "Well, will you look at that! Livin' proof that big things come in small packages. Never seen so much meat on a skinny runt."

I lewdly flexed my dick. "You like peters, Big John?"

"Well, I think *you* do, kid. I've been watching you since you started workin' in that filthy joint on Main Street. I was just waitin' for you to get outta line."

"You had this planned?"

"Had you under surveillance, put it that way."

I wrapped my fingers around my cock and slowly jacked it. I could tell I was turning the cop on. That made me even hotter.

"Wanna feel my dick, *sir*?"

"What I want to feel is those virgin lips on *my* meat."

That said, Big John unzipped and flashed me his cock. It was a fat lump of uncut flesh.

"Play with it. Get it hard."

Reaching over, I grabbed his cock and tugged on the foreskin. It started to grow, *really* grow. With the glossy head out of the hood it was massive, not much longer than mine but a lot thicker.

What made me even more horny was his uniform, and his girth. Don't know why, but I've always been fascinated by big

guys. Maybe it was the chunky neighbor who bounced me on his belly when I was a tyke. Maybe it was the image of Santa as a jolly old man. Maybe it's just the fact that I'm so skinny. All I know is that more beef means more to love, more meat to grab onto.

To tell the truth, I'd dreamed of the day I'd get to play with a real man's dick. But I never thought it would happen. Not in this hick town. And certainly not with a stud cop by the side of the road. I was in my glory – like a wet dream.

"Wanna suck on it?"

"Oh, yes, *sir*."

"Like to suck dicks?"

"Never done it before."

"Oh, that's right you are a virgin. But you'd like to, right?

I never wanted anything so much before in my life as to suck on that blueberry cop's big piece of meat. I was about to make my dream come true, and I leaned over and parted my hungry lips. I licked, then nibbled on the head.

He moaned. "Can I spot queer boys or what?"

No one had ever called me that before and I winced. But it was the truth.

Suddenly, he grabbed me by the hair, pulled my mouth away.

"Hey, we gotta be safe."

I watched spellbound while he fished a condom out of his pocket, bit open the foil and sheathed his fat prick in latex. "Come and get it, Billy."

I dove on his fat prick like it was a lollipop. It surprised me that the rubber had a minty taste. What did I know about condoms? Gangly high school boys carried them in their wallets hoping they'd get lucky with some pussy. Not me.

"Oh, yeah, lick it."

I ran my tongue up one side of the prick and down the other, then grabbed hold of the throbbing shaft and opened my mouth.

"Suck it. Yeah! Christ, yeah."

With my head buried in his crotch, the hefty cop was bouncing up and down on the seat and battering my tonsils. Somehow I managed to control the gag reflex. I soon felt his cock get steely hard.

"Gonna shoot, kid. Gonna blow in your mouth. Keep sucking it. Oh, yeah, I'm close!"

In spite of the rubber I felt his cock blow, gushing wads of spunk. I'd done it! I'd actually sucked a cock, a real macho man's cock, a cop's cock – and gotten him off.

I was so horny I wanted to fist my prick and shoot, but the cop shoved my hand away. How I loved that meaty paw, and the sound of his heavy breathing.

I wrapped my arms around his barrel chest as far as they'd go and rested my head on his belly, all the while watching his cock in the condom that was full of cum.

He peeled off the rubber and slung it out the window, then deftly fitted another one onto his cock. I had a sore jaw from the size of his meat, but I'd gladly have gone down on him again. That, however, was not what he had in mind. He slid my jeans and shorts down my legs. I loved it when he stroked my body and soon he was kneading my bare buns. Not only that, he was poking a thick finger into my ass.

"Want me to stick it to you, Billy?"

"I dunno. You're awfully big. I could never handle a cock that size – it would rip me apart."

"C'mon. I know you want it."

He had my number. I'd have done practically anything he asked. I was just kind of scared about getting fucked.

"God, it's been ages since I had any boy-butt. And I've never had a looker like you, Billy my boy. C'mon, boy, give me your cherry."

How could I refuse? It would happen someday. Why not now? Why not with Big John, who made my balls tingle just by looking at me?

He pulled me over on top of him. Next thing I realized, he was spitting on his paw and smearing it in my crack.

When he went to stick me it hurt like anything. It felt like a knife in my guts. But the very idea that it was the big cop's club up my butt thrilled me.

With the head of his bloated prick rammed inside me, I went wild. I'd never felt anything like it. Once the pain subsided, I humped his dick and slipped my hand inside his uniform, I rubbed his furry chest. Rolling my head from side to side, I bounced around, feeling in control. I clenched his cock with my

bounced around, feeling in control. I clenched his cock with my butt muscles and the smell of his Brut aftershave, combined with his body sweat, got me hornier than ever.

"Such a hot, tight boy-pussy. Oh, here I come...now!"

Despite the rubber I felt him shoot hot cum-pellets inside me. My butthole contracted. Just my prick rubbing on his belly in that gabardine uniform got me going, and I gushed, spraying cumdrops all over his shirt, even on his badge.

"Clean up your mess. Use your tongue."

After I licked him off, he kissed me and feeling his bristly mustache sent me into orbit. Snug in his embrace, I agreed not to tell anyone about what happened.

For many months, when I got off work, I'd see Big John in his cruiser. Sometimes he'd just toot his horn. Other times, he'd flash his lights at me and I'd drive out into the country with him behind me. He'd lash out at me for speeding and reckless driving and I'd be made to suck his fat prick and take it up my ass to avoid a ticket.

It ended only after I graduated and left town to be on my own, but Big John made me a cop-sucker for life.

AMONG THE MISSING

John Patrick

Of all the boys I thought I'd never see in Tampa on a rainy night like this and of all the places where I would count myself lucky to run into him, there he is. He's waiting in line at the 7-Eleven on Kennedy Boulevard, on the strip where the hustlers let it all hang out. Having spent two hours at the bar and finding nothing, I am heading home. I have stopped to get a cup of coffee to brace me for the long drive.

It's an awkward moment when I catch his eye. Vince looks startled, then smiles. "Big John! Hi!" There is a way a hustler smiles that embraces your whole body, congratulates you for being so hard up as to have to pay for their company.

We wait in line together, both with coffees, he with a chocolate eclair.

"Dessert?" I ask as he starts to stick one end of the eclair in his mouth.

He nods as the creme filling gushes from it, oozes out one side of his mouth. It is an oddly erotic moment and I feel my cock stiffen in my trousers. I want to wrap my mouth around his penis the way he's wrapping it around the eclair.

We move slowly towards the cash register. It is Friday night and many are buying lottery tickets. Even long after midnight. He has nearly finished the eclair by the time the young black girl checks us out. As always, I pay for everything.

"Thanks," he mutters, then takes a swig of coffee.

Outside in the dark, he moves easily toward my silver-blue Mercedes. He remembers it. "Nice ride, man."

"It needs the top down. I hate it when it rains."

Seeing his jeans hugging his perfect buns in the orangey light that streams from the store windows, and my wallet fat from the cash machine, I desire him all over again. But things have changed. I could see that as we waited in line. He hasn't made a porn flick in two years. He looks messed up, in need of a haircut, a good solid meal.

I remember his last message. I came home and the answering machine was blinking: "John, pick up, please. I need you to

wire me some money..."

It seemed he was always out of town, out of his mind, out of money. And he breathed his message into the phone with such pained pauses that I knew he was near the bottom of his list of the johns who had, one way or another, supported him for years. He needed to get back to Florida, to live again with Fred, the farmer near Orlando. I had glimpsed the man briefly one day in a shopping mall parking lot when he dropped Vince off to spend his first weekend with me. I saw the look of pain, of desperation in the pudgy man's face as Vince got out of his pickup truck and walked towards my car.

Vince was the brightest thing ever to cross that parking lot, I thought at the time. A compact Italian stripper who had parlayed a few good moves into a short-lived career in gay video and, from there, a couple of good years hustling.

Now, in the rain soaked parking lot at 7-Eleven he is no longer bright. He appears soiled, tossed aside by men far richer than I for younger, prettier boys.

I swing open my car door. "Can I drop you somewhere?"

"I thought you dropped me a long time ago," Vince says with a crooked smile.

"Hey, I called but you had already left."

"Yeah, I'm always leaving."

"I thought you were always coming - "

As he's getting into the car, his smile is broader now. "Not as often as I used to."

"Join the club."

As I start the car, he punches the cigarette lighter. When it pops up, he lights a cigarette, coughs.

He exhales. I look at him. Suddenly everything about him now seems out of focus, as if I had just come out of a chlorinated swimming pool.

Vince's dark eyes become smaller, mild, distant. "I got a room here, paid up for tonight," he says, pointing at the motel across the street.

His last trick rented a room, left him the key. Or maybe it was the first trick; how many tricks has he had today? I wonder, but then I'd rather not know.

"Yeah, I gotta get back to Orlando tomorrow, then I go back to New York. I'm gonna dance at the Show Palace. You ever

been there?"

"Once. Didn't care for it."

Hollywood, San Francisco, Miami, Tampa, Orlando, New York. He's now flying low between landing points and praying for luck. He has always lived in his own present tense, no real sense of the past or the future.

In the cheap room at the Tropic Breeze motel that reeks of sweat, piss and Lysol, I sit on the edge of the bed. He stands before me, stripping off his clothes.

Now in the dingy, dank room, I remember the full beauty of all I had fantasized about long before Vince ever came to see me. Every time I would take one of his videos from the shelf and gaze upon the cover, especially the one where two blond boys cling to that beautiful tight body, that crotch so enticingly bunched in a jockstrap. After I spent a couple of days with him, I would recall with fondness the many happy hours I spent slipping his jockstrap off his body, kissing his olive skin, sucking his cock.

But tonight he wears no jockstrap, no underwear at all. After he drops his jeans and steps from them, he tosses his long dark curls back and presses his crotch into my face. Looking up into his eyes, I change my mind, feeling that the years have been good to him. His face is still unlined and, as I run my hands up and down his thighs, I see the lean, muscular body is still tight, smooth, unblemished. I begin sucking his cock, a cock that now smells of Ivory soap. Thankfully, he washed it after his last trick. It is not a big cock but is in perfect proportion with the rest of him. As the cock hardens, he begins twisting with joy and groaning with delight. His head is turned so that he can watch the blowjob in the mirror. He stretches, arches his hips upwards. He has always loved watching others pleasure him and themselves.

Panting, I take my mouth off the cock completely and reach down and dig out my own cock from my pants. Soon his hand covers mine. I let go of my cock and he strokes it with one hand and takes his other hand and puts it on top of my head. I know the twitching, the swelling of his cock is the prelude to orgasm. He throws back his head and groans. He strokes my cock furiously, wanting me to come before he does. I take his cock back into my mouth, even though the precum is dripping

from it. I run my tongue gently around the cockhead, pulling against the underside to get all of it inside my mouth, and play with his lightly furred balls. I push him into me, grab his ass. The full, throbbing length of him is now in my mouth, down my throat. My nose buried deep in his pubic hair, he starts to come. I pull my mouth off and his jism flies everywhere, hitting my eyes, my cheeks, splattering my pants. I hug him to me, suck on his balls. He rubs his fingers into my head, moans.

I kiss his balls, pull back, kiss his hard belly, his navel, work my way up to his perfect pecs. I suck one nipple, then the other. If I hadn't come, if I didn't have to go home right now, I would ask him if I could fuck his ass.

Still, cupping the buns with my hands, I find myself saying, "Have you started to take it up the ass?"

"Yeah, I had to. Sooner or later you have to, ya know?"

"Yes, I know." I remember the last time, how much I wanted to fuck him. But he didn't get fucked. He only fucked. Guys or gals, it didn't matter. I turn him around so I can look at his ass in the mirror as his body is pressed against mine. I kiss his bare shoulder as I stare at it. It is red, as if he'd just been whipped.

I run my hands across it, stick a finger in. He is loose and moist, as if he has just been fucked. Remembering his penchant for dirty talk, mostly about cunts he'd fucked, I felt no compunction about saying, "Feels like somebody was just here."

He chuckles. "Yeah, about an hour ago."

"Bet it didn't take him long – "

"I don't let it take long. I got bills to pay."

Vince's sphincter resists at first, then easily parts as I push the fat, spongy head of my cock into him. It soon disappears into his asshole, followed by a couple of inches of hard cock. He reaches back and parts his cheeks for me and I slide deeper into the warmth of his well-fucked hole. I begin to pump my cock in and out, going a little deeper with each shove. Finally he lets out a deep gasp as my cock slips in to the hilt, my balls slapping against his.

Vince keeps urging me on, and soon is almost out of control, groaning and crying out as I ram it deep into him.

"Was the last one as big as this?"

"Hell, no," Vince cries. "Not many as big as you."

I am so turned-on at the thought I fucking this porn stud at a bargain price that I am soon shuddering, filling the condom. Vince is writhing and bucking with each spurt of my cum, crying, "Oh, yeah, yeah..."

I run my fingers through his wild curls and kiss the top of his head. "God, I've waited two years to do that."

We collapse, my cock still firmly buried up his ass. Our rest is short; soon he is lifting me up, causing my still half-hard dick to slide out with a juicy "plop."

As he climbs off the bed, I squeeze the full, rich globes one last time. "I hope you won't keep me waiting another two years."

"No," he says, staggering to the bathroom.

I count out three twenties and lay them on the dresser. Then I add two more to the pile. For old times' sake. It was worth it.

"Thanks," he says as he returns to the room, sees the cash. "Can I have one of your cards? I lost my address book again."

I hand him my business card. He sticks it in his wallet alongside the cash.

As we stand at the door of the motel, he hugs me.

"Have fun in New York," I tell him.

"Yeah," he says brightly.

I stroke his ass one last time before we leave the room. "Can I drop you somewhere?"

"No, thanks."

I start the car and, as I pull out onto the boulevard, it begins to rain again. I flick on the wipers. I watch as he slowly makes his way across the street, then pauses as a car slows beside him. He bends over, talks with the driver. He gets into the car and is gone. Just like that.

I almost miss him already. Yet I know this is the end. When a boy like Vince, a boy with a largely invented past and no future, walks out of your life, even though he was never really in it, he just goes. Gone but not forgotten, joining the many others who are simply "among the missing."

SOMEONE BOUGHT
THE HOUSE ON THE ISLAND

Ken Anderson

Kevin had hardly been able to bide the time. Throughout the week, he ate little, yet was charged with excitement, throwing himself into work. By Friday, he was leaner and primed, as well as preened, fussing over the least detail of his trim appearance.

"Gee," Helen, his mother, said, smiling. "I don't think I've seen you *groom* this much for Ary." His girlfriend.

"This man's got class, Mom," Kevin replied. "I wanna make a good impression. Besides," he said, "I think I can talk 'im into a big landscaping job."

"If you reel 'im in," commented Paul, his father, pouring a Scotch, "I'll give you a ten-percent commission."

"If I reel 'im in," Kevin declared, "he's mine!"

Around nine o'clock, the twilight at the lake had the yellow transparency of a topaz; the lake so still, in fact, the only sounds were the purl and drip of the paddle, the hoarse incantation of the frogs. Bats, like bees, were swarming over the cove. Approaching the point, Kevin began to hear music, then saw the island swing into view, from his angle a smooth, tree-studded dome silhouetted against the drowsy afterglow of the sky. He recognized the music as "Siegfried's Rhine Journey."

He landed on the beach, then took out the canoe and headed up the steps. A sundial and a concrete planter of papyrus were placed symmetrically on either end of the terrace. A high-powered telescope stood beside the planter. The central set of doors was open, and the curtains billowed inward with a breeze. Kevin brushed one aside, coming face to face with the German shepherd. Kevin stood still, and they stared at each other. He noticed the design on the dog's brows – a perfect brown butterfly. Dieter came out of the bedroom, and his eyes widened as if with amazement.

"Oh, hi, Kevin. How are you?"

"Fine, and you?"

"I'm running a little behind with dinner."

"That's all right," Kevin smiled. "For some reason, I'm not all that hungry."

"I can fix that."

"This is Rome," Kevin said, meaning the dog. "As in Italy?"

Kevin had seen the dog several times but had heard him referred to by name only once, when Kevin had spied on Dieter and others at the wharf three weeks before.

"No, Roehm, as in Ernst Roehm."

"Ernst Roehm?"

"As in Third Reich. Look him up in your history book."

Kevin stepped forward, and the dog lowered his head to be petted. The hair on his head came to a strange little point.

"Hi, boy," Kevin said. "How're you?"

"They make such fine guard dogs, don't they?"

Dieter suggested that they settle in the kitchen, and passing by the dining area, Kevin noticed the glass vase of lilies, Crimson Beauties, on the table.

"Have a seat," Dieter offered, and Kevin straddled the bench of one of the two rough-hewn picnic tables.

On the table was a big bowl of blackhearts and sauce for a Cherries Jubilee. On the counter, Dieter had set a bowl of peeled shrimp, a bag of flour, sticks of butter, an eggplant, onions, and two bottles of pepper, one red, one white. Dieter grinned at Kevin, then began cutting an onion on a cutting board.

"I'm glad you dressed casually," he said. "I opened up the house."

Kevin was wearing teal shorts, a yellow Izod, and tennis shoes with white socks; Dieter, black shorts, a grey T-shirt, and a pair of Blucher moccasins.

"Let me help you with something."

"Oh, no," Dieter said. "Just sit and talk to me." When the Wagner was over, he asked, "What kind of music would you like-- The Beardless Boys, The Punks, GWM; Britten, Tchaikovsky, Poulenc?"

"I kind of like the quiet," Kevin said. "Such a great night. Looked outside?"

"Quite peaceful."

"Someone told me you were in the chemical business."

"Well, yes."

"What kind?"

"Pharmaceuticals, actually." When he had finished chopping the onion, he said, "My main interest. Though I'm also involved in what you might call security systems."

"Security systems," Kevin thought. "Not much need for them around here."

Dieter raked the onion into a bowl, then said, "Can never tell."

"How'd you wind up buying the house?"

"I'm opening a plant in Atlanta, and I'll be here a few years. So I found a place there, but wanted a somewhere to get away – something convenient, yet secluded."

"You can't get much more secluded than an island."

"Yes, the closest house is yours."

Kevin thought he caught something excited, even tremulous in Dieter's voice, as if he were having to go to some trouble to restrain it.

"It was a bargain," Dieter added, wiping his hands on a dishcloth. "Houses in this area are quite reasonable. Oh, I haven't offered you anything to drink. Let me go downstairs and pick out a bottle of wine."

When Dieter headed for the stairs, Kevin experienced deja vu, but could not conjure up a memory to explain it. He got up and strolled into the living room, surprised by a detail he spotted. There were two sofas back to back at a slant across the area, one facing the fireplace, one facing the central doors. On the one facing out lay a black vest and what looked like the sock he had lost. He picked up the sock to examine it, the green stripes around the top, then, dropping it, picked up the vest, which, from the weight and padding, he realized was bullet-proof.

When Dieter came upstairs, Kevin asked, meaning the sock, "How'd you know this was mine?"

"I didn't."

"I apologize for snooping around. Didn't know anyone had moved in."

"No problem."

Kevin had scaled the back wall to sunbathe nude on the upstairs deck, but scampered off when he heard the boat pull into the boathouse. He had dropped the sock on the way to the woods.

"No problem at all."

Dieter moved to the bar and began opening the wine.

"I'm sort of the caretaker of the place."

"Caretaker," Dieter repeated.

"I used to play here all the time when I was a kid."

"Finding the sock was an auspicious omen," Dieter claimed. "I knew I'd made the right choice."

Kevin puzzled over the statement, thought of asking him about it.

Instead, he dropped the vest and asked, "You wear this?"

"I have an enemy or two," Dieter smiled, popping the cork. "Oh, not so much me personally. What I represent."

"Which is?"

Dieter gestured with the corkscrew, then said, "Oh, how can I say this modestly? Wealth, power?"

Kevin did not quite make the connection.

"Did you know the Moores?" Dieter asked.

"Oh, yeh," Kevin blurted, strolling to the bar. "Like grandparents. They moved to Miami for a few years, but moved back when Mrs. Moore got liver cancer. She wanted to spend her last year here."

Dieter handed Kevin a glass of Cabernet, then said, "I understand."

"She died when I was about eleven, I guess, and Mr. Moore died a year or so ago. Snake bite, but the doctor said he died of a heart attack."

Kevin sipped the wine, then leaned on the bar, staring into the sink.

"Tell me about yourself," Dieter asked. "How does a strapping youth like you spend the summer?"

Kevin stood up straight, smiling.

"I work for my dad. Landscaping."

Kevin was aware that Dieter was eyeing his arms and legs.

"Keeps you in shape."

"Yeah," Kevin laughed. "And I swim. I *love* to swim. I can swim for miles."

"We must go swimming."

"Tonight?"

"Don't you swim at night?"

"Oh, yeh, all the time."

They eyed each other, sipping wine.

"You wouldn't happen to need any landscaping, would you? The place is pretty stark. I could take care of it for you."

"Not a bad idea," Dieter mused.

"I think I've outpaced my dad as far as design goes. I'd do a great job."

"Sure you would. We'll talk about it."

"He's not willing to try much."

"And you are?"

"Yeh, sure," Kevin claimed. "It's an art."

Dieter filled their glasses, then took the bottle to the kitchen counter and reached a small saucepan. He unwrapped two sticks of butter, then placed them in the pan and turned the burner on low. Kevin had followed him, then half leaned against, half sat on the end of the table directly behind him.

"You seem like the healthy, all-American type," Dieter commented, his back to him. "You date?"

"Not at the moment," Kevin said.

Dieter picked up his glass and propped against the counter, facing him.

"I broke up with my girlfriend a couple of weeks ago."

"How sad."

"Not really," Kevin blushed.

They sipped wine.

"You a virgin?"

"A virgin?" Kevin pondered. He could not believe that Dieter had asked him that, but admitted, "Yes."

They stared at each other.

"But more from rotten luck than qualms. I'm game."

"Good."

"I'm no angel, if thinking about it counts."

The butter started bubbling, and Dieter set down his glass and began whisking in some flour.

"I sit on the stairs sometimes at night while my parents do it," Kevin confided. "It's a good thing I can't see into the room."

Dieter looked at him over his shoulder. They laughed.

"I don't know why I'm telling you this."

"That's all right," Dieter said, setting the pan aside, then turning off the burner. "You can tell me anything you like. Your juiciest secrets."

He moved to the bar and, his back to Kevin, lit a cigaret, slipping the lighter into his pocket and blowing smoke toward the ceiling.

"Sex isn't bad," he said, turning, leaning against the bar. "Americans are warped by their Puritan heritage, but sex isn't bad. Besides, it's a major step in discovering yourself. You won't have much idea of the adult inside till you take that first, instinctive step."

"The sooner the better," Kevin laughed nervously.

Dieter smiled, then looked aside pensively. Kevin got a whiff of the smell and realized that Dieter was smoking pot.

"The heart is sort of an ultimate dark lantern," Dieter said, not looking at him, "giving off light only for those who are blind. You must see with its light if you are to find your way through such a deep and perilous realm as love."

"I'm sorry, Dieter," Kevin apologized. "I didn't follow you."

Roehm had wandered into the room, then sat and stared.

"Roehm would make a wonderful guide dog," Dieter explained. "And – "

"So does the heart. Gotcha." When Dieter took another hit, Kevin asked, "You gonna offer me a hit, or do I have to beg?"

"Of course," he said, extending the joint. "I'm a little surprised. You seem such a – babe in the woods."

"Oh, I've smoked before," he admitted. "A couple of times. Never did much for me, though."

Dieter smiled shrewdly.

"This will. Thai. Make you forget who you are, who I am, where you live."

"Promise?" Kevin grinned.

He drew on it and held his breath, handing it back. Dieter drew on it and passed it to him again. Then Dieter bent over, touching his toes.

Looking up, he said, "Forcing the smoke to my head."

He clasped his hands behind his back and faced the floor, then stood, exhaling. Kevin imitated him, and they smoked the

joint down to a roach. Dieter dropped it into an ashtray, where it trailed a thin, blue string of smoke.

"How old are you?" Kevin asked point-blank.

"Three hundred and eighty."

"You mean thirty-eight," Kevin smiled.

"No," Dieter replied. "Three hundred and eighty. I was born under the reign of the mad king Rudolph II, in a little town called Geheimnessbach, a farming village in the Schwarzwald."

They stared at each other.

"You're a vampire," Kevin joked.

"And vampires must feed on people, Kevin," Dieter leered. "So be careful. I admire your innocence, but – "

"Geez, you're playing mind games with me," Kevin laughed, holding his forehead. He looked up: "Guess I'll have to whip out my cross."

"The basic assumption behind the, uh – cross – in vampire stories is that it represents goodness, which, of course, isn't always true. Some of the worst episodes in history took place in the name of, uh – Christianity. The Spanish Inquisition, the Crusades, the brutal rape of the West. The Catholics and Protestants were killing each other when I was born. They're still killing each other-- from Northern Ireland to Lesotho. No, the cross is useless until it means something other than stupidity, intolerance, and hate."

Kevin looked around the counter for garlic.

"If you're a vampire," he countered, "then why do you wear that vest?"

"Being shot would present some practical problems."

"What's it like sleeping through centuries?" Kevin scoffed.

"Like sleeping one night," Dieter brooded. "A cavernous night in which a dream is as long as a life followed by another dream and another. Only when you wake, your muscles are a little stiff, and you find people wearing the most ridiculous outfits."

They laughed.

"I've seen you in the daytime," Kevin said.

"That story about not going out in the day – a myth. But you should know that from the Stoker tale."

"Oh, yes," Kevin exclaimed, the drug's first rush over-

whelming him.

"But," Dieter quipped, "why go out in the daytime – "

"I know, I know," Kevin blurted, "when you can go out at night."

Both laughed so hard they cried, and as Kevin bent over the table, he noticed the bowl of dark-red sauce.

"I imagine this must be what blood tastes like," he mused, "to a vampire."

"Must taste like to a vampire," Dieter repeated. Kevin pictured splattered blood, but could not get as far as tasting it, when Dieter said, "It tastes like Cherry Marnier, as sweet and rich as a fine liqueur, and just as it's about to clot, like Cherries Jubilee, thick and sweet – cloying, yes, yet superb."

"I must try it sometime," Kevin smirked.

"Yes," Dieter joked. "Over ice cream." He seemed to be trying to compose himself, then asked, "What is this, an interrogation?"

"I may as well find out as much as I can while I can. How many chances do I get to interview a vampire?"

He dipped two fingers into the bowl and smeared the sauce on his throat, tempting Dieter with it.

"'Good morning,'" Dieter enunciated with a Slavic accent.

"'I had cut myself slightly,'" Kevin quoted, recognizing the scene from Stoker. "'He suddenly made a grab at my throat. I drew away, and his hand touched the string of beads which held the crucifix.'"

"'Take care,'" Dieter recited. "'Take care how you cut yourself. It is more dangerous than you think in this country.'"

Roehm got up and strolled from the room. When Kevin laughed, Dieter took his hand and, catching him off guard, sucked the two sticky fingers into his mouth, staring up at him with iridescent eyes.

"Geez," Kevin chuckled, referring to the grass. "This stuff's good. I've never hallucinated before."

Dieter glanced at him again, but his eyes looked normal, grey. He stood, holding Kevin's hand, then released it.

"Kevin," he sighed. "I do wish you'd quit blurting that – expletive."

"What, Geez?" he stressed, teasing him.

"What about a swim?"

"Now?"

"I think it would be fun, would level us off, wash the blood," he joked, "I mean sauce, off your chin."

"OK," Kevin smiled, picking up a dishcloth. "But I don't have a suit."

Kevin wiped his throat, and Dieter left, then returned with two black Speedos and two big, white towels.

When he handed a suit to Kevin, he said, "Nothing more elegant than black."

Dieter began to undress, first the T-shirt, then his shorts, revealing a great physique, as well as a perfectly drawn tan line. Kevin had never seen an uncut cock, and the strange sight moved him strangely, stirred inchoate feelings in his groin.

"Modest?" Dieter asked, pulling up the suit.

Kevin exhaled through his nose, stripped, and stepped into the suit. They took off their watches, laid them on a table, and picked up the towels.

The path to the south beach was soft with pine straw and splotched with shadows – draped down the hill, like in a long, moonlit ribbon. All around them, frogs croaked and crickets thrilled, pumping their pulse through the sultry vein of the night. Big windchimes dangled lazily from a pine, and to Kevin, their languid clank gave the island a sacred, magical feel. He felt in tune with the place, as if time had gone back, as if he and Dieter were Cherokees in breech-skins on the way to some secret rite.

At the beach, they dropped the towels onto a bench and waded into the water. Waist-deep, they tipped forward into relaxed, perfectly timed strokes. At first, the water felt cool, but Kevin soon got used to it, and swimming toward the open lake, he caught a warm, bath-like current. He treaded water, then dipped beneath the surface, breast-stroking down through the gloom. Then he just hung in place, fish-like, letting the soothing fingers of the current massage a sweet, light joy from his limbs. High above, the sheer, blue fabric of the surface wavered and twinkled. Arms out, legs apart, Dieter floated there like a corpse, like an angel sleeping on a patch of sky. Kevin thought of himself as Dieter's shadow, a pale reflection in the dark, translucent mirror of the depths.

One scissor kick, and Kevin ascended, angel-like himself,

grabbing Dieter's ankles. Dieter arched backward, breast-stroking down so that they wheeled smoothly, easily, like synchronized swimmers, one's face lifting from the water, then the other's. Kevin let go, treading water, waiting for Dieter to come up. But Dieter grabbed his foot, yanking him down so that they hovered face to face, holding each other by the arms just a foot or two underwater. They rose, and as they broke the surface, Kevin, exhilarated, laughed.

"Wow, this is great," he gasped, paddling to stay afloat.

"Yes, it is."

With a kick, Kevin tipped onto his back. Dieter turned onto his back, gliding beside him, and they rested that way, gazing straight up at the stars, Altair, Vega, Deneb...not a flat chart, as the night sky had often appeared to Kevin, but a three-dimensional glimpse into space. They floated there a-while, rocked by the waves, gazing at the stars quietly, then Kevin lifted his arm in a slow back-stroke, then another. Dieter followed, and when they neared the beach, they rolled over, slipping into free style. Kevin held back, treading water, watching Dieter finish the last few yards in a graceful series of strong, even strokes. Then Kevin swam in and waded out, aware all at once of his weight.

Dieter stepped from his swimsuit, wrung it out, and tossed it onto the bench. He picked up a towel. Kevin stripped and toweled off, his body firm and keen from the swim. He glanced toward the moon low in the east, a moon so big and bright he could see the details of its craters, seas, and hills.

"Just think," Kevin said, indicating the moon. "Armstrong and Aldrin played golf up there."

Dieter smiled at the moon, wistful.

"What's that glow over there?" he asked, nodding toward the south.

"Atlanta," Kevin said, wrapping the towel around his waist.

"Didn't think you could see it from here," Dieter mused, flipping his towel over his shoulders.

The tiny, blinking light of a plane lifted from the skyline.

"Ready?" Dieter asked.

They turned toward the hill, slowly walking up the path. Halfway to the house, Kevin stopped by a pine, touched the bark, and laughed. His erection was holding up the towel, like

a tent pole.

"Is this where you – ?"

"What?"

"Is this where you suck my neck?"

Dieter dropped his towel, then stepped forward. Kevin stared at him, Dieter's face eclipsed in an aura of moonlight. A breeze stirred the woods. The chimes clanked.

They embraced gently, like a father and son, and Dieter rubbed Kevin's back and shoulders as if to warm him. He kissed his neck tenderly, once, twice, then fell on it hungrily, and they staggered quietly against the tree, all the sinews of Kevin's throat, all the muscles of his shoulder, all the fibres of his gripped being – drawn irresistibly into the scalding vampire bite of Dieter's mouth.

"Oh, man," Kevin sighed rapturously. "Oh, man, oh, man."

Kevin's towel came undone against the tree, dropping to the ground. Dieter stepped back, then knelt on one knee, an arm resting on the other.

Kevin's Diary
Saturday, August 30

Dieter just knelt there in front of me awhile, staring at my cock as if fascinated by it, as if he had never seen one or there were something new or different about it. A vampire must stare at the contours of a nice, juicy neck the way he was staring at it. And, of course, it was staring right back at him, pointing straight at his mouth. A compass needle pointing north couldn't have pointed more directly toward where it was drawn.

When he put his hand on my groin, I was all touchy and ticklish, and when he squeezed the base of my cock, it ballooned even more, threatening to come in a dangerous, yet delicate sort of way. I knew it wouldn't take more than a lick or a kiss to get me off.

When he finally went down on me, I was so steel hard it hurt. I mean it really hurt. I had the worst case of blue balls I had ever had – the buildup, like a geyser, of seventeen years – and my cock felt like one big, fat, stretched-tight vein. I couldn't help grabbing hold of his hair, couldn't help groaning

– it hurt so much, yet felt so good at the same time.

At first, my whole body flexed. I felt like one big bicep flexed doing curls, but the more he sucked me, the more I relaxed. Wave on wave of warm sensations washed over me, lulling me into a state of warm, womblike paralysis, the kind of passivity that vampire victims must assume, at first hypnotized, then paralyzed by the act of literally nursing someone.

My legs shook, my thighs began to quiver, and when I came, the pain was like the exquisite torment, the incredible pleasure the victim must feel when the canines puncture the vein, and the blood starts spurting out the way my hot come did, spurt after steamy spurt into Dieter's mouth.

And he was loving it the way that a vampire loves blood, I imagine, groaning over it the way a vampire groans over the wet, inflamed wound, wallowing in my crotch as if he could never get enough of the gory taste of it, the salty smell of it, the sweet, addictive drug of it.

Man, if this is what it's like being a vampire victim, suck on.

ETHAN'S APOLOGY

David Patrick Beavers

Ken sat in the outdoor gallery of the coffee house, sipping a stinging cup of Kona and reading about the history of Berlin, completely oblivious to the prattling voices of other patrons nearby. The plume of smoke from his cigarette drifted up from the ashtray into his eyes. A blind hand adroitly crushed the butt.

"Got a smoke, man?"

The words sort of filtered into Ken's ears, but his brain almost immediately disregarded the noise. He turned another page in his book and continued reading.

"Maybe he's deaf," another voice said.

"Yo! Got a smoke, man?!" the first voice shouted.

Damned noisy people, Ken thought to himself as he went back and scanned the previous page in an attempt to reread a pertinent paragraph. He automatically fished another cigarette from the pack in his shirt pocket. A hand swept down like a hawk after its prey, snatching away the cigarette.

"Thanks man!" the voice said.

Ken whipped around only to see the forms of three young people, two guys and a girl, walking away. He saw a rather smug looking youth with buzz-cut red hair lighting up his cigarette. He turned slightly, catching sight of Ken. He sneered and snickered. The young girl, who looked trust-fund trendy in her designer grunge clothes, pointed at Ken as her shrill laughter pierced the air like the sound of a falling bomb. She was laughing so hard, she had to steady herself on the shoulder of the redhead. The other young man seemed to try to laugh, but Ken could tell the boy really wasn't finding this funny. As his two friends turned to hurry on, this young man lingered, slowly walking backwards, as his innocent, wide dark eyes, locked onto Ken's. The boy finally hung his head low and turned away, hurrying to catch up with his friends.

Ken let a weary sigh slip through his lips as he lit another cigarette and went back to his reading. His eyes ran over the words, page after page, yet when he paused to take another sip

of his tepid coffee, he realized he couldn't remember any of what he'd read. Instinctively, his eyes turned away from the book, from the gallery around him, and fixated on the people walking along the sidewalk, some of the passers-by scarcely a foot away from him. The coffee house gallery was designed to draw people together. The patio section of the gallery adjoined the concrete walk, a three-foo- high, wide-topped wall being the only barrier between patrons and pedestrians.

The parade of foot traffic often brought him into contact with friends and acquaintances from various places he frequented. Most of the guys he saw, though, were cronies from his gym. A few others were acquaintances, friends of friends whom he'd met at dinners or functions or in casual passing. Men who, like himself, were most often single with histories of previous relationships that for one reason or another failed. Single men in their thirties and forties who were forever looking for some optimal ideal of a lover - one that was mature, one with shared interests or a similar past, one with the mind of a forty-year-old matched with the body of a twenty-year-old. That kind of combination was rare to find. Is rare to find, he thought. He'd basically given up the chase, settling for occasional sexual encounters with guys who were as horny as he and just as disinterested in pursuing anything beyond sex. Sex that was safe. Sex that was so unlike the unbridled hedonism he'd experienced in his own youth.

Every now and then he'd spy a man around his own age whom he'd allow himself to have a brief fantasy about. A fantasy of a lifetime commitment that would be over with in a matter of nanoseconds. Then he'd go back to his books, back to his work, or back to whatever conversation was the order of the day.

He flipped back through the pages to begin re-reading the words he'd read blindly. He lit another cigarette, took another sip of his coffee and focused on the print of the page. And he read. Read with intent. Read with comprehension, blocking out everything around him.

"What's it about?" the voice asked.

Ken didn't quite hear the words, but he was a bit taken aback when the young man with the wide, dark eyes sat down in the vacant chair opposite him. Ken glanced about for signs of his

two snickering friends. "Pardon me?" Ken said.

"The book. What's it about?"

"You didn't sit to talk about this book," Ken said softly, yet directly. The young man looked incredibly young. Too young. The lad's dark eyes were really a brilliant ruby-brown, fringed with long, ebony lashes that women would do more than kill for. Sad eyes. Innocent eyes. As puppyish as a Golden Retriever's. Long hair, a honey-hued brown with flecks of auburn, was blunt cut just below his chin. Delicate pale skin set off the arch of deep brown brows and full, pale lips. The young man was prettier than a girl might be.

The youth toyed with the buttons on his oversized gray flannel shirt, then tugged at the collar of the navy blue T-shirt. "Maybe I did," he said.

"It's about Berlin," Ken said. "About its evolution."

"Cool," said the young man. "My parents have been there. Said they really liked it."

"Maybe you might like to buy this book for them as a present," Ken said.

"Maybe," he said. "Sorry about my friends..."

"Well, you've shown you've more character than they," Ken said.

"I'm Ethan."

"Ethan?" Ken said. The kid looked like an Ethan, Ken thought. Old school name for a new school kid. Obviously, his parents were quite young as well. Some time in the mid-to-late seventies, citified or educated parents started pulling out the lists of archaic names to bestow upon their children. "I'm Ken. Not Kenneth. Not Kenny. Just Ken."

"Like in Barbie and Ken?" Ethan said with a smile.

"Something like that," Ken said.

"Can I bum a smoke?"

"You hardly look old enough to have a diploma, let alone smoke," Ken said.

"I'm eighteen," Ethan said.

"Right," Ken said.

Ethan shifted around in his seat, pulled a battered billfold from the back pocket of his thrift store chinos, and flipped his drivers license onto the table. "Card me, if you want."

Ken studied the license. Ethan Johnathan Greene. Greene

with an "e." Date of birth - October 1, 1976. Ken almost let out a laugh. "A bicentennial baby."

"Missed the hoop-la by a couple of months," Ethan said as he stowed away the I.D. and his wallet.

"I was getting ready for the S.A.T. when you were born."

Ethan shrugged. "We all gotta do that."

Ken pulled the pack of cigarettes out of his pocket and set them on the table. "You in school?"

"I'm a senior," Ethan said as he stabbed the filter of the cigarette between his lips, then produced his own lighter. "I should've been placed a year ahead, but my parents wanted me to be the oldest in my class, instead of the youngest. The way I see it, it ended up not mattering that much."

"Well, I never had that problem. My birthday fell in the middle of the school year in the dead of winter," Ken said.

"Why Berlin?"

"What?"

"Why're you reading about Berlin?" Ethan asked.

"Why not?"

Ethan smiled slightly. "Why not?"

"Well, I'm glad that you stopped by to make amends," Ken said.

"You want to get back to your book," Ethan said.

"I don't want you to feel obligated to stay," said Ken as he gulped down his now-too-cool coffee.

Ethan wasn't sure that he wanted to leave. He'd felt bad about his friends just snagging the cigarette, then laughing at Ken. There wasn't any reason for them to be that mean-spirited. Still, he knew they were waiting for him to join them at the burger joint up on Robertson Boulevard. Then again, he was tired of hanging with them. They were always doing something stupid. Dean and Tammy could be an obnoxious duo, and they usually were. They lived to make fun of people, even when there was nothing about a person that warranted their antics. He thought Ken was attractive. He looked like a refugee from the seventies, with his shaggy, dirty blond, surfer haircut, Saturday morning stubble and those crisp, green eyes. Tanned skin with the fine lines of experience framing his eyes, creasing his forehead. He looked young, yet he looked old. Sort of that young-old look that mature men with boyish faces get. He also

noticed Ken's hands. Large hands. Weathered like a day laborer's, with callouses and scars. Ethan noticed the scars on the lower portions of Ken's ring finger and pinky on his left hand. Those markings made Ethan feel his youth. Like he was some fresh piece of clay scooped from the earth, still waiting to be molded. Into what, he wasn't sure.

Ken couldn't help but notice that Ethan wasn't leaving. The boy seemed to be staring intently into a microcosm of space. He studied the young man's eyes, trying to access where this young man's train of thought was headed. He swallowed down the last of his coffee and set the mug down on the table with a decided and purposeful thud. Ethan seemed to snap back to reality.

"Are you all right?" Ken asked.

"Yeah," Ethan said quietly. "What happened to your hand?"

"My hand?"

Ethan grabbed hold of Ken's left hand, gingerly splaying the fingers to better observe the scars. "These scars..." Ethan continued.

Ken let out a nervous laugh. "My own stupidity," Ken said. "Chopped them with a rather big knife."

"On purpose?" Ethan asked.

Ken had to think about that. He'd never been sure if he'd done it purposefully or not. "I honestly don't remember," Ken said. "It was so long ago. I was nineteen. Young, full of vodka and speed, I think, and quite stupid. I remember being angry about something, maybe at myself... Anyhow, me and a very large, very sharp and very heavy piece of cutlery had a disagreement of sorts."

"Pretty heinous," Ethan said. "Must've been pretty wild'n fucked up back then."

"The times, or me?"

Ethan just shrugged as his gaze fixed on the scars, as his finger traced the thick trails of smooth flesh. "Pretty fuckin' heinous."

Ken felt a weird tingle shoot from his fingers, up through his arm, then course through his torso as it bulleted to his crotch. His cock began to inflate. He calmly pulled his hand back from Ethan's grasp, hoping his swelling member would shrink away

again. "Heinous is a good word," he said.

"Kind of sad, don't you think?" Ethan said.

"Sad... Bad... It happened. That was then, this is now," said Ken.

"Now..." Ethan parroted. "Now... Is smart. Yet, now.... kind of sucks, ya know?"

"It's just different," Ken said. "At least you know ahead of time what... dangers... there are. You can take precautions."

"I know," Ethan said. "But at least for a time, you guys had freedom."

"Of sorts," Ken said. "No scenario's perfect, though."

"Is your scenario perfect now?" Ethan asked.

"Meaning?" Ken began to wonder if he was being set up by the young man. So many kids had ulterior motives these days, he thought. Target a pigeon to pluck, to beat up. He didn't want to set himself up to be in a crossfire of any sort, let alone to be a target.

"Someone tucked away keeping the home fires burning for you," Ethan said.

"Are you sure you're eighteen?" Ken asked. "That's not a typical eighteen-year-old's question."

"What's typical?" Ethan asked. He felt as if he didn't really know what typical was. He had straight friends. He had gay friends. He had bisexual friends. Even though most of them were "open" about these things, it still didn't prevent tongues from wagging when the person in question was out of ear-shot. Dean liked to work the gay guys in this area of town, getting them to buy him things or dinners or whatever, yet Dean never so much as let any of them cop more than a squeeze of his ass. To Dean, these men were patsies just waiting to be conned. Tammy was his girlfriend. She always played the part of a fag hag - her term - hanging with Dean, to keep their hustle going. Dean liked the game. He liked his gains. Yet he didn't have much of anything good to say about the men he conned. To him, they were all idiots. When Ethan first hooked up with Dean and Tammy, he knew Dean was hustling, but he thought Dean was actually putting out in trade. He'd just assumed that Dean was bisexual until Dean tried to teach him the tricks of the trade. They'd played out a scenario, with Dean as the john and he as the hustler. When Dean pressed for a kiss in return

for a favor granted, Ethan really kissed him. Dean knocked him aside, as if Ethan had just spit battery acid into his mouth. Dean spat and cursed and called him a stupid, naive fuck, while Ethan tried to will his raging erection into submission. Ethan had laughed at himself and played the dumb fool, the ignoramus. Dean was appeased and forgave Ethan. Ethan felt stupid for being so naive; felt resentful that Dean felt there had been some action that needed forgiving. Quite often when he and Dean and Tammy were out on the strip, running their scams, Ethan found himself feeling connected to their marks. Ethan found many of them attractive. He tried to pull a con once, but when push came to shove, he found that he wanted to slip into his mark's arms, to feel the man's strength, his solid form, his masculine smell. A few guys near his own age had hit on him, but he wasn't attracted to them, or at least as attracted to them as he was to the older men. He had started to get aroused when he was touching Ken's scars. Had he held the man's hand any longer, he was sure he would have cum in his shorts. But Ken had pulled his hand away. He wasn't interested, Ethan thought. Not in him.

"Typical," Ken responded. "I'm not sure anymore."

"So?" Ethan persisted. "Do you?"

"Do I what?"

"Have someone tucked away?" Ethan asked.

"That's a rather personal question," Ken said. "But, no, I don't. Don't think I want anyone. Too much maintenance."

"No kids, then," Ethan said.

"I didn't say that."

"You have kids?"

"You ask a lot of questions," Ken said as he closed up his book and stuffed it into a soft, leather bag.

"Is that bad?"

"No," said Ken as he slipped on his jacket. "If you're sincere."

Ethan felt his stomach drop through the seat of his chair as he realized that Ken was leaving. "You gotta go?"

Ken felt weird. The young man's question seemed to be more of a "stay and talk" plea. Like the kid was really interested in hearing about his thoughts and views and whatever. Ken smiled begrudgingly. "Part of the package of being an old fart

like me is having to take responsibility. I've got things that I have to do."

"Maybe I could help you?" Ethan said, not really believing he'd said it.

"Your friends are waiting for you, aren't they?"

Ethan sighed. "I suppose..."

"I suppose... You suppose..." Ken said as he slung the strap of the bag over his shoulder. "It was nice meeting you, Ethan." Ken extended his hand.

Ethan took Ken's proffered hand, squeezing it firmly as he shook it. His crotch immediately stirred again, almost shooting into a full erection. In that moment, he didn't want to let go.

Ken felt a bristling, cobalt blue charge of cold electricity shoot from his hand, up his arm and down to this gut. It scared him. Scared him because he'd never felt this kind of energy with someone so young before. Young men had never really appealed to him. He never felt connected to them. Even when he was young, he sought out the company of older men. Men. Then the realization flashed in his mind like a supernova. What if the young man was as he once was? Looking for someone older. Ken shook the thought from his mind. Young men were pretty, but had never been to his suiting. He liked men, not boy-men. Men with forms of kid-covered marble. Men with hairy legs, calloused hands, chapped lips and five o'clock shadows. Men who were not fragile. Youth is fragile, he thought. Think of all the men he'd had. Men old enough to be his father, to be his grandfather even. Young men, like Ethan, were pretty boys. Boys with wants and needs and... God, he thought. He'd already done all that this young man needed to do.

"You come here much?" Ethan asked.

"What?"

"Here," Ethan said as he finally let Ken's hand go. "Maybe I'll see you here again?"

"Maybe," Ken said as he pocketed his cigarettes. "Your friends are probably wondering where you've disappeared to."

Ethan nodded slightly. "Catch ya later, then..."

Ken nodded and walked away.

Ethan stood a moment longer, then sat back down, watching Ken shrink into the distance as he hurried on. He could tell that

Ken had broad shoulders. Strong shoulders. And a full, firm ass that gently stretched the denim of his jeans. Ethan's cock was straining beneath his shorts. Straining to be touched.

He suddenly shot up out of his seat and hurried from the gallery out onto the sidewalk. He shoved his hands into his pockets and clipped along at a pace that was almost running, all the while keeping his eye trained on Ken. Finally, he freed his hands and ran to close up the distance between himself and this man - this man whom he found attractive as well as intriguing.

By the middle of the third block, he was trailing Ken by about ten yards. Somewhere along the way, Ken had slipped the earphones of a Walkman on. Ethan felt a bit reassured by that as it gave him the chance to bail if he suddenly chickened out. He wasn't sure, though, what he'd be chickening out of doing? He'd only had sex twice before. Once with a girl he dated when he was a Sophomore and once with a guy just a bit older than himself. They'd tricked in back of the guy's mini-van. A rather hurried and uneventful experience it was. For him at least. He'd expected it to be more fulfilling, more sensational. But all the two of them did was to kiss a bit while they jacked-off. But this guy, Ken, excited him. He wasn't sure why. But, then again, who can explain attraction, he thought.

He watched Ken disappear around the corner. Ethan slowed down his pace, cautiously. He knew that around that corner there were just a couple of shops, then the rest of the street was a residential section. Mostly apartments and condos. Very little foot traffic on the sidewalks. And no stores to duck into to hide.

As he came around the corner, his eyes sought out the familiar dirty blond hair. Like he'd swallowed a gut full of ice, he froze. Ken was scarcely twelve feet from him. His back was to Ethan. The headphones were draped around his neck as he was talking to the guy who ran the small video store. Jeff, or Jerry or something like that. He was a nice guy. Nice looking. But he'd hit on Ethan more than a few times. Ethan had always just taken the pseudo-seductive comments with a grain of salt and a grin. Other guys thought Jeff, or Jerry, or whatever, was hot, but Ethan found him to be too pretty. Forced pretty. Hair frosted and cut neatly like some trendy topiary on an estate's

grounds. Jeff, or Jerry, or whatever, was forever packing his gym-built body into tacky lycra bike shorts and tank tops, even in the middle of winter, to show off his wares and his tanning salon bronze-toned skin that always shone like he'd swabbed himself with olive oil. Even his eyebrows were plucked and shaped into mannequin reality. Forced beauty wasn't real beauty to Ethan. It was unnatural. Non-human. Ethan wanted to run away, but his feet and mind seemed to have separate agendas.

"Hey, doll!" Jeff, or Jerry, or whatever, called out.

Ken turned around. He seemed quite surprised to see Ethan standing there. His blank stare suddenly turned into a bright grin. "Hey, little dude."

Ethan felt the heat of a thousand degrees crisp his face a brilliant crimson. "Hey," he said flatly.

"Haven't seen you in awhile," said Jeff, or Jerry, or whatever. "Got loads of new films in."

"I heard," said Ethan.

"So?" said Ken. "You're a videophile?"

"What?" asked Ethan.

"Maybe Jeff can tell me what you young kids watch," said Ken with a slight laugh.

"He's not typical," said Jeff. "Likes the art-house works."

"Such as?" Ken asked Ethan.

"*Menage, Edward II, The Last of England, Pretty Boy, Bette Blue*, you know..." Ethan answered.

"He's even rented Pasolini," said Jeff. "*Salo* even."

"That's pretty heavy," said Ken.

"He still hasn't checked out *Pink Narcissus*," said Jeff.

Ethan shrugged. "Maybe one day. When I've nothing better to do."

"Well," said Jeff with a capped-tooth smile, "looks like that day is today."

"Maybe I'm not really in the mood for a vid, today," said Ethan as he collected his calm and joined them. He looked directly at Ken. "So, what're you renting?"

"Nothing, today," said Ken as he stared into the boy's eyes, trying to read whether this was a coincidental meeting, or not. His sight drifted a bit for a fraction of a second, running a scan up and down the young man's form. Even with the baggy

flannel shirt and baggy pants, Ken could sense the boy was slight, but lean. Sort of a delicate hardness, like fine bone china.

Ethan swept his hair out of his face, wishing a customer would come along or something would happen that would drag Jeff back into his celluloid den. "Business slow?" he asked Jeff.

"So-so today," said Jeff. "Nice days like this, everyone heads out to the pool or to the beach to catch a few rays." He leered at Ethan. "A little sun would really be an extra asset on those cheeks of yours."

"Tanning makes you wrinkle faster as you get older," said Ethan.

Jeff's leer turned into a short-lived sneer. "Not if you tan properly."

"Well," said Ethan. "At least I don't have to worry about tan lines."

Ken let out a loud guffaw. Jeff seemed a bit irritated by the outburst. "You're a fine one to scoff, Captain Leatherface."

"I don't care about my wrinkles," said Ken.

"Natural wrinkles are less noticeable and more... attractive than smooth skin that looks like it was polyurethened," said Ethan.

"Come back and tell me that in twenty years, oh Prince of Youth," said Jeff. "No amount of shade's gonna keep that delicate skin of yours wrinkle-free."

"But I won't be worried about it," said Ethan.

Jeff laughed loudly. "Right. Come see me in twenty." He gave Ken a quick hug, then waved idiotically at Ethan. "I've got tapes to rewind."

"Bye, Jeff," said Ken.

"Bye," Ethan tagged.

Ken cocked an eyebrow at Ethan as he slowly began to walk on. "I think you might've hurt his feelings."

"He's a bit... much for me sometimes."

"He means well..." said Ken.

"Right," said Ethan sarcastically. "Like when it's just him and me in his store. He's always saying lewd shit to me, trying to get me to go into his office or the bathroom."

"He's lonely," said Ken.

"He's horny," Ethan said.

"That, too."

"He's as bad in some ways as Dean is."

"Dean?"

"Yeah... My friend with the cigarette business."

"Ah..."

"You live around here?" Ethan asked.

"Yeah..."

"By yourself?"

Ken's slow pace slowed even more. The kid's scamming, he thought. Even if he's not, he's too, too young. He didn't want a man-boy or boy-man or whatever they're called. "Do you live by yourself?" he asked Ethan.

"No," Ethan said with a slight laugh. "If my folks have their way, I'll be livin' at home 'til I'm forty."

"That's good," said Ken.

"Yeah... I know," said Ethan, a bit begrudgingly. "Most of my friends' parents are divorced an' shit like that. My mom sometimes says she thinks she'n my dad are genetic mutants 'cause they like being with each other."

"That's lucky. They're lucky," said Ken. "My folks divorced when I was thirty. They'd spent a lot of years disliking each other."

"That's too bad," said Ethan. "How old are you, anyhow?"

"Thirty-seven," said Ken. "Truly old enough to be your father."

"He's forty-one," said Ethan. "My sister's twenty-one. She's up at San Francisco State, studying physical therapy."

"What about you?"

"Me?"

"Yeah, you," said Ken. "Plans for college?"

"Dunno..." Ethan said.

"Not sure about what you want?"

"Dunno..." Ethan said again. "I wanna know a lot about a lot of things, but I'm not sure what I'd want to focus on. Doesn't seem like there's really a thing like a career to be had out there."

Ken stopped at the walkway of an old quadraplex. He was home. He was home with this tag-along boy in tow. He wasn't sure what to say or do as he'd never found himself in a situation quite like this. "Well, you've walked me home."

"What do you do for a living?"

"Landscape architect," said Ken. "Not a lofty profession, but it's generally enjoyable."

"So, you must have lots of plants?"

"Not a one," Ken said.

"Bullshit," said Ethan.

"Believe what you want."

"Show me." Ethan was surprised by his own brashness. He felt that icy lead sensation weighing down in his gut as his cock flushed alive with a surge of coursing blood.

Ken was at odds with himself. His mind kept saying to politely dismiss the young man and head inside. His crotch, though, had a mind of its own that was slowly eroding his logical mind. He smiled nervously, then led on.

As they went up the stairs to Ken's second floor unit, Ethan felt trickles of sweat stream from his underarms and down his side. The low din of his pounding heart sounded like ocean waves slapping at a rocky shore in his mind. He wondered if Ken could sense his nervousness.

He let a throaty giggle slip as Ken escorted him into the living room. Ethan had expected to see something either orderly and masculine, or a surfer's pad, consisting of ratty, disposable furniture with beer bottles and empty pizza cartons all around. But Ken's living room was neither. It was just different. Two of the main walls were painted a deep, navy blue. Two other walls were a very dark red. Each stick of furniture was somewhat unique - each standing out and commanding attention. Stained oak antiques, some heavy pieces of golden-hued teak, a deep green and cream-colored oriental rug. A hodge-podge of paintings and framed pictures were unevenly spaced on the walls. While the room was a bit cluttered, it all seemed to work well together, making Ethan feel at home. And, there were no plants.

"Well?" Ken said.

"I like it."

"It's a bit of a mix, but everything has a history, for me at least. I like having it all around me," Ken said. "I can sort of pinpoint times in my life by looking at that chair, or that ashtray, or that lamp."

"I haven't got a history," Ethan said.

"Not a full one yet," said Ken. "But that comes with time."

"Time goes slowly," said Ethan.

"Doesn't when you're older."

"So I've heard."

"Want something to drink?"

"Sure," said Ethan. "Got any diet stuff?"

"Cola," said Ken as he led Ethan into the dining room then kitchen. "And cranberry juice, bottled water, coffee, tea, and milk. Non-fat, though."

"Blue milk," said Ethan.

"Blue?"

"Looks kind of blue to me."

"Like chalky rinse water," said Ken. "Tastes about the same." He handed Ethan a can of diet cola, then poured himself a glass of bottled water.

"Thanks," said Ethan.

"So? Is it what you expected?"

Ethan shook his head as he forced down the fizzing drink. "Kinda expected something more gay, ya know?"

"Gay?"

"Everything sort of matching like some designer showroom."

"Never did like that look," said Ken. "If you're gonna live in a house, or whatever, you should live in it, not keep it on display."

Ethan stepped into an adjacent hallway. "Bathroom down there?"

"End of the hall," said Ken. "I even have a small service porch. More of a closet, really, but it holds a double stack washer and dryer and all the housecleaning tools."

Ethan nodded and headed down the hall to the bathroom. As he stepped inside and flipped up the lid and seat of the commode, he debated whether he should shut the door or not. He decided not to as he loosened his fly and let his swollen prick fly free. As he took a finger-hold of his cock, he felt that bristling wave of static energy rip through him. The kind of brilliant wave that he got as he came close to cumming. The harder he focused on peeing, the harder it became to force his urine out through his rigid prick. The titillation he felt about his exhibitionism was quelled by his need to piss.

He tucked himself back into his pants, shut the door

completely, then slipped his pants down again, turned on the faucet and sat down on the toilet seat, letting his mind go blank and leaving his dick tucked down between his thighs, pointed toward the water in the bowl. After what seemed like forever, his cock relaxed a bit. A steady stream of urine flowed from his bladder, the relief almost orgasmic.

Ken didn't want to intrude on Ethan, so he busied himself in the kitchen making a pot of coffee. He heard the pipe rumbling slwoooooosh of the flushing commode. In an instant, Ethan was back in the kitchen.

"I'm making some coffee," Ken said. "You want some?"

"Sure. Thanks."

Ken pulled out a chair at the small dinette, then set an ashtray, lighter and an open pack of cigarettes on the table. "Have a seat," he said. "How do you take your coffee?"

"Black," said Ethan. "Cream'n sugar tastes better but it makes me queasy." He started to sit, then stopped and removed his flannel shirt, draping it over the back of the chair. As he sat, he swept his hair back out of his face again.

While Ethan's gesture was innocuous, Ken couldn't help but look. The pale, slender arm tugged the wide, over-sized sleeve up, allowing Ken a glimpse of flesh. Smooth, tight flesh. A cocoa-colored nipple peeked out briefly. Ken restrained a rising sigh. Such a beautiful young man, he thought. He removed the coffeepot from the burner and slipped a mug in its place. Hurry this coffee klatsch along, he thought, before he did or said something he might later regret.

"Have you always been a landscaper?" Ethan asked.

"No," said Ken. He slipped the first mug from the burner and set another in its place. He set the filled mug down on the table. As he turned, Ethan hooked his finger beneath Ken's belt buckle stopping him.

"I like your belt," Ethan said as his finger tip traced the worn brass.

"It's older than you are," said Ken as he gently pulled away to trade out the coffee pot for the mug on the burner.

"What're you? A thirty-two waist?" Ethan asked.

"Thirty-three," said Ken. "You work in retail?"

"No. My sister does. Besides, the label on your jeans says thirty-two."

"Cotton stretches," said Ken as he leaned against the counter, sipping his coffee.

"You have a lover?"

"No," said Ken. "Most men my age are busy looking for someone buffer or... different."

"Younger, you mean."

"That, too," said Ken as he snagged a cigarette from his pocket and lit it.

"I get lots of older guys hitting on me," said Ethan.

"You're comfortable with that?"

Ethan shrugged. "What's comfortable?"

"I don't know," said Ken. "Back in my day, when I was your age, I probably freaked about it."

"Older guys hit on you?"

Ken had to think about that a moment. Did they hit on him, or did he hit on them? He really wasn't sure. What he did remember was that many of the ones he wanted were either closeted or straight. "It was just a different time," he said. "Sexuality was exploding and expanding all over, yet there was a lot of the old thinking and taboos to keep us a bit scared."

"It's still scary," said Ethan.

"You're gay?"

Ethan just nodded. "I guess I'm still not comfortable with it, though. Don't talk about it with my friends. Much, anyhow."

"That's not uncommon," said Ken.

"What kind of guys do you like?" Ethan asked.

"Average guys," said Ken. "I like directness. Guys who like being guys and not girls."

"Me, too," said Ethan.

"What about you?"

"I like men. Like you," Ethan said directly, though he felt his whole body flush an embarrassing red.

Ken's stomach fell into his crotch. His cock immediately swelled. He felt himself blush as vividly as Ethan had. "Well," he stammered. "I might be a lousy lay," he quipped.

"I wouldn't know," said Ethan.

Ken shifted a bit, then set down his coffee mug. "Excuse me a second," he said. "Gotta use the head."

Ethan's heart pounded with anxiousness. Hot-cold sweat trickled down his sides again as his straining dick shifted itself

uncomfortably in his shorts. He wasn't sure what to do. He wasn't sure whether Ken's response was good or bad, whether he'd just made a fool out of himself or not.

His mind raced ahead so fast that he acted without thinking. He pulled off his T-shirt and wiped away the sweat. The coolness of the air pinched his nipples erect. A wave of goose bumps swept over his torso and back, making his tits sting. He suddenly felt awkward and scrawny. He heard the toilet flush, the waste water rushing through echoing pipes. Panic overtook him. He grabbed his flannel shirt and threw it back on.

As he tugged at the tails, Ken returned. Ethan busied himself, re-rolling his sleeves. "Your bladder feel better?" he asked.

"Better?" Ken repeated as he stared blankly at the exposed expanse of flesh framed by the panels of the flannel. Smooth, pinkish pale skin was stretched taut over the youth's slender body. His chest was deceptively wide, with just the tracing of pectoral definition. A slight trail of fine brown hair led from his navel to a region hidden by baggy, cotton cloth. Ken's throat was suddenly dry, though a flood of saliva washed through his mouth. He swallowed hard. "Yes," he said. "Better. Thanks."

Ethan could feel Ken's intent gaze. His erection strained painfully. His legs tingled with a sudden numbness forcing him to almost fall back onto the seat of the chair. As he clumsily steadied himself, he jostled the table, sloshing coffee from the disturbed mug. Without thinking, he grabbed the mug with one hand and slapped his T-shirt down on the spilled liquid. He froze rather awkwardly, realizing he'd just used his T-shirt as a rag.

"Shit," he muttered.

Ken took the soaked shirt from him as he quickly wiped up the rest of the mess with a dishtowel. He immediately pitched both shirt and towel into the sink and filled the basin with cold water.

"It'll be all right," Ken said. "A quick wash in cold bleach water should take the stain out."

"God, I can't believe I just did that," said Ethan.

"I've got other T-shirts, if you need one," said Ken.

"I'm such a fuckin' boner, sometimes."

"It's only a T-shirt," Ken said. "Let it soak for a few

minutes."

Ethan parked himself in the chair. He lit a cigarette, then rested his elbows on his knees as he let the nicotine steam out in a forceful stream. "I'm sorry."

"Nothing to be sorry about."

Ethan sighed. "I guess I just get nervous..." he started. He censored himself with another drag from the cigarette. He caught sight of a small puddle of coffee on the floor. "Got another rag?" He nodded to the wet spot.

Ken tore some paper towels off a roll, then kneeled down to blot it up. As he wiped the floor, Ethan impulsively laid a gentle hand on the back of Ken's head, stroking the silky, thick, shaggy hair. Ken froze. Ethan's fingers burrowed into the blond softness. Ken steadied himself on outstretched arms, succumbing to the pleasant massage of his scalp, then neck. He sighed almost inaudibly as he turned his head slowly to feel Ethan's stationary palm against his cheek, then lips.

The feel of Ken's breath upon his hand sent another wave of goose bumps rising over Ethan's body. His entire form trembled slightly with that tingle of excitement. The cigarette found its fire killed in a cup of cooling, black liquid as his smoky hand joined the other, cupping Ken's cheeks, feeling the soft, yet bristly sensation of new whiskers glazing his face.

Ken's eyes slowly pulled away from the soft, warm palms and followed a path to Ethan's eyes. So clear. So bright, yet soulful. Youthful. It scared him. Excited him. Seeing in Ethan the reflection of himself so many years back when he was young and wanting. Wanting a man. Now he was the man and here was the lad who wanted him.

Ethan slid from the chair onto the floor with Ken. His fingers slipped around Ken's chin, then snaked through his hair as he drew him close. Wanting to taste his mouth, to feel the roughness of whiskers scrap against his own chin, his cheeks. His soft, full lips pressed against Ken's. His tongue pressed through into Ken's mouth, finding its eager mate.

Gentle exploration turned rough as hunger fueled greedy feasting. Ken's hands clamped down hard-on the sides of Ethan's head, grabbing fistfuls of thick brown hair as soft as eiderdown. Ethan's arms slipped down awkwardly to wrap around Ken. Excited hands slid all around Ken's broad

shoulders and back. The heels of young palms kneading his muscles.

Ken instinctively balanced himself, then rose up easily, holding earnestly onto Ethan's slim body, picking him up. Their lips parted. Ethan smiled, then folded himself over Ken, hugging him hard. Ken's arm swept down beneath Ethan's rear, holding him fast.

"I want you," Ethan whispered.

Ken just closed his eyes and pressed all of the young man against him. He could feel Ethan's heart beating in time with his own. His lips bit down on a small patch of white shoulder flesh. Ken's tongue slowly licked up the lad's neck to his ear. He felt a tremble surge through Ethan.

Without another word, he carried Ethan down the hallway into his bedroom. The tangle of sheets on the unmade bed made it that much more inviting. As he kneeled onto the mattress and laid Ethan down, the old box springs creaked. Ethan started to snicker.

"It's the bed. Not my back," Ken said with a laugh.

"I like your back," Ethan said as his fingers unbuttoned Ken's shirt.

Ken hovered over Ethan, nuzzling the youth's neck, then shoulder as Ethan finished loosening Ken's shirt, pulling the tails out from his pants. Ethan's hands pressed against Ken's wide, solid chest, then ran over the broad, meaty pecs. Hair as soft as corn silk held a lingering scent of Ivory clean and smoky green - outdoor green - woodsy... husky... Pale tan nipples pinched oblong over the cut of the muscles. Ethan pressed his face into Ken, inhaling the smell of him, relishing the heat, the softness of flesh and the firmness of muscle below. His whole body tingled violently as Ken's warm, damp tongue slowly traced a trail over his collar bone, then down, into his underarm.

Ethan's hands slipped up beneath the opened shirt. His arms wrapped around Ken. He wanted to feel the strength of this man's back. His broad shoulders. The subtle sloping curve that dipped down, then rose again beneath the cotton of cloth to meaty buttocks, full and round and pliant. Blind fingers found the deep crevice between ass cheeks. A sweaty, slick sensation of fuzzy warmth.

Ken growled low as he shoved his face into Ethan's armpit, as his hips rose up off the youth's crotch. He pulled the exploring fingers from the crack of his ass, up above the lad's head, exposing the downy bush of dampness, greedily lapping up the heady scented wetness. Ethan squirmed, releasing a pleasurable gasp. Ken took hold of the boy's other arm and pushed it up, beyond his head, then feasted on his young man's other savory pit.

Ethan writhed as each sweep of Ken's tongue washed away his apprehension. His fears. He wanted to lose himself, to feel the totality of this new sensuality. His need to give all of himself, his desire to please his new-found man, gave each portion of his anatomy a mind of its own. His head bobbed up, his lips parted to unleash a wanting tongue, wanting to again taste this man's hot mouth, while his legs wound around his man's thighs, squeezing them tightly.

Ken caught the glimmer of desire, of love-starved lust, in the youth's eyes. Ethan's soft lips beckoned his own. Ken's arms slipped beneath his boy's back. He drew him up to press the young man's slim chest against his own. Four hands spoke the same silent signs as two, then two slipped shirts from their forms.

Ethan marveled at the solidness of his new man's torso. Eager hands slowly explored the fine, pale brown hair, as soft as talcum, that insulated Ken's chest, that blazed a delicate trail down his abdomen, then slowly spread east and west below the shadowy indentation of his navel. The road map of the Y chromosome led Ethan's fingers on a random course, feeling the hard stomach, kneading the slight rise of love-handles that Ethan immediately loved. Innocuous grips of security, of stability, of comfort for him. He wrapped his arms low around Ken's waist and hugged him hard as he pressed his face into the crook between his man's shoulder and arm, breathing in deep into his lungs, into his core, the scent that belonged to this new man.

Ken leaned into Ethan. He eased his young lad back down onto the mattress, then slipped down and removed the youth's shoes while he blindly kicked off his own. Then he peeled away his socks, then his jeans. His thick, rigid cock and heavy balls strained against the dark blue cloth of cotton briefs.

Now Ken slowly removed Ethan's socks, then gently massaged the lad's warm, moist feet until all residual tension in the young man's body melted away like butter on freshly made toast. Ethan started to unfasten his pants, but Ken stopped him.

"I'll do it," he said.

Ethan submitted, lying back flat on the bed. He closed his eyes as he felt Ken unfasten his pants, unzip his zipper, then slowly slip his trousers down, also peeling away in the process his last, remaining boundary - his underwear. Though he could feel his own erection slap up against his belly, his fear crept back into his mind, whispering that his body, was so slight and boyish that his new man would reject him. But Ken's touch didn't stray away. Ethan felt his foot being manipulated again by strong, firm fingers. He felt his bare sole being pressed against the cotton pouch of his man's crotch, full of beefy hard cock and full scrotum. Ethan's toes reflexively manipulated his man's full genitals, while his man's fingers and palms plied the flesh of his calves, then thighs.

"I want to feel you on me," Ethan whispered.

Ken slipped up atop his lad, blanketing him gingerly, keeping the bulk of his weight supported upon bent elbows. "You've such incredible eyes," Ken said. "I could easily cum just staring into them."

"Lie on me," Ethan said softly. "All of your weight."

"I might crush you," Ken said with a smile. "That wouldn't do either of us any good."

"I want to feel all of your weight on me," Ethan whispered. "Please..." Ken slowly eased himself down until his body covered Ethan's, pressing the youth's form deep into the bed. Ethan wrapped his legs, his arms, tightly around Ken. His mind reeled under the crush, as if the pressure alone was an intoxicant. Again Ethan's fingers made their way down Ken's back, beneath the waistband of the briefs, then into the clammy, deep crack of his full, full ass, probing the depths until a fingertip traced over the furry, puckered opening of his hole. Ken shivered slightly and groaned as his ravenous need fused his lips to Ethan's. As their snaking tongues entwined, coaxing their mouths to secrete warm wetness, Ethan's finger slipped into his man's asshole, exploring its tight, hot depths. Ken's

hips slowly gyrated, grinding his crotch into his young man.

He felt Ethan's finger slip out of him as they broke their kiss. He licked Ethan's nose, then sucked it gently. Ethan's manipulative finger, sweet with the faint scent of its exploration, pressed against his lips. Ken pulled slightly away to gaze at Ethan's beautiful face. The young man smiled, then wrapped his lips around his probing tool and sucked it slowly. Ken took hold of Ethan's hand and eased that digit from the youth's mouth then swallowed it whole himself.

As he finally let Ethan's finger slip from between his lips, Ken slid down the lad's body, letting his tongue leave a glistening trail of slick saliva upon his young man's chest, then stomach, then groin. Ken nuzzled Ethan's crotch, allowing his eyes to feast on the youth's sleek cylinder of maleness. He had a beautiful erection, Ken thought. His boy's prick was slender and long, pink with the glow of eager youthfulness, and left whole from birth. A delicate lip of foreskin wrapped gently around the head, almost as if protecting it. The swelling glans throbbed slightly as a drop of precum oozed from the slit. Ken stared at the dewy drop for the longest time, then his tongue reached out connecting with the sticky wetness, and lapped it up with a single flick.

Ethan shuddered. The head of his cock was sensitive. The feel of Ken's tongue brushing over it almost sent his balls reeling and a load of thick, steaming wetness shooting through the chamber of his rod. His fingers combed through Ken's shaggy hair, easing him back.

"You okay?" Ken whispered.

"Very," said Ethan. "It's just... New."

New, Ken thought. He liked the sound of that. New. Virginal. Though he didn't think that his young man was all that new to this. If he was, then his instincts were all on target. Ken slipped himself between the boy's legs, easing them apart. His dexterous tongue lifted the soft glans into his mouth and Ken swallowed his lad whole. Ethan's long shaft seemed to strain and stretch even longer, pushing itself all they way down into the hot, tight throat.

Ethan's whole body tensed suddenly. His legs wrapped around Ken with a vise-like strength as his torso arched forward and his hands slammed Ken's head deep into his

crotch. With a guttural groan, Ethan's abdomen contracted tightly and he lost control.

Ken felt globs of thick, scalding cum jet down his throat. His head started bobbing furiously as his lips and mouth began pumping the lad's cock to suck every last gram of Ethan's syrupy juice out. Saliva flowed freely, warm and sticky, almost lathering the youth's genitals. Ken wanted to drink down all of this boy, yet he wanted to keep his young man hard and alert. He wouldn't allow Ethan's cock to deflate.

Ethan had never shot a load with such intensity before. Nor had his cock stayed rigid after cumming. But, he was still hard. Painfully hard - as if every atom in his member was straining to explode. He felt tears well up in his eyes. Tears born of this new sensation. His cock felt right and happy with its new sheath - Ken's throat - Ken's entirety. Hot and wet gave way to clammy and cool as his erection slipped from Ken's mouth.

"Geez, fuck," Ethan sighed. "I'm sorry..."

"For what?"

"Coming in your mouth like that," Ethan said. "I shouldn't have."

"I allowed it," Ken said. "It's all right."

"I don't have anything," Ethan began to add, "like, you know..."

"I didn't think so," said Ken as he drew himself up onto his knees and hoisted Ethan's legs up over his shoulders. His face pressed down into the crook between the young man's splayed thighs, and he slowly bathed his boy's scrotum, nibbling and suckling the delicate testicles tucked away in the fleshy flesh sac. His large, thick hands plied the small, square buns, kneading the tissue. His nose slid down a bit, inhaling the heady sweetness of his boy's small, rosette hole. His tongue found the puckered patch to be as tight as a new button-hole. His lips pressed around the lad's sphincter, kissing it, sucking it lightly, while his tongue painted delicate swirls of solvent spit over the tiny ridges of flesh.

Ethan's entire body turned to jelly, all lickerish and submission and dough, wanting to be molded, to be formed by this man - his man. He felt the rush of escaping tension all around his groin, all around his ass. His tight asshole relaxed to allow Ken's tongue entry into him. All the way in, he

thought as he felt Ken drilling deep in him.

Ethan shifted slightly, his head lolling from side to side, the tangle of long hair curtaining his sweet young face. Ken could sense his lad floundering. Wanting. As he ate out his boy's ass, he grabbed hold of his young cock, swollen and red, straining again with the sting of impending release. He pumped his lad's dick with deliberate, firm strokes that built in momentum until his motion was rapid and he could hear the slapping-whip of the boy's prick flesh. Ethan's breathing become deep, rushed and labored with sporadic grunts. Spurts of watery jism sprayed up, splattering on him. On his hair. On his face. On his hand like a live lava flow. Ken's mouth instantly moved to feed on the sweet, young cum, cleaning away every last trace.

Ethan's legs slowly slid from their perch atop Ken's shoulders as Ethan's arms reached up. He pulled Ken back down onto him again, his own soft lips and wet tongue eager to taste himself in the mouth of his man. He kissed Ken voraciously. A complete feeding frenzy. His tongue scoured his man's mouth completely, then lapped up residual drips of his own cum from his man's face, his hair. His arm slid down between their bodies. His hand slipped between their groins. His fingers took hold of Ken's huge, burning rod and he guided the massive head down between his thighs to his spit-slickered hole.

He felt another rush of static, electricity rush through him as he shifted his hips and pushed himself down onto his man's swollen, burning cockhead. It hurt for an instant. A sharp, stabbing pain.

"Ethan..." Ken whispered. "Don't..."

"I want it," Ethan said softly. "I want you... Want to feel you in me."

"Slowly..." Ken said. "Very slowly... Breathe slowly. Deep, deep breaths. Relax..." He kissed his young man again and again as he lifted himself up slightly. A free hand gently massaged the soft of Ethan's groin area, his hips, his lower abdomen. He felt the biting tightness of Ethan's sphincter relax its grip on his glans. He eased his shaft into his lad with very deliberate care, stopping completely when he saw Ethan wince even the slightest. They continued to kiss, to feel their forms, as Ken slowly made his entry until he was finally in. All the way in. "Just relax your ass for a moment."

Ethan felt as if he was being stuffed. But he liked it. It seemed like Ken's cock was all the way up into his stomach. He took slow breaths as Ken had said to do until his lower region was completely at peace. He clamped his ass hard around his man's prick. A dull pain shot through him.

Ken immediately withdrew himself. "You all right?"

"God, you feel good in there," Ethan said with a smile. They kissed again.

"You wanna fuck me?" Ken asked.

"I've never... ya know?" Ethan said.

Ken smiled. "I know..." he said as he lowered himself down into Ethan's groin, nuzzling his sticky, sweet meat. Ken's tongue probed beneath the juicy prepuce protecting the lad's glans. His lips wrapped around the tip of Ethan's cock and he sucked the plump head into his mouth.

Ethan shuddered. It was as if he'd inserted his cock into the meat of a warmed melon. He felt himself expand and stretch in the slick, moist chamber that was Ken's mouth. His nuts went taut, drawing up into him as he felt them churning, already ready to expel another load of his milky liquid. His arms swept down to gently cup his man's cheeks as his limber torso rose up and folded softly over this man who made him feel so good. His groan was almost a purr.

As Ken slowly eased himself up, Ethan rose like a willowy branch lifted by the wind. Ken wrapped his hard, thick arms around his boy's lean trunk and squeezed him hard. He wanted his young man's imprint fused to him like a brand. He realized then that he was branded. He wanted to wear Ethan's mark.

Gravity and inclinations lowered them back down onto the bed. Ethan stared up into Ken's eyes, reading his thoughts; hoping that Ken could read his as well. He felt Ken's sturdy, hard thighs slip over his own. Ken cradled him with a bent arm as he leaned in to kiss him. Watery lips and starving teeth and probing tongues melted together as he felt Ken's large, rough hand sweetly grip his rigid cock. Within a moment, he felt the tight, tight pressure bite down gently on the head of his cock, then slowly engulf his entire shaft as Ken lowered himself onto him. Then into him. All the way in. Ethan felt ligh- headed with a euphoria he'd never before experienced. As Ken slid up and down his length, Ethan's heels dug deep into the mattress,

his knees tented stiffly and his hips began to instinctively buck, thrusting his prick deep into his man's tight, warm ass.

Ken scooped his arms beneath Ethan and swiftly rolled the two of them over. He wanted to let his boy bottom him out - completely. Primal instincts overtook Ethan. His hips bucked furiously, pounding Ken's fleshy ass with accelerating momentum.

Ken devoured Ethan, his greed and need fueled by the slap - slap - slapping sounds of hips blasting his spread buttocks as his own cock rubbed vigorously against his youth's stomach, pumping his shaft inadvertently.

Ethan suddenly pried his face from Ken's as bracing arms shot his torso up and he gasped loudly as he slammed himself into Ken to climax.

Ken grabbed his own cock and yanked it once. His balls erupted. Thick spurts of creamy, steamy jism spat from his prick, splattering over Ethan's stomach, over his own chest. Ethan suddenly collapsed on him, melting like sun-softened ice cream all over him. An arm cupped the youth's rear, holding him, holding his spent member inside him.

Ethan felt Ken's other arm clamp down about his shoulders, hugging him. He knew that he wanted to know this man better. He knew he wouldn't be returning to run with his friends on the street. He knew he had a purpose here. He knew he wanted to love this man.

BETWEEN HIS THIGHS

John Patrick

An hour ago I was rocking between Doug's thighs spread wide and now he flies away on a jet, his ears plugging up with a dull thrum. Beneath him, I am driving home with the top down, punching the buttons on the radio.

"Do you have to go?" I asked as he finished packing his suitcase.

"Yes."

"I wish you could stay."

"I'll be back."

"It's been fun, this weekend. I'm so glad your flight was cancelled."

"And your's arrived on time."

He put down his suitcase and came over to the bed. "Come on. You gonna take me to the airport or not?"

"If I can fuck it one last time."

He grimaced. "Hey, I just showered. I'm all dressed. I'll miss my plane."

I reached up, unzipped his pants and, as I dragged it out, it grew hard in my hand. I settled for sucking it again. It was a splendid cock, one of the nicest I'd seen in years. A full eight inches at least, cut, with a nice sucking head. I moved my hand back and forth over it as I sucked, getting the rhythm going that I had found pleased him.

When he first saw the pool, he had to dive. He was straightforward and undramatic about stepping into his dive. The board seemed to bend in two under his muscular weight and then to fling him toward the blue sky. He attempted a forward two-and-a-half, tuck position, but failed to untuck completely before entering the water. In a moment he was hoisting himself out and heading for the board to try again. All the pieces seem to fit together perfectly. And he really was a good diver.

When he came over, dripping and fit, toweling his hair and shoulders with my huge lavender towel, his smile seemed very

white, his skin very rosy, and his presence rather welcome. He was pleased with the dives he had accomplished and my obvious admiration. He was remarkably well-made, with goldenskin, lit by the late-afternoon sun, defined muscles swelling over slender bones, a cloud of dark hair. He was so beautiful that you could not help attributing to him all of your favorite virtues. I had remarked about his beauty, and it seemed to him a senseless thing, as if it had gained him nothing in the way of kinship, or real intimacy. Oh, there had been many passionate moments, to be sure, but he said he never remembered any of the men, *really* remembered them.

He was shy. I pulled his bikini down and just swallowed it. It took awhile, he was still dubious of me, a so-called "therapist" who picked him up in the lounge at the airport. I had just returned from Chicago, a week with the folks for Thanksgiving. I was horny as hell, and I'm afraid I felt like rushing things.

When I returned to the house, he went out to the pool while I walked around throwing open the windows. I had always done that. Even as a boy returning home from college, first thing I would open all of their windows. "Get some fresh air in the place," I muttered, wondering if my vengeance frightened them. How could they know how much I hated being closed up? I think my mother knew. One time she said to me, "I feel like if I ever started crying, I would never stop. If I ever started running, I would never come back." Poor woman, she did neither. She lived her life on the verge of tears, on the edge of running away.

I believe that when we begin to accept things that we do not agree with, it is the beginning of the end. I would prefer to do without than to accept anything less than what I wanted. That's why I spent a week in the Windy City without a single fuck. I had several opportunities but, after awhile, my heart wasn't in it. I felt cross and tired, bought a lot of clothes I couldn't afford at Marshall Field's and knew I wouldn't need when I finally went home. On the plane, I felt temporarily safe, suspended between decisions, strung between states. I was invisible, and I could do anything. I breathed in deeply, savoring the feeling.

After I landed, heading towards the baggage claim, I spotted him. He was sitting in at a little round table in the bar, smoking

a cigarette, a full drink in front of him. He was exactly my type: smartly-dressed, too pretty to be a man and undoubtedly well aware of it, probably approached more times than he could count by predators like me. The place was jammed. Heavy snows had caused all flights to the Northeast to be cancelled or interminably delayed. I went into the lounge, got a drink, stood beside his table for a moment, long enough for him to notice me, and then I asked him if the seat next to him was taken. "No," he said. His brown eyes met mine and he smiled; I knew I was halfway home.

He told me he had a rotten time in Florida. It rained and was overcast most of the seven days he was vacationing. It was his first time on Longboat Key and he was shocked at the prices. He was a computer programmer and travelled a lot but he'd never seen prices like those anywhere. "It's season," I told him. "Come back in September or October. Everything's half off."

"Everything?"

"Yes, even therapy," I answered. I told him I was a massage therapist, which seemed to fascinate him. I had gotten into massage after I had wrenched my shoulder lifting weights. It was natural for me to take up Swedish massage since my mother was part Swedish and I was named Sven, although I am known by my friends as Steve. The description in my ads: "Blond hair, blue eyes, athletic build," keeps my answering machine constantly busy, especially during season.

"How much does this therapy cost?" Doug asked.

"Depends on what the client needs."

He nodded. "What do most clients need?"

"To be touched."

He smiled and finished his drink. It was obvious he was stranded and didn't want to go back to Longboat Key. The airline was putting him up across the street.

"Terrible place," I said, finishing my own drink. "There was someone murdered there a few weeks ago."

"Got any suggestions?" he asked, his knee pressing against mine.

I am sick of these clothes, I want to get home, jump in the pool. I try not to think of Doug, at the shallow end of the pool,

the sweet smell of his cock as it hardened and how I went down on it. When he came it was as if he hadn't come once during his whole vacation.

After our swim and his blowjob, we dressed for dinner. I sensed our time filling up with possibilities of things we could do together. He told me my therapy was wonderful and wondered what more I did. "Later," I said. He wanted to treat me to dinner on his American Express card; that was only fair, he said, so I picked a little Italian place where the most expensive entree is $8.95. We had a bottle of wine that cost $12. Then he ordered another bottle. Since he was nearly drunk by the time we left, my getting him into bed was an easy matter: he simply fell onto it. I removed his clothes, piece by piece, kissing, licking, nibbling on each body part as I went along. By the time I got to the cock, it was semi-hard and dripping precum. But I left it alone. I wanted to find out just how far I could go with him. He told me he hadn't been active for long; he thought he should get married and almost did. His gay experience was limited and he didn't even go to the bars while he was staying on Longboat Key. I have found nearly all of my married clients have a penchant for getting butt-fucked and I quickly found this was what Doug wanted more than anything. I did no more massaging, I was too horny for that. I got nude and then slid between his thighs. He had not even seen my cock at this point and when I greased him and pushed apart his thighs, he opened his eyes and raised his head. "Oh, God, I'm not going to be able to take that."

"Oh yes you are," I said, as I slid the head in, paused, then lowered myself over him fully. I kissed him full on the mouth as my cock went all the way in. He bit my tongue, but his hands moved to my ass and held it as I began. When my mouth left his, he began gasping, pleading for me to take it slow. I knew he was hurting, but he wanted it; it was what he'd been waiting all week for.

The next day he told me, "There was a young guy at the hotel who brought me breakfast a couple of mornings. I thought I might see him some other time but I never did."

"I bet you find something nice in every city you visit."

"Sometimes. But always in a crazy way, like the way we

met, just by chance."

"You don't go to bars in all those places you visit?"

"Sometimes, but most of the time, by the time I finish work, I just can't get excited about going out partying."

But partying is what we did, if you can call it that in my sleepy little town. We have only three bars and the crowds are usually dull, and that night was no exception. After staying in the last bar only ten minutes, Doug said, "I'm glad I've seen them but I know a place where they give a great massage, at least that's what they tell me."

I realized I hadn't given him the full treatment, just the first blowjob, the fuck, and then another blowjob earlier that day when he finished his diving. "Well, I guess it's about time."

I drive carefully, checking the rearview mirror, listening to the radio, remembering his name, his address, even his phone number.

We had not drunk much in the bars and Doug was sober and eager. After having an orgasm earlier in the pool he was in no rush; he was willing to put himself at my mercy. But I wanted him a bit more ready than he obviously was. When we returned to the house, he went directly to the bedroom, stripped and jumped in bed. I took my time in the bathroom and when I finally emerged, wrapped in my robe, he had rolled over on his side and was dozing. I pushed him all the way over and climbed on him. After pouring a little rose oil into my palm and rubbing my fingers together, I began making love to his taut young body. I stroked his muscles, listening for tightness, slowly penetrating the places where I found it. At one point, he said, "Oh, that's great, right there." I stayed there, in the small of his back, for awhile before moving on to the firm, slender buttocks.

Before long, my oily fingers probed his anus, readying him. He murmured as I inserted one, then two fingers, lightly screwing him. He lifted up, begged me to go deeper, but I left him like that to massage his legs and feet. He moaned repeatedly as I spent extra time on his feet. After several minutes of stroking, rubbing, kneading, pressing and vibrating, I rolled him over. His erection was inviting, oozing precum

again, but I by-passed it, placing my thumbs between his eyebrows and pressing, drawing my thumbs across his skin until I reached his ears. As I stretched his ears upward, I contorted his face into a smile, and then I kissed him. A long breathy sigh came from his lips. "Oh, fuck me."

My mouth crushed down on his, my tongue slipping inside easily, exploring, thrusting, then teasing and tasting. I reached out and brushed both palms against his manly chest, covered with a light carpet of hair, feeling the thud of his heart beneath them. His eyes widened in amazement as my practiced hands twisted his nipples until they were aching and taut. Suddenly, I drew away and shrugged out of my robe, dropping it casually to the floor. He squirmed beneath me, trying to bring his ass to meet my now throbbing cock.

I went from one nipple to the other, in no apparent rush as one hand caressed the tip of one unoccupied pec while my tongue worked the other.

"Oh, please, fuck me," he pleaded. "Fuck me!"

My hands were on his thighs now, stroking them lightly. My fingers inched closer to his erection, but not quite touching it. He thrust his pelvis toward me and moaned.

In a low rumble, vibrating against him, I murmured, "What a cock," and I opened my mouth and took him in, swirling my tongue around his shaft. I moved slowly, tantalizingly, taking it in and out of my mouth. My hands worked his cock, moving the wetness of my saliva up and down as he began easing in and out of my mouth. He flinched again as I took over again, working my magic. At the same time, I thrust two fingers into him, moving in and out slowly and expertly. He began to shudder, climaxing in warm gushing waves.

I got up onto my knees and brought my lips down to him. When I began to nuzzle him, he gave a slight shudder and pushed himself against me impatiently. His breathing quickened and finally I rolled him over and gently, pushed him down onto his stomach. With my hands, I maneuvered him up on his knees. My rigid length brushed against his buttocks and he gasped. First my fingers slid in again. He rocked against them, wanting it all.

Slowly, I pressed myself into him, thrusting gradually until I was in to the hilt. A wave of uncontrollable desire raced

through me as he ground himself against me, clenching his hands into the sheets.

"Oh, yes!"

I began to thrust in and out slowly.

"Faster," he murmured. "Please, faster. Oh, god!"

My rhythm began to pick up. My hands slid to his now fully erect cock, pressing and squeezing. I slapped against him, hard and fast, my breath coming in gasping heaves. He moaned as the heat built up inside him, coming closer and closer with each thrust. And then, as I was pumping into him as hard as I could, he came again. It was even more powerful than the one I'd brought him to with my tongue. Growling, I gave one more powerful thrust and collapsed against him, shuddering.

After a moment, I rolled over on my side, bringing him with me. He nestled against me, spoon-fashion. Our eyes closed. We slept peacefully till dawn.

Yes, we climbed to the heights that second night. It is the fuck I will remember most. Doug was funny; he said it wasn't natural the earth should tremble so. And I believed that he too thought certain dreams last longer than a night.

Now, remembering those two glorious days between Doug's thighs, I reach my turn-off on the highway – and drive right by.

FIRST PORN

Peter Reardon

"I have a favor to ask you," said the familiar voice on the other end of the telephone. "But I can't talk about it over the phone. I'll pick you up at your place. Can you be ready in twenty minutes? I need to show you what I want done..." The voice lowered to a whisper, " ...Or more precisely *who* I want done."

The urgency in the voice of my old friend Dixon Lish intrigued me. He gave me no clue as to what the favor was, but I told him to come over anyway. I knew it had to involve some gorgeous young thing. I knew Dixon too well to think it could be about anything else. He was obsessed with male youth and beauty and his considerable wealth had given him the leisure time and the resources to pursue it full-time. Dixon had inherited a chain of luxury hotels and apartment buildings along the strip in Fort Lauderdale. These provided him a disposable income of over a million dollars a year and the use of a two-story penthouse on top of the most exclusive oceanside condo. It was at the penthouse that I first met him in 1975. I was 18 and the new kid in town, just beginning my first term at the Art Institute of Ft. Lauderdale and I was thrilled to be invited to one of his infamous parties. Jimmy, the skinny, good-looking kid from school who invited me promised there would be plenty of drugs and drinks and beautiful people. Jimmy said our host was interested in new talent from the art school. The way Jimmy said the word "talent" as he fixed his eyes on my crotch made me think that he wasn't referring just to artistic ability.

Jimmy and I arrived at Dixon's penthouse after midnight. ("That's when the fun really begins," Jimmy said.) The apartment's ocean view was spectacular but the scenery inside was even more breathtaking. In the center of a cavernous living room a dozen young guys were dancing to the heavy throb of early disco . There wasn't an unattractive boy in the bunch.

In a dark corner, two kids who looked young enough to be

in junior high were passionately sucking on each other's faces, oblivious to the rest of the party. A slender blond wearing only a microscopic bikini and jewel-studded dog collar glided over and offered me a drink from a tray he was holding. As I took a glass, he winked at me. My eyes followed the jiggle of his shapely ass as he darted off to refill his tray. That's when I caught my first glimpse of Dixon Lish. He was a baby-faced pear-shaped man in a silky crimson kimono. His impressive bulk crushed a huge cushiony pillow as he sat surveying the party like a lecherous sultan. On the table in front of him was a china plate with a small mountain of white powder piled on it. A hunky, red-headed boy sat in his lap snorting up lines of the powdery stuff, finally stopping to lift his shivering head to give Dixon a wet, sloppy kiss on the mouth. The blond in the micro-bikini drifted over and joined in the fun.

I had never been to such a queer party before. Jimmy interrupted the action to introduce me to Dixon, who welcomed me by offering an enormous spoonful of coke. I graciously accepted and as I leaned over to snort it, the thin blond suddenly stuck his tongue in my ear. The drugs hit the back of my head and I could feel the boy's hot breath on my cheek. He was more than cute and very willing so I impulsively grabbed him and kissed him long and hard. Dixon pulled the boy's bikini off and the party degenerated into a total orgy. During the course of the night I had my cock sucked and my ass fucked by three of the most attractive boys at the party. The night climaxed with me and a handsome Latino named Ricky taking turns fucking Jimmy on the penthouse balcony under the stars. When the morning sun finally peeked over the horizon I was feeling utterly debauched and wasted. I could hardly walk, for more reasons than one. It was a perfect introduction to the decadent lifestyle of Dixon Lish.

I became a regular fixture at Dixon's parties. Because we both shared a passion for youth and beauty, Dixon and I developed a sort of friendship, the shallow but intense kind of relationship that hobbyists with mutual interests share. He became a patron as well, often commissioning me to paint or photograph some beguiling boy with whom he was currently obsessed. He admired my work, claiming that no one could capture the erotic essence of young male beauty like I could. Of

course, I managed to seduce most of the subjects he sent to pose for me but I never told Dixon this because I considered getting my models "in the mood" a regular part of my artistic process.

Now, five years after that first party, Dixon was calling me. I hadn't heard from him in a few months. I'd just ended a long, stormy relationship with a gorgeous but difficult boyfriend. I missed the easy and uncomplicated kind of sex I used to have with the horny teens at Dixon's. I was busy working on my first one-man show of paintings for a Miami gallery when I got his call. I needed a break from work and Dixon's mysterious request, whatever it was, promised a chance for some dirty fun.

I didn't have to wait long to find out. Dixon's big blue Continental appeared in my driveway a few minutes later. He was wedged in tightly behind the steering wheel, looking even fatter than the last time I saw him.

"Get in," he barked impatiently. "We're going for a ride." He sounded like a sissy thug in a B-movie. His eyes burned with sinister purpose. He was a man with a mission. I hurriedly got in the car and Dixon whisked the Lincoln briskly out of the neighborhood.

He pointed the long blue car east down Sunrise Blvd. towards the ocean. Soon we were on Highway A1A cruising slowly south along the Lauderdale strip. Neither one of us spoke. Dixon appeared to be in the grip of some nameless obsession. We were almost in sight of the Marlin Beach Hotel when he abruptly turned into a multi-story parking garage. We reached the top level and he brought the car to a stop at the edge of the building overlooking the restless blue Atlantic. We had a perfect bird's-eye view of the gay beach. Four stories below, directly across the street, was the notorious "kiddie corner" where the hustlers that were too young to get into the sleazy Poop Deck bar would hang out and try to get picked up by anybody with a car and a few spare dollars.

Dixon brought out a pair of binoculars and looked down on the street below.

"Yes! Yes! Yes!" he squealed excitedly. "He's down there now! Here, take a look down there, across the street, by the

tree. He's what I brought you down here to see."

He thrust the binoculars towards me. I looked down through them, over the steady stream of cars on the strip, past herds of pink tourists towards the tall royal palm tree Dixon pointed to with his chubby finger. Three boys were loitering around the tree which served as the hub of gay hustling on the strip. Two of the boys were skinny dark-haired delinquents that looked like they probably learned how to give blow-jobs in reform school. They weren't very appealing. But over to the right, near the tree, was a sight that caused my heart to skip a beat. It was a boy who looked no older than 16. I refocused the binoculars to be sure I was seeing right. He leaned against the tree in a pose of crude glamour. Ringlets of golden hair fell around his shoulders and fluttered slightly in a lazy breeze. Dark wayfarer shades covered his eyes but left enough of his face exposed to let you know it was uncommonly good-looking. He would have been pretty had he been a girl, but as a boy he was absolutely stunning. He was short, about five-seven, with a lean, compact build that went spectacularly well with his boyish good looks. Tiny brown nipples peeked through a gauzy tank top that wasn't trying very hard to cover his well-defined swimmer's physique. He looked too good to be down there on that hustlers' corner. Too fresh and radiant and pure. Exactly the sort of innocent boy that Dixon would love to corrupt. But he had better work quickly, I knew. After all, this is swinging Lauderdale, baby, and nobody stays fresh or radiant or pure in this town for very long.

Dixon jerked the binoculars away from me and gazed down at the boy posed seductively under the palm below.

"Isn't he just scrumptious?" he said. A bubble of drool appeared in the corner of his mouth. God, he was disgusting but at least he had excellent taste in younger men.

"Sure, he looks edible from head to toe but that doesn't explain what you wanted me for," I said. "If it's about golden boy down there why don't you just go over and pick him up? He doesn't look like he's too busy right now and if he's looking for business he's standing in the right spot."

"Ah! That's the trouble - he's just a tease, a junior hustler wannabe," snorted Dixon unhappily. "I tried to scoop him up the other night but he pretended not to even notice me. Take

a look at this big blue monster I drive, how can anyone not notice me? All the hungry rent boys in this town know me and they know I pay cold hard cash for hot hard cock. Believe it or not, I've even had some of them fight over who gets to go home with me. They know Daddy has lots of sugar, but I couldn't even get him to look at me. Behavior like that is so unprofessional."

I took a good look at Dixon. He looked plumper than I had remembered. Large, gaudy chains of gold jewelry glittered around his thick neck. He reeked of money. He didn't reek of class or refinement or elegance, just money. Lots of money. And in this little corner of the world that's almost enough to get whoever you want. Almost.

Dixon gave me a frustrated smile and went on talking.

"That's where you come in. I did some checking around and found out all about the beautiful brat. His name is Shane and he's from Iowa or Indiana or one of those horrible midwestern states that grow a lot of corn. He's been in town almost three weeks and he's staying at Fred and Bam-Bam's place."

Fred and Bam-Bam were two notorious hustlers who ran a call-boy service from a seedy apartment a few blocks from the beach. Their place was a magnet for all sorts of lost boys and more than a few wound up peddling their asses on the strip for the profit of Fred and Bam-Bam. They were evil, sleazy pimps and Dixon used their services often.

"Here's what they told me. He's really 18 but he looks a lot younger, doesn't he? He acts straight but Fred says he's queer as a three-dollar bill. He's only had one boyfriend - back in Iowa or wherever - and he hangs out here looking for a rich, good-looking sugar daddy. He's tricked with a few guys - young junior executive types-and he's gotten as much as $100 just to let himself get sucked off. Considering his looks, you know it's not going to be long before some handsome playboy with a taste for young stuff is going to drive by in an expensive sports car and sweep him off his feet and take him away from here forever. I'm realistic enough to know I'm never going to get him but that doesn't mean you can't try."

"What are you getting at?" I asked, puzzled. "The kid's awfully cute but I've never paid for sex before and I don't

intend to start now. Anyway, what thrills could you get from having me get into that boy's pants?"

"That's the favor I want ask of you. Actually, it's more like a job, if you can call getting paid a few hundred dollars for picking up a beautiful young boy and having sex a job," said Dixon.

"Okay, you've got my interest. Exactly what devious plan have you hatched in that diseased mind of yours?"

"You know how to operate video tape equipment, don't you?" asked Dixon.

"Sure! Hell, I took a production course at the Art Institute this summer."

"And you've seen a few pornographic films, right?"

"I've seen a few dozen at your place!"

"Then you know what I like. What I want you to do is pick up that star-to-be down there, whisk him off to the studio I've set up in my building and make a hot little video for me. Something I can use for those lonely nights when jerking off is my only outlet."

I was intrigued by the idea but didn't say anything. The plan seemed rather unsavory, but there was sex and money involved and that was an unbeatable combination. I grabbed the binoculars and looked down towards the corner again. The boy was still there leaning alluringly against the rough gray shaft of the palm tree.

"What kind of budget do you have for this production?" I asked in my smoothest professional voice.

Dixon reached in the glove compartment, brought out a fat envelope and threw it in my lap.

"Look inside there," he said in the same sleazy whisper I heard in his telephone call.

I opened the envelope and counted ten crisp hundred dollar bills. Tucked in behind them was a folded piece of paper. I pulled this out and read the crude hand-written note:

1. Each person must give and receive at least one blowjob.
2. The younger person must get fucked by the older person.
3. Each person must have at least one orgasm on camera
4. Bonus $$$ for kissing, rimming, and finger-fucking.

"Since I'm financing this production, I want some control

over the content. These are some general guidelines." His whisper grew louder. "I don't want just another lousy jack-off tape. I want some hot sexy action. You're a creative person. You've got the looks and style and smarts to do this job. Now you've got the money and facilities, too, but that's not all. I've leased a Porsche for you to pick up your starlet in. I thought you needed a flashy car to help complete the rich young stud package that the boy will no doubt find irresistible. You're not camera-shy are you? I want you to direct and co-star. I'm sure you're clever enough to know how to do both."

It was an offer I couldn't refuse. I needed the money. I fingered the bills one more time and stuffed the envelope in my shirt pocket. I shook Dixon's hand and said: "Congratulations, you are now a film producer! Don't worry, I'll make a work of art."

"Fuck art! Gimme hardcore smut! Something that will get me hard and keep me hard! I want a cocksucking, ass-fucking epic!" Dixon was almost shrieking. He looked and sounded just like a big blustery Hollywood producer.

The fat wad of cash felt warm and comforting inside my shirt pocket. It was enough money to get any horny kid, hustler or not to perform for the camera. I stroked the top of the envelope nervously. Visions of hard cocks invading smooth tight asses danced in my head. I was giddy with excitement. I was going to direct a porno film! I just hoped my leading man would cooperate, because I planned to have lots of gratuitous, dirty sex in this production.

"So, when do I start work?" I asked.

"The sooner, the better. He's only here on weekends. He's got a job at Burger King on weekdays. Can you believe a boy who looks like that actually works? Did you see that bulge in his basket? That's the real home of the whopper!" Dixon laughed and then said seriously: "Today's Thursday, you should get down here just after dark tomorrow night, Fred and Bam-Bam said he'll be here for sure. In the meantime, I think you should go get familiar with my studio.

Dixon and I cruised out of the parking lot and drove back to his place. The studio he had set up occupied a large apartment on the tenth floor of his building. It was sparsely furnished, just

a few chairs and a kingsize bed in the middle of the main room. There was video equipment everywhere. Two expensive-looking video cameras were on rolling tripods on either side of the bed. Each camera was hooked up to a monitor on a dolly, so one could see what was being taped while it was recording. There was another monitor and a professional editing board in the corner of the room. On a nearby table were a dozen blank video cassettes. It was a first-class set-up. I knew I could do quality work in a studio like this.

"Ah, when did you get all this stuff?"

"I've had this for a couple of months. I thought I'd make some home movies of some of my little friends. But I don't really know how to work all this technical stuff. I guess the only equipment I really know how to operate is a big, stiff teenage dick." He giggled like a naughty schoolgirl.

Dixon left me alone in the studio while I played with the lights and cameras and editing board. I quickly got the hang of it and spent the greater part of the afternoon studying some of Dixon's porno tapes. Watching them, I got lots of interesting ideas. When Dixon finally drove me home that evening, I had him swing by the Pink Pussycat sex boutique so I could pick up a few props for tomorrow's shoot. I made him wait in the car while I selected an assortment of merchandise that would be perfect for the type of movie I was planning. I was a director with a vision and that vision demanded just the right kind of toys.

The next evening was cool and crisp; a perfect mild winter's night in Florida. The studio was ready and so was I. A few minutes past sunset I got a call from Dixon. He had just driven past the kiddie corner and our boy was in his usual spot.

I inspected myself in the mirror. I was squeezed into a pair of tight blue jeans and a striped T-shirt stretched across my upper body. I thought I had never looked better. Those strenuous workouts of mine were doing some good and I had no reservations about appearing nude on camera. The image of Shane lounging enticingly beneath the palm tree kept appearing in my head. Since he was blond and boyishly cute and I was darkly handsome, I thought we would make a great screen pairing, especially with our clothes off.

Dixon's leased Porsche sat waiting in my driveway. He certainly didn't skimp in the luxury auto department. It was a beautiful machine; glossy black with an expensive leather interior that had an almost erotic texture and smell. I started the car and sped off into the night, ready for adventure. As I zipped along A1A, I began to understand the connection between cars and sex. When I stopped at a red light, a carfull of beautiful girls began flirting with me. As I drove towards the gay beach, men turned their heads to watch me pass. I could feel the thick wad of Dixon's money bloating my wallet. It was exciting to have so much money to spend exclusively on pleasure. I was feeling young, rich and beautiful as I approached the corner where I hoped to find Shane waiting for Mr. Right to drive up. The tourist season was in full swing and the strip was crowded with people looking for cheap thrills and fun. Traffic slowed to a crawl in front of the Poop Deck. The line of cars inched forward until I could clearly see a group of boys loitering around the palm tree at the edge of the block. Some were standing together looking restless but one figure stood alone, a small golden vision beneath the hazy glow of the streetlight. It was Shane.

Just at that moment, I could swear I heard Connie Francis warbling from a car radio: "Where the boys are... Someone waits for me." I'd heard it a hundred times before; after all, it was the unofficial theme song of Fort Lauderdale, but this time it had a delicious new layer of meaning.

Luckily, a space opened up right in front of the tree and I whipped the Porsche up to the curb with great panache. My appearance caused quite a stir among the assembled rent-a-boys. By nature, boy hustlers are simple creatures, attracted to shiny objects such as expensive sports cars and solid gold cokespoons. But I hoped it was me, not my car, that was getting them excited. One of the skinny dark-haired boys I'd seen the day before strutted up and poked his head into the car.

"Wanna date?" he said brazenly. His eyes moved across the interior of the car, studying everything inside. He put a grimy paw on the car door like he was waiting to be invited in. I paid him no attention. "Hey, there's a party in my mouth, wanna come?" he asked, giving me a slutty grin. He was the type of

street trash that would suck your cock all night long just for beer and cigarette money. I didn't like him. He was dirty and nasty and he was blocking my view, so I told him: "Do me a favor and call your friend over here." I pointed to Shane, who stood looking cool and unapproachable just a few yards away

"Hey, Shay-nuh, somebody wants you," the dark-haired boy yelled before shuffling off to solicit his next potential victim.

I took out one of the hundred dollar bills from my wallet and cupped it discreetly in my hand. Shane ambled over with deliberate slowness, as if he couldn't decide whether or not I was real. He peered into the passenger's side open window and looked me over, saying nothing.

"Wanna go for a ride?" I asked, letting the edge of the hundred dollar bill peek through my fingers. This got his attention.

"How far are you going?" he asked.

"All the way," I said as I moved the money temptingly across the car seat towards him.

He took about a half-second to consider my offer and said "Okay, let's go."

He slipped into the front seat and I eased the car out into the sluggish flow of traffic and headed towards Dixon's studio.

"Hi, I'm Peter," I said in a friendly voice as I put my hand out. He gave me a firm handshake and broke into a bashful grin.

"Glad to meet you. I'm Shane," he said, squirming uncomfortably in his seat. He tugged at the snug crotch of his supertight shorts trying to give his balls some breathing room. He certainly wasn't wearing enough clothes to conceal his considerable charms. He had on a colorful short sleeve shirt buttoned up halfway. A small crucifix hung around his neck and dangled across his tanned, hairless chest. He had looked good from a distance, but up close he was dazzling. He had the kind of unspoiled beauty that's often sought after on the strip but rarely ever found - he had a smooth-cheeked babyface with warm brown eyes and big, pouty lips that looked like they'd feel very good wrapped around my cock. The wind blew his hair around and the faint smell of cologne drifted over from where he sat. I was getting a hard-on looking at him so I thought I'd better distract myself by making small-talk.

"Aren't you a little cold in those clothes?" I asked, not knowing what else to say.

"Hell, no! I'm from up north. It's snowin' like hell where I come from."

"So you moved to Florida to get out of the snow?"

"No, get outta the house. Actually, my folks kicked me out. Anyhow, I'd heard Lauderdale was a happenin' place, so here I am," he said matter-of-factly.

"Do you mind if I ask why your parents kicked you out?"

He tossed my question around in his pretty head for a few seconds, tilted it thoughtfully, then said: "They caught me getting it on with my stepbrother, so they threw me out. I mean, it's not like we're really related, is it? He's a couple years younger than me, but he looks older. He's one of those big kids that looks 21 when he's fifteen. He made the first move on me, but since I'm the older one they thought I forced him to put his dick in my mouth. What a joke!"

He laughed bitterly and began fidgeting with his tight shorts again. They were a problem and needed to come off as soon as possible. I'd see to that once I got him back to the studio a few blocks away.

"So, do you like Lauderdale?" I asked.

"It's a freaky place, man! I've never had so many people try to get into my pants." He said this with incredibly boyish excitement. "Yeah, back in Indiana you're not considered good-lookin' unless you're a big corn-fed jock. Shit, I'm just this little guy from Kokomo. But I come down here and suddenly I'm getting offers right and left. Guys wanna pay me to let 'em suck my dick, so I let 'em. But I'm not a whore like that dude who first ran up to you back there. That's Bill. We call him Dollar Bill 'cause he'll do anything for a dollar. Me, I'll only go with guys that I like – and I won't do just anything."

"That's good to know. So, what makes you think you like me? You hardly know me."

"Well," he began then paused like a salesman trying to search for just the right words to say to close a big sale. "You have a nice smile and you have a nice car – and you have a nice hundred-dollar bill."

I pulled into parking garage entrance of Dixon's building. I

killed the engine and in the cool dead silence I brought out the hundred-dollar bill again and said, "What'll you do for this?" I waved the money teasingly in the air. It had a dirty green color under the bad fluorescent light of the garage.

He looked at it, bit his lip then said, "What do you have in mind?" He didn't look at me. His eyes remained glued to the hundred-dollar bill.

I took another bill and added it to the one I was waving, then another and another and another until I was shaking a handful of money in his face.

"If I'm paying for it, I get to be the boss, understand?" I said spreading out the bills like a fan. "Is this enough to get whatever I want?"

He said nothing, just stared wide-eyed at the money. He was under its spell. I could feel any resistance fading now.

"I don't do any kinky stuff, okay? "

"Look, I'm not a sex freak. This is the first time I've ever paid for it. I believe in making love, not buying sex. But I really want you to spend the night, so money is no object. It has to be you, no one else. Don't ask me to explain."

He reached for the money I was holding. He tugged at the bills but I didn't let him have them yet.

"Look, I'm not going to hurt you, in fact, all I really want to do is make you feel really good. But if you take this money, you have to do whatever I say. Understand?" I paused. I was still holding the money tightly and he was still pulling at it. "You trust me, don't you?" I flashed a warm, reassuring smile and he smiled back.

"Okay, it's a deal. I'm all yours for the night."

I finally let go of the money and he struggled to stuff the bills into the pocket of his tight, skimpy shorts. "Sleeping with a young, good-lookin' guy like you hardly seems like work anyway."

"I don't think we're going to do much sleeping," I said. I gave him a naughty wink and we got out of the car and took the elevator up to the studio.

I unlocked the door and let Shane go in ahead of me. There was an impressive stack of video recording gear set up around the bed in the center of the room. A large jar of vaseline, a stack of gay skin magazines and a couple of towels lay

indiscreetly on the nightstand by the bed. It seemed obvious that this was a place where sex videos were made.

"What do you use all this stuff for?" Shane asked dumbly.

I came up behind him and whispered softly in his ear: "You and I are going to make a little movie."

He pulled away from me and turned around.

"You mean a dirty movie?" he asked. He crinkled his cute little button nose and drew his eyebrows together in a worried expression.

"What's the matter?" I said dryly. "Isn't $500 enough for a screen test?"

"Yeah, sure, five hundred's a lot of money but I wasn't expecting to make a porno film. I'm just a little surprised, that's all. Jesus Christ, I haven't even been in this town three weeks and I'm living in a house full of spaced-out queers, letting strange guys suck my dick for money and now I'm making my first porno film. Man, if anybody back in Indiana found out they'd all think I'd gone to hell in a handbasket." He laughed mischievously, then asked: "Who's gonna see this movie anyway?"

"It's for a private collection. Just one person besides me will ever see this tape. He's an older gentleman, a good friend who suffered a horrible disfiguring accident and is now unable to have a regular sex life. His appearance scares people away." (I was glad Dixon couldn't hear this!) "He asked if I could make a video for him. He shares my taste in young men, so when I saw you I knew you'd be perfect." It was a good story. It made my job seem like a noble enterprise instead of just a dirty bit of teen sexploitation. And Shane bought it, too.

Looking at me with warm expressive eyes, he said: "Wow, I had no idea... I just thought you might be some rich pervert – no offense – who likes to make kinky films. I guess he must really be a good friend if you're gonna go to all that trouble for him. God, it must be horrible to be messed up like that."

He moved close to me and ran a playful finger down my shirt towards my belt. "I think it's awfully nice for you to do this for him." His voice was low and sultry now. He was getting friendly, five hundred dollars worth of friendliness. "I promise you'll get your money's worth out of me."

"I know I will," I said, pulling him to me and giving him a

long, soulful kiss that degenerated into a frenzy of sloppy tongue-play. We locked lips for a few delirious minutes until we both collapsed breathlessly onto the bed. The boy definitely knew how to kiss! (And I thought hustlers didn't like to do that.) I wondered what else he knew how to do. Those tempting lips of his were just inches away. They were soft and warm and supremely kissable. I could be easily entertained by them for hours. But, dammit, I had a video to make, so I summoned all my willpower and got up off the bed.

"You're distracting the director," I said, half-seriously. "Now get up and get ready, we've got a movie to make."

He obeyed my command and hopped to his feet. He started taking off his clothes - what little there was of them. He unbuttoned his shirt and tossed it on a chair. Next, those tight shorts were peeled off and he kicked them playfully across the room. He stood before me now totally naked, wearing only his tiny cross necklace and a wide unselfconscious grin. The pinkish brown color of his sun-tanned skin made him look like a nude blond Indian. My eyes were instantly drawn below his tan line to an area untouched by the sun. There a thick cock of mouth-watering proportions hung semi-erect from a tuft of dark pubic hair. It was a cock worth looking at, so I stepped back to get a better view. Shane shook his hips and the thing wiggled about like a lewd sausage. I was ecstatic. I'd found the perfect package. He had the slim body of an adolescent boy with the full-size cock of an adult pornstar. I had definite plans for him and his horse meat.

I grabbed a package from a nearby table and tossed it on the bed next to him.

"Get into those," I ordered. "And don't worry if they're a little too big, you'll be naked again soon enough."

He unwrapped the package and a pair of boy's pajamas fell out. Little rocket ships that looked like sleek silver penises decorated the fabric. It looked like something a ten-year-old might wear. Shane went to the mirror and held the pajamas up to his chest as if he were in a clothing store deciding if he liked them.

"Check out these little designs. These are for kids, man. Why do you want me to wear these?" he whined.

"Because I want you to look as young as possible –

remember this is a sexual fantasy - and you represent all the pent-up sexual energy of youth," I said in my best arty-genius-film director's voice. "The video will start with you in bed asleep. You've been having hot, sexy dreams and you wake up with a raging hard-on that needs immediate attention. Then you pick up one of those porn mags by the bed and start jerking off and I'll join you and we'll improvise from there. If you perform well, there'll be a bonus in it for you. That means taking directions. If I tell you to suck my dick, you'll suck my dick; if I want to fuck your ass, spread your legs and prepare to get fucked. Understand?"

Shane gave me a startled look. Apparently no one had ever talked to him like that before. The prospect of being used as my sexual plaything before the cameras must have excited him because I noticed his half-erect cock poking through the unfolded pajamas he held loosely in front of him. Without further comment he quietly put the pajamas on and did a brief runway twirl before the mirror. He looked ridiculously young in his rocket-covered pajamas and the enormous cock peeping through the unbuttoned fly added just the right touch of illicit eroticism to the total picture. He presented himself to me for approval. The compliant softness in his fawn-like eyes that told me he understood that I was in the driver's seat and the growing hardness of his cock told me he was ready for the ride of his life. I pushed him gently down onto the bed and turned on the camera lights. The bed glowed under the harsh lighting. It was showtime!

"I know these are kind of bright," I said. "But once the taping starts you won't even notice them. Because I'm cameraman and director and performer that means between scenes I'll have to get up and move the camera dollies around the bed to get interesting new angles. It might interrupt the flow occasionally but I'll edit the scenes together so it looks like continuous action. So just act naturally and remember, I've also never made a porn film before so we're both going to lose our video virginity together."

I turned the monitors on and positioned the cameras on Shane. He stared into the lens, tossed his hair back in a parody of a dumb starlet pose and blew me a sensual kiss. I watched his image fill the monitor screen. To call him photogenic would

have been faint praise. The camera loved every inch of him. I zoomed in for a close-up. He peered at me seductively through a strand of hair that fell Veronica Lake-style across one eye. The ceiling fan blew open his pajama top just enough to show one pink nipple peeking out from behind the little rockets. He made a tight circle with his lips and flicked his tongue in and out in a way that suggested he was eager to suck my cock. Unfortunately, that was going to have to wait a few minutes because I planned to start the production with a short solo sequence featuring Shane pounding his astounding prick..

With the tapes rolling, I had Shane go through the motions of waking up and discovering his urgent hard-on. It stuck out like a meaty baton from the open fly of his pajamas. He grabbed a magazine from the nightstand and began energetically jerking off to pictures of nude musclemen. He was a very natural, unselfconscious performer. He stroked his big cock with such youthful exuberance that seeing him on the monitor was like watching a surveillance camera planted inside a horny teenage boy's bedroom. From behind the cameras, I warned him not to come until I gave him the signal. He responded by relaxing his furious jerking to a slower, more measured pace. His balls were visible now and they looked like fuzzy pink fruit as they bobbed up and down with each vigorous stroke.

I detached one of the cameras from the tripod and circled the bed while Shane continued massaging his meat. His cock looked impressive from every angle. Watching him work on it was a voyeur's delight. He played to the camera without making it obvious he knew he was being recorded. When I had taped about five minutes of really hot solo footage I decided it was time for me to join the fun. I replaced the camera on the tripod and then positioned both cameras at opposite ends of the bed while Shane, completely absorbed in his own pleasure, kept beating off with a smooth unhurried rhythm. I started to describe the erotic situation I wanted us to act out: "Pretend I'm your best buddy... I walk in and discover you jerking off. It's gets me so excited that I take off all my clothes and join you in bed and we begin sucking each other's cock. Got that?"

Shane opened his eyes and nodded his head weakly, without missing a stroke. I entered stage left and Shane acted shocked

and surprised (he'd been caught jerking off to a gay porn magazine by his best friend!). He dropped the magazine and I picked it up and opened it to a photo that showed a guy with cum all over his face sucking on a thick, veiny cock. I studied the picture and showed it to him. He got the idea, he was going to have to suck my cock just like the guy in the picture. I stripped off my clothes and stood before the bed in my underwear. Shane sat up in bed and pulled me closer, his lips just inches away from my cock. My erection pointed towards his mouth but was trapped inside my briefs. Shane took hold of the elastic waistband with his teeth and stretched it out, then down. My hard cock sprung out with a resilient *boing* right into his face. He didn't have to be told to suck it, he popped it right into his mouth and started earning his money. He tickled my cockhead with a wet tongue and ran his lips across the length of my boner like he was playing the harmonica. Then he opened his mouth wide and tried to stuff the whole thing inside it.

I watched on the monitor as his blond head bobbed up and down. I looked pretty good on video: The camera made my cock look bigger and the lighting improved my skin tone but something was wrong in the picture - Shane still had his pajamas on. I pulled my cock out of his mouth and pushed him onto the bed. I didn't even bother unbuttoning his top, I just ripped it off and tossed it dramatically behind me. Next I undid his pajama bottoms in the same brutal manner, leaving him naked and panting under the hot lights.

I climbed onto the bed and started to work on his magnificent prick. He squirmed with delight as I tugged on his balls while I gave his long cockshaft some spit and polish. He took hold of my cock and we awkwardly maneuvered ourselves into a 69 position. Now we were both trying to shove our cocks down each other's throats. Shane managed to swallow most of mine but his formidable slab of teenage meat presented me with a greater challenge. It was ridiculously large. Every time I put my lips around the thing I felt like a midget puffing on a giant cigar. There it was, in my face, demanding attention, while the cameras recorded everything for posterity. This was my chance to show off my cocksucking prowess, so I opened wide and Shane pushed nearly half of it into my mouth. I

thought I was going to choke to death, but at that moment I couldn't think of a better way to go. My lips stretched painfully around his thick cock as he fucked my face with a skillful sensitivity I wouldn't have expected in someone so young. I reciprocated by cramming my cock even further into his hungry mouth. He licked and stroked and kissed it with great tenderness that developed into hot impassioned sucking. There we were, two naked boys with our mouths full, putting on such a torrid display of cocksucking that it would make most porn loops seem tepid in comparison. Suddenly, Shane started climaxing in my mouth. I spit his cock out just as he spurted a geyser of jism across my face. His cum dripped from my cheek in thick pasty gobs. Now I knew how that guy in the porn magazine felt.

Meanwhile, Shane kept my cock in his mouth while he jerked me off with one hand. I could feel the cum churning in my balls and a warning tingle told me that at any second it would be my turn to decorate Shane's face with a heavy load of hot spunk. I pulled my cock out of his mouth and a gush of warm white liquid splashed across face. Shane kept jerking on my cock until the last heavy drop fell like syrup onto his lower lip then he popped my cock back into my mouth and licked it clean with great care.

I was really impressed by Shane's performance. He obviously loved to suck cock and even better, he looked good doing it. I'd found a real diamond in the rough, a cute kid from Indiana who wasn't shy about getting down and dirty on camera. Dixon was going to be very pleased. And there was more fun yet to come. I'd discovered Shane knew how to please a man with his mouth: Next I wanted to find out what he could do with that beautiful little butt.

Since we both were rather messy I suggested we take a shower together and clean up. There was a shower in the studio. I washed him all over, not missing any nook or cranny. I wanted him to be fresh as a daisy. While he dried himself off, I set up the cameras for the next scene. He came out of the bathroom swishing a fluffy towel across his rear end. His cock had shrunk back to almost normal size and it hung limply above his plump balls.

"You ever been fucked?" I asked bluntly.

Shane didn't even blink at this question, he just kept polishing the firm mounds of his ass with the bath towel.

"I let my stepbrother do it to me a few times. He used to make me pretend I was a girl. When he fucked me he made me say stuff like 'Your cock feels so good inside me!' or 'Oh yeah, fuck my pussy hard!' It was kinda humiliating but it was kind of fun, too. He was rough on me sometimes - he just wanted to get his rocks off - you know how kids can be."

I smiled knowingly at this last statement. Yeah, I knew how kids could be - I'd been on the receiving end of countless teenage stud-pups who were in such a hurry to orgasm that they forgot I was supposed to come along too. But Shane didn't have to worry about that with me - I planned to drive my hot rod down his back road and I was going to make sure he enjoyed every inch of the ride.

I went over to him and ran my fingers gently through his hair. He smelled fresh and clean after his shower. The minty smell of soap floated in the air. I whispered into his ear what I wanted from him in the next scene. In a flash, he hopped agreeably onto the bed and got into position. That beautiful butt was up in the air, ready to get the fucking of its life! It was a golden moment custom made for video porn. I quickly repositioned the studio lights and fetched the hand held camera. Shane wiggled his booty for the camera while I zoomed in and focused. He took a slim, spit-soaked finger from his mouth and ran it teasingly along the crack that separated the pale twin globes of his ass. With both hands he spread open his asscheeks and revealed his greatest treasure: a dainty pink hole surrounded by a wispy halo of brownish fuzz. It was a true ass connoisseur's delight: a butthole with genuine star quality, a rosebud of such beauty that it begged to be explored by fingers tongues and cocks. I was fascinated and let the camera record the scene as Shane the burlesque exhibitionist contracted and expanded his asshole for my amusement. Obviously, Shane was more than ready. His ass was hot and my dick was hard and the cameras were in place. It was time for action.

I ordered Shane to take the vaseline and lube up my stiff cock, which he did immediately. He was as obedient and helpful as a boy scout and twice as cute. He spread his legs wide and, holding my greasy prick in one hand, tried

unsuccessfully to guide it inside him. My cock was too big and his butt was tighter than a nun's pussy. It was like trying to park the Goodyear blimp in a baby's mouth. It was going to take some serious prep work before I'd get all eight inches of my cock in there. I thought I'd try my tongue first to loosen him up a bit.

I nudged my tongue into the crevice and began wetting down the fine hair around his tight pink slot. Shane went crazy with delight, moaning wildly every time I tickled his back door. After my tongue had gotten his hole nice and moist I started to work a finger in slowly. His opening wouldn't yield at first, but soon he relaxed and I squeezed about half of my middle finger in. I massaged his snug passage with great tenderness. His moaning grew louder and more intense the deeper I probed. He was enjoying it, but I could tell it was going to take something bigger than a finger to get him ready to take my cock.

Luckily I had planned for just such a situation. The shopping bag full of toys I'd purchased the day before lay within arm's reach on the nightstand. Keeping one hand busy finger-fucking Shane, I reached out with the other and brought the bag onto the bed, accidently dumping the contents in the process. A couple of serious-looking, medium-sized dildoes tumbled out and fell next to Shane, who flashed me a lusty grin between moans. He knew those dildoes were going up his ass.

I delicately withdrew my finger from his butthole and began smearing a generous glob of vaseline on the smaller dildo. When it was sufficiently slick I parted his asscheeks and started pushing it in carefully. Shane drew in his breath sharply as I worked the dildo in further and further until half of it had disappeared between his bubble-shaped buttocks.

Shane gasped and groaned as I gave the dildo a playful little twist, possibly from pain but more likely from pleasure since he kept spreading his legs wider and wider. I slid it up and down his chute while the unblinking eye of the camera preserved every ecstatic shudder of his firm young body. The dildo slipped in and out of his narrow channel with increasing ease. His ass was now primed and ready for a real flesh-and-blood cock.

I went into him gradually. He relaxed the ring-shaped muscle of his ass and my big throbbing cock was soon completely

inside him. It was like entering a warm, velvety dream. I fucked him slowly at first, letting him get used to my prick moving in and out, in and out. I nibbled on his earlobe as he made soft little musical noises whenever my cock rubbed against his prostrate. It was tender and leisurely lovemaking and we were both enjoying ourselves immensely but I needed to rev up the action for the video. The sex needed to be more athletic, more visually exciting. Keeping my dick planted up his ass, I rolled him over onto his back. His legs went over my shoulders and I pumped his tight rump with intense piston-like strokes. Sweating under the hot glare of the studio lights, we tried more positions than there were on a day-glo zodiac sex poster. We generated so much heat I expected us to burst into flames at any minute. During one delirious moment as I was screwing him doggie-style I began slapping the cheeks of his ass. (I'd seen this done in so many porn films I just had to try it). Shane apparently dug the rough treatment: With every playful little spank he pushed his butt backwards to try to take in more of my cock. This sweet young kid from Kokomo was turning out to be a truly insatiable bottom.

"Your cock fills so good inside me," he moaned. I guess he got a lot a practice saying that late at night to his stepbrother back in Indiana. Yet he said it with such conviction that I believed him. I may have paid him $500 but I wasn't forcing him to say he enjoyed getting his "pussy" reamed.

I turned him onto his side and lifted his right leg up like I was opening a pair of scissors. The videocam had an excellent view of my tool plugging his talented butthole but I didn't care anymore about the cameras or the movie or even Dixon's money. I wasn't working for Dixon now, I was busy working on Shane's orgasm. I wasn't going to stop fucking him until his cock erupted with spurts of molten teenage spunk. The boy had amazing staying power - it took several more minutes of earnest fucking before he finally climaxed. It was worth the wait, however, because he delivered a truly impressive cum shot. A supernova of semen exploded from his cock in three or four mighty blasts. Hot white globs fell like melted pearls across the smooth expanse of his chest. Considering he had just come about an hour earlier I was shocked at the amount that gushed out from his phallic volcano. I kept pumping my cock against

his prostrate until his deluge slowed to a dribble. He was finished; now it was my turn to get off. I withdrew my cock from his now stretched-out asshole and holding it like a fleshy firehose I squirted a foamy load all over him. My juice mingled with his as my cock dripped across the toned flatness of his stomach. In a moment of inspired perversity I crawled over Shane's sprawled body and holding his head back I forced my used dick into his mouth. To my surprise, he sucked on it without protest even though it had been up his ass just minutes before. He was either incredibly submissive or he really wanted that cash bonus I'd promised him if he did exactly as I wanted. He cleaned it off with the eagerness of a sweet-toothed kid licking the frosting off a cake knife. When he finished, I gave him a long, passionate final kiss. I could taste the faint saltiness of my cum on his lips. It was the perfect way to end the video.

I wiped off Shane's body with a soft fluffy towel then got up and shut off the cameras and lights before collapsing next to him on the bed. Exhausted from sex and drained of semen, we cuddled for a while, then fell asleep in each other's arms, as snug as two spoons in a silverware tray.

I woke up the next morning with Shane's head resting on my chest. His soft blond hair fell around my shoulders and I could feel the warm mist of his breath against my neck. It was a nice way to wake up. I finally roused the sleeping angel and we got up and took a shower together. Then we dressed and went out for breakfast.

From a corner booth in a Denny's on the strip, I watched as Shane devoured a huge breakfast hearty enough for a lumberjack. His appetite didn't surprise me, after all, he was a growing boy who'd just been fucked all night long. Making a porn film can certainly work up a healthy appetite.

He cleaned off his plate and gave me a long, dreamy look with his big brown eyes. He wore the delirious, glazed expression of smitten schoolboy. Under the table, his feet brushed against mine in a tentative game of footsie. I liked him and I think he liked me. Or maybe he liked my money or my car or my bogus rich stud persona. I wanted to be honest and set him straight about me, that I was just a struggling artist without a million bucks or a flashy Porsche or an expensive

condo. But that could wait, right now I was enjoying his attention too much.

"So did you enjoy being a star last night?" I asked. He kept stroking my leg with his foot and gazing at me silently.

"My ass hurts this morning," he said with a naughty grin. He wasn't complaining; he sounded like a proud athlete discussing sore muscles the day after winning a big race.

"Yeah, breaking into show biz can be rough," I said with a laugh. Just then I remembered I'd promised him a bonus. I still had $500 of Dixon's money. Shane had proven to be an extraordinary performer and he certainly deserved more money. I took the five bills out of my wallet. I could get more for myself from Dixon.

"Here's that bonus I promised you," I said, sliding the money discreetly across the table towards him.

He looked down at the cash and blurted: "That's $500!" He quickly tucked the bills into his pants.

"You earned it," I said, putting my hand on top of his. "Now you've just made a thousand in less than 24 hours. You know, you're awfully cute, but don't think you can make this kind of money every day. You need to take this money and get your own place. You shouldn't be living in a house full of hustlers (I'd been to Fred and Bam-Bam's place - it was a real den of sleaze). I know it seems like fun to get paid for sex but you could catch VD or get hurt or just get burned out and ugly. I've seen it happen a hundred times in this town. You need somebody to take care of you."

My speech sounded like it belonged in "Rain," that Somerset Maugham story about the priest and the whore. I fucked him and now I wanted to save him. Shane looked at me with wide unblinking eyes. I guess he was surprised that I even cared.

"Yeah, I suppose you're right," he said seriously. "I could never be a real whore like that kid Bill you saw last night. I guess I like myself too much to let just anyone have me for money."

"Hey, I like you too much to let just anyone have you, too," I said stroking the top of his hand affectionately.

Shane called our waitress over and asked to borrow a pen and some paper. He scribbled something on a scrap of paper

and folded it into my hand. I read it and smiled, then placed it in my pocket.

I paid the check and drove Shane towards Fred and Bam-Bam's apartment. I stopped a half a block from the place and pulled the Porsche over to let him out in front of a bus bench that had old gray-haired woman sitting on it. Before he got out he leaned over and gave me a scandalously long kiss on the mouth. The old lady's eyes popped out of her head. I guess she wasn't used to seeing two guys kiss. It was fun being shocking.

"Don't forget that note!" shouted Shane as I drove away. In the rearview mirror I watched him shuffle hesitantly down the sidewalk. He walked as if he were a little saddlesore. I certainly had done a lot of bareback riding on his ass the night before.

I went back to the studio and spent the rest of the day editing the tape of the previous night's action. It took me about six hours to shape the raw footage into a classic piece of gay smut. For an amateur production it was a scorching erotic epic, I had to break a couple times during editing to jerk off. That was good indication that my first effort as porn director and co-star was an unqualified success. I phoned Dixon with the happy news and he insisted I bring the tape over immediately. I duped a copy for myself and then I was on my way.

Dixon met me at the door wearing a purple caftan as big as a circus tent. He looked like a big excited grape as he grabbed the tape out of my hand and dragged me into the living room. The tape went in the player and Dixon plopped onto the couch, breathless in anticipation. Within seconds the opening sequence flashed onto the screen. I'd created a two-minute intro by editing the hottest moments of the tape together in a series of arty dissolves. This torrid trailer showed Dixon that I'd fulfilled all his requests and then some. It was all up there on the screen: rimming, cocksucking, finger-fucking, ass-reaming. The sequence ended with a montage of slo-mo cum shots. Hot jism seemed to drip right off the screen.

Dixon watched the intro then abruptly paused the tape. I could tell he was genuinely aroused, a bubble of drool appeared on his lower lip. It wasn't a pretty sight.

"My god, that's fucking hot!" blurted Dixon. "You're obviously a video genius and a major stud, too. I can't wait to see the rest of it- you might want to leave now unless you want to see a big fat man play with himself."

"What about that bonus you promised? As you can plainly see from the tape I've done more than meet your guidelines."

"Oh, I suppose fucking the sweetest ass in town wasn't enough?"

"Hey, it was a dirty job but somebody had to do it." I replied. "Anyway, genius studs don't come cheap - no pun intended"

"What'll it take to get you out of here so I can jerk off in privacy?" He asked anxiously.

"How about $200 and letting me have the Porsche until Tuesday?"

"Okay, okay - just don't put a scratch on it," he said as he took the money out of a thick wallet lying on the coffee table. He didn't give a damn about the money, all he cared about now was getting his rocks off with his video date. He pushed the bills toward me in an impatient gesture of dismissal. "Tuesday. No later! Now get the hell outta here, I've got a terrible itch I gotta scratch."

As I rode the elevator down to the garage, I fingered the keys to the Porsche with one hand, Dixon's money in my pocket with the other. My budding career in porn certainly had its rewards. Now that I had the use of the car and some spending money I was ready for fun and I knew exactly who I wanted to have fun with. I pulled out the scrap of paper Shane had given me in the restaurant and re-read it:

Call me when you want to make another movie -
Next time I'll do it for free!
XXX OOO,
Shane 555-1980

SLENDER FORMS

Patrick Dome

"Mildly obscene," Johnny said while slowly sliding one hand across his taut belly, "though a tad on the skinny side." Nestling and rubbing against the side of my bed, I said, "But it feels right and oh, so good."

The room was a blue-gray haze, as if this could not be happening, and it felt like we were miles away from our ward, until I heard the retarded man in the Panama hat laugh; and when I realized he was watching, I knew this was no dream.

The laughter woke some of the others and brought their attention to the corner where we were furiously attacking the bed with stone hard cocks.

We had crossed the line from hushed, private movement to careless, unwavering masturbation. Johnny's sweaty balls, rubbing across a clean white pillowcase smooth from starch, were unwittingly edging towards my face.

I could smell the sweet scrotal odor – immediately thinking of a garden I once walked through that had the strangest smelling flowers and now I think that they smelled like Johnny's balls. I moved my head away as his hand, covered with his own saliva, moved to his cock and he began stroking himself.

Then a force stronger then Johnny's biceps – both richly tattooed with purple and red flowers – extended my tongue out flat, ready to taste salty liquid that formed like silver drops on the long, curly hairs.

The moon shone bright above, though just a crack of light made it through the closed shutters.

My attention moved for an instant to the barely visible bodies in the room that were propping up, moving around and perhaps all squinting to get a clearer look at us in the corner.

But my eyes were focused only six inches away as my open lips moved in closer, while my mind transplanted us to the top of a hill under more satisfying and open moonlight, more tempting air, and perfect seclusion. But we remained firmly planted in the room filled with reasonably sane psychiatric war

casualties mixed with reasonably sane crazies. But I did not care what earmark I was given, as long as my bed was next to Johnny's. After three months of watching his sheets twist around his constantly fidgeting body each night as he restlessly slept, or of watching his thick, powerful hands lift a spoonful of mushy oatmeal to his succulent mouth each morning, we were now sweating together as we twisted across the mattress.

I watched Johnny's ass move rhythmically to the tune of his masturbation; he was truly a graceful fucking animal. For a moment I closed my eyes and thought of Johnny in the exercise room, standing in the corner with a cigarette while constantly pulling the edges of his bright blue workout trunks. We all attended the exercise hour, but Johnny never participated – Johnny, with the most supple and tightly woven body in the hospital, watched the rest of us with a timid, boyish face.

He was painfully shy, yet his sublime features belied such a stigma.

Like a hundred boys I wanted to get close to in school gyms, Johnny was my entire adolescence standing before me – but with the biggest bulge in gym shorts I'd ever seen.

There was, despite his sheepish grinning, a constant thrill in his eyes; his frightened eyebrows softened his strong masculinity to perfection.

I thought him always to be holding in a warehouse of unused power. Each day in the gym I climbed one of the ropes; my cock got harder each time I pulled my thighs up to match the distance my hands had reached. And I continuously watched Johnny on my way up towards the steel beams in the ceiling, until the only thing to see was the top of his somewhat shaggy soft brown hair and his filthy, shuffling sneakers.

When my head was into the rafters, I pulled and stretched until cum released into my shorts, then weakly slid back to the floor mat with blurry vision and the thick sulfurous smell of semen as it saturated my jockstrap. Walking a little clumsily past Johnny, I ritually patted his bare back, my sweaty palms sliding for a instant on his milky skin. Now in bed, my sweaty hands were stroking my cock and one of Johnny's thighs.

His eyes were closed, lost in the reverie of masturbation and fantasy, as my mouth dared move in closer.

When the courage finally hit me, as if the fear of how he

might react had melted from his heat, my mouth grabbed hold of his balls and sucked in deep, taking in a massive dose of power.

My tongue could separate and move them around and around. I gave them life, so now I could manipulate them.

They were now out of Johnny's control.

And how did Johnny react? He seemed to accept their birth unto me with a moan that could not have escaped the deepest sleepers in the room.

My eyes opened but with Johnny's thighs rubbing against my face they could see nothing else.

He moaned again to the gray shadows watching us from the scattered hospital beds. Johnny had once told me that his mother painted the kitchen walls lavender and the cabinets black and that he hated it.

I thought it sounded like an interesting combination, and when I told him this he began to change his mind about it.

He pulled on his thick, shiny hair and sheepishly said, "well, it really was elegant I guess," as if he had been totally wrong to say it was ugly.

Johnny, my sweet vulnerable boy, what would it take to make you cry for me in the night?

If I covered myself in lavender, set against my black hair, you would see it: lavender and black are exquisite to fuck.

Johnny, it soon became evident, relied on me and my opinion; whatever I said about music, art, nature, or anything was the truth he had been seeking.

Johnny was my body, my sweet brother, my voyeuristic youth. I was Johnny's eyes, wisdom, and the resolution to his ambivalent feelings.

I could tell him what to wear, what musical composers to like, what books to read; I could have told Johnny anything except what I really wanted him to believe: that he should give me his cock, I wanted it so badly. But then, caught in another intellectual conversation, I managed to convince him of the art of masturbation in times such as ours, with no women around. Johnny, Johnny, Johnny...agreed to do it quietly in the dead of night, long after the others fell asleep.

I said, "the moonlight can do crazy things," and he said, "fuck, man, we're two guys...we're just gonna see who can

give the biggest load, right?"

I could taste the night and I could taste Johnny as the tattoo on his left arm screamed at me: "Don't fuck with us, man! Keep your fuckin' hands to yourself." But now my hands weren't doing anything; the walls of my mouth and tongue were doing everything.

What did the god-damn skeleton tattoo have to say about that?

Too bad, I said, too bad.

Johnny and I were practically doing it.

Then his hands gently brushed my shoulders as it reached for my head.

His big, beautiful hands grabbed my head and started to pull it away and I was petrified and excited, ready to die silently in the night.

Johnny twisted his hips and sat up as his hands carried my whole body with my head; there seemed to be no effort as he lifted me through silent air.

I always knew that someday it would end like this – silent, no violence, at the hand of someone who is perfect and exciting. What really happened: Johnny pulled me up to meet his eyes, piercing intensely through the flat grayness.

Sweat poured from him, delectably sweet to meet.

As his thick fingers roughly massaged my cheeks, I saw a few tears sit at the edge of his eyelids before dropping down his cheeks. I died – Johnny crying and not me? – but came instantly alive again as his hands moved slowly across my chest around to my back, then finally pulled me in for the big kiss that found our tongues wrapped like snakes as our bodies rolled noisily across the bed. In the meager moonlight, Johnny's flesh was like a carnival. I rolled over it and over it, sliding on the sweat, and tumbled on my head while looking at his face that was not at all passive, but radiant and happy.

I tore his tongue out with my teeth and bit my way across his muscled arms.

The skeleton tattoo now screamed with agony as I ripped at the flesh, unable to heed any more of its warnings.

We were doing it! He was not inside me, but so close it felt like we were one. We pushed our bodies together tighter and tighter, the two cocks like melting iron, rubbing between our

bellies. Our kiss became so deep I thought maybe we were coming together in our mouths.

But our flesh was binding from semen that poured out of the two cocks like a slow fountain between our bellies.

It only took that powerful embrace to bring us to the point of sweet agony – agony because I wanted to scream my guts out as my cum flowed into the barely existing space between us.

And Johnny's cum was so warm I thought my chest was on fire. We did not loosen ourselves until our senses began to take in the world around us.

Fear crept into me as we unfastened our grips and semen stretched and fell as Johnny lifted himself up. The dark room around us was scurrying and it took some believing to see that the man in the Panama hat, Jessie, was standing over us, his hand covered with his own cum.

He looked sexy that moment, not crazy.

He looked at us and laughed, and we started to laugh too.

"Jessie, Jessie," I whispered, "what are the others thinking of all this?"

Jessie stepped aside and some of the shadows in the room were moved slowly with cadence as Jessie stifled his laughter.

Johnny, Johnny, and Jessie too ... I got up on me knees and grabbed Jessie's cock and squeezed the rest of the cum out of it.

He shook with delight as I playfully pulled him by his cock into the bed.

The next day, Johnny seemed more distant than ever. At breakfast he pushed oatmeal around with his spoon but didn't put any in his mouth; when I looked his way he nervously reached for the tin cup and took a swig of the strong bitter coffee. At the morning exercise he stayed stringently alone, allowing no one into the bubble that surrounded him. Johnny, Johnny, what happened in these few lonely hours since you rubbed your cum all over my ticklish belly?

While climbing the rope my adolescent heart was breaking to watch Johnny standing alone, looking down at his shuffling feet, while my cock nearly exploded just thinking of how it was with Johnny – his strong hands holding my ass while his mouth seemed to scream for me from the inside out. Was it just

with Johnny – his strong hands holding my ass while his mouth seemed to scream for me from the inside out. Was it just a dream? Was it only that high school fantasy playing tricks on me?

Each time my legs lifted up toward the ceiling semen seeped into my shorts as I looked intently at Johnny down there on the floor. He lit a cigarette and looked up at me. Our eyes met for just a moment before he snubbed his butt in an ashtray and quickly ran out the door. Johnny, don't leave me hanging here!

My heart pounded wildly and, as all equilibrium left my body, my hands let go and, falling into darkness, I reached out for Johnny's cock that loomed in front of me like the holy grail. I dreamt of Johnny's house, entering his bedroom as tenderly as if it were his mother's womb. This was the secret place that would unlock Johnny's shyness, and his slipping away from what I knew was in his heart. There was his bed covered in a soft green blanket. I lifted it to find a letter in a faded yellow envelope. My hands trembled to discover just who had broken Johnny's heart. I picked up the crumbling paper as Johnny grabbed me from behind, threw me against the wall, and screamed, "Don't even think of entering here or I'll fucking kill you!"

I yelled back, "Johnny, you know I won't hurt you!"

When I woke to see Johnny's face just inches from mine, no longer averting my gaze, I knew I was still dreaming. Johnny put his hand under the bed sheet and massaged my balls with his powerful fingertips. I felt as if I was climbing to heaven, and Johnny was my rope. Then his boyish smile changed into mock anger; "You fuckin' scared me and everyone else! What made you fall like that?"

"Johnny, I ... I'm sorry, but ... I thought it didn't mean anything after all. It just hurt so much."

"Not mean anything? Fuck ... you just don't know ..."

Johnny looked like a boy about to ask for the biggest present in the world from Santa Claus; "You see, kid, I just realized that I want to go all the way and it scared the shit outta me. But the thing is ... I really want you to fuck me." Knowing that I could have died not knowing that Johnny wanted my dick up his ass brought tears to my eyes. He looked at me like a hungry monster wanting to be fed, and I looked despairingly at my foot

hanging from the ceiling in a cast. "Johnny, when I'm out of this thing I swear I'll ..."

"I can't wait for that. I want you inside me right now."

"Johnny, you are a crazy bastard. Look at me! And someone might hear us!"

"Don't worry, Kid, I could never hurt you, and ... just shut up; I'll make it work."

With that Johnny leaned over and started to kiss my mouth. My cock got hard before our tongues met. Johnny untied the string on my pajamas and pulled and tugged at my cock while I reached into his jeans and pulled and twisted at his balls.

I started to moan but Johnny covered my mouth. "Shut the fuck up! If they catch me like this you know they'll send me away for good!"

Johnny then took off his jeans, exposing his erection, and climbed up onto the bed, straddling with his feet. The mass of male power looming above me in the darkness lowered down and hovered over my waist.

Johnny covered his hand with saliva and lubricated my dick and then, guiding with his strong fingers, pushed it into his asshole without any hesitation. I could see in his face that he felt a lot of pain, but he was taking it like the fucking man that he was. But soon, as he moved his ass up and down, the pain in his face turned to ecstasy – and I felt like a bullet shooting through Johnny's heart.

The movement of Johnny's hips grew in intensity, up and down up and down as semen dripped out of his cock onto my chest. Drops of it landed everywhere, even on my cheek as this thrusting of Johnny's body remained powerful but amazingly silent.

We held our hands in a vice-like clasp as he took my cock deeper and deeper and harder and harder causing all sense to leave my brain. I kept thinking of Johnny's mother's house again, the richness of lavender and black in this darkness, and the song that Johnny's mother would sing to him ...

Little, little boy, don't lie to me
tell me where did you sleep last night?
In the pines, mother, in the pines
where the sun never shines ...

Thinking of Johnny naked on a bed of pine needles made me moan. Johnny slapped my face hard, and from them on I suffered this silent fucking night inside Johnny for nearly an hour as he would take me to the edge and make me scream in my head to let me erupt. Like flashes of purple light came scenes of Johnny and me outdoors, way beyond the electric fences, somewhere out in sublime sweet darkness.

These pictures brought me to an ecstatic flood of tears; I looked up at Johnny and saw tears in his eyes as well. Some were shed for the sweet pain he felt from his first fuck, but there were some shed for me, I know, as his eyes looked straight into mine with the deep deep mating of our souls. I held tight to his thigh and squeezed at the Celtic cross tattooed there.

Johnny was the only guy in this place with leg tattoos, another emblem that made him so irresistibly different than the rest of us – that made Johnny more fucking great than my high school dreams could ever conjure.

I lifted my head and sucked hard at the tender skin, smelling the sweat dripping all over Johnny's legs. Every experience of love Johnny ever felt in his life was oozing through his pores and I was swallowing all the past loves with my tongue. Just like we men were all united in this place through our dreams of one day getting out, so was I now connected to the world out there through these unknown contacts that I was so grateful to for delivering Johnny to me at this very moment, for any reason good or bad.

Johnny moved the tide back and forth endlessly until my cock finally exploded. At that moment his semen sprayed in every direction as his body shook all over and toppled onto the floor making the wall vibrate. Here was Johnny, the strong, silent fucking machine, standing naked, still with an erection, in a panic of what was about to happen because there was nowhere to escape.

The door of the infirmary opened. A shaft of bright florescent light filled the room of mostly empty beds. Johnny's eyes looked green in the glow, his naked body trembling like a nervous cat. I looked at his face, my Sir Galahad who found his Holy Grail in my erection, for perhaps the very last time. Our eyes met just as two men grabbed Johnny's arms and pinned

him against the wall.

Suddenly I heard the door close and a hushed voice call my name, followed by stifled laughter. A thin silhouette moved toward me in the darkness and then I saw the face of Jessie underneath his Panama hat, with his never-ending goofy smile and bony masculine face. He reached over and squeezed the last of the cum from the hole of my dick.

"Jessie, what the fuck are you doing here?"

Jessie giggled again and turned toward the wall where two guys were taking turns pummeling their dicks into Johnny's asshole.

Jessie sat on the edge of the bed. My eyes still on Johnny, I pulled and tugged at his quivering cock. I knew Johnny was not enjoying what was happening, but it was a lot more comforting to me than having him taken away from me.

BURNING BRIDGES

David Laurents

I closed the lid of the toilet and sat. The ceramic brought goosebumps to my skin as I leaned against the tank, pressing up against it to absorb the cold into my shoulder blades, the small of my back. October and it was still as hot as August or July, the sun blazing during a drought. They promised me it never got this hot when I was thinking about moving to San Francisco from New York City. But then, a lot of promises had turned up empty, I reflected, as I stood and turned on the tap. I dipped a wash cloth into the sink, soaking up the cool liquid. Elliott... I held the cloth up to my lips, letting it drip against my neck and chest, cold. Oh, Elliott.

I hadn't seen him in months. I had moved to Oakland so I wouldn't run into him accidently on the street, had given up all that was familiar so I wouldn't see him at our favorite haunts in San Francisco. I know I didn't get very far away, but I couldn't bear the thought of being away from him. I was still madly in love with him. I knew he probably had my address, my phone number. But I hadn't heard from Elliott since the night I walked out on him, when I found him in bed with another man.

I ran the towel under the tap again, and pressed it against the back of my neck, reveling in the feel of the cold, wet cloth.

My rage knew no bounds that night. It welled up inside me, a searing pain in my gut, burning like I was on fire. And suddenly my anger burst free, setting fire to items at random as I ran from the apartment. The thought of someone else making love to Elliott, other hands running across his body...

I leaned forward and stuck my head under the tap, but the image of Elliott's body stayed before my eyes. I imagined they were my hands pressed against his flesh again and opened my mouth to nuzzle one of his large, dark nipples. I bit down on my shoulder, running the cold cloth down my body, between my legs. I cupped my balls, remembering the feel of his mouth on my cock, our bodies pressed together in ecstasy.

I grabbed the bar of soap from its dish and pressed it to my

groin, rubbing it back and forth along the length of my cock until it had produced a lather. I remembered when Elliott and I had showered together the first night we slept together. He was in New York on a business trip. Was it two years ago, already? I remembered every detail: our first lovemaking, deliciously awkward as we explored each other's bodies, uncertain of everything but our desire for each other. I let the soap slip between my fingers into the basin, and reached for my swollen, lathered cock instead. I remembered the taste of Elliott's skin, the salt of his sweat under his armpits, his balls, the sweet flesh of his cock. I remembered the feeling of being inside him, the half-closed look on his face as he lay below me, his hands on my hips, pulling me towards him.

I could not hold back any longer and sat down, hard, on the toilet as I began to cum, shooting pale white arcs against my chest and stomach, legs. Beside me, the roll of toilet paper bust into flames. I ignored it, still stroking my cock as it spasmed with pleasure.

I am lying in the top bunk. They are the bunk beds I had as a child. I look about me and find that I am in my room at home, except everything looks odd. I step on the ladder to climb down, when the rung snaps under my weight. I fall, snapping each of the rungs as my legs push towards the floor. Am I grown so big, since last I slept here? I catch my breath, then lean down to pick up one of the broken ladder pieces. They are candy canes. I lick one to prove by its peppermint taste that I am right. This is what is odd: everything is made of candy.

I walk into the hall and hear noises downstairs, follow them into the kitchen. My mother is cooking. She is dressed all in black and has a big wart on her nose. On her head she is wearing a large, black witch's hat. "Good morning, dear," she says. "I'm making myself some breakfast." She points to the corner near the stove. "Would you like some?"

Elliott is chained to the refrigerator. He is naked, gagged, his hands and legs cuffed. I cannot help thinking he looks like he's ready for a B&D session, even as I open my mouth to protest. "You can't eat him," I say.

"What's the matter?" my mother asks, cackling like I have

never heard her do before. "Don't you want to share with your mother? His flesh is sweet enough for you to eat, isn't it?" She crosses to where Elliott is bound. He tries to shy away from her, but the chains prevent him. She turns to look at me and grabs him by the balls. I know it hurts, because Elliott stiffens, his back suddenly hunched. "You eat his meat, don't you?" She shakes his flaccid penis for emphasis, violently tugging it. "You eat his meat all the time."

Suddenly, my mother throws open the door of the oven. It is enormous, like a huge, gaping maw. Inside, the coils are so hot that flames leap up from their orange filaments. I rush forward to stop her, but she throws Elliott into the oven and shuts the door. I try to open the door, but it will not budge. The light is on inside, and I press my face against the glass, desperate to at least see him one last time before he burns. Behind me my mother cackles on and on, her voice as high and nasal as a smoke detector.

The bed was on fire! I jumped up, pulling the blankets with me. Reflex made my fingers shy away from the heat. By force of will, I grabbed the burning linen, flipped them over, and smothered the fire.

But it was no use, I realized, as I sat naked on the floor amid the smoldering bedding. The smoke detector cried overhead. The whole apartment was on fire!

I struggled into a pair of jeans, even while thinking that this was no time for modesty, and ran down the stairs. Fire raged up and down the street. I cringed from the heat, awed and overpowered by the strength of my anger. What a dream of Elliott I had been having! Everything was on fire, from my block all the way to the Hills!

I felt my insides suddenly wrench with guilt. I had to make sure everyone got to safety. It was my fault if they died!

I heard shouts for help to my left. The neighbor's house was on fire, the roof crumbling in. I rushed into the building without hesitating, following the shouts. The heat was incredible, like standing in an open furnace. My jealousy-induced parakineses was no help in protecting me from fire. All it did was cause damage, cause harm.

Even with Elliott. Elliott was afraid of my anger. Afraid of *me*.

That's why he hadn't called. He was too afraid to face what it meant, my love for him.

The shouting woke me from my memories. I rushed upstairs and into a bedroom filled with smoke. "Over here!" a voice shouted, "Help me! Over here!"

I stumbled towards him. He was trapped beneath a fallen beam. I struggled to push it off of his legs. Come on, I berated myself, lift! You caused this fire! Adrenaline surged within me and I managed to lift the beam, holding it on my shoulder as he scrambled out from underneath. I reached out with one hand to help pull him free.

"Get your hands from me, faggot," he shouted, swinging a fist at me.

I dropped the beam, ducking the blow. I felt a chill in my bones, as the adrenaline burning along my muscles froze.

"You're disgusting. Take advantage of a man trapped in a fire." He stumbled toward the door, turned and spat. "Pervert," then slammed the door behind him.

I was in shock. Why had I bothered? I had saved his life, and all I got in return was hatred. I wished for a moment that I had left him trapped beneath the beam.

No. This was all my fault! As full of hate as he was, I wasn't ready to kill him, wasn't prepared to be responsible for his death.

His, and how many others?

I saw Elliott's face before me, inside the oven. I tried to reach him, but the glass was in the way. I banged against it with my fists, but it would not budge. I cast about me blindly, looking for something, anything, to break the glass. My fingers closed on a pipe, and I swung it desperately at the oven, hoping I wasn't too late.

I choked suddenly, as I gulped in huge lung fulls of smoke. I stared blankly at the wooden door in front of me.

Elliott? Where had Elliott gone?

I was still in the burning house. Elliott wasn't there. He hadn't been there at all, but was safe from the fire, miles away.

But I still heard his voice, calling for me.

"I'm coming!" I shouted, my voice tearing my throat. Panic surged through me; I had to get to him, save him from the fire. My spark burst forth, incinerating the door. I could feel the

intense heat as I ran through the now-open frame, but I didn't care. I had to find Elliott, I had to save him. I ran down the stairs, out into the street.

Where was he? I heard shouting to my left, turned towards my own apartment. I saw the man I had saved, ignored him. I could still hear Elliott calling my name; where the hell was he?

Suddenly, the door to my building flew open and Elliott was there, shouting for me. I rushed to him, practically threw myself at him. He held me in his arms, arms that were so comforting and familiar I couldn't help but believe he was real.

"You're safe," he said, hugging me so tightly my chest hurt. "I'm so glad your safe."

I began to cry, an overflow of fear and frustration and happiness, and then passed out.

. . .

I could feel the flames licking at my skin. I was on fire burning up but I had to go on I had to save them this was all my fault I had to find Elliott I had to save Elliott!

And suddenly he was there with me, holding me, cradling me in his arms, shielding me from the flames. His hands were deliciously cool, draining away the heat.

"But we have to save them," I said, trying to push him away. "This is all my fault!"

"Shhhh," Elliott crooned. "You're safe now. Nothing is your fault. It was an electrical fire. Up in the hills. You had nothing to do with it. Because of the drought, it got out of control."

I stopped struggling. Electrical fire? Not my spark. Not my fault at all. I wanted to laugh with relief! I thought of the neighbor I had saved. Did I regret it? Risking myself for the sake of preserving his hatred?

No, I realized. I didn't.

I opened my eyes and looked at Elliott. His concern was obvious as he stared down at me, as he held me against him. I never wanted it to end, wanted to remain frozen in that moment, forever the object of his full attention. I was afraid that if I looked away, even for a second, everything would fall apart and I would suddenly wake up from a smoke-induced

hallucination and find that I was still trapped in a burning building.

But I could feel cloth beneath me, and finally I tore my eyes away from him to look at my surroundings. I was in Elliott's bed. In our old bed. Everything was as I remembered it. He hadn't changed a bit. I even pressed myself up onto my elbows to peer into the corner by the closet and laughed when I saw his dirty socks and underwear in a pile.

I lay back against the pillow again and closed my eyes for a moment, simply for the pleasure of opening them again to find Elliott before me. He really was there, still holding me, still running his cool hands along my body, draining the heat away. We were both naked. I wondered what had happened between the fire and waking up here, wondered if perhaps the last few miserable months had been nothing more than a nightmare. But then I coughed, my throat still raw from the smoke, and I knew that Elliott had found me in the fire, had brought me home and nursed me until now. I knew that he still loved me.

Tentatively, I reached out with one hand and pressed it against his chest, over his heart. His skin was as cold as marble, or perhaps it was that I was burning up. I let my hand drift, luxuriating in the cool feel of his body as I explored its familiar planes, in the feel of his hands along my body, my chest, arms, thighs, draining away the heat. It was as if he was absorbing my spark, all my built-up anger and frustration. And I surrendered to the sensation.

I sat up, pulling him towards me. My tongue was stone-dry as it entered his mouth, but he didn't care and, after a moment of kissing, it was soon wet.

My hands ran up and down along his chest, which felt like a Grecian pillar, solid and safe; I clung to him. He pulled away for breath, and I kissed my way down his smooth neck and chest to his nipples, those large, dark nipples that had haunted my dreams.

I ran my tongue around them, moving from one to the other in figure eights. Small tufts of hair grew in rings at their edges, the only hair on his smooth chest.

I let my hands fall into his lap to his cock, swollen with desire and anticipation. His hands ran through my hair and down my back.

I licked the strong muscles of his abdomen, working my way towards the sweet flesh of his cock.

I felt his mouth wrap around my own cock, moist and tight.

I wanted to consume him with my passion, to devour every last piece of him.

Unbidden, my mother's voice from my nightmare echoed in my mind as my tongue was about to touch his cock: *His flesh is sweet enough for you to eat, isn't it? Don't you want to share with your mother?*

I shook my head, trying to clear the voice from inside my skull.

Elliott sat up, concerned. "Are you okay? Did I hurt you?"

I looked into his face, at his loving concern and felt there could be nothing wrong with the world.

I pulled his head towards me, kissed him deeply, my tongue pressing far into his mouth. "I love you," I said, grinning like a baby from happiness.

He smiled back at me, and winked. "Likewise."

I laughed out loud. He hadn't changed one bit!

I turned and eagerly buried my head in his crotch, licking my way down his shaft to his balls. My tongue thrilled at the familiar taste of his skin. I could hear Elliott's catch of surprise as I took one testicle into my mouth, which turned into an almost-purr in his chest as I began to suck on it gently. I let it drop from my mouth and rubbed my face back and forth along the length of his wet cock, letting it slide against my cheeks, eyes, chin, neck. With one hand I reached for his nipples, teased them with pinches and twirls. With my other hand I lifted his cock to my lips. Even his swollen, throbbing cock felt cool, inciting my own desire as the heat of my spark drained away.

I felt Elliott's mouth on my own cock, pumping up and down its length, his lips tightly clamped. It felt like he was going to suck the fire from me! We fell into a rhythm, in unison in sex, life, everything. I tried to hold back, to make the moment go on forever, but I crested over the wave into orgasm, crying out in pleasure.

A moment later, Elliott came, too, cum shooting up at me; I bent my face to catch his warm seed on my nose, eyelids, chin. We shuddered, and I felt an intense fulfillment that was soured

by only one thing.

I looked about me nervously, wondering what my spark had set on fire. But nothing in the room was burning. I smiled, turned around towards Elliott, kissed and held him tightly.

. . .

We walked down to the Embarcadero and stood together at the water's edge. The Oakland hills were glowing like the coals after a barbecue.

I kicked off a shoe, let it drop, splashing water onto the reflected image of the flame. I stepped from Elliott's embrace and dipped a toe into the water, to prove to myself how cool it is, how wet it is, orange and red from the fire and the lights. I had to prove to myself that I had escaped the flames as I had finally escaped my anger at Elliott.

I thought of my life on the other side of the Bay, in Oakland. I was perfectly happy to step back into the life I had left behind when I ran away instead of staying to talk. Life seemed so perfect right now, I never wanted it to end. It didn't have to, I thought. All I needed to do was forgive Elliott. He had proven himself when he came searching for me in the middle of the blaze. And he had forgiven me, for leaving him, for my anger, my dangerous spark.

To my left, three people conversed in French, leaning against the rail and smoking. Ash drifted before me, dropping to the water. One of the tourists laughed loudly and I began to shake.

Elliott put his arm around me and turned my face towards him. "Likewise," he said, and kissed me deeply.

When we came up for air, I focused on the tip of the tourist's cigarette, and let go of my anger, forever.

Our arms around each other, Elliott and I turned our backs and walked home.

BOY

Edmund Miller

Box of sweets, compacted lay,
Your skimpy-sideburned youth
Suggests a slick and hairless chest
And restive late pubescence.
Your Greek and little nose
Reveals your restless organ grows
No more than those
Exquisite parts of ancient Greeks
Remembered in their arts.

WHAT GOD LIKES TO WATCH

Antler

If one is observant of boys
One can see specimens with erections
  They're unable to straighten out without drawing attention to
  them,
Erections in their longpants or shorts,
Humorously obvious prongs
Throbbing as they walk along trying to conceal them with
schoolbooks, hoping no one will notice.
But you haven't been a boylover for 25 centuries for nothing.
Yet so sly
No boy glancing frantically around
  as he tries hiding his crotch with his books
Catches you eyeing the magnificent risen boypenisgod
  arching bent straining pulsing awkward
  making it get even harder bonerprong in Levis.
This is what God likes to watch.
This excites God – why else would
  God have created it?
Not an unwished-for uncontrollable prankish boyboner
  escapes you, its blushing owner
  returning from trackpractice in early autumn,
  its sensitive sophisticated inquisitive
  13-year-old mulatto boy who plays classical violin,
Not even the 14-year-old with his portfolio of watercolor
paintings,
  nor the 15-year-old proudly flaunting atheist
  secretly shy for his bestfriend's kiss
  who shies from him daydreaming
  quarter-hardon
  half-hardoning
  three-quarter-hardoning
  full-fledged hardonbongdong
A simple matter to take care of
  first things first
  on getting home.

How many erections does a boy have a day?
How many boys with erections can you see in a day?
Good questions to ask.
As they used to employ people to count
   the number of cars that went by,
A new job niche in society comes into being
Sly boy-erection-gazers of the World –
It turns out this was your job all along
See, poets and poetic license
   are a boon to the Job Creation Think Tank!
Voila! In a second's epiphany
Antler creates full-time jobs
   for a million boy-crazy souls.

NOTE:

The following novel has been extensively edited
from the original manuscript to
meet the current needs of the publisher.

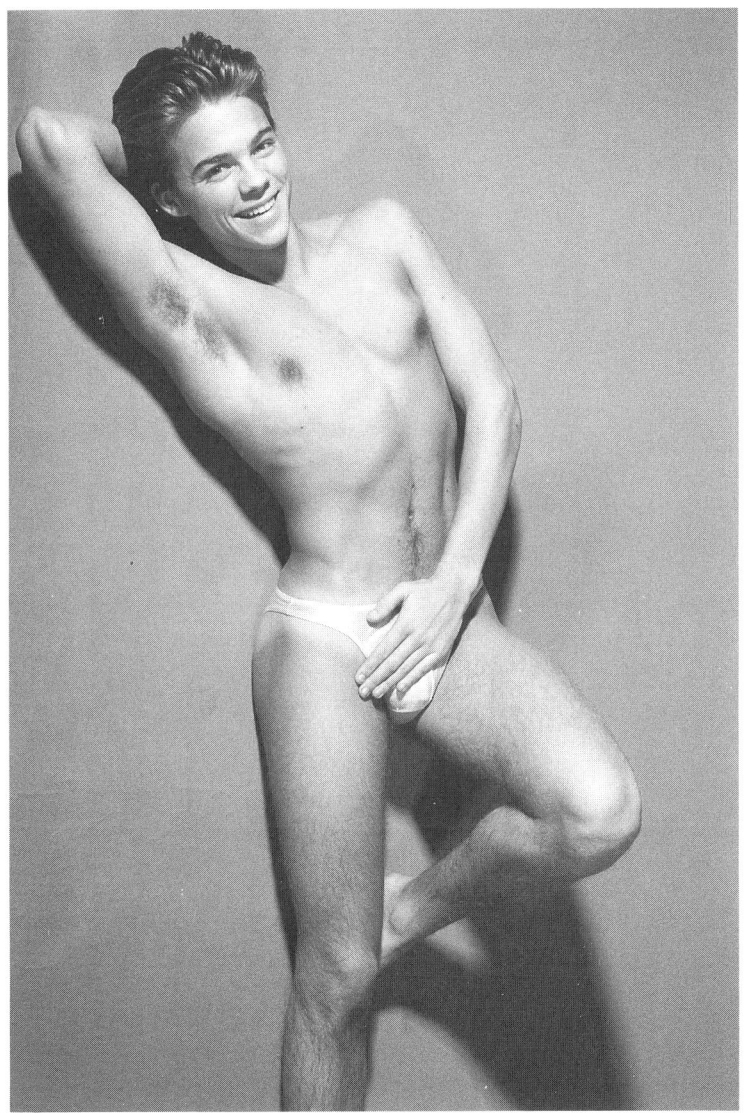

THE YOUNG AND THE FLAWLESS

A Novel by
JOHN C. DOUGLAS

STARbooks Press
Sarasota, FL

*"He said something once that shocked me.
I thought about it for years.
He said only two things in life really interested
him: sex and his work."
-Bob Raison about his longtime friend,
the great film director George Cukor*

1

Furiously chewing the stump of an unlit cigar, Larry Davis, the director, waddled over to where Danny Murphy and I lay, naked and covered with sweat, on the rumpled double bed.

"It won't work, goddamn it!" he growled, waving the wet end of the cigar at my slowly wilting erection. "People pay to see that thing sliding in and out, Pete. No matter how I shoot it, they're gonna know you ain't really got it in there."

"Talk to Danny boy," I sighed. "I've been ready to shove it in for the past hour."

It was no lie. For nearly sixty minutes, I had been crouched behind the boy's rearing bottom, giving the camera a full view of my stiff cock, then pretending to slide into his anus and begin humping him. The trouble was that Danny had adamantly refused to let me actually stick it in, and I had to slip it between his legs, letting it ride against his balls as I hunched in simulated sodomy. I was about to develop a stone ache from frustration.

Ordinarily, Larry would have replaced the kid with a more cooperative performer, but Danny was one of the prettiest of the available crop. Eighteen, but looking like fifteen, blond, and with a magnificent body, Danny had the chicken hawks in the audience creaming their jeans, and Larry figured that watching me ram all ten inches up his tail would really drive 'em wild.

But Danny insisted that he had never done it that way, preferring to use his mouth when satisfying his partners. It was true, he had sucked a mean cock, but that's only half of the game in reel life.

"How about it, kid? You're costing me a fucking fortune here!" Larry was so agitated that for the first time in my memory, he lit his cigar.

"Kick in some more," Danny said, "and I'll let him do it."

"Shit!" Larry groaned, beginning to puff away. "Look, Danny, you've got four scenes with Pete, so I'll spring for a hundred extra each time you let him stick it to you. Okay? But

not a cent more. And I'll expect some cum – got it? Cum! When he finishes, you come!"

"What if I can't take it all?"

"You'll take it. Shit, they all start out sayin' that, but they keep comin' back for more." He pointed the cigar at me again. Ashes fell on my leg. "Fuck the holy shit out of him, Pete!"

"You're the boss." I found myself half-hoping that Danny would protest. It would make screwing him even more exciting.

"You ready, kid?" Larry asked.

Danny nodded uncertainly. It was obvious that he wanted my dick. His cute seven-incher was standing up like an eager soldier, and his eyes kept jumping from Larry's face to my cock.

"Okay, we'll have a full shot and two cameras on cover for closeups. Don't worry about them. Just give me some real action, and I can edit it any way I want. We've got one hell of a story, and I want it done right."

Story? Well, the script wasn't exactly adapted from a current best-seller, but I had to admit that it was the nearest thing to a dramatic vehicle Larry had ever attempted. Usually, it was a case of man meets boy, man and boy suck and fuck, and roll the credits. This time, for a change, I had the chance to do something other than show off my big prick. In fact, a couple of scenes called for some honest-to-god acting, as I was playing the part of a private dick hired by a wealthy man to rescue his nephew, played by Danny, from kidnappers. As usual, we were shooting everything out of sequence and starting with the sex scenes.

"Please, Pete," Danny murmured. "Take it easy."

I placed my hands on his slender hips and let the head of my cock rub his smooth belly. "Relax, kid," I whispered back.

Larry called for lights, and Danny and I were suddenly alone on an island of brilliance. There were ten other people in the high-ceilinged warehouse Larry used as a studio, but we were able to ignore their presence, and play out our assigned roles.

"Cameras!" Larry ordered, and waited for the three operators to announce that they were up to speed. Then, from behind the lights, he cued us with, "Action!" But that wasn't really necessary because we were already making love.

Placing my hands on Danny's lithe waist, I urged him toward

me just enough to let the heads of our dicks touch. Although he was nervous and apprehensive, the youngster still had a beautiful erection; I felt the heat of it against my cockhead. Danny's arms slid about my neck, and I moved my own hands around and down to clutch his firmly rounded buttocks.

"You're a gorgeous creature," I said, my voice a little on the husky side. It wasn't acting. I was horny for this kid.

His lips parted as I covered them with mine, and his tongue swirled into my mouth in a torrid kiss. I backed off just enough to let the camera capture our fencing tongues, and Danny's hips worked more rapidly to rub his prick against mine. We both knew that the second hand-held camera was down there capturing every move.

Gently, but firmly, I pushed him down onto the bed, lowering myself atop him as he spread his shapely legs. A shiver ran through his body when he felt my cock against his balls. I knew he was expecting me to slide down and force my prick into his virgin asshole, but I had already decided to rewrite the script. I figured the best way to warm him up for the big finale was to continue the oral action m a bit longer..

Slipping lower in the bed, I ran my tongue over his left nipple, licking it until it reared up like a big eraser, and Danny gave a little groan of pleasure. Then I paid the same oral tribute to his right tit, fastening my lips about the small circle and sucking it as I licked.

"Oh," the boy murmured, his fingers running through my hair. "That feels so good!"

Danny's chest was hairless. In fact, I doubted that he was yet into shaving, for even his cheeks were smooth, with just a trace of soft down. My cock was throbbing like crazy as I worked my way lower, wriggling my tongue into his navel and making his hips squirm. His prick was rubbing against my chest, the head nudging my chin.

I glanced over at Larry, who was motioning me to get on with the fuck, but I wasn't about to pass up anything as inviting as Danny's dick. Anyway, doing it this way would relax the boy, and he would be more cooperative when I finally penetrated that hot little ass.

Danny must have sensed my reasoning, for he created his own lines. "Turn around so I can get to your dick!"

My cock bobbed and wiggled as I moved about to lie on my side with hips even with Danny's head, and my own head hovering just over the boy's prick. I licked my lips and fitted them over the plum-like head, my tongue flaying the delicious glans.

"Oh, God! That feels ... UMMMMM!"

His last word was muffled as he drew the big knob beyond the soft palate and into his throat. It took all of two minutes to ease the boy onto his back so I could straddle his face and feed my dick in and out of his mouth, quite literally fucking it. Meantime, I was nursing his tasty young prick sliding my lips all the way to the base with each bob of my head.

Some boys, no matter how much they love to suck cock, never learn how to relax their throat so they can take a big prong really deep. But Danny was not just taking all of my prick, he was swallowing while the head was buried in his throat, and the contraction of those soft hot tissues about my glans was driving me wild. My balls were tightening with every stroke of my cock through those greedy lips and over that swirling tongue, and I knew that I was dangerously close to orgasm.

One of the requirements of porn is that you show the prick as it spills its load of cum. It's frustrating to the actors, but audiences demand it. Larry would expect both of us to pull out before we came, so the cameras could capture the sight of the big event from several angles.

I could sense Danny was only seconds away from coming for his hips were grinding like crazy, and I could feel his cock swelling and jerking.

As for me, I've had a lot more experience at control, so I could hold back longer than the kid. Raising my head so that my lips slid up and off of Danny's dick, I arched my back and looked back between our bodies to where my own cock was plunging in and out of the boy's mouth.

My balls were pressing and spreading over his nose and eyes with each thrust, and Danny's chin was working madly as he sucked.

"Let's both come," I panted. "I'll swallow yours, but I want you to save mine. Don't swallow it, okay?"

I expected Larry to interrupt us, for there was nothing like

this in the script, and only I knew what I had in mind. Maybe Danny did, but all I got from him was a little grunt that let me know he would hold my semen in his mouth.

I nursed his cock hungrily, no longer trying to hold back the spasms of ecstacy that surged through my balls. Danny's hips hunched wildly, ramming his cock up into my mouth each time my lips slid down the shaft, while I fucked his throat with almost savage thrusts, each one more delightful than the last.

"UMMMMM!" Danny moaned, his hips jerking and his cock swelling in my mouth. My tongue ravaged the slippery glans and I felt and tasted the first salvo of that delectable cum, the cum jetting against my tongue with youthful force.

Almost at the same moment, ecstacy churned in my balls and my own cum spurted into Danny's mouth. We both sucked even harder as our pricks delivered the rewards of our nursing, and I swallowed greedily as the youngster's cum spilled down my throat.

Over the furious pounding of my heart, I could hear Danny's moans of frustration as he fought back the urge to swallow my load.

Slowly, patiently, I milked the lad's cock with my lips and fingers, stripping the last drop of savory cum from the still-hard shaft. Then, very carefully, I slid my lips up and off, and raised my upper body by placing my hands on either side of Danny's hips.

One of the cameras was right in my face, so I made a big show of licking my lips to demonstrate my enjoyment of what I had just done. Then I planted a kiss on the head of Danny's dick.

"Now here's what we're going to do – "

Quickly I explained what I had in mind, and Danny, with my cock and my cum still in his mouth, listened and grunted in understanding.

From behind the lights, I heard Larry's muted growl, but he made no move to stop us as we rolled onto our sides and Danny carefully opened his mouth wide, permitting me to pull my prick out, its entire length coated with cum.

Licking the stray drops from his full lips, the boy rose to his hands and knees, his thighs spread for my mounting, and I knelt behind him, the camera so close it was almost touching

my cum-slick dick. Our positioning was perfect, and the head of my cock nuzzled Danny's anus. I put my hands on his hips and pressed just enough to let him feel what was about to enter him.

"Oh, god!" he groaned, his body tensing. "Your cock's so big!"

"Just relax," I soothed him. "Let me in there."

Holding his hips for leverage, I arched my waist, thrusting my hips forward, feeling the delightful yielding of Danny's sphincter as the glans forced its way into his virgin asshole.

Earlier Danny had inserted a special suppository in his anus, but even with that and the lubrication of my semen, it was difficult to work my cock into him.

"Oh, god!" he cried, his naked body writhing in a desperate effort to evade the penetration of his tight rectum. But my hands held his pelvis in place and I pushed my cock deeper into the hot corridor, feeling the clinging tissues ripple and churn as his anal muscles contracted and relaxed, trying to adjust to the painful invasion.

With about half the length of my prick inserted in him, I stopped pushing, and waited for him to calm down. Slowly, delightfully, his rectal muscles relaxed about my dick, and he drew a long, shuddering breath.

He gave a different sort of cry when I pulled my cock back to where the corona of the glans tugged at his anal ring, for the swollen head had massaged his prostate, and rubbed it again when I thrust the shaft back into his ass, even deeper than before. "Jesus..." he gasped as I worked my prick in and out, frictioning and filling him again and again, my big balls pressing his own tender orbs with each thrust.

I leaned over Danny's back, my hips continuing their rhythmic hunching, my dick pistoning in and out, and I hissed, "What am I doing to you?"

"You're fuckin' me!" he groaned, his neck arching as he raised his head as if baying with lust, and I buried my own face in those soft curls.

I raised my upper body and worked my knees farther beneath Danny's rearing hips, enabling me to drive still deeper into that convulsing asshole.

"Do you like being fucked in the ass?" I panted, my belly

slapping his lower back as I pounded him.

"Oh, god, yes!" he cried. "Give me that big cock!"

Larry was getting all the footage he wanted, and I was getting my best piece of ass in a long time as Danny's hips twisted violently to provide extra friction to my thrusts and withdrawals.

I tried to think about something other than how good it felt to drive my prick in and out of the boy's asshole, anything to make the fuck last a little longer, but it was getting too good for both of us.

"I'm gonna come!" Danny panted, and I knew that one of the cameras would zero in on his jerking dick, for it wasn't often Larry got a shot of a boy shooting his load simply from being screwed. Most of the time, either the kid masturbated while taking it up the ass, or his partner stroked the boy's dick during the fuck. Danny was about to get off from simply the pleasure of having my cock rammed in and out of his ass. I hunched harder and faster as I headed for orgasm heaven. "Work that sweet ass!" I cried, my hips pumping like crazy and my balls slapping his with little plopping sounds. "Show me you really want it!"

Danny twisted his head about so that our mouths could reach each other, tongues darting and licking as I continued to probe his hungry tail with my throbbing prick.

"Uuuggghhh!" Danny gurgled, his body jerking as the pleasure intensified. I felt his rectal muscles spasm about my cock, chewing and sucking, as I reamed him.

His asshole convulsed as his prick spurted the first volley of cum, and ecstacy jolted my balls, squeezing the cum out and up through my still driving cock.

It took a supreme act of willpower to wrench my dick out of that greedy asshole and let my cum blast onto Danny's arched back. Usually, I would grab my cock and stroke it, milking the cream out, but not this time.

All I did was press forward so that my balls rubbed the crack of his ass. My cock jerked and spurted like a fire hose gone berserk, spraying the thick liquid all the way up to where his blond curls met his back.

My groans of pleasure were not faked, and neither were Danny's as he felt the shower of cum on his fevered skin.

"Jesus! I wish that dick was in my mouth!"

Quickly I rocked back onto my haunches. "Turn over, kid!" I said harshly, and he rolled onto his back, his legs slipping between mine so I could straddle his waist. He lifted his head as I lowered my hips and eased my prick between his eager lips, letting his tongue coax the last spurt of jism from it.

With a groan of contentment, I slid my cock into his mouth until my balls were pressed warmly against his chin.

"UMMMMM!" Danny moaned.

I've made enough porn films to know that was the moment for the music to swell and the scene to fade.

Only when Larry yelled "Cut!" did I pull my dick out of the boy's mouth and roll onto my back beside him. He turned that pretty face toward me and licked his lips, giving me a smile that contained both gratitude and promise.

"Just imagine," he murmured, so softly that only I could hear him. "I'm gettin' paid *double* for this!"

2

The next day, Larry scheduled the second fuck scene with Danny and me, only this one included Keith Landers, a dark-haired beauty, veteran of six or seven fuck flicks. Keith had wanted to be paired with me for a long time and his eagerness was a turn-on.

Larry gave us our instructions, leaving a lot of room for improvisation, just as he had before. The action took place shortly after the scene we had completed the previous day. I had rescued Danny from his kidnappers and we had stopped at a motel to fuck. Upon leaving, we spotted an attractive boy, Keith, painting one of the rooms, and hastily convinced the lad to go join us in the room we had just vacated.

I left Keith and Danny together while I went to the bathroom. When I returned to the room, dressed only in my briefs, they were writhing against each other and I had a bulging erection. Larry took a loving closeup as I pushed down my Jockeys, letting my cock smack up against my belly before settling down at a thrusting angle.

Danny was kissing his way down his new friend's naked body, and he finally dropped to his knees before him, fondling the boy's dick before taking the oozing head into his mouth.

The two were right in front of the bed, and while Danny began sucking Keith's cock, I stepped up behind Keith and slipped my arms about his waist, palming his pectorals, while pressing my prick against his bottom.

Prior to the scene, both boys had lubricated their assholes so they were ready for action. I rubbed my cock in the crack of Keith's ass while Danny worked on the boy's hard-on.

Impulsively, I said to Keith, "Put one foot up on the bed." In this position, he could spread the cheeks of his ass and give me greater access to his ass. Careful not to dislodge his dick from Danny's mouth, he lifted his right foot and placed it on the bed. Now Danny fondled his balls as I gripped the base of my cock and steered the head into position, the tip pressing Keith's asshole. I had to really push to force the head past his

sphincter, and he gave a little cry of half-protest. But soon, as I slammed my prick into his ass, he was throwing his head back and almost sobbing with pleasure. All the while, Danny was sucking away on his prick.

Gripping Keith's hips, I fucked him with full length thrusts, and Danny timed the slide of his mouth down the boy's prick with my hunches. Each time I buried my dick in his ass, Keith's cock was rammed to the balls in Danny's convulsing throat, and three cameras were capturing every delightful moment, including our mingled gasps, grunts, and groans.

Keith had been instructed to pull his cock out of Danny's mouth before he came, and to shoot his load on the boy's face. I was supposed to yank my prick out at the last minute, and spray my semen over Keith's lower back.

A few times I've shot my wad into a partner's bottom or throat, and kept right on with the scene. The other guy took it and played dumb, understanding that the next time, he might be on the giving end. Of course, if you're the type who wilts after the first orgasm, you can't get away with a stunt like that. But I can come four times without losing my hard, which is why I get picked for so many films.

In this case, Keith was the first one to pass the point of no return. I could feel the hot tissues of his colon chewing on my dick as I slid it in and out, and I fucked him harder, slamming my pelvic arch against his bottom.

Danny could feel the sudden swelling and throbbing of Keith's cock, so he increased the speed and force of his busy mouth.

"AHHHH!...UHHHH!...UHHHH!"

It was Danny who pulled his lips off of the jerking prick just as the cum blasted from the tip, the cream splattering against Danny's lips and chin, and the boy licked some of it in with an eager tongue.

Keith's orgasm was echoing in his intestinal sleeve, and each spurt of his cum made his asshole contract about my dick, an effect that heightened my pleasure. I fucked him even faster, grunting with the increasing joy, feeling the pleasure become ecstacy that boiled in my balls and raced upward through my driving cock.

I forced myself to pull my prick out of his spasming ass, and

I moved quickly around to aim the head of the shaft at Danny's face.

When Keith, looking down, saw what was about to happen, he dropped to his knees and began licking Danny's mouth and chin, his tongue gathering up his own semen just as my cum spilled out to join his. Some of it sprayed into both boys' mouths, and they claimed it with whimpers of delight.

Their mouths fastened on the head of my cock, their tongues massaging it and flicking against the other, they managed to lick up most of my cum, with Keith recapturing his own spent sperm from Danny's face.

Before they were done, each boy had taken my dick into his mouth, drawing it deep. I was already aware of what an excellent cocksucker Danny was, but I now learned that Keith was equally skilled, for he was able to swallow while the head of my cock was between his tonsils, a feat which sends the most exquisite thrills through any dick that experiences it.

"Cut!" I heard Larry cry. "Good work guys! You fuckin' almost gave *me* a hard-on!"

For Larry, that was the supreme compliment. But I happened to know that one of the things that turned him on was watching a guy eat cum. Sometimes I wondered if Larry ever did that. He never discussed his personal sex life, and although I knew a few fellows who had spent time with him, they never talked about what it was like.

I patted Keith's butt. "Hot ass! We'll have to do that again!"

The boy's lips curved and he showed me the tip of his tongue. "Anytime you want it," he purred. He looked at Danny. "The same goes for you. That tongue of yours is too much."

Danny grinned back. He was the only one who hadn't shot off, and he still had a terrific hard-on. "I'll bet you do a good job, too."

Larry saw Danny's prick and said, "Let's not waste that. Get a fucking camera over here. Go on, kid," he told Keith. "Take care of it for him. He owes it to me."

Without hesitation, the boy lay down on the bed and held out his arms to Danny. "Come on, lover," he urged. "Fuck me in the mouth!"

Danny gave me a helpless look and knelt astride Keith's

chest. Keith's hands gripped Danny's buttocks and pulled his hips forward, taking the strutted cock into his hungry mouth.

Danny didn't hesitate. With a groan of pleasure, he drove his prick into Keith's throat, jamming his balls against the youngster's chin, then grinding his hips to friction the head of his dick against the pulsating tissues. Keith's mouth made a wet, sucking sound as Danny's dick slid in and out, his hips pounding, and his balls slapping the boy's chin and throat.

Keith had wanted to be fucked in the mouth, and Danny was giving the youth exactly what he had asked for. Keith sucked noisily and greedily, swallowing repeatedly as his saliva mingled with Danny's precum. Danny's hips worked faster, and Keith moaned with anticipation.

My own prick was stiffening again and Larry shouted that it was time Danny earned the extra money he had been promised. I mounted the lad and shoved it in him. His ass jerked and the buttocks tightened, and he pulled his dick back to where Keith was sucking just the head. His hips trembling, Danny held that position just long enough for Keith to massage the glans with his magic tongue, tipping him over the edge. Stifling a cry of ecstacy, Danny drew his cock out of the boy's mouth, holding it poised about an inch from the parted lips. His semen jetted into Keith's open mouth, some of it landing and clinging to his lips. After the last spurt of cum shot from his cock, Danny eased the head back into Keith's mouth and let the youngster suck it dry.

All through this, my cock never left Danny's ass. After he came, I pulled out and ordered them to get on their stomachs on the bed and I alternately fucked them. They kissed each other feverishly while I kept at it until, at last, I came again, splattering my jism on each of their buttocks. Then we collapsed together on the bed, me in the middle. They kissed me and each other even after Larry yelled for the cameras to stop rolling.

3

Whenever my schedule permitted, I'd drive up to the cabin on Lake Arrowhead my Sugar Daddy, an executive with a music publishing firm, let me use. I savored the remoteness of the place, while not having to give up any of the comforts of a condo in the city. Once a month or so, I would go there for a long weekend with Sugar Daddy, a size queen, who never asked any more of me than to worship my cock. Now with Sugar Daddy out of town, I would be able to enjoy some solitude. Or at least that's what I'd planned.

Dusk was just settling in as I pulled off the freeway to make my trek up the mountainside and spotted a slim young hitchhiker. He wore a worn, dirty pair of Levis and was carrying a jeans jacket in his hand. Covering his feet, and much of his legs, were badly scuffed cowboy boots. He was trudging down the road in the opposite direction, heading for the freeway. While I'd had a pretty strenuous afternoon, and was looking forward a rest, this was too good to pass up. I made a fast U-turn and, as I approached him, he lifted a hopeful thumb.

I halted my maroon Buick Roadmaster beside him and lowered the power window. He leaned down to rest one tanned arm on the window ledge. I found myself staring at his girlishly pretty face, framed by thick black curls, and a pair of full lips.

"Where you headed?" I asked, admiring his hairless pecs with their prominent nipples.

"L.A.," he answered, his voice one of those sultry types that seems caught between adolescence and maturity.

"Why?"

"Why not?"

"Hop in."

He tossed his backpack and jacket in the back seat and climbed in next to me. I made another U-turn.

"Hey," he said, turning around, watching the freeway disappear behind us.

"I've got to make a little stop before I go back to the city."

"Oh."

After I told him my name and he introduced himself as Mark, I asked him where he was from.

"Up near Sacramento."

"Nice area. Why'd you leave?"

"I just got fed up with my folks." He admitted he was tired of hearing what was going to happen to him if he didn't believe as they did.

"And what *do* they believe exactly?"

"In Jesus. They think *everything's* wrong."

"Oh, like what?"

"Sex stuff mostly."

"I didn't know Jesus felt that way, but what the hell do I know." I chuckled. "What do *they* say Jesus doesn't like?"

"Like jerkin' off," he said innocently. "Stuff like that."

"You do that a lot?"

"Shoot, yeah," he said with boyish enthusiasm. "Two or three times a day."

I took a deep breath, reminding myself that the boy could be real trouble. He told me he figured if he was going to start rebelling L.A. was the place to do it. "Hundreds a day get off the bus," I told him. "What do you plan to do when you get to L.A.?"

"I'll find a job," he said confidently.

"Doing what?"

"Washin' dishes maybe," he shrugged. "Moppin' floors. I don't care what it is. I ain't got no trade or nothin'."

He stretched his legs. The bulge had grown even bigger. My cock started doing pushups in my slacks. "Tell you what," I said. "You can stay with me tonight at my cabin and tomorrow we'll go back to town and I'll call a few people, see if I can find a place for you."

"I ain't looking for no charity," he protested.

"I don't look at it as charity."

He considered that for a long moment. Then he nodded. "Long as it ain't charity."

"No, it ain't charity, and I'll enjoy the company tonight."

"I don't want to put you out none," he said.

"It's okay," I assured him. "It gets lonesome up at the cabin

sometimes."

"Yeah," he sighed. "I been lonesome a lot myself. Ma and Pa ain't never let me have no real friends. Kids at school make fun of me 'cause I ain't got nice clothes and stuff."

He studied the passing scenery for a few minutes. Then, he asked, "What kinda work you do, Pete?"

"I'm in the movie business," I told him.

This really got his attention. "Movies? Honest? You an actor?"

"Oh, not a very good one," I said, smiling. "But I get by."

"Man, I'd sure like to see one of your movies. I'll bet you're real good. You sure got the looks."

"Thanks. I've got some tapes at the cabin."

"You mean, you got a VCR machine?"

"Yeah."

"We ain't never even had a television. Pa says they're a sin, and anybody that watches one will go to hell."

"Well, hell's gonna be pretty damn crowded."

He laughed heartily and started to slip out of his boots.

The turn to Lake Arrowhead was just ahead. I slowed the Buick, explaining I wanted to pick up a few things at the convenience store. Mark had just gotten out of his boots and was massaging his toes so he said he'd wait in the car. I bought bread, cold cuts, cereal and milk and, after setting the bag on the back seat, I climbed back behind the wheel, sneaking another look at the boy's lithe torso. Now I noticed he had developed an even more significant bulge in his jeans. I decided he must have been thinking about me while I was gone.

When we reached the cabin, I switched on the lights and he followed me into the kitchen. The cabin was really a small house, with four rooms and a bath.

"Man, you must really be rich!" he said, looking about as he crossed the room. He had left his boots at the front door and his bare feet sunk into the rug. "I ain't never seen nothin' like this."

One wall of the living room was filled with an entertainment center and book shelves. A sectional sofa hugged the opposite wall, flanked by massive end tables, and fronted by a marble-topped coffee table. There were two chairs, one a cushiony recliner, the other an easy chair that matched the sofa. A wet

bar graced one corner, topped by a well-stocked cabinet.

I started putting things away. "Make yourself at home," I said, watching him examine the digital controls on the microwave.

"What's this?" he asked.

"An oven."

"Really?"

I showed him how it worked. His fascination with everything made me realize just how quickly I had taken the trappings of wealth for granted. "Like to see the rest of the place?"

He nodded eagerly, and I motioned him back through the living room and into the master bedroom. He stopped just inside the door, his eyes wide. "Wow!"

The circular bed, twelve feet in diameter, took up almost the entire room. Piled with soft, baby blue pillows, it was an invitation to every position imaginable in the game of love.

Pointing to a closed door, I said, "And that's the bath."

As he walked over to the bathroom, his ass swayed sensuously with each step. My prick swelled in anticipation, and I felt my balls tighten.

When he saw the mirrored bathroom, with a king-sized whirlpool tub, he gaped for a minute, then turned to face me. "Can I take a bath, Pete? I really feel dirty now with all this pretty stuff around here."

I chuckled. "You'll find towels in there." I gestured toward the cabinet. "And you can use one of my robes. I'll lay one on the bed for you."

He embraced me. "Nobody's ever been this nice to me, Pete," he said, his voice almost cracking.

I pulled away. "Hey, I'm gonna have a drink, you want one?"

"Ain't never had no liquor. That's another thing Pa says'll send you straight to hell."

"Well, like I said, it's gonna be pretty damn crowded there," I smiled. "But at least you'll be able to watch TV!"

I left him in the bathroom, closing the door before he dropped his jeans. The kid's naivete was making me hotter by the second. In the bedroom, I stripped down and took two robes from the closet, both silk, one blue (Sugar Daddy's), the other red. I donned the blue one, and laid the other on the bed.

At the bar, I dropped four ice cubes in his glass, two in mine and put two jiggers of Jack Daniels in each. I put a splash of water in his glass. Sipping my drink, I turned on the television.

He seemed to take forever in the shower, but the wait was worth it. Boys who just come from their baths seem to look as if they have been primed and ready to fuck and Mark was no exception. His dark curls were still damp, and his smooth cheeks were glowing as he entered the room, bundled in the red robe.

"This sure does feel nice, Pete," he said, crossing the room. One hand stroked the silk along his left thigh.

"You sure you won't join me?" I lifted a glass to him.

"Well, okay." He nodded. "I wanna try everything Pa says is wrong! At least once!"

"Your drink's on the bar over there."

He took a tentative sip, closing his eyes as his taste buds sampled the bourbon. He swallowed, then gave a little shudder. "Boy!" he said, staring at the whiskey. "No wonder people like this stuff. It makes me feel warm all the way to my toes."

"It helps me relax. That's why I come up here, to relax and do as I damn well please."

"Reckon it's nice to do that. I always wanted to do all kinds of stuff, but my folks wouldn't let me."

"Like watch TV." I patted the cushion next to me on the couch. "Come, sit."

He sat down and stared at the screen. I had put my first film,"Brother Lust," which had recently been converted to video, in the VCR. It had been on for twenty minutes. Two scenes had already played. I was in the last scene.

"Wow!" he said.

"Wow what?"

"I ain't never seen nothin' like that."

"You ain't seen nothin' yet," I chuckled.

By the time my scene began, Mark was visibly aroused, rubbing his crotch through the silk. When I appeared on the screen his jaw dropped. "It's you! That's you!"

"Peter Hardee, that's me."

Finishing his drink, he set it on the coffee table and remained bent over, his eyes glued to the screen. "My god!" he cried

when my cock was exposed by my older "brother." As my cock grew with my partner's heated sucking, Mark gasped.

I opened my robe and let the real thing loose. He watched the scene intently for a few moments, then gave me a sidelong glance. I smiled. His eyes dropped to my cock, laying semi-hard against my thigh. His eyes bugged.

"Go ahead," I said, "you can touch it."

Tentatively his fingers went to the shaft, lifting it up, admiring it. "I can't believe this," he breathed.

I grabbed him and brought my lips to his.

"Ummmm!" he moaned, his body quivering as our tongues danced. He opened his mouth wider, letting me explore at will. He squeezed my now hard prick.

One of my hands found the sash of his robe and loosened it, baring his young flesh.

"Oh, Pete!" he gasped as my fingers slipped between us to cup his balls, gently squeezing them, then climbing to encircle the swollen hardness of his prick. "Oh, that feels so good!"

I dropped to my knees and leaned forward, pulling him to me so that my lips could caress his right nipple, my tongue teasing it with dainty flicks. Then I fastened my mouth over it and sucked, making him cry out.

After a few moments, I licked my way down over his firm belly, dipping the tip of my tongue into his navel, my chin grazing the head of his cock. I bypassed the beauty, and kissed his thigh, running my tongue through that moist crease between thigh and belly, then lapped gently at his young balls.

"Ohhh!" he whimpered, his prick jerking in my grip.

Almost reverently, I lifted my head and pressed my parted lips against the delicate triangle, just below the inverted "V" of his glans, drawing a gasp of ecstacy from the youngster, his body quivering and jerking, his hips scooting lower on the couch.

I looked up into his eyes. His long lashes were fluttering uncontrollably. The light was reflected in the brown irises, making them sparkle. His tongue circled the full lips.

"Want me to suck it?" I asked softly, letting him feel the words as my warm breath bathed his cock. My fingers teased his balls and squeezed the strutted shaft, drawing a pearl of jism from the tiny slit.

He could only nod his eagerness for a continuation of the thrill my oral caress had produced. My own prick pulsed with shared excitement as I opened my mouth and slipped my lips over his huge cockhead, tasting the pre-cum and feeling his satiny smoothness yield to my swirling tongue.

He cried out with delight, his hips pushing upward, and his hands reaching to run fingers through my hair, then urge my head down, pushing my mouth onto his swollen dick.

My cheeks hollowed, and he cried out again as he felt the hot suction, my lips beginning that delightful sliding, my fingers moving down to the base of the column, so I could take the entire length in my hungry mouth, letting the head invade my throat.

I sucked him with a slow rise and fall of my head, letting my mouth relax as I took his cock deep, then sucking hungrily as I pulled back until only the soft-hard head was still behind my teeth. His hips worked in perfect harmony with my bobbing head, pushing the cock into my mouth until the knob was against the back of my throat, then retreating to draw it almost free.

Again and again it spilled those little globs of jism, and I blended them with my saliva, savoring his youthful passion, swallowing the mixture as if blending his essence with mine.

"Oh, Pete!" he panted, his hips lifting and quivering as my tongue swirled and licked the head of his prick before taking it full-length again. "I'm gonna come!"

I squeezed his balls just hard enough to let him know that I understood, and I sucked even harder to assure him I wanted his load. Soon his cock swelled in my mouth, and his cum spurted against my tongue and palate. I took his prick deep as it jetted and chills raced through my belly, making my own cock throb.

Even when his hips relaxed on the couch, I followed him down, still nursing his dick for that one final drop of cum. His fingers stroked my hair, lovingly now, and his gasps of pleasure became the heavy breathing of satisfaction.

"Oh, Pete!" he managed, his voice ragged. "I thought I was gonna die!"

I pulled my mouth off his cock, but kept my lips against the head. "Was it that bad?"

"Oh, no, it was that good! I never knowed it could feel that good!"

"I'm glad."

"Did you like it?"

"I loved it," I said, running my tongue around the sloping glans. As I lifted my head to look at the television again, "Brother Lust" had ended and the screen had gone blue.

4

After another drink, I steered him into the bedroom. I took off my robe and got on the bed. I spread my legs, and my prick reared up in readiness. Mark stood on the carpet, his own dick stiff and eager.

"My god," he said, staring down at me with disbelieving eyes. I began stroking it.

He placed one knee on the bed, bracing his weight on extended arms, his hands on either side of my hips. Slowly, almost reverently, he brought his other knee to rest, kneeling between my thighs. He lowered his head, moistening those full lips with a slow sweep of his tongue. But, instead of taking my prick in his mouth, he pressed his beardless cheek against it, rubbing the swollen glans the way a playful cat rubs against a convenient leg. Then, while I arched my neck to watch him, he pulled back just enough to bypass my cock, his tongue licking out to caress my hairy balls, tracing the outlined orbs with its tip.

"Yeah!" I groaned, spreading my legs wider, and pushing my hips upward. Without hesitation, his tongue reached beneath my sac, lapping at the perineum, and flicking dangerously close to my anus. If the kid wanted to go farther, I wouldn't have objected, loving to feel a boy's mouth on my ass, his tongue forcing its way inside. But I didn't believe Mark was quite ready for that just yet. Anyway, I wanted his mouth on my cock. I had a king-sized load of cum that would provide him with a worthy initiation.

He took his time, although I could tell from his heavy breathing that he was eager for my meat, and, now and then he moaned, betraying his lust. He licked his way back to the base of my prick, then up the shaft, his tongue flicking back and forth, making the shaft sway and bob. Just as he reached the slit, I felt a surge of pleasure, and a glob of jism oozed from it. He took it into his mouth, giving a little grunt of satisfaction.

Having just tasted his first cock, he was ready for more. One arm at a time switched positions, transferring his weight to his

elbows, freeing his hands to explore my balls while he used his mouth on my prick.

One hand encircled the wrist-thick base, holding the shaft with its slight donward curve near the tip, firmly in place, his wet tongue lapping at the plum-like head.

"Ummm!" he murmured.

His smooth cheeks hollowed, drawing another glob of jism up through the swollen shaft. His tongue gathered it, spreading it over the glans, and he pulled my cock farther into his mouth.

"Suck it! Suck my big dick!"

He didn't need any more encouragement. He was now doing what he had always wanted to do, and all I had to do was relax and enjoy it.

I had been much younger than Mark when I sucked my first dick, and I will never forget the taste and feel of my second cousin's cock, and the thrill of knowing that I was producing such pleasure.

Mark's mouth was sliding up and down my cock, his tongue flaying the soft underbelly, and flicking at the head each time he pulled back. It was incredibly good, and, since there were no cameras rolling, I made no attempt to slow my mounting pleasure.

Mark gagged trying to take it all – that would be something we could work on for hours later. However, he was adept in other areas. One hand still played with my balls, and the other now reached under them to tease my anus, one fingertip gently scratching the striated circle as he sucked harder and faster.

"I'm gonna come!" I panted, my hips thrusting to match the bobbing head. "Don't stop, baby! Suck that cock!"

My warning only made him suck me harder, his lips and tongue demanding that flood sperm. He snorted as he sucked, his head moving in a little circling as he mouth-fucked me closer and closer to orgasm.

Pleasure spiraled into ecstacy, and my cum spurted against his tongue and palate. He moaned and began gulping noisily and hurriedly, as if afraid it might somehow escape his sliding lips. My hips thrust upward, shoving the head of my prick deep in the boy's throat as the last few jets emerged. He took it all, swallowing again and again, even after the last drop had been sucked from my prick. He had been initiated, and he

didn't want it to end. He held my prick in his mouth, gently nursing it, and running his tongue about the head, urging me to a renewed hardness. Finally he freed his lips, then moved down to pay homage to my balls again.

He lifted his head and looked up into my eyes. His tongue licked slowly across his upper lip, and he gave me a lazy smile. His fingers curling about my cock again, he asked, "Did I do a good job?"

"Perfect, baby," I answered.

We went back into the living room and had another drink. I put my second film, "Big Shooters," in the VCR. While I had only done a sixty-nine with my "brother" in my first film, in this one I had my first on-screen fuck. The kid I had the pleasure of seducing was no virgin but he acted like one. Cuddled in my arms on the couch, Mark watched the scene intently. When it was over, I put my hand on his thigh and asked, "Now, do I get some of *your* ass?"

He hesitated, his brows knitting. "Oh, I want to," he said, "but I'm more than a little scared."

Scared or not, he followed me back into the bedroom.

He crawled atop me, his naked body pressing urgently against mine from chin to tingling balls. Our mouths fused in a long, delicious kiss.

"Get the tube of jelly out of that drawer." I pointed to the nightstand. "We'll get that little butt ready." He fumbled in the drawer and finally withdrew the tube. Uncapping it, he scooted down to kneel between my spread legs and began greasing my cock. My fingers caressed his hair as he spread the lubricant over the full length of the column. I held out my hand and the boy squeezed a generous glob of jelly onto my fingers. With my free hand, I urged him upward until he was straddling my hips, and I could reach his virgin asshole.

He gasped as my finger slipped into him, and again when I added a second digit, wiggling them about to loosen him. "Ummmm!" he sighed, his eyes closing and his lips parting. "Oh, that feels good, Pete."

"Let's see how it feels with my prick in there," I said, guiding his bottom into position with one hand, and steadying my cock with the other. I felt his quivering hole touch the tip.

Transferring both hands to his hips, I began pulling him down, feeding my distended prick up into the hot embrace of his young ass.

He held his breath, his fingers gripping my pecs, and finally I felt the sphincter yield.

"UHHHHH!" he groaned.

I began pushing my dick into his ass, soon filling and stretching the tender corridor with its heat and hardness.

"Oh, Pete!"

"Easy, kid!" I urged, penetrating him more deeply. "You can take it!"

He closed his eyes. His teeth were clamped together.

"Take it all, baby!" I grunted, and his hips dropped still lower, pushing that torrid grip farther on to my rearing prick. The slippery canal spasmed and undulated, and he cried out as he felt his asshole fill with hard cock.

"That's it, baby!" I gasped, for his bottom now rested on my pelvis. The little virgin had taken it all! His whole body trembled as he worked his hips in a slow grinding, savoring the feel of the shaft deep within him. He cried out when he began pulling his ass upward, the sensitive tissues clinging to my cock and massaging it with hot squeezes, and he reversed direction while at least half of the rod was still inside him.

"UHHH!" he bleated, beginning a pumping of his hips that sent his asshole sliding up and down my prick, making me groan with pleasure and thrust my own hips upward to ram into him. His head was thrown back, his lower lip caught between his teeth as he fucked my cock, his rectum tightening and relaxing.

"What are we doin', Mark?" I panted, watching his distorted features as he savored his first fuck. I loved asking this question more than anything.

"We're fucking!" he gasped, without hesitation and without looking down. "You're fucking me in my ass! Oh, god!"

The boy's dick was jerking each time he took mine into his ass, and the spasms of his rectum were increasing in frequency, signaling the nearness of his orgasm. I held back my release as he rode my prick savagely, grunting each time my cock speared his asshole. He tried to speak, but the excitement was too intense, and he could only gasp when his hips jerked, his dick

swelled, and I felt the hot constriction of his colon. My own cock responded by flooding his ass in almost perfect rhythm with his coming.

Minutes later, in the shower, I fucked him again, bending him over and ramming my prick deep in his ass with powerful thrusts. I didn't come, but it was a most enjoyable session. I learned a long time ago that it isn't necessary to reach an orgasm every time you screw. Just sliding my dick in and out of his sopping ass and embracing his willing body was pleasure enough.

We slept late on Saturday morning, waking to shower and then fall back onto the big bed, where I had him lie back and pull those graceful legs up, draping his ankles over my shoulders, permitting me to fuck him face to face. His hips responded to every stroke with a wild grinding that sent jolts of pleasure through my driving cock.

His kisses became totally uninhibited. He sucked my tongue, chewed my lips, and eagerly swallowed my saliva. And, between the savage thrusts, he begged me never to stop fucking him. I promised I wouldn't.

We came together, his cum shooting up over his naked chest and belly. When I let my prick slip out of his ass and lowered my body down onto his, we kissed with an almost tender passion.

"I love for you to fuck me, Pete," he whispered, licking my lips, his arms tight about my neck. "You can do it anyway you want to, and anywhere."

"Even in front of a camera?" I asked, my eyes searching his.

"Boy, I'd like to have a picture of you doin' it to me. I really would."

"Well, there's one way to get one. If you're serious I can probably get you a part in the film we're makin' now. You need a job, and the pay's good."

"*Me*, in a movie?"

"Why not, man?"

"God, I couldn't take money for lettin' you fuck me," he protested. "I love that big dick!"

I chuckled. "Look, the money's for lettin' 'em have the

privilege of filming the action. Oh, and you'd have to make it with other guys, too."

"Where'd you be?"

"Right there. See, sometimes they have three or four guys doing it to each other at the same time."

He stared up at me for a moment, then grinned. "I'll think about it."

"That's my boy." I reached down and took hold of his cock, feeling it stiffen in my grip. "There's another thing."

"Oh?"

"Yeah. You gotta be able to fuck as well as get fucked, and this dick looks like it'd enjoy that. Would you fuck me?"

"Could I?" I thought he was going to cry. "Oh, god, can I, Pete?"

I released him and greased his erect dick. I rolled onto my back, shoving a pillow beneath my hips. "Come on, show me what you can do with that beautiful prick!" He was a little awkward, but his eight inches of cock was more than enough to make me grunt as it slid into my waiting asshole. As I flexed my anal muscles about his prick, he cried out again and again. As much as I prefer being the reamer, I don't mind getting fucked one bit when the one fucking me is as young and flawless as Mark was.

Looking down into my face as he poured the meat to me, his limpid eyes told me far more than he could put into words. Still, he tried: "Oh, man, I love you!" he gasped, his hips pounding, and his cock making little squishing sounds as it slid in and out of my ass. "I love you!"

"It's okay, kid," I panted, my own hips working beneath his. "Just fuck me!"

After his initial blast, he gave me a few extra jabs to make sure he delivered the full load. I looked up into his flushed face. "Scoot down there, kid," I said breathlessly, "and suck me off."

It took only seconds for his mouth to pull my semen up through my throbbing cock, and he sucked it with joyous moans, swallowing until I was drained.

He was still nursing my prick when I said, "Let's have breakfast, then we'll drive back into town and get you some decent clothes."

He started to protest, but I suggested that he could pay me back from his wages earned on the film set.

In response, he released my dick, then slid upward to let me taste my own cum on his full lips. "You really think they'll hire me?"

"I guarantee it. Larry Davis is always lookin' for fresh meat."

5

To some people, it may have appeared that what Larry was looking for most of the time was trouble. It seemed he always had at least one case pending in a court somewhere. Although he said he was careful to check the ages of his actors, now and then he said a boy would fool him, and the shit would fly. So far, he had never been convicted, and he had begun checking more carefully. He squinted at Mark's driver's license and pursed his pudgy lips in concentration. Then, as though asking for a reference, he said, "Okay, let me see your cock, kid."

Mark looked at me. I smiled. He kept his eyes on mine as he unzipped his fly and pulled out his prick. He shifted his feet farther apart, placed his hands on his hips, and looked at Larry.

"Can you get it hard?" Larry demanded, chewing on the ever-present cigar.

"Sure," Mark said, turning slightly and staring at me. Slowly he lowered his brown eyes to my crotch.

"Goddamn!" Larry exploded. "Pete, you got this one trained!"

It seemed like it. Mark's cock was rising, reaching a throbbing erection within seconds.

"Now, Pete says you'll do whatever I want. Is that right?"

"Yes, sir," Mark nodded, "especially if it's with Pete."

Larry snickered. "You're not the only one hooked on Pete."

Larry explained the portion of the plot we'd be shooting that day. "Pete," he said, "you're lookin' for a guy who's sort of a scoutmaster, taking six boys on a camp-out."

"Doesn't that present an age problem?"

"Hell, we don't mention ages," he shrugged. "It just so happens that all these kids look a lot younger than they are. Just like Mark, here. Shit, he could pass for fourteen or fifteen."

"What about the other boys?" I asked. "Do I know any of them?"

"I doubt it. Believe it or not, we're basing some of this on the life of Claude Anderson, who runs a kinda nudist camp on a

farm north of here."

"Any cherry?"

"Just two. The others have played around some, he says, but they're pretty green. Hell! That's what I want!"

"What about the two virgins? They ready?"

"They're thinkin' about it," he said. "And they know we'll be filming their first time. Shit! Pay 'em enough and they'll do anything! You know that, Pete."

"Some you don't even have to pay."

He gave me a wicked grin. "Yeah, I ought to charge *you* for doing this shit!"

While we shot most of the interior scenes in the warehouse, we did the outdoor stuff on Larry's ranch in Malibu. We got paid extra for the time and mileage so nobody minded the drive a bit.

Larry led me and Mark to a pile of backpacks in a corner of the overgrown lawn. To one side, there was a three-sided, roofless structure with an aging sofa. It was built like that so the cameras could shoot from outside, and to take advantage of the natural light. When not in use, it was kept covered by a big tarp. This was to be the site of my first seduction of Mark.

An assistant took Mark's measurements and hurried off to return with a scout uniform that hugged his crotch and bottom most suggestively.

While we waited for the others to join us, Larry went over the script again, as if I needed to be reminded.

"Pete," Larry said, "your character's looking for a kidnapped boy, and you've had a tip that the guy who heads this group may know something."

"I know, Larry."

"Yeah, right. And do you know you're gonna follow them through the woods, and grab Mark when you see him?"

I nodded.

"Am I supposed to put up a fight?" Mark asked, arching his eyebrow again.

"Do whatever feels right," Larry shrugged. "You're at the back of this bunch, so Pete can pick you off real easy. Once he gets his hand over your mouth, so you can't yell, he starts groping your crotch."

The boy grinned. "I like that part."

"Yeah, but don't show it too quick. Make him work for it," Larry said. "The idea is that he gets you into the shack, and asks you about Claude, the scout leader. It also gives us another sex scene."

Minutes later, we were joined by the five boys and Claude, a slender, pleasant-looking guy in his late 20s with long, wavy brown hair. The youngsters were already wearing their uniforms and had begun putting on their backpacks. I felt a rush of anticipation as my eyes drank in the incredible array of inviting young flesh. Larry was right. I *would* have paid *him* for the privilege of fucking these pretty teenagers. But I wasn't about to turn down my paycheck.

Introductions were made, and Larry took Claude and me aside, motioning to the camera crew where he planned the first shot. Claude was having trouble keeping his eyes above my waist. He had one of those heart-shaped mouths that seem to be begging for a big dick, and I found myself wondering just how talented those fleshy lips were.

"Claude," Larry explained, "I want you to lead the boys along this trail." He pointed towards the worn path that wound through the woods. "Pete will be hiding behind that big rock over there, and when the group passes, he'll grab the last one. That'll be Mark. The rest of you pretend you don't see or hear anything unusual."

"Sounds easy enough," Claude nodded. "Does Pete ball the boy?"

"No, just a blowjob," Larry answered, "in that shack back there. While we're doing that scene, you guys go back to the house and relax. If this works out, we'll use Kyle with Mark this afternoon, and then bring Pete back in."

Claude hesitated. "You know Kyle's cherry?"

"Everybody is once," Larry grinned. "Don't worry. Mark's a little green, too, and Pete knows how to pluck a cherry."

It was my turn to grin. "Who's the other virgin?"

Claude looked at the group of youngsters and his eyes indicated a red-haired cherub with an ass that threatened to split his clinging shorts. "Freddy," he said. "He and Kyle have never actually done it, but they're thinking about it."

"Let's get on with it," Larry said impatiently. "Pete, you get

behind that rock, and when they march past, you grab the boy. We'll cut then and set up for the next scene."

Claude gathered the boys around at the spot Larry indicated, and I took my position behind the big rock, listening as the cameras were placed and everyone got ready.

Larry called for cameras, then yelled, "Action!"

Claude led the six boys, Mark in the rear, down the trail. One camera caught their approach, another shot me lurking behind the rock, and the third followed their progress along the path, concentrating on their cute asses.

Mark, as he had been instructed to do, began to lag behind the others until some twenty feet separated him from Kyle, whose lusciously curved rear was swaying with every step.

The moment Mark passed, I stepped out behind him, grabbing him about the waist and clamping one hand over his mouth. The boy struggled realistically, and I had to use real force to drag him back down the trail toward the shack. His movements worked that firm young ass against my cock, and I developed an instant hard-on, anticipating the next scene, when I would hump him to a ball-draining finish. I had screwed him at least six times over the weekend, but I was still hot for that tight ass.

"Cut!" Larry yelled, and I took my time releasing the boy. Mark seemed in no hurry to pull away, now that the struggle was unnecessary. Mark looked over his shoulder at me. "This is gonna be fun," he said softly, rubbing that firm bottom against my swelling dick. Cameras and equipment were shifted to the three-sided shack where we were to perform, and Larry joined us.

"Okay," he said, chewing on the unlit cigar. "Mark, I want some resistance at first, even while you answer Pete's questions. Then, once you give in, show me some real action."

Mark and I took up our positions, and I pulled that firm rump back against my cock again, one hand on the boy's mouth.

When Larry gave the order, I dragged the kid over and pushed him down onto his knees on the sofa. Using the arm I had about his narrow waist, I slipped my hand down to cup his balls, feeling the hardness of his cock through the thin shorts.

"I'm not gonna hurt you, kid," I said gruffly. "I just want

a few answers."

"Let me go, damn you!" His whole body was arching as he struggled. "Who the hell are you, anyway?"

I explained that I was a private eye, and that a boy had been kidnapped, probably by the leader of the troop Mark was in. Mark denied knowing anything about it. I forced him down all the way and pushed my body over his. We fought some more before I kissed him. Before long, I was unfastening his shorts, and working them down over his hips. His cock sprang free, fully hard and erect. I curled my fingers about it, making him groan with pleasure. He rolled over onto his back and h He let his body relax a little, and I stripped his shorts completely off, then opened his shirt, giving me access to his prominent nipples. I leaned over him and applied my lips and tongue to one tasty tit, then the other. The youngster closed his eyes and moaned softly.

One of the cameramen moved in to get a closeup of my oral assault, and another trained his lens on my fingers as I opened my own fly. I kissed my way down the silky skin of his flat, firm belly, and his hips stirred and his prick jerked invitingly.

I pushed my own trousers down, and a cameraman captured a closeup of my cock, straining to be freed from my Jockeys. Mark, pretending to see it for the first time, stared in fascination. I eased my hips forward, and the tip of my prick brushed the youngster's chin. His tongue reached out and his head lowered to lick the head. His whole body shuddered. His lips parted and slipped over the head of my dick, and he began sucking with noisy tugs.

After I came, we sat on the sofa and continued the dialogue. The leader, Mark told me, had brought a new boy to their clubhouse, and had warned them not to tell anyone about him. He was a runaway, and had been abused by his father.

As Mark talked I was fondling his balls, and digging the tip of my tongue into his navel.

"Have you talked with this boy?" I asked, my mouth moving to his prick.

"No," he said, "but Kyle has."

6

Larry was happy with Mark's first blowjob, caught by the camera in close-up, my heavy load puddled in the middle of his belly. He was also pleased with the reaction shot of Mark's face, with some of my cum flowing down his pointy chin.

Now Larry began explaining what he wanted us to do next. I had already warned Mark not to try to make sense out of the scenes, but simply follow Larry's directions. I also explained that we would eventually shoot what seemed like hours of nothing but closeups of my cock sliding in and out of his asshole, viewing it from every possible position.

"They're used as fillers," I told him. "When you put all the scenes together, there's always something missing, especially in the sex scenes. So the editor has a lot of footage he can choose from, matching it with the particular scene."

What Larry had scheduled next was the sequence where Mark leaves me, after agreeing to talk Kyle into meeting and talking with me about the new boy. Mark and I had only a few lines, ending with him throwing his arms about my neck for a big, juicy kiss, and a closeup of my hands squeezing his cute ass.

"Okay," Larry told us. "Let's break for lunch. Then, we'll shoot Mark and Kyle here at the shack." He pointed that cigar at me. "That's when you catch them chewing on each other, and use that dick to make Kyle talk, among other things."

"Do I end up screwing him?" I asked hopefully.

"Does the pope shit in the woods?" Larry snorted.

Although Mark had done a good job emptying my nuts in our scene on the couch, I was anticipating initiating young Kyle properly.

The caterer's truck delivered a raft of fried chicken and raw veggies, and jugs of iced tea. They set up tables for us on the lawn. I slipped in between Mark and the nervous Kyle and settled down on the bench with my well-filled tray.

"I've seen a lot of your pictures," Kyle said. "I never thought I'd actually meet you."

"Why not?"

"'Cause you're a *big* star!"

"Big for sure," Mark interjected.

"No, not really," I countered. "You kids are the stars. I'm just the lucky guy that gets to play with you. The audience is interested in you. To them, I'm just a big cock." I knew this wasn't entirely true, but I wanted them to think it was.

"I guess you can tell that I'm a little scared," Kyle admitted. "It'll be my first time."

"You can always back out," I said.

"No way! I want to do it. I just know it's gonna hurt like hell."

"No." I waved a chicken leg. "Just ask Mark. A couple of days ago, he was just starting out."

The boy looked past me at Mark, his eyes questioning. "Honest? You'd never done it before?"

"All I'd ever done was jerk off. Pete showed me what I'd been missin'."

"Don't worry, Larry'll give you a little suppository to put in your butt. That'll make it real slick and relaxed."

"You sure?"

I squeezed one of his bare thighs for emphasis. "Scout's honor!" Then I let my hand slide up to where my fingers could give his dick and balls a brief squeeze. I felt his cock start stiffening. This promised to be fun.

In the scene, Mark had talked Kyle into meeting him at the shack where I had let him blow me, intending to talk the boy into cooperating with me.

The cameras were rolling when I approached the set. Both Kyle and Mark were naked, and playing with each other's dick. Mark was teasing his companion by running his tongue into the boy's ear.

Both youngsters sported hard-ons, and I was pleased to note that Kyle's prick was larger than I had expected. I estimated the swollen hardness at about sevenuncut inches, and Mark was skinning it back and forth with obvious relish.

I slipped over beside Larry, next to the wide angle camera, and watched the boys as they exchanged a long kiss, their hands still busy on the stiff dicks.

"Cut!" Larry called. "Just hold your position, boys. I want

to move in a little."

The big camera was moved forward about ten feet, and Larry squinted into the view finder, shouting orders, finally grunting his agreement with the composition.

The other two cameramen took up positions before and at the end of the couch, ready to move in at Larry's signal.

"Okay," Larry instructed the pair, "Mark, you're gonna go down on Kyle. You sure as hell shouldn't have any trouble with that. And Kyle, when it starts feelin' really good, you work around to where you can get Mark's dick in your mouth. Got it?"

Kyle appeared skeptical, but he nodded his agreement. Mark answered with a grin, making it clear he was indeed looking forward to going down on Kyle.

"Cameras!" Larry barked, and waited for an assurance that both cameras and recorders were up to speed. Then, "Action!"

Kyle gave an audible gasp when Mark dropped to his knees and took the boy's stiff cock into his mouth, his lips sliding all the way to its base with one quick bob of his head.

For a few moments, Mark worked up and down the sizable shaft, making Kyle's hips squirm and bounce responsively. Then, just as Larry had instructed, Kyle lay back on the sofa, and Mark moved up, without losing his oral grip, to straddle the lad's head, his own prick nudging Kyle's waiting lips.

One of the cameramen dropped to the floor, crawling in to shoot on a level with Kyle's head as he slid his tongue out for his first taste of cock, the tip touching Mark's glans just as the first pearl of jism oozed from the slit.

It was my guess that, Kyle, like Mark, had already tasted his own cum, so he knew what to expect. His visible reaction was just what Larry was hoping for. He swallowed, licked his lips, then pushed his head up to take Mark's dick between them, his little moan cut short when Mark's hips pushed the full length into that inviting mouth.

I expected Kyle to gag with his throat full of hard dick. Instead, I saw his neck swell and convulse, and realized that he was swallowing. That's a trick only a few boys can master, and I knew Mark was receiving a rare treat. Mark's head bobbed faster, and his cheeks hollowed with suction, nursing the rearing shaft of Kyle's dick, while his own hips rose and fell,

fucking the youngster's mouth with full-length strokes.

I moved to one side, ready to walk into camera range on cue. That cue was the last spurt of Kyle's cum onto his arching belly, and from the way his hips were grinding, it was not too far away.

"UMMMMM!" was all the boy could manage with his mouth full of Mark's prick, but Mark quickly released his prize and raised his head far enough for the lens to capture the jetting cream that arced up, some of it splattering against Mark's chest, but most of it raining down on Kyle's own heaving middle.

It would not have surprised if Mark had come then, for his dick was being sucked relentlessly by an over-eager boy. Instead, his head was thrown back, and he was almost snarling in his effort to hold back his orgasm.

Out of the corner of my eye, I caught Larry's wave, and I walked onto the set, planting my feet apart, and placing my hands on my hips.

"Well! Well!" I said, staring down at the two supposedly startled youngsters. "Look what we have here!"

Mark lifted his hips, pulling his cock out of Kyle's mouth, and they both gave me frightened stares. Kyle's tongue made a slow, arousing circle of those full, reddened lips.

"Oh, god!" was his hoarse cry.

"What are you gonna do?" was Mark's line.

"Well, now," I drawled, moving a step closer, and making it obvious that I was enjoying the sight of two naked young boys who had just been eating each other. "I think Mr. Baker ought to know about this," I said, using the scripted name of the scout leader.

"No!" Kyle said, sitting up and swinging his feet off of the sofa. "Please don't tell him! He'd tell my father, and he'd kill me!"

Mark chimed in with, "We'll do anything, mister! Please!"

I moved closer to Kyle. "You know a new kid around here? A blond about your age? Somebody who just joined a few days ago?"

He hesitated, a slight frown wrinkling his forehead. "I'm not supposed to tell anybody about him."

"Okay," I shrugged. "Then we tell your old man that you're

sucking cocks out here."

"No!" he said quickly. "Okay. Mr. Baker brought him out to our clubhouse a few days ago. He's keeping him pretty close, but we got to be buddies right off."

"Did he tell you who he is?"

"No. He says Mr. Baker told him to just stay there and keep his mouth shut. He acted like maybe he was scared of Mr. Baker."

"This Mr. Baker," I prompted. "He ever fool around with you?"

"You mean..." He made an awkward gesture that took in both his own naked body and that of Mark. "You mean, like this?"

"Yeah," I grinned. "He ever feel you up, or make you suck him off?"

"No," he said, shaking his head. "This is the first time I ever did anything like this." He hesitated, then went on, "I think Mr. Baker may do it with some of the other boys. And I know that some of them do it with each other."

"So, now here you are."

"Yeah," he said slowly, refusing to meet my eyes. "We've done this a few times. but we wouldn't want anybody to know about it."

"Tell you what," I said, reaching for my belt buckle. "You two want to keep this a secret, and I got a hardon watching you go after each other's dick. Let's make a deal."

It was Kyle who managed a shaky, "What kind of a deal?"

I pushed my trousers and shorts down, kicking off my loafers, then shedding my shirt to stand naked, my prick sticking out like a salami roll. The two youngsters stared at it, the cameras zooming in for a closeup.

"I keep quiet about you two, and you do exactly what I tell you. Have we got a deal?"

Mark was first to say, "Okay."

Kyle hesitated. "Please, mister. I'm scared!"

To Mark, I said, "Suck me, get it nice and wet."

As Mark stood up, Kyle asked, "What are you gonna do?"

"Just relax, pretty boy," I told him. "I'm gonna give you something you'll never forget."

Mark licked my cock, leaving it liberally coated with spittle.

He turned toward Kyle. "He's gonna fuck you in the ass," he said calmly. "Don't worry. You'll love it."

"But it's too big!" Kyle protested, staring at my slippery prick. "I can't take that!"

"Turn around, kid," I said. "Get on your knees and brace your arms on the back of that thing."

Kyle was almost sobbing as he obeyed, that delightfully curved bottom arching in readiness. He looked back over his shoulder at me.

"Oh, god!" he gasped. "Please, don't!"

"Just spread your legs, and shut up," I growled, moving to stand behind him, my dick aimed at that inviting little circle between his buttocks. I could feel the heat of it on the head of my cock before I ever touched him.

I put one hand on his hip, and he flinched.

"No, no, please!"

"Relax," I told him. Then, to Mark, I said, "Why don't you lie down and nibble on his dick while I fuck him?"

It wasn't in the script, but Mark picked up on it without hesitation. He lay down on the sofa, raising himself on one elbow, and claimed Kyle's cock for the second time.

Before he could recover, I used my free hand to hold my cock steady, and pushed the big head into that virgin asshole, feeling the sphincter yield, then grip my pole just beneath the flared rim of the glans.

"UHHH!" Kyle yelped, his hips trying to evade my grip, a movement which pushed his own dick farther into Mark's eager mouth. "UUHHHH!"

The second cry came as I forced about four inches of hard prick up into his tail, freeing my other hand to grip his hips for leverage as I began pumping in and out. His ass was tight, but that coating of semen and Larry's suppository let me slide in and out, frictioning the nerve-laced circle and the tender tissues inside.

The head of my cock rubbed his prostate, and with each thrust, his hips jerked, the little cries now those of pleasure as he discovered the thrill of having his young ass packed with throbbing cock. Mark was making a little slurping sound as he sucked Kyle's dick, his head braced against the back of the sofa as the youngster's hips were pushed forward by my thrusts. I

was giving him almost all of my prick, and his hips were grinding to increase the pleasure of our sliding flesh.

Kyle was getting almost the full treatment for his initiation. The only thing better than being fucked and sucked at the same time is to have still a third cock in your mouth.

I fucked the kid for several minutes, making sure Larry was getting plenty of footage from every angle, trying hard to think of something other than how good it felt. Too soon I was dangerously close to coming, but I wanted the boy to come first.

As if reading my mind, Kyle gasped, "I'm gonna come!" His hips were twisting and thrusting and Mark evidently started sucking even harder, because Kyle's sphincter chewed on my cock, the convulsions matching the spurting of his cum into Mark's mouth.

I kept hunching as long as I could, but it was too good to last, and I felt the hot seizures begin, forcing my semen up through my jerking cock, the first jet lancing deep in Kyle's asshole. It was all I could do to pull my prick out and spill the rest on the youngster's back and between those perfectly rounded buttocks.

Two cameras took loving closeups of my spurting cock, and I delivered a full load of the thick cream, some of it trickling down to coat Kyle's anus. It was too damned tempting to resist. As the last drop of cum oozed from the tip of my dick, I slid it back into the youngster's ass, driving it in until my balls were jammed against his, holding it there while his hips writhed to work his colon about the still-throbbing invader.

"Cut!" Larry yelled. He was grinning. We had just captured a bit of sexual magic on film.

Claude had agreed to appear as the leader of the group of boys. "Type casting," Larry called it. But I knew the main reason was because it was cheap; Larry was paying for the boys so he got their leader for free. Larry took Claude and me aside and first explained to us that the opening sequence and the finale were to be filmed at the very end, to accommodate Bill Morrison, a distinguished-looking guy in his late thirties, who was cast as the uncle. Then he went on to describe how, in the script, I located a couple of the kid's friends, and learned that

the lad often hung out near a bar on Fifth Street, in a block notorious for hustler traffic.

The bartender admitted seeing the kid outside a few times. He looked at the photo the uncle had given me, and told me that the boy had been seen a lot with Kitty, a teenaged drag queen, a frequent customer of the bar. It was through Kitty that I would learn of the kid's relationship with Mr. Baker, who, Kitty would tell me, was trying to purchase a large farm for his group of what he called "naturists," some of whom were still undecided about their sexual preferences.

For my meeting with Baker, Larry was using his own living room as a set. According to the script, I had come to the house to question Baker concerning his association with the kidnapped boy. Larry had Claude and me rehearse the lines several times until we were comfortable with them. Then it was time to shoot the scene.

At first, Baker was uncooperative. "Just because I've seen the boy a few times doesn't mean that I kidnapped him," Claude, as Baker, told me.

"Who said he's been kidnapped?"

"You did."

"No. I said he was missing. And I have a witness who will swear that you brought him here."

Claude started to say something, but suddenly it seemed as if all the air went out of him, and his shoulders sagged. "Goddamn it! I told the kid it wouldn't work. It's too fucking obvious!"

I settled back in the chair and stared at him. "Want to tell me about it?" I said. "Or would you rather talk with the cops?" That was another thing that would never happen.

"It was the boy's idea! I told him we'd get caught."

"You left a trail big enough. I think you wanted to get caught."

He shrugged. "Hell! I'm not cut out to be a crook."

"Just a baby-fucker. Right?"

His head jerked up and he glared angrily. "That's a damned lie! All these boys are over eighteen!"

"Yeah, sure," I said. I finally got him to admit the kid was there. "Yes, he's here. Willingly, of course. It was his idea that we could get his old man to come across with the money, and

we could pay off the mortgage on this place. We're about to lose it. That way, we'd all have a place to stay and do whatever we wanted."

"There's just one catch. That ransom note makes it extortion, and that can cost you a few years."

"But, it was all a big joke!"

"I doubt that the judge and jury will do much laughing."

He looked as if he might start bawling any moment. It was easy to see how he could have believed that the kid's plan would work out without a hitch. What he didn't know was that the uncle wanted nothing to do with the cops.

"Maybe," I said, "we can work something out."

"Anything! I'll do *anything* to settle it!"

"Before we discuss that, I want to make sure the boy is safe. Let me see him, and talk with him."

"Cut!" Larry shouted. "Print it!"

"Take tomorrow off," Larry told Mark and me as we were leaving. "I want both of you fresh for Wednesday. We've got some hot stuff coming up."

"Oh?" I asked.

"Yeah, it's a scene that comes after you've talked with Claude."

"Who's in it?"

"You, Mark, Danny and Kyle." He gave Mark a wave of that cigar. "Think you can handle three guys?"

"Guess I can try," the boy grinned. "Sounds like fun."

"Good, then I won't have to pay you!"

"What?"

"Just kiddin', boy."

7

As Mark and I settled down in the Buick, I asked, "Well, how'd you like it?"

"It was great," he answered. "It's what I've always wanted to do, and here I am gettin' paid for it."

"Guess your folks would be pretty upset."

"Good." He put his hand on my knee as I nosed the car into the early evening traffic. "You know," he said, his hand crawling up my thigh to press the bulge of my balls just enough to make it feel good. "I don't give a shit what they think!"

We rode in silence until I pulled into the parking lot of a supermarket, and motioned him to come with me. Inside, we loaded a cart with things I thought we needed, and I asked him if there was something special he'd like to eat.

He leaned close and whispered, "Yeah, and you've got it between your legs."

"You can call that dessert," I said. "You like chicken?"

"No, I like men."

"I mean, to eat."

"That's what I mean."

"Okay."

We headed for the deli section and ordered a huge whole fryer. I sent Mark for rolls and butter. He came back with them – and big jar of honey. The aroma of barbecued chicken filled the car as we sped through the gathering dusk, pulling up at the cabin at a quarter past ten. After showering, we watched television as we dispatched the food from the deli. Then Mark played bartender, pouring two tall bourbons over ice, and handing one to me where I sat on the big sofa.

"Time for dessert, and know what I'd like?" he asked, dropping down beside me.

"I can guess."

Seated, Mark's robe slid up to show plenty of thigh, and his hairless legs drew my eyes like twin magnets.

"Promise you won't laugh," he said, and I made the motions

of crossing my heart. He grinned, and took another long swig.

"I'd like to pour honey on your dick," he said hesitantly, "and lick it off. Then, make you come."

I nodded my appreciation.

"It's somethin' I heard about when I was about ten. Some boy said he read it somewhere, and I started thinking how I'd like to do that with somebody I really liked."

"When you were just ten?"

"Sure," he answered. "I can't remember when I didn't want a dick. It was just that there was never anybody I could talk to about it, and nobody to do it with."

"Yeah," I argued, "but when you were ten, you wouldn't know what to do with a stiff pecker."

"I knowed you could suck one," he insisted.

"Knew. Not knowed. *Knew*."

"Okay, I *knew*. And I *knew* some boys stuck it in each other. I heard 'em talkin' about it, and callin' guys like that sissies."

He ran his hand beneath my robe, his fingers curling about my semi-erect cock. "How old were you, Pete? I mean, the first time you did it with another boy."

"My first was a cousin. He was about fifteen, and he was visiting us during the summer. He came home late one night half drunk and when he got into bed he just lay there naked, playing with it. He thought I was asleep. Well, I just did what I wanted to."

"You sucked him off?"

"Damn right! And I knew what kind of sex I wanted. I was only twelve but I was, well, pretty well developed."

"Did he fuck you?"

"Later. And before the summer was over, I was puttin' it to him. It was then I realized I had a bigger dick than almost anybody."

"Yeah, can here I am with it," he said, taking my cock in his hand.

Our robes slipped away and we embraced, mouths meeting in a kiss that was both gentle and insistent. Hands roamed, caressing and exploring, and our cocks stiffened in readiness.

"I'll get the honey," Mark whispered, his tongue just brushing my parted lips. "I'm gonna like this."

"I probably will, too," I whispered back. "Especially if you

smear a little on my balls."

While Mark got the honey from the kitchen cabinet, I put a thick towel on the bed, stripped off the robe and lay naked, legs spread, my cock already half hard from thinking about the boy's plan. I was also wondering if Larry would be interested in working a scene like that into a movie. He set the jar down long enough to shed his own robe, then opened the honey, knelt between my legs and tilted it over my dick.

Now, it's impossible to pour honey on your cock and balls without getting some of it in the pubic hair around the base as well and Mark wasn't stingy with the sticky, syrupy goo. It felt funny, oozing down from the glans, and my dick swelled a little more from the feathery caress of the liquid. He poured an extra glob on my balls before recapping the jar and placing it on the table. Then, licking his lips in anticipation, he leaned back on his heels and stared down at my honey-coated cock.

"Man," he murmured, "that sure looks tasty."

I didn't answer. Instead, I spread my thighs a little farther apart, and reached for him. The boy bent forward, and I caught his hair with both hands, guiding his head down until I felt that warm wet tongue begin its eager licking up the ventral ridge of my prick.

Having a boy licking your dick is always exciting, but the extra tongue effort in gathering up the honey makes it so much better. I gave a little grunt of delight.

"Like it?" he asked, pausing just long enough for me to assure him that I did. Then, he went back to his cleanup chores, moving up to that little "V" and giving it special attention.

"Don't take it off my cock," I said, pulling his head up so he had to look at me. "Clean up my balls." I raised my hips a little, and he went to work on my sac, drawing my balls into his mouth, one at a time, and working his tongue over the rolling nut, swallowing the mingled honey and saliva with audible gulps.

It took a while to lick the cum from about the base of my cock, and he stopped several times to pull a hair from his teeth. My prick was jerking like crazy when he finally lifted his pretty face, licked his lips, and stared at my honey-coated shaft.

"Now, get on your belly and spread your legs."

"Oh, shit!" Even as he said it, he was rolling over and pushing that inviting ass up in readiness. I mounted him with a little grunt of anticipation, pressing the sticky head of my dick against his puckered anus.

It took real pressure to force the glans past that tight sphincter, but Mark had already learned the trick of relaxing his asshole by pretending to force the invading cock out.

"OOOHHHH!" he moaned, feeling my prick sliding into his ass, but held back by that molasses-like grip. "OHHHH!...That's so good!"

It was better than good, and a little like screwing in water. It was impossible to slide in and out very fast, so I fucked the youngster with slow, full-length strokes, feeling the resistance on every inch of my cock, just as Mark was feeling it tug at his intestinal lining and that delicate anal circle.

His hips twisted and hunched, and he whimpered with the added pleasure of our coupling, his asshole squeezing as I slammed in and out, the ecstasy climbing with every stroke.

I didn't warn him of my orgasm, but his own began when he felt my prick jerk and swell. His anus tightened, and he gasped my name again and again as my cum gushed into him.

I was in no hurry to pull out of him, and he didn't want me to. We lay like that for several minutes, my face buried in his hair and my chest pressed against his back. Now and then, his muscles tightened, squeezing my cock, and I moved my hips to jiggle the still-hard shaft inside him.

"I love it when you fuck me," he murmured. "It's fun doing it with the others, but you're special."

"So are you," I said, my lips moving against one delicate ear. "That is one sweet ass."

He giggled. "Yeah! Especially now!"

After showering, we slept spooned together, my prick pressed into the crease of his buttocks, and it was still there when I wakened at nine-thirty.

Mark, become quite the cook, prepared breakfast while I studied the script for the next day's filming. Then, as we ate, I described the scene to him.

"Unless Larry changes it," I said, "Kyle fucks you, while you suck my dick, and Danny sucks yours."

His shoulders executed a little shiver. "I still can't believe it. Just a week ago, the only sex I'd had was jerking off. Now, I'm gonna do it with three guys!"

"You sorry?"

"No way! I'd take on a dozen if one of them was you, Pete."

"You're a sweetheart. You're prettier than most girls. You've got one hell of a little body, and you have no inhibitions."

"What's that mean?"

"It means you'll do whatever your partner wants."

"That's like a hang-up?"

"Right," I nodded. "I don't think you have any."

He arched one eyebrow. "Guess not." He fiddled with his fork for a moment. "What's this guy Danny like?"

"He's young, pretty, a lot like you. Until a scene we shot just the other day, he'd never been screwed."

"Had he sucked dicks before?"

"Yeah. That was his thing. I was the first one to fuck him, though."

"Like me. Except I'd never done either one."

"Now, you're my favorite cocksucker."

He grinned. "Just what I want to be. That, and your favorite piece of ass."

I got him agree that there would be no fucking that day, that we both should be ready for the scene Larry had chosen. We would simply enjoy everything the lake had to offer: swimming, sailing, hiking.

That night, after watching television for a couple of hours, and limiting ourselves to two small glasses of wine, we stripped, showered, and fell naked onto the bed, our bodies pressing and our arms embracing, satisfying ourselves with a series of delicious kisses.

Just before we drifted off to sleep, Mark insisted on sliding down to kiss my semi-erect cock goodnight, letting the glans slip into his mouth for one delightful moment.

"You know," he whispered, moving up to place his head on the pillow beside mine. "I think I'm in love with your big prick."

"Go to sleep, Mark," I murmured. "Remember, we promised we were going to save it for tomorrow."

"Selfish!" But there was humor in his voice as he said it.

8

Except for the cameramen, soundmen and the light crew, all the others were told to take the rest of day off, leaving Mark, Danny, Kyle and me stripping for another first for Mark. If the idea of taking on three men had begun to make him nervous, he didn't show it, and his cock was hard when he stepped out of his shorts.

"I'll swear he's got a pump on that thing," Larry growled. "Wish he'd teach all you guys how to do that."

Inspiried by Mark, Danny was semi-erect, and Kyle's dick was almost as hard as mine. The four of us stood beside the bed, anxiously awaiting Larry's instructions.

"Kyle," Larry ordered, "I want you and Mark across the bed, down at the foot. Start out side by side, then, Kyle, you get on top. Pete, you and Danny get up at the head of the bed, but facing the other way."

He waved the big boom camera into place over the bed, and we took our places, Danny, pressing that firm naked body against mine with more eagerness than the script called for.

"Don't forget," I whispered into his ear, my hands roving over his smooth buttocks, "you haven't been screwed yet. Don't be too greedy."

"Okay," Larry said, "you can wing it, once you're all in the mood. Just end up the way I told you."

In moments, Kyle was on top of Mark, dry humping him, and Danny was doing his best to swallow my tongue, while his hands fondled my balls and my cock, and teased my anus. All that wriggling around brought us together, and our hands reached out to explore each other, playing with one prick for a moment, then finding another to skin back and forth.

Danny rolled onto his back, and Mark quickly straddled the boy's chest, aiming his cock for Danny's open mouth. I rose to my knees and worked my way around to where Mark could lean forward and capture my prick with his eager lips. Kyle, pretending to lubricate his dick with saliva (actually, Mark had

greased his ass earlier), knelt behind Mark, and pressed the head of his tool against the youngster's anus.

Four cameras were busy. The big boom job over the bed, one wide angle to catch the full bed, and two portables, moving about to record the scene from any direction Larry chose.

As for us, once we got into position, we tried to forget about everything but the sheer pleasure of what we were doing. Mark grunted when Kyle's dick slid up into his ass, and he took it all, his lips tightening about the base. From the muffled moan Danny gave, it was clear that Mark had hilted his own dick in the boy's throat, a move that Danny had admitted he loved.

The next several minutes were filled with grunts, groans, sighs, and the juicy slurping of three sliding cocks, two in wet, hungry mouths, and the third in Mark's tight, slippery asshole.

Danny, greedily sucking Mark's dick, was also pumping his own, and working those slender hips as his hand raced up and down. Kyle, hunching in and out of Mark's ass, leaned forward to offer me those full, moist lips, and we shared a tongue-writhing kiss as we poured the meat to my young friend, making him fuck Danny's mouth even faster.

Having his ass reamed, his dick sucked, and a big cock massaging his tonsils, all at the same time, was more than Mark could control. He sucked my prick harder, snorting each time he drew back to take a breath, and I could tell from Kyle's avid kisses that Mark's asshole was chewing on his cock, which made him hunch harder and faster.

Mark managed to yank his dick out of Danny's mouth, but not before the first spurt was delivered onto the boy's eager tongue. His orgasmic spasms, transmitted to his colon in the form of rhythmic squeezes, triggered Kyle's cum, and the youngster's semen shot up into Mark's asshole with powerful force. My own prick jerked, and the ecstacy spread like white heat through my balls, my cum gushing into Mark's sucking mouth, to be gulped down with noisy swallows, just as Danny was ingesting his.

It was all I could do to pull back and shoot the last few spurts onto Mark's chin, and Kyle's features contorted as he struggled to withdraw from that torrid ass and spill his load onto Mark's naked back. Likewise, Mark's own cock spilled its cream, spraying it over Danny's mouth and chin, while Danny's

dick shot off onto the bed.

The hand-held cameras caught it all, and it wasn't until all four cocks were drained that Larry finally called an end to our mini-orgy.

Having showered and dressed, I was waiting for Mark when Larry plopped down in a chair beside me. He lit his cigar. " I need a favor," he said.

"Who do you want killed?" I asked, fanning the smoke away from my face.

"It's Claude," he said. "It's the kids. I just have a funny feeling about it. Like, maybe I'm borrowing some trouble I don't need."

"I think I understand. What do you want me to do?"

He took the cigar from his mouth and squinted at it, as if it contained the answer. "You keepin' Mark with you?"

"Yeah. You blame me?"

"Shit, no! But maybe he can help you."

"With what?"

"I want you to nose around out there at that camp, or whatever it is. You and Mark could just drop in, for a little fun and games."

"When am I supposed to do this?"

"Tomorrow," he answered, shoving the cigar back in his mouth.

Mark joined us at that point. I stood up, and Larry gave the boy's butt a playful feel as we walked away. Mark shook his head, that one eyebrow tilting questioningly.

"We've got a little job to do for our lord and master," I told him, leading the way out into the late afternoon sunlight. "Playing detective."

In the car, weaving through the rush-hour traffic, I explained what Larry wanted, and the boy eagerly agreed to do anything I suggested.

As we climbed into the Buick, I asked, "So, how'd Kyle's dick feel?"

"Good, but I liked the one in my mouth a lot more."

9

By eleven the next morning, following the directions Larry had given me, we turned off the highway onto a dirt road that led to Claude's farm. It was already unseasonably warm and threatened to be downright scorching by mid-afternoon.

The road curved around a grove of tall trees, and we saw the weather-beaten two-story clapboard house. "Well, I've lived in a lot worse," I said, and Mark agreed.

One of the boys, cute, curly-haired, wearing only a pair of faded cutoffs, stood, legs spread, on the porch.

"That," Mark said quietly, "is for eatin'."

"You eat it! I'll fuck it!"

We were both chuckling as I halted the car, and the youth came down the steps to greet us. He had the lips writers often call "cupid's bow," full and moist. The crotch of his cutoffs bulged promisingly.

"Hi," he said. "You here to see Mr. Anderson?"

Mr. Anderson? I wondered what I had wandered into.

The kid introduced himself as David and we said we were friends of Claude's. He led us into a high, wide hallway, then up the broad stairs to the second floor. There were five doors leading off the upstairs hall, but only one was open. From it came the hesitant pecking of a typewriter.

Claude was hunched behind a desk older than himself, his fingers hovering uncertainly over the keys. He looked up as we entered, and his handsome face broke into a welcoming smile.

"Well, what brings you out here?"

"I bet you can guess."

"Looking for more virgins?"

I nodded. "Right. Mind if we look around a little?"

"Of course not." He nodded at David. "Why don't you show Mark around?"

I gave Mark a permissive wink, and the two youngsters left the room together, exchanging little looks of mutual interest. I had to smile as I turned my attention back to Claude. I hadn't

really noticed it before, for I had been busy admiring his young friends, but the group leader was rather sexy, and looked younger than his years.

I rested one thigh on a corner of the desk, quite aware that it tightened the slacks across my crotch, and saw Claude's eyes shift downward. Deliberately, I shifted to sit on the corner of the desk nearer him, and widened the angle of my thighs. His tongue flicked out to run suggestively about his lips, and he drew in a long breath.

I asked him what he was trying to accomplish with his "farm." As he talked about how he sought to get young runaways off the streets, give them a home life that was accepting of their homosexuality, I began moving a few inches closer, sliding my butt along the desk top.

He swallowed hard and his hands gripped the arms of the chair. His eyes became fixed on my bulging crotch.

Finally he rolled the chair back and I saw that he was nude – and he had a splendid erection

"Well," I said, "I see you were expecting us."

"No, not exactly. We go bare in the house. It helps the boys grow more confident."

"You certainly practice what you preach. Look at how *confident* you are," I said, reaching out to seize the shaft of his stubby cock.

"It's just that I've seen every picture you've made."

"But this is real life." I stroked his cock.

He squirmed in his chair. "But you came here looking for virgins and I'm no virgin."

"I was hoping you weren't. I like a little variety."

"So do I."

His fingers were trembling as he unfastened my trousers and freed the still-growing shaft of my cock. He stared at it, only a couple of inches from his nose. As his fingers encircled it, his other hand dipped beneath to free my balls, exposing me completely to his hungry gaze.

"Man alive, I've never had my hands on one this large," he murmured, hovering over my dick as if undecided what to do next. "I'm not sure I can..." His words trailed off.

"Sure you can." His lips were plump, but it was true that Claude's mouth was small. That meant it would feel extra good

when my prick slid into it. I really hadn't planned on this, but I wasn't about to pass up a good blowjob. His hand tightened on my cock, and his tongue slid slowly, lovingly across the slippery head, finally to lick away the tiny drop of jism that seeped from it.

He gave a moan of surrender then, settling himself more comfortably in the chair, adjusting his head and neck for the oral assault. He licked me again, leaving the head coated with saliva, and took a deep breath. I stood over him and watched him pay homage to my cock.

"Damn!" I groaned as Claude's lips slipped over the glans, and he took it down to the base. I could feel the sensitive head rub past his tongue and palate, then felt the warm, wet and gentle embrace of his throat muscles as it slid between his tonsils and deep in his throat. I grabbed his hair and pushed his head down. He gagged and I released him.

He began twisting his head, adding a screwing motion to the caress of those oral tissues and that flicking, licking tongue. He compounded the offering by swallowing just as the cockhead was buried deep in his throat.I was helping by hunching into his mouth, and pulling his face against my crotch again and again. I didn't have to ask if he wanted to take my load in his mouth.

Anyone who sucked as avidly as he did was anxious for the result, and I was about to give it to him. All I did was pull his head down and ram my cock deep in his throat one last time, letting the convulsions tip me over the edge and into a swirling, knee-weakening ecstasy of orgasmic release. My balls tightened, and my cum spurted against his palate and down his throat. Alternately, he gulped and moaned as he swallowed, jacking himself off at the same time, his cum splashing onto his hairy belly.

He took his time releasing my cock, carefully licking the top four inches and the head, his fingers tugging to force the last drop from the slit. Only then did he look up into my face.

"Shit, if you could bottle that," he whispered, "you could make a fortune."

"And you could give lessons," I said, stowing my cock away and refastening my trousers.

"Well, to be honest, it was even better than I expected."

"I'm glad."

He stood and tugged on a pair of bikini trunks. "Want to look around the place?"

"Love it," I said, following him into the dim hallway, my eyes drawn to his hot ass, idly wondering if any of these boys were fucking him. When he stopped at the top of the stairs, I patted his bubble butt. "Somethin' else I'd love – "

"I'm afraid I'm like Freddy, I need time."

"Well, whenever you're ready."

"Thanks."

"I wonder where Mark is," I said.

"With David. We'll look for them now," he answered as we descended the stairs.

One wall had been knocked out downstairs, creating a large area he had furnished with three sofas, four easy chairs, and about a dozen huge pillows. In one corner, a large screen television set and a VCR were flanked by bookcases.

"When do you have time to read?" I chuckled.

"We don't screw all the time," he grinned back. "The boys have to read a book a week, and make a report on it."

We stepped out onto the porch. "What do you hope to get out of all this?" I asked him. "Playing nursemaid to a bunch of lost boys can't be a picnic."

"Well, I guess it's compensation. I had a rough time as a boy. My parents disowned me because I was gay, and I didn't have many friends. Oh, I knew a lot of guys who would hit the sack with me in private. But, in public, they pretended to be homophobes. I like to think I'm giving these boys a chance to be whatever they want to be."

"And you're getting a lot of young ass."

"Sure. I won't deny it. But I don't force my attentions on any of them. Just like Freddy and Kyle. They wanted time to decide just what they really felt, and I told them not to worry about it. They were welcome here, so long as they accepted the others the way they are."

"How do you pay for all this? Teenagers eat their weight in junk food every day."

"It was easy, at first. I inherited a few bucks from an uncle who just happened to be gay."

"Did he fuck you?"

"Every chance he got."

"How old were you?"

"I was old enough to like it, and I instigated it several times. Anyway, he left me his money, and this old place. Trouble is, it's mortgaged, and I'm running out of cash. That's why I made the deal with Davis. These boys enjoy having sex so they might as well get paid for it, in a controlled way. I don't want them out hustling. What they make will help keep us afloat a little longer."

We walked into the front yard.

"Where the hell is Mark, by the way?"

"I imagine if he gave David the slightest hint, the boy went down on him."

"Remind me to check the water out here," I laughed.

Suddenly Mark and David came around the corner of the house, Mark's arm about the youngster's slender waist.

"What've you two been up to?" I asked as they approached us.

"Nothing, so far. Just lookin' around. It really is a farm. These guys are workin' hard."

I grinned. "They're workin' *hard* all right." I turned to Claude. "How far is it to the nearest restaurant?"

"About three miles. Why?"

"Well, I'm starved. Let the kids wash up, and I'll treat the boys to whatever they want."

Before Claude could speak, I held my hand up, palm out. "Hey, whatever's on the menu!"

10

At the restaurant, the waitresses let us push two big tables together so all eight of us could be seated and were delighted when I told them it wouldn't be on separate checks.

I sat across from a boy introduced to me as Andy. He had dreamy eyes, framed by long lashes, and a highly kissable mouth with full, pouting lips. His blond hair was wavy and shoulder length, and his body reminded me of some Greek statues I've seen. He didn't talk much, but I discovered he, like Danny, hailed from Mississippi, and had run away for the same reason as Mark: Zealously religious parents who insisted that his homosexuality was a one-way ticket to hell.

Mark was seated next to me, but he was deeply involved in conversation with David. Freddy and a little blond named Billy sat at the other end of the table, along with Kyle, who gave me a smile now and then, letting me know he hadn't forgotten who introduced him to anal intercourse.

Andy noticed where I was looking and said, "You like Kyle a lot, don't you?"

"He was a pleasure to meet, let's put it that way."

"Now the pleasure's all ours," Andy snickered.

"He's hot isn't he?"

"Thanks to you. You know, before he was with you, he wouldn't do anything. Now you can't keep him down, not that we'd want to."

As I sliced the tough ham in my omlette, I asked him what part of Mississippi he hailed from.

"North," he said. "My folks had a little place out from New Albany. That's pretty close to Tupelo."

"Well, you're about as far from Tupelo as you can get now, aren't you?"

He looked at Claude with fondness. "I was about to give up when I met Claude. I couldn't find a job or nothin'."

Claude was talking across the table with Mark, and seemed to be ignoring my conversation with Andy. Leaning closer, I asked, "Did Claude offer you help in exchange for sex, Andy?"

He frowned. "No way!" he said sharply. "I offered, but he wouldn't let me. Said I could stay as long as I wanted, and I didn't have to do nothing."

"But, you finally did?"

He wagged his head again. "Yeah, but Kyle is my favorite right now."

I gave the waitress a fifty dollar bill, telling her to keep the change, and Andy drew a deep breath. "Jesus!" he hissed.

"She's gotta live. Most of her pay is in tips."

"Wish I had money to hand out like that."

"Stay with Claude. He'll have you makin' the big bucks, I just know it."

Mark, Andy and David rode back to the farm with me in the Buick, while the others shared the van with Claude. Andy sat close to me on the front seat, his firm thigh pressing mine and moving, now and then, as if to remind me it was there. Finally, I dropped one hand to rest on his warm flesh, and he quickly covered it with his, urging it upward toward the bulge of his crotch. I stopped just short of his cock, and let my hand slip down between those slender thighs.

He moved his hips restlessly, and scooted closer, making me glad that I hadn't bought the Buick model with bucket seats.

"Do you like to kiss and hug, Mr. Hardee?" he whispered.

I glanced up at the rear view mirror before answering, "You mean like those two?"

He gave a quick glance at the back seat, where Mark and David were locked in a fierce embrace, their mouths fused, and both hands busy between them.

Turning back with a grin, Andy said, "Yeah. Like that."

"Sure. But you'll have to call me Pete, not Mr. Hardee."

His thighs squeezed my hand as he grinned and said, "I'll bet I can make Pete hard."

"You know, I believe you can."

When we returned, Claude told everyone it was time for a "nap." Andy led me to what appeared to be the master bedroom, with two double beds. Mark and David followed us. Claude took Billy, Kyle and Freddy with him.

I found Andy in the nude even more attractive; his uncut prick was perfectly formed, and almost as large as Mark's.

"Just hold me for a few minutes," he urged, pulling me down beside him on the bed. Beside us, Mark and David were already nursing each other's dicks, head to toe, with Mark on top, his hips thrusting that cock deep into David's willing throat.

Pulling Andy's warm body against me, I ran my hands over his youthful curves, squeezing his firm buttocks and caressing the smooth inward curve of his lithe waist. His soft lips parted for my kiss, his tongue twisting and probing, searching my mouth as his arms tightened about my neck.

"I missed this," he whispered, " when I was little. I never got hugged and kissed."

Our bodies shifted, adjusting to various positions, different parts of our bodies pressing and moving. My lips found his dainty nipples, sucking them gently, while my tongue lapped at their stiffening tips, making him moan.

His mouth paid homage to my pectorals, nursing like a baby as his hands slipped lower, fingertips caressing my throbbing cock and swollen balls. His kisses moved lower, that warm, wet tongue pausing to dip and twist in my navel.

Then, lower still, to lick hungrily at my inner thighs, pretending, for the moment, that my prick did not exist. All the way down to my knees, the boy applied that wet mobile tongue, then kissed his way upward with little butterfly caresses that made my hips squirm and lift.

His mouth found my balls, drawing the hairy eggs in, one at a time, to roll them about with his tongue, coating them with saliva, and sucking just enough to make me groan with pleasure, and push my hips higher, pulling my knees up to my chest.

Andy took the unspoken hint, burying his face in the cleft of my buttocks and flicking the tip of that bold tongue over the nerve-laced circle of my anus.

Beside us, Mark and David were sucking each other like two starving calves, slurping and moaning as they reached for matching orgasms. But Andy received my full attention when his tongue stiffened and bored into my asshole, sending a jolt of hot pleasure through my belly.

The youngster was in no hurry to leave, and I wasn't about to dislodge that probing muscle. I flexed my sphincter, and

Andy let me feel the gentle suction of his pursed lips, his tongue fucking in and out, slowly and luxuriously. I've had enough experience to tell when a boy is enjoying his work, and he definitely was!

Soon Mark and David were in the midst of incredibly noisy and almost simultaneous orgasms, shaking the bed with their hunching hips and bobbing heads.

Gurgling gulps signaled the ingestion of the cum, and, with little pause, they scrambled about for Mark to kneel behind David's arched back, slipping his still-hard cock into his partner's ass.

Now Andy reluctantly pulled his tongue from my asshole, kissed his way over my balls, licked the vein from the bottom to below the slit, and paused to look up at me. I don't know what the kid planned to say, but I reached down and pulled him up until he was lying atop me, his legs spread and his stiff cock pressed against mine. His limpid eyes seemed to begging for approval, companionship, and understanding. There was no need for words. My arms drew him closer, and I kissed him long and hard, our tongues swirling and our hips writhing with mounting lust.

Like many boys, Andy was starved for affection, and sex offered an acceptable substitute. I instinctively knew that he would have gone down on me at the very start, if I had suggested that. But, I wanted to give the lad at least a sample of simple companionship, and he responded with a near sob of happiness as he nestled in my arms.

My hands explored his naked body, then my fingers teased his anus, then moved lower still to caress his balls as they rested against mine.

His smooth cheek rubbed my jaw as he placed his mouth against my ear, his hips still working that hard cock over mine.

"After I suck you off," he whispered, "will you fuck me?"

"You like to be fucked?" I asked, fingering him.

"More'n anything!" he breathed, his tongue flicking my ear. "But, I love to suck dick, too."

"If you suck me off first, we can last longer when I screw you. Show me how much you want that big prick."

Eagerly, the youngster slipped down to lie between my legs, his fingers toying with my balls while his tongue ran lovingly

about the flared rim of my cockhead. Then, slowly, his lips slipped over the tip, drawing the knob in until it was just behind his teeth, where he began nursing the dick. The feeling was intense, for his tongue lashed the sensitive head as he sucked with short, powerful tugs, drawing a spurt of jism through the throbbing column.

My hips pushed upward, and Andy's head lowered, his throat taking a good deal of my prick. As the boy mouth-fucked me, Mark and David changed positions. Mark was face down, while David hunched away on top of him, shaking the bed with his deep thrusts into Mark's bottom.

Raising myself on elbows, I asked the busy Andy, "Where's the K-Y?"

He managed to pull his lips free to answer that it was in the nightstand drawer. He returned to my cock as I twisted about to find the tube.

Squeezinga glob onto my left palm, I ordered, 'Turn over, Andy. I want some of that cute ass."

"Let me make you come like this!" he panted, his fingers gripping the base of my cock, and his lips moving against the oozing tip. "I want your cum, Pete!"

"You can suck it later. I want to fuck!"

With a little grunt of surrender, he rolled over onto his belly, and spread those girlish legs. Reaching back, his fingers parted the cheeks of his adorable ass, and I used one, then two fingers to lubricate the entrance, making him groan when I forced them into him fully.

The rest of the jelly I spread over my swollen cock before swinging into position, one knee between the youngster's thighs, the other beside him, so that I lay half on top of him, while Andy was almost on his side.

Sensing my intent, he raised his upper leg, holding it in the air as I pressed the head of my prick against his anus, and pushed. He muffled a cry as he felt my entry, for I doubt that the boy had entertained a cock so big before.

"I'll take it slow," I promised. There was a brief resistance before he relaxed his sphincter and let my dick slide into him.

His upper body twisted about, and even as I began fucking him, my lips found his waiting mouth, and his tongue swirled about mine in a torrid kiss.

After several minutes of this, he hissed, "It's so good, Pete!" "I'd like to push my balls in there, too," I panted. "That's a hot ass."

It didn't last much longer for the youth had brought me close to orgasm with that skillful mouth. Now, my dick sliding deep in his clenching asshole with every stroke, I could not resist the sweet pangs of my approaching climax.

"Fuck me, Pete!" he gasped between those tongue-stabbing kisses.

It was then I noticed that our two companions had broken off their own coupling to join us. Mark wriggled down to where his mouth could take Andy's throbbing prick, and David buried his face between my buttocks and began licking my asshole. This sent me over the top, and the boy's own dick spilled into Mark's mouth, and David's tongue worked feverishly in my butt. As I pulled my cock from Andy, Mark and David seized it and wouldn't let it go until I was hard again and able to fuck each of them. After awhile, Andy wanted it again. Then there was a knock on the door and David got up to let the rest of the gang into the room.

As Claude approached us, his cock swinging back and forth tantalizingly, the boys scampered out of the bed. "Well, Pete, I'm ready," he said, getting on his knees on the bed. I lifted myself up so that I could mount him.

Every boy in the room watched with glittering eyes as my cock began stretching Claude's anal passage. He butted his hips back at me, driving me into him all the way. My chest smeared his back with sweat as I drilled his ass. He reared up and finally hot splatters of cum spurted from his cock. "You sure were ready," I joked.

While the other boys stood around us jacking their cocks, Kyle rushed onto the bed to take Claude's place. I got behind him and when I nudged him with my cockhead, his anus puckered with renewed fear. He grimaced as the big head squeezed past his ass-ring and he gritted his teeth as I began slowly sinking the shaft. When my pubic hair finally brushed against his buttocks, I hugged him to me and whispered, "That's it."

The other boys moved in closer. Claude lay on the bed, playing with Kyle's cock as I fucked the boy. The other boys

now stood tight to the mattress, their cocks jutting at me. Soon the heady sound of cocks being beaten echoed all around us.

My fingers tingled as I wrapped them around Billy's thick prick. I peeled back the foreskin, exposing his cockhead, slick with precum. I licked it as hard, throbbing cocks surrounded me, some of them touching me, and I knew what I had to do. I sucked each of them as I slammed into Kyle. Still shy, Freddy backed off slightly when I moved my mouth to his cock, but Mark pushed him forward, sending his lovely erection sliding into my mouth.

After sucking Freddy for a couple of minutes, I cupped Mark's big balls with my left hand and heard approving grunts. I held onto Mark's shaft as I bent my head and opened my mouth. Mark squirmed when I licked his slit. Then I took it deep. I almost choked on his tasty meat. I became intoxicated by the heady smell of his crotch, now steamy with sweat and spent cum. Sucking my lover while my cock was plunging in and out of Kyle, I was in heaven.

But Mark quickly backed off, pulling his cock out inch by inch, dramatically, to the delight of the others. Once it was completely free, I leaned over to capture it again. Mark face-fucked me, slipping it back in again, over and over, and I let out a long, deep groan. Cocks were again pressed and bumped against my shoulders and face. I went back to Billy, and his foreskin slid back and forth in my mouth.

David dropped behind me and opened my sweating asscheeks. The boy's sharp, hot tongue sent a flinch through me, and I twisted and writhed as he licked at my anus. Still sucking Billy's cock, I let out another long, low growl.

David lifted up, his arms holding my waist, and began riding my hips, forcing me deeper into Kyle. I thought for a moment David was going to stick his prick into me but he was content to push it up and down my crack. I let out another moan as Billy came in my mouth. I savored the beef-jerky flavor and I grabbed his balls, squeezing until I got the last of it.

David kissed my shoulder blades as I came inside Kyle. Claude, still working Kyle's dick, was soon taking his load. Exhausted, I pulled out and fell back, watching as the boys covered me with their spunk. The scene was surreal, making me wish I had brought along the crew to capture the whole

thing on film.

"I'll be back," I vowed to Claude.

"Any time, big man," he said, kissing me full on the mouth. "Any time at all."

11

When I told Larry that Claude was exactly what he appeared to be and that I saw no boys at the farm that might cause any trouble at all, he was relieved. "Do any *recruiting*?"

I grinned. "A little."

"Tell me about it later. I want you to meet Kitty."

I shrugged. Mark chuckled, "Here Kitty, here Kitty," and wandered off to help the crew set up the lighting for the sex scene between his lover and a transvestite.

Larry led me into one of the several dressing rooms in the warehouse and when I saw Kitty/Kenny was tempted to ask him to immediately to show me his dick; it was almost impossible to believe that he wasn't a girl. He had shoulder-length hair, a slender waist, long, exquisite legs, and a fantastic ass. But that was just part of the package. He was also blessed with daintily arched brows, a delicate nose, and lips that seemed constantly pursed. His icy green eyes were like deep pools you wanted to dive into and drown. In all of my film work, I had never been paired with a transvestite. I had worked on the same picture with several, but they were either stage dressing, or someone else got to enjoy their favors. Always game for a challenge, I was looking forward to this.

Kenny extended a carefully manicured hand when Larry introduced us, and I felt the long nails tease my palm. I gave an exaggerated bow and brought the back of the hand to my lips.

"Oh," Kenny, simpered, batting those long lashes. "You're a real darling. I've heard about you."

"And I've heard about you," I retorted, staring at the twin mounds that poked tiny fingers against the thin blouse. "Are those real?"

"Of course, you naughty boy! I spent enough on hormones and surgery. They'd better be real."

"Okay!" Larry groaned. "Let's cut the shit! You two can swap measurements on your own time. Let's get some film in the can. All right?"

Kenny gave a very feminine toss of the head. "Well! This is

no way to treat a lady!"

Ignoring the comment, Larry outlined the scene for us. Talking about the missing boy with Kenny at the bar, I became infatuated and when he asked me to go home with him I did. Luckily, there was no dialogue to contend with. If we felt the urge, Larry added, we could exchange comments about our actions.

"One more thing," Larry said. "Let Kitty suck it awhile, then give it to her from the rear. But when you get ready to come, let her have it in the mouth again, pulling it out just as you start to shoot."

Kenny waved one hand theatrically. "I don't see why I can't just swallow his cum. It's so wasteful when it just spills like that."

"It's good for your skin," Larry snorted. "Rub it in."

"Oh, I know that, you silly man! How do you think I keep such a lovely complexion?"

While the crew got everything in order, Kenny and I stepped to one side, and began to neck.

"How did you get rid of the beard?" I asked, kissing those flawless cheeks. Even the closest shave couldn't make them that smooth.

"Honey," he purred, moving his hips suggestively, "I spent a fortune on that, and to keep my pussy just as pretty."

"Your pussy?"

"Oh, poo!" Kenny pouted. "I suppose you'd call it an ass."

"Boy pussy. I love boy pussy."

"Oh, you sweet thing! We may be here indefinitely!"

Larry summoned us, using his cigar as a baton, and directed us to a point outside one wall of the set. He indicated the door.

"When I call for action," he said, most of his attention focused on me, "enter through there. You can wing it from there. After you close the door, all I want is heavy sex. If I see something I don't like, I'll let you know. Just remember to freeze when I say 'cut', for I may want to pick it up from there."

We nodded our understanding, and, as Larry moved away, Kenny whispered, "You'd better kiss your balls goodbye, Pete."

"Why?"

"Because I'm gonna suck them right out through your dick!"

"Lights!" Larry called, before I could think of a sharp answer. The motel room sprang to life under a battery of lights. Whatever we did would be faithfully recorded by the all-seeing eyes of four cameras.

"Cameras!" was the next command, and men and machines sprang to attention.

"Action!"

Following him into the room, I carefully closed the door, then took him into my arms, feeling those firm breasts nuzzle me and his hips press the swell of his own cock against mine. It was a strange feeling, but one charged with eroticism. My prick began to stiffen immediately.

His eyes, wide and deceptively innocent, threatened to swallow me up, and his lush lips parted for my kiss. With his tongue dancing into my mouth, he tasted even more delicious than I had hoped.

My hands roamed over his body, tracing the indentation of that supple waist, then cupping the pronounced swell of those magnificent buttocks, fingers working the short skirt up so I could caress him. My lips drifted down the graceful neck, and I deserted this ass to unfasten the skimpy blouse, exposing those miraculous tits, their small nipples already hard and tilted for my mouth.

Kenny sighed and his back arched as I licked, my hands squeezing the mounds as if seeking to draw sustenance from them.

Some transvestites wear a cup over their genitals to disguise their arousal, but Kenny's cock was already tenting the front of his skirt, and when I helped him out of his clothing, a thin, seven-inch cock snapped up to stare at me, while a pair of promising balls hugged its base.

Whatever he had done to the area around his asshole, he had not removed the dark curls of his pubic thatch.

His fingers helped me with my own undressing, and we feasted our eyes on each other, his widening when he saw my big cock for the first time.

Larry hadn't indicated exactly how we were to proceed, but Kenny's thrusting, uncut prick could not be ignored. Dropping to my knees on the rug, I let my hands cup his firm rear, while

my tongue paid lip service to his erection.

Licking my way upward from his balls, I pushed back the skin and took the mushroom head into my mouth, sliding my lips almost to the root of his dick.

"Ummmm!" Kenny murmured, his hands pulling my head still closer. "You know the way to a girl's heart!"

I wouldn't have minded spending more time on that delicious meat roll, for the single surge of jism was most tasty. But, Larry wanted it otherwise, and it was wise to put business before pleasure.

Releasing Kenny's dick, I kissed my way upward, over his smooth, slightly rounded tummy, and paused for one more taste of his tits. Then I urged the boy back onto the bed, following him to straddle his waist, and slide my cock between his breasts.

Kenny's hands pushed the mounds from either side, shaping a valley for my prick, while his neck arched, and his tongue extended to flick daintily at the head each time I thrust forward through the warm clasp.

That mouth was too inviting. Lifting my hips, I eased upward, and Kenny's lips parted to claim my swollen prick, relaxing his throat so I could slide all of my prick into that warm wet embrace, and bounce my balls against his chin while the head nuzzled the back of the boy's throat.

I stroked in and out a few times, but I knew that I wouldn't be able to keep from coming if I kept fucking the boy's mouth. He wasn't kidding about pulling my balls loose; Kenny's expertise was beyond question.

I pulled my cock out of his mouth, and his hands clawed at my hips, urging me back. A glance at the youngster's eyes told me he really wanted some more of my dick, and I couldn't deny him.

Turning onto my back, I let him crouch between my legs and go down on me again. Looking down at him, as his head rose and fell over my middle, what I saw was a lovely young girl, for each time he drew back, I caught a glimpse of those cute breasts. It didn't make it any easier for me to hold back when Kenny started moaning as he sucked. Kenny's ass was already slick and ready, but I didn't want to pull out of his greedy mouth. Still, duty called. "I want some ass, Kitty!" I grunted,

forcing Kenny's head up, an action he resisted, trying to recapture my saliva-coated cock.

"Get on your hands and knees!" I ordered, "and spread those cheeks for me!"

Kenny knelt in the center of the bed, swung his ass into position. The youngster lowered his chest, reached back with both hands, and parted those firm, velvet mounds, revealing the tiny, striated circle that was the gateway to paradise for so many. While I seek out virgins, at the other end of the spectrum, sticking it in an accomplished whore is almost as big a thrill.

Cameras were almost touching my hips as I placed one hand on the boy's back, and gripped my swollen cock with the other, steering its tip until it pressed the hot entrance.

"This will be a first," Kenny murmured, his cheek pressing the pillow as he stared back at me. "I've never been fucked by a dick's dick...UNNNHH!"

He never got to finish the pun, for I shoved my prick into that tight little ass, forcing the head past the sphincter, and burying half the length inside him.

Larry's little suppository had lubricated the channel, but it was still gripping my cock like a lover's fist, and the anal muscles were contracting with a rippling motion that began at the well-stretched anus, then rolled inward like a series of squeezes, until the tissues were sliding about the well planted knob.

With five inches of dick in there, I could reach around that slender waist and urge Kenny to raise his torso, bracing himself with both arms extended. Then, I grabbed a firm tit in each hand, and literally pulled the youngster onto my prick, moving my hips in a grinding motion as the hot, slippery embrace slid farther down my cock, chewing and sucking until I was all the way in, my balls were squeezed against his.

I'll admit to a touch of bisexuality in my makeup, and that part of me was suddenly enjoying the best of both worlds. The body beneath me could well have been that of a girl, for those breasts were the real thing, the nipples responding to my fingers by swelling and pulsating. But when it came to getting fucked, Kenny was all-boy. I've known girls who don't mind having anal sex, but they simply cannot respond the way boys

can. Boys can provide a thrill that even the best intentioned girl can never duplicate, and Kenny was demonstrating this to me once again. "UHH!...UHH!" became a litany, accentuated by the sound of slapping flesh when my hips collided with his arched bottom, and by the wet slurping sound of my prick sliding in and out of that juicy asshole. I tried holding back but every thrust was carrying me closer to the inevitable orgasm.

"Jesus... Oh, God!" he screamed, his face slammed into the pillow, and his body writhing, his own prick jerking, its powerful spasms reflected in his contracting colon.

"I'm gonna come!" I gasped.

It took every ounce of willpower I possessed to tug my cock out of Kenny. I reared back on my heels while he scrambled about to face me, his mouth claiming my prick. He drew the full length of my prick down his throat just as the first spasm of orgasm smashed through my loins. He drew back, and his fingers gripped my cock, milking it in time with the powerful jetting. Then his tongue darted out to lick the head as the last dribbles escaped.

Even as Larry was yelling "Cut," Kenny was opening his mouth to take my dick down his throat once again.

12

According to Larry's production chart, we had more than fifty percent of the film in the can. That's why I was upset when Larry called me into his office and told me, "I'm runnin' outta cash."

"I thought you had your usual deal with the distributor."

"I do, but they want me to cut the budget. I can't. No way am I going to cut the budget."

"I don't understand."

"It's the fuckin' videos!" he growled. "Any bastard with a camera can turn 'em out by the dozens while we're trying to make one lousy film!"

"How about the ranch? Can't you borrow on that?"

"Shit, I'm in hock up to my ass already." He leaned back in the chair and drew a long breath. "Just once in my fuckin' life I wanted to make one damned picture that was a little better than the usual shit. Just one!"

"Hey, you've made some damn good stuff."

He shrugged. "But I can't take that to the bank. If I was putting this crap on tape, I could raise the money. But porno theaters are closin' like a virgin's legs. Now I'm supposed to cut the budget."

"How much would it take to finish it the way you want it?"

He stared at me for a moment. "If I cut every goddamn corner possible, it'll still take another twenty grand."

It was my turn to take a long breath. Then I said, "How 'bout if I buy half the picture for twenty grand."

"Where the fuck are you gonna get that kind of money?"

"I've been lucky. In his will my pa left me some stock. It's doubled, and doubled again. I can borrow on it if I need to." Little did Sugar Daddy know how I was going to put his generosity to work for me.

"I don't know."

"Hey, I figure I'll wear out my welcome sooner or later, and I might as well move into the producer's chair while I can."

"In other words, you want to be my partner?"

"Why not? That'll look good: A Davis and Hardee Production."

He chuckled. "At least you put my name first."

"Have we got a deal – partner?"

He nodded. "Have I got a choice?" He climbed to his feet. "I'll get the papers drawn up. When can you have the cash?"

"As soon as I can get to the bank."

I had a feeling the picture, still untitled, was several cuts above the usual porn flick, and was certain my investment would pay off. Still, I knew the future was in video. Larry was like a farmer who still plowed with a mule, pretending that tractors were just a passing fancy. But I was convinced I could make my new partner see the light sooner or later.

I left Larry's office to find Mark. He was talking with one of the cameramen, a good-looking guy in his early twenties. I waved him over, telling him we were going to the bank. His eyes widened when I explained what I was about to do. To him, a twenty grand was a fortune. It was to me, too. But I didn't think of it as a gamble; porn was here to stay and I wanted to be more of part of it.

The bank's parking lot was almost full, but I found a spot between a Mercedes and a battered pickup, easing the Buick in with just enough room to open the doors. Mark and I made our way through the waves of heat to the cool interior of the bank.

I went to my safe deposit box and took out all my stock certificates in Sugar Daddy's company, then found an officer who gladly wrote up my loan. Within minutes, the money was in my checking account.

Back at the warehouse, Larry had just finished shooting Danny and Keith in a series of clips he could use for fill later. He had Keith suck Danny's dick in just about every possible position, standing, sitting and lying. Each shot would be carefully filed, and used as needed. The boys took off for the showers and I waved Larry toward the office.

Larry let Mark and me enter the room first, then closed the door behind us.

I sat down at the desk, wrote him out check, and handed it to him. He stared at the check, still not believing it. I thought

he'd ask if it was good but he didn't. He took a deep breath and put the check in the center drawer of his desk. Turning to me, he said, "I'll have those papers ready in the morning."

"No rush. We've got a deal. Is Kenny working today?"

"I guess you could say that. He's labeling some of the film we just got back from the lab. Why?"

"Well, if you don't need us we'd like to borrow Kenny until tomorrow."

He gave me a teasing frown. "If you spend the night with both of them, you won't be worth a shit tomorrow."

"Trust me."

"You're the boss now, Pete."

"It's just that I've got an idea I want to try out."

Nodding resignedly, he said, "Well, go for it, partner."

I told Mark to wait while I talked with Kenny. Exchanging greetings with the crew, and the two boys I had enjoyed only days before, I walked across to the cutting and editing room.

Kenny was, as usual, in drag, but with a different approach. Perched on a stool as he ran the film through a small viewer, he was wearing an ultra-short skirt, a skimpy blouse, and, except for a pair of dangerously high heels, looked for all the world like a schoolgirl.

He turned at my approach and fluttered his false lashes at me. "Hey, Prince Charming, where's your big white horse?"

I cupped my crotch. "Right here, baby. Wanna ride it?"

He licked his lips. "Only after I eat it."

I stopped about a foot from him. "How would you like to spend the night with Mark and me at my little cabin in the mountains?"

"How much are you going to charge me? A night with you two would be cost more'n I could afford."

"It's a party, Kenny. Just a party. You do like to drink, don't you?"

"My middle name is Fish," he said, shifting those shapely legs and showing a disturbing length of a luscious thigh.

"Finish up whatever you're doing. It's time to party!"

A manicured hand darted out to cup my balls, squeezing gently. He pursed his lush lips and sucked in a long breath. "What we did on camera was just a sample, sweetheart. Tonight, I'll take you to heaven."

"Oh, and don't forget about Mark."

He cackled. "Oh, honey, it's a poor girl who can't handle two men."

When I told Mark that Kenny would be spending the night with us, and his lips curved in an excited smile.

"Anything you say. I still have to pinch myself," he said, "to keep from thinkin' all this ain't just a dream."

Kenny came tripping across the big room to join us, swinging a large purse and swishing his hips. Mark pursed his lips in a soundless whistle of appreciation, and Kenny gave him a flirtatious smile. "I know what you're thinking."

"What?"

"What all you dirty men think about. You probably want your dick sucked."

"No," Mark grinned. "I'd rather have a piece of ass."

"Oh, my god! A real man!"

To the casual observer, we were two men and a very pretty girl, crossing the sun-drenched concrete and piling into the Buick. Kenny slid in between Mark and me, letting that short skirt climb all the way to his crotch. His breasts jutted out, and Mark kept stealing looks at them.

"Does it feel good to you?" he asked innocently. "I mean, when a guy sucks on them."

"I'll show you, you pretty thing," Kenny said, "when we get to Pete's place. You want to chew on one for me?"

Mark groped himself. "You wanna chew on this?"

"Honey," Kenny said, smiling broadly, "I'll eat that thing like a big stick of candy."

13

Mark held the door for Kenny as he climbed out of the Buick, clutching Mark's arm as he teetered in his high heels.

"Oh, stud, you're a real gentleman," Kenny said, giving Mark a sultry smile and rubbing those firm tits against the boy's arm.

As I unlocked the door, I said, "I'll bet you don't say that when he rams his dick up your ass."

Kenny pretended a look of shock, his full lips rounding. "Mark and I will make *love!*" he announced haughtily. "That's something you big porn studs just wouldn't understand."

I let them precede me into the cabin. I teased, "Hey, while he's fucking you, will you suck my prick?"

"I prefer to say I'm making *love* to your big dick," Kenny joked, tossing back a stray curl. Mark, who I was happy to see was finding more and more things funny these days, chuckled and headed for the bar. He set out three glasses and began preparing our drinks.

I sank into one of the easy chairs. "How would you two like to help me with a little experiment?"

Kenny licked his lips. "Experiment? You mean there's something the big porn stud's never done?"

"Yeah, I've never directed a movie before."

Kenny lifted the glass Mark delivered to him. "Direct away, honey!"

Mark asked, "What do you want us to?"

"Nothing out of the ordinary. I'm just going to use a video camera, and give Larry an idea of what I'm capable of."

"I'm ready for my close-up, Mr. Hard-ee," Kenny joked, striking a pose.

"What I'd like to do is set up in the bedroom, and film you and Kenny. I'll shoot it without sound, and tell you exactly what to do as we go along. Later, we'll edit it, and add all the grunts and groans."

"Sounds like fun," Mark grinned. He put one arm around Kenny's slender waist, his hand moving upward toward one

breast. "How 'bout it, Kenny?"

Kenny moved his hips suggestively. "I knew better than to trust you two nasty boys. A girl agrees to have a little social drink, and ends up gettin' fucked."

"Let's get the lights rigged, and check a few angles."

"And curves," Mark added, rubbing his hand over Kenny's shapely rear. They followed me to the front closet, and helped carry the lights and camera tripod to the bedroom. I chuckled remembering the number of my times Sugar Daddy had used the camera when he first bought it, shooting cassette after cassette of my dick. Then he grew bored with the camera and never used it again. I decided to leave a copy of what I was about to film in the VCR with a big thank-you note.

Kenny had some experience on a set, and Mark followed his suggestions as they arranged the lights, eliminating shadows on the big bed, while I sighted through the video camera and decided just where I would position myself for the best shots.

Kenny said, "It'd make us feel a lot better, Pete, if you got undressed." Mark nodded his agreement.

"Okay," I said. "But I want to shoot you both taking your clothes off, so I'll strip now."

By the time I stepped out of my shorts, my cock almost hard from anticipation, Mark's crotch was bulging, and Kenny's skirt showed a definite tenting.

I had them move to the far side of the bed, while I got down and aimed the camera up at them from the far side.

"Okay, give me a long embrace, and a juicy kiss, and feel each other up."

As the kids pressed their slim bodies together, I moved around the bed, eye glued to the viewer, letting the tape drink in their lush curves. I caught the play of dancing tongues as they kissed, and captured the exchanged caresses as hands groped and squeezed their swelling cocks.

Mark used one hand on Kenny's ass, while the other cupped one of the small but perfect breasts, fingers teasing the nipple, while Kenny, in turn, concentrated on Mark's thrusting prick. They undressed slowly and seductively.

"Sit down on the bed, Kenny, and let Mark stick his dick between your tits." Then I added, "And don't look at the camera."

I needn't have bothered with the warning. My stars were too intent on making me – each other – happy to do anything other than follow my instructions.

Obediently, Kenny lowered his ass to the bed, and pulled Mark close, letting his cock slip between his breasts. His head dipped, and when Mark pushed forward, his tongue licked out to flick the head of that swollen organ.

Mark's asscheeks flexed, his hips thrusting to drive his dick through the valley between Kenny's enhanced pectorals.

Through the viewer, it looked for all the world as if Mark was enjoying the favors of a young and very pretty girl.

"Take it in your mouth, Kenny," I said, moving closer to catch the gleam of moisture on the youngster's lips as they parted to receive the head of Mark's cock. Kenny already knew, and Mark was rapidly learning how to adjust to the camera's demands, keeping arms and hands out of the way, so the lens could view every action.

I captured each lovely movement as Mark's dick slid into Kenny's mouth, his balls spreading against the youngster's chin as he held the head between Kenny's tonsils for several ecstatic seconds.

"Mouth-fuck 'im!" I directed, feeling my own prick swell as I watched the ass cheeks tighten and the slender hips hunch that cock in and out. Kenny's fingers clutched Mark's buttocks, urging the boy to shove that hardness deeper and his jaw worked with obvious suction, his cheeks hollowing repeatedly, making Mark grunt with delight.

For the next hour, I recorded every move of the two horny youngsters, guiding their actions and mentally applauding the way they responded as if each step was a personal decision.

Mark fucked Kenny as just I had, doggie fashion, and then again with the boy's legs over his shoulders as he piled that well-fucked ass

Eventually, knowing exactly what would excite Larry the most, I told them what I wanted. Gracefully, the pair separated, their cocks wagging as Mark lay back on the bed, and Kenny mounted him, quickly impaling his ass on Mark's dick, and riding it with full length bouncing, his augmented tits jiggling as he took the cock deep inside him again and again.

Mark's hips thrust upward, slamming into that greedy ass

each time Kenny came down on him, and he gasped with pleasure as the strokes became faster and faster.

"I'm gonna come!" Mark cried.

Immediately, Kenny lifted his hips, pulling his ass up and off the rearing cock just as it jerked and spurted its white cream over Mark's chest and belly.

Kenny's fingers went down to grip the throbbing prick, milking it with gentle tugs until the last drop rolled down the slope of the glans. Then, while I moved still closer with the camera, the boy leaned over and licked hungrily at the head of Mark's dick, sucking it into his mouth to claim every trace of the orgasmic flood. Releasing the cock, he began licking up the spilled cum, drawing it in and swallowing it. Only when he had cleaned every bit of the cream from Mark's chest and stomach did he return to that still-hard cock, and swallow it to the balls with one slow, deft movement.

I laid the camera on the floor beside the bed, and knelt behind Kenny's arched body, guiding my own swollen dick into the boy's delightfully tight asshole.

He grunted as I entered him, then again as I began stroking in and out. But, he kept sucking, for he knew that, this time, Mark could come in his mouth.

Later, so did I.

14

When I showed the tape to Larry the next day, he was non-committal until we reached the scene where Kenny gobbled up Mark's cum.

"Goddamn!" he howled with delight, teeth clamped on the ever-present cigar. "This is so fuckin' realistic I can't believe it."

"It does have an immediacy about it, doesn't it? And it's so much cheaper."

"Shit!" he sighed. "Make it cheap. Cheap, cheap, cheap! That's all I hear these days. I guess that's all that matters. It just don't seem like a fucking movie when you got nothing but tape."

I flicked the control to turn the television set off and halt the VCR. "Nothing," I shrugged, "but money."

"Okay," he said reluctantly. "Maybe we'll go for it on the next one. We'll see what we can do with tape nobody's done before."

I chuckled. "Now you're talkin'. You know, if we don't, we both may have to go to work for a living."

For a change, Larry had no fuck scenes scheduled for the day, and we did a lot of looping for scenes we had already done. Looping is just repeating the dialogue and sounds that are on the original. Quite often, the original has a lot of background noise that makes it unusable, so we simply would redo the sound portion.

When we knocked off for lunch, Larry instructed the film crew to regroup at the Pink Slipper at two o'clock. I was to bring Kenny and pick up a kid named Kevin, who was a bartender at a popular hustler bar on Sunset and was playing the bartender in our little movie. Mark, of course, tagged along.

After collecting Kevin at his apartment, we had lunch at Falcon's Liar, a small cafe just three blocks from the Slipper. Kenny said it wasn't fancy, but the food was good, and the

prices reasonable. As we ate, we discussed the scenes we were to do in the bar.

While we talked, Kevin couldn't keep his eyes off of me. He was in his late twenties, but appeared much younger because, standing, the top of his pretty blond head barely reached my chin. He had also taken very good care of himself: His gym-toned body was a work of art. I found my cock stirring with interest as I watched the way his pouty lips shaped themselves into an inviting circle just before he spoke, which was seldom because he seemed to be genuinely in awe of me.

The dark, seedy bar was on one of a side street, flanked by manufacturing plants and offices of wholesalers who couldn't have cared less about the patrons coming in and out of its doors.

"I spend a lot of time here," Kenny said as I parked in the small lot beside Larry's equipment van. "The men who come here appreciate beauty."

I gave one curved asscheek a quick squeeze. "Yeah, most of us just appreciate somebody who knows how to give good head."

He feigned shock. "I hope you don't think I'd do something like that!"

Kevin snorted. "Quicker than a cat can lick its ass!"

We were laughing as we entered the bar. Mark began helping the crew, Larry took Kenny aside to coach him on some of his lines, while Kevin and I found ourselves alone for a moment.

I said, " I can tell we're gonna have to get together."

"Oh?"

"Yeah. I can tell."

He looked away. "I don't know – "

I put my arm around his waist and pulled him into me. "But I do."

He looked up into my eyes. "Well, tonight's my night off."

"You're on."

"What about Mark?"

I hesitated. Then I said, "Maybe I can get Kenny to keep him company."

We shot the scene seven times before Larry was satisfied, and I took the opportunity to remind him that if we had been

using video tape, it would have cost a lot less. To which, he grunted and chewed his cigar a little more vigorously.

After we called it a wrap at five-thirty, I had my first chance to ask Kenny about spending the night with Mark. He smoothed his dress over those cute tits, and gave me an impish smile. "Why can't Mark spend the night at my place?"

"Okay, why don't you ask him?" I countered, and watched the boy wiggle those incredible hips as he walked over to where Mark was coiling an electrical cord, trying to make himself useful.

Mark came over to me later, a confused look on his face.

"I'm going over to Kevin's tonight," I told him. "I didn't want you to get lonesome."

Mark put one hand on my arm. "Save some for me, Pete," he said in a near whisper.

"Plenty to go around, kid. Plenty."

"Got that right," Mark said, groping me.

"Where would you like to eat?" I asked Kevin as we got into the Buick.

"Anywhere suits me," he answered, fastening his seat belt and settling in the seat. Still a bit shy, he stared out the window.

We passed a Mexican restaurant. I slowed the car. "Feel like this?"

"Suits me," he said, watching a panhandler working the crowd waiting for the light.

At the restaurant, after the first Margarita, Kevin began to loosen up. He asked me, "How'd you get into this business?"

"Believe it or not, it was a woman who got me into it. Not long after I moved here, I answered a casting call for a soft-drink commercial, one of those where a bunch of kids are playing on the beach and swigging some soda. The director, a girl named Parker, took one look at my crotch in the tiny swimsuit I was wearing and called me aside. She asked if I'd ever thought of doing porno. Her eyes drifted down to the bulge and she said I was obviously equipped for it."

He grinned.

"Well," I went on, "I didn't know what to day. I looked away, trying to think of something, and then she asked me

what was wrong. I blushed and came right out with it, that I wasn't into girls. Then she asked, 'How 'bout women?' 'Them either,' I had to admit. But she accepted that with a smile, and told me she knew some guys who were making films with just guys in them. Shit, and I thought all porno was hetero!"

"I think they were for a long time."

"Anyway, I got the job. I found out later this Parker woman got a finders' fee for sendin' guys to the director. All I had to do was let three different guys suck me off. Larry saw the flick and hired me for one scene, and then I did another, and we've been stuck with each other ever since."

I speared the last bite of the chili-coated tamale and popped it into my mouth. "How 'bout you, Kevin?"

He blushed. "Actually, it was Kitty - Kenny, I mean - who talked Larry into using me in a picture about eight months ago. I'm just one of those out of work actors in Hollywood, and as long as it's just lines, I can handle it."

"No action?"

"I'm too old for that now. And besides, I don't have what it takes."

"Like what?"

"Like what you've got, man. I've seen all the Peter Hardee pictures."

"The real thing is better."

"That's what I was hoping."

I paid the tab, ignoring the flirtatious stare of the cute Mexican cashier, and waved Kevin through the doorway. His hand brushed my crotch as he passed, and I felt a sudden rush of desire for the little guy.

Darkness had fallen and the clouds that had moved in from the ocean hid what was supposed to be a full moon. As usual, the bulbs in the street lights were broken, and only a dim halo spilled from the restaurant windows. There was no sign of life in the area.

Side by side, we rounded the corner of the building, and I gave a sharp gasp as a hulking figure, the features indistinguishable in the darkness, loomed in front of us.

I felt something hard and metallic ram into my belly, and a harsh voice grated, "Gimme your wallet, man!...Both of you!"

Hearing this sent a ripple of fear down my spine. "Don't

shoot! Here's my wallet!"

I made as if to reach for my hip pocket, and managed to step back about a foot, feeling the muzzle of the gun retreat from my gut.

Suddenly, Kevin's right hand came down across the man's forearm, almost invisible in the blackness, while the left swung, catching the man's chin just as his finger tightened on the trigger.

The sharp crack echoed from the side of the building, and I cried out, the combined sounds masking the man's gasp as he staggered backward, arms flailing. Before he could recover, Kevin brought the toe of his left foot up between the guy's legs as he bent forward, his face meeting Kevin's right knee with a terrifying thump.

Kevin took one step back, and kicked again, his toe connecting with the guy's throat, and he crumpled to the concrete, the gun clattering across the broken pavement.

"Jesus!" I gasped, clutching Kevin's arm. "Did you kill him?"

"I hope so," he growled, shaking his head.

I put my arm around Kevin's slender waist. "My hero!" I cried, mimicking the tone of Kenny's wail.

"Mean streets, man."

"For a little guy you sure pack a wallop."

He grinned. "You ain't seen nothin' yet."

I spotted the gun. Taking my handkerchief from my pocket, I picked it up, drew back, and sailed it up onto the flat roof of the low building.

We raced to the car. As I swung out into the street, my headlights flooded the sidewalk. The man was beginning to stir, arms moving tentatively, and knees flexing. "He'll live," Kevin said.

It wasn't until I'd had a couple of stiff bourbons and relaxed on the couch at Kevin's apartment that it really hit me: We could have been killed.

"I can't get over the way you decked that guy," I said, eyeing him over the rim of my glass.

He stood and began unbuttoning his shirt, revealing a flawless chest with tiny nipples just begging to be kissed.

"Just lucky. I grew up in New York. I've seen worse than

that, believe me. If he'd been a little quicker, we'd have been dead meat."

"Speaking of meat," I said, bringing my hand to the bulge at his crotch.

"Can I undress you, Pete?" he asked in a soft voice.

"After you finish. I want to see what I'm getting into."

He grinned at the silly pun. His right hand fumbled with his belt and zipper, then pushed the slacks down over his thick thighs. His dick snapped upward in release, small, but in perfect proportion with the rest of him, and definitely ready for action. He stepped out of his pants, then turned, slowly and teasingly, to give me a good look at his firm ass. When he faced me again, he was jerking his cock, the tip oozing a drop of jism.

I finished my drink, set the glass on the table, and said, "Man, that was good. I've never had a bartender fix me a drink in his own home before."

"I'm not really a bartender."

"I know, you're just an out-of-work actor who has to make a living." I stood and embraced him. "Then you can understand. I'm an actor, too, just trying to make a living."

"But some of us are better equipped for their roles than others," he said, groping me. When he found I was hard, he led the way into the bedroom. He halted beside the big bed, turning to reach for my shirt buttons, while my own hands explored his body, tracing the curve of his waist and stroking the dainty nipples, feeling them stiffen responsively.

My shirt removed, Kevin unfastened my belt, and eased the zipper of my fly down, then used both hands to push my slacks and my Jockeys past my knees. My fingers laced through his straight hair, using him for balance as I stepped out of the puddled cloth to stand naked, my prick sticking out like a gnarled limb, the veins pulsing.

He took my cock in his hand and began stroking it. It was then I saw bruise on his hand. I grabbed his wrist. "You're hurt, Kevin."

"It's nothing," he said, watching me draw his hand to my mouth, lips and tongue soothing and caressing the faint discoloration.

"Come here," he said, forcing me to release his hand, and

lifting his face to mine. We kissed and my tongue reached for his tonsils while my hands cupped and squeezed that tight little ass, fingers easing between the buttocks to explore his anus, making his hips jerk as I teased the nerve-laced entrance.

When I freed his lips, they moved immediately to fasten over my left nipple, sucking and tonguing as his hands roamed over my waist, hips and bottom.

"If you can suck cock like you suck tongue," I murmured, jamming my prick against his belly, "you'll pull my fuckin' balls out."

I urged him down onto the bed, pulling his sleek body atop mine, spreading my legs so he could work his hips between them, rubbing that throbbing dick over the swollen hardness of my cock. We kissed again, then he kissed his way down over my throat, pausing at my pectorals, licking and nursing the nipples, then working his head beneath my left arm to lap at my armpit.

"Hmmm," he murmured, his words muffled as his tongue licked at the moist, hairy hollow. He lifted himself on extended arms to look down at my cock, which was standing almost straight up. "God, Peter Hardee's in my bed. I can't fuckin' believe it!"

"Believe it!" I moaned, pushing him down to his belly between my spread legs, his warm, moist breath fanning my balls as he inhaled the scent of my freshly-scrubbed crotch.

His arms were on either side of my hips, his hands forcing their way beneath my buttocks, pulling me up to meet his mouth as he sucked one ball at a time, drawing them in to roll them about with that mobile tongue, and teasing just enough to make my hips squirm.

He licked my thighs, running his tongue up along that sensitive inner curve, then burrowing into the crease between thigh and leg. He moaned as he kissed his way over my balls and urged my hips higher, enabling him to lick the area between balls and ass. His fingers tugged at my buttocks, spreading them, and I shoved my pelvis still higher, inviting that hot tongue to slip farther back, an invitation the youth accepted with a groan of eagerness.

It was then that he shifted his arms to the inside of my thighs, and I draped my legs over his shoulders as his mouth

framed an oval that fastened greedily about my asshole, his tongue forcing its way into that tender channel, wet, hot and twisting to massage the nerve-laced circle.

"Oh, Kevin!" I grunted, shoving my ass still higher, and his tongue began a feverish fucking motion, driving into my anus, then wriggling its tip inside me. It didn't take much of that to make me grab his hair and urge him back to the throbbing shaft of my cock, and he licked his way up the pole until his tongue was fluttering about the head, savoring the pre-cum that seeped from it.

"Oh, suck it, Kevin!" I cried, and gasped with pleasure as his lips slid down over the head of my prick, and his tongue began dancing over the slippery glans.

My hips thrust upward, and he relaxed his mouth to let me drive my cock into it, the head sliding past his palate and burying itself deep in his throat. He held it there for several seconds, while my hips strained upward and my balls rolled against his dimpled chin. Then, as I pulled back, he sucked my dick with hungry pulls, his tongue lashing it as soon as the head was within reach of that darting tip.

Kevin was a moaner, something I particularly like in my partners. It was obvious he loved sucking cock, and that made it feel even better as I drove in and out of his hot, wet mouth. He swallowed repeatedly as the mixture of saliva and seminal fluid gathered about my thrusting prick, but some of it seeped from the juncture of lips and shaft, and trickled down to dampen my balls and his caressing fingers.

The pleasure was mounting, and I was tempted to blast my load into that willing throat. But I had been admiring that hunky body all evening, and I wanted to feel the thrill of his tight little ass on my prick.

Again I grabbed his hair, tugging his lips upward. He spluttered a protest, but I silenced him with, "Raise up, Kevin, and sit on my cock!"

"No," he said. "I can't. I'm sorry. I've tried a couple of times but guess I'm just not built to take it."

"You're a virgin?" I was astounded.

"Yeah, and likely to remain one."

"How old are you, Kevin?"

"Twenty-nine."

"A twenty-nine-year-old virgin living in Hollywood! I can't believe it!"

"I'm sorry. Believe me, if I could take it, it'd be Peter Hardee's dick I'd want."

That was small consolation at that point, but I was too hot to worry about it. "Just finish what you've started, Kevin. We can talk later."

And he did, going at it as if he was trying to make up for the fact he couldn't get screwed. He slid his lips up and down the shaft for several minutes, cheeks dipping as he sucked. Every now and then he let my cock escape his mouth, and his hand gripped the base, holding it like a candy cane, his tongue licking up, around and over it.

I began shuddering. His eyes closed as he savored the full extent of my load, swallowing it all.

"Wow!" I said, letting him know I wasn't a bit disappointed in him.

Still, when he crawled up into my arms, my cum dripping from his lips, he was frowning. "I'm sorry."

"Nothing to be sorry about. That was incredible."

We kissed and I held him in my arms.

After a few moments, he said, "I want to try it with you. I really do."

We kissed again. If he was willing, I was ready. Or at least would be in a few minutes. I took a quick shower and when I returned to the bedroom, he was on his hands and knees, his ass in the air. "This way?" he asked.

I laughed. "No. You have to sit on it. That's the best way to start with this thing." I wagged my cock at him.

"Bring it over here," he said.

He sucked it again with his arms wrapped around my waist. When it was hard again, I got on my back and he mounted me. After greasing himself, he slowly eased himself over it. Eventually his asshole reluctantly accepted the head. His pretty face was contorted with strain, full lips tight across clenched teeth, and eyes squeezed shut. He tilted his head tilted back as he slowly impaled himself on my prick. His hands clutched my pecs for support, every muscle in his asshole rippling as he took my cock deeper and deeper. The tight embrace swallowed about half my dick, then, after resting a few seconds, he took

it all down to the balls.

"Christ!" he gasped, his hips twisting, trying to adjust to that unprecedented filling. "You're so damn big!"

I grinned. "And that damn ass feels so good," I said, pushing my hips upward, and gaining a little more depth.

"UHHH!" he bleated, eyes closing again, and hips squirming. His legs flexed, and I felt that hot grip slide upward, sucking and chewing on my prick as it pulled almost off, keeping only the swollen head inside, the sphincter squeezing it and sending pulses of pleasure through my balls.

"Fuck it, Kevin!" I urged, and his hips began rising and falling above mine, working that virginal ass up and down my cock.

"Let me come in your ass!" I panted, my fingers gripping his thighs, nails digging into the smooth skin. Thrusting up to meet that descending asshole, feeling his warm balls spread over my pubic thatch, I screamed, "Oh, Kevin!"

His right hand gripped his own dick as well as mine, and a shiver of resignation ran through his hunky body as he accepted my demands. His hand moved faster, and he rode me with a more rapid hunching, each embrace of my dick sending a fresh wave of ecstasy back through my balls.

"I'm gonna come, Pete!" he panted, his back arching, his hips still bouncing to spear his asshole with my rearing cock. "Oh, Pete!" He twisted his hips, grinding his ass about the jerking, swollen shaft. His fist tightened about his own dick and he cried out as the cum jetted out and onto my belly. Each orgasmic spasm tightened his asshole about my cock, and it was my turn to grunt with pleasure when my own cum spurted deep in the teenager's thirsty bottom, each volley making his hips gyrate and his asshole seem to actually suck my throbbing dick. Somehow, without pulling my cock out of him, I managed to roll him onto his back, his legs over my shoulders, and I began fucking him, driving my prick in to the balls with each thrust.

After about a half an hour of this, I set him free. He was exhausted, but happy, and we slept wrapped in each other's arms.

16

With the sun pouring in through the curtains, Kevin entered the bedroom fresh from his shower. I coaxed him back into bed and went down on him, taking his prick in my mouth while it was still limp, and tonguing it to a full erection. Then, as he clutched my hair and cried out with pleasure, I sucked him to a delicious orgasm, milking his cock until his balls were drained.

"You didn't have to do that," he panted, when I finally moved up to share the taste of his cum with him.

"I just wanted to suck you off."

"I'm late for a casting call. You know, out of work actors spend most of their days making the rounds."

"Fuck me before you go."

"I'd love to but I'm really late."

"Maybe another time then."

He looked away, lost in thought.

"You'd like that, wouldn't you?" I asked.

"Yeah," he said finally. "But I can't."

"Oh, now what?"

"I have a lover. He's on location right now, but he's coming back tomorrow and I'm moving in with him."

"God, you're full of surprises."

"So are you. I never thought Peter Hardee would be such a nice guy."

I smiled. "That's me, Mr. Nice Guy. But you know what they say about Nice Guys."

"I never believed that. Look at you, the biggest porn star in the world."

"Yeah. At least I'm finishing first in something."

He stopped me from feeling any sorrier for myself by kissing me. It was a warm, tender kiss. A kiss of farewell.

When I returned to the warehouse, Kenny and Mark still hadn't showed. I discussed the day's scene with Larry, but kept an eye on the door. Finally the boys arrived and I raced over to

them, pushing Mark into a dark corner.

"Hey," he said, "what's goin' on?"

I took him in my arms and kissed him harder than I had ever kissed anyone. When we finally came up for air, I said, "No matter what happens, just remember, you're my lover."

"What?"

"You're my lover. I've never had a lover, but you're my lover. Got that?"

He was trembling. "I guess."

I grabbed his shoulders and began shaking him. "No guessing. You're my lover." I was squeezing his arms, digging my nails into his tender flesh.

"Please, Pete. What's gotten into you?"

I let go of him, stepped back. "I'm sorry. I had a terrible night."

I went on to tell him about the hold-up, about how Kevin kicked the shit of the man. He listed intently, tears forming in his eyes. "You coulda been killed," he sobbed.

"Now do you understand?"

"Sure, Pete."

He said it half-heartedly. Of course he didn't understand – not really. I didn't understand it fully either. "I want to fuck my lover, now!" I screamed.

"Here?"

I shook my head. "No, at home. We're going home."

"Now? But you have to fuck Freddy."

"Fuck Freddy." I started to laugh. It was nervous, crazy laugh. "Yeah, fuck Freddy. Okay, I'll fuck Freddy – "

He smiled. "And then we can go home and you can fuck me all night if you want to."

I couldn't help it. I loved him so much at that moment I started to cry, and I hadn't cried in years. I took him my arms and held him. "My lover," I murmured.

"My lover," he echoed, his hands patting my ass. "Now, go fuck Freddy."

17

According to Larry's script, Freddy wanted desperately to lose his virginity to me. He had finally made up his mind that I should be his first partner in anal sex. "Art imitates life," Larry joked as he led Freddy to where I was sitting with Mark and Kenny on two bales of hay that had been brought in to make the set look like a barn.

"I just hope I don't mess it up," Freddy said nervously.

"You'll be fine," I said. "Just do what I tell you as we go along."

"What if I get excited and come? I mean, before I'm supposed to."

"That'd make Larry happy. Just do what you feel like, but remember that we have to let the camera see us come."

Larry waved us forward, just out of camera range. He took a good look at Freddy. "You really ready for this, kid?"

"Yes, sir." His eyes searched mine before turning back to Larry. I winked. "I'm ready," he told Larry.

The cameras rolled, signals were exchanged, and the boy and I were cued. Together, we entered camera range and tumbled down onto the hay, arms about each other. It seemed perfectly natural to guide the boy's hand to my crotch, and I felt his fingers curl about the swelling hardness he found there.

We helped each other undress, and the sight of my erection bulging in my Jockeys turned Freddy into a wild child. As he sucked the cock through the cloth, I knew Larry had found a gold mine: Freddy appeared much younger than eighteen, and, once he was naked, he looked younger still. His cheeks were beardless, and his chest showed no trace of hair, the little nipples distended in arousal. His lips, full and moist, were parted to display even teeth and the tip of a pink tongue. Green eyes were almost hidden behind long lashes, and his dainty nostrils quivered with each deep breath.

He was only five-six, and with just a few added pounds, he would have been chubby. As it was, that perfectly curved body was an invitation to a sexual feast. His sizable dick was erect

and jerking with excitement when I pulled him against me and covered his tasty mouth with mine.

Somewhere, somehow Freddy had learned how to kiss; for he did his best to swallow my tongue, our hands exploring and caressing each other's body.

I couldn't resist the chance to nibble on those dainty nipples, and dip my tongue into the delicate hollow of his navel. And, since it was rubbing my cheek against the oozing tip of his cock, I turned my head just enough to take the head of it in my mouth.

Freddy had obviously not expected that, and his entire body trembled as I sucked his cock with tongue-swirling tugs. He moaned.

Finally he came up with his own dialogue: "Let me suck it! I want to taste that big cock!"

I didn't want to release his dick, for it was both exciting and delicious. If not for the cameras, I would have sucked that young meat to a spurting finale. But the script demanded that our positions be reversed.

I raised my head and kissed him again, giving him a sample of his own cum in my saliva. Then his lips trailed down over my chin and throat, paused to pay homage to my prominent nipples, gently nipping them before he pulled my Jockeys away and slid down to lie between my spread legs, fingers playing over my cock and my balls, and his warm, moist breath bathing the slitted knob.

At hand was the scene Larry most wanted to capture on film: the boy's first oral encounter with a stiff cock, and the first time he felt a hard cock invade his virgin ass. And Freddy was giving the leering eyes of the cameras a brilliant performance, for the boy was not acting.

Just for an instant, he raised his head and looked up into my eyes, a silent admission that he no longer considered this to be part of a motion picture. It was, his sultry look told me, an act of passion between him and me. He wanted my prick, and I wanted him to suck it. It was that simple.

Holding my cock with his fingers about the wrist-thick base, he kissed the tip, gently and experimentally, his tongue reaching out just far enough to taste the delicate musk of the clear jism that seeped from the pink slit.

His eyes closed, savoring the initial thrill, and his throat moved, swallowing the mixture of saliva and seminal fluid. His tongue reached out again, licking across and around the shiny crown of my prick, wetting it and making the shaft throb with that feathery caress. He retreated to bury his face between my thighs and lap hungrily at my hairy sac, and I pushed my hips up so the camera could see his mouth work its magic as he licked farther back.

I drew my knees up, spreading them apart, giving the boy access to that tiny circlet of nerve-laced tissue, and his mouth fastened over it, his tongue stiffening to force an entry. My prick jerked at the feel of that wriggling heat and wetness in my ass.

Most boys work up to ass sucking, but Freddy was trying it before ever taking my cock in that hot young mouth. Some boys never do it, insisting that it is disgusting, while others love to fuck with their tongues. Freddy evidently was of the latter persuasion, for he was sucking and moaning as his tongue stabbed my anus again and again.

I recall a scene in one of the films I did, where I shot my load while a cute youngster tongue-fucked me just as Freddy was doing. It wasn't supposed to happen that way. Just like Freddy, the boy was supposed to play around down there, then move up and go down on my prick. But, he kept working that talented tongue, and it felt so good, that I couldn't hold back the spurts of cum.

Of course, I was relatively new in the business then, and had little control over my emotions. Since then, I've learned to hold back and give the cameras plenty of footage. But Freddy was creating a miniature tornado in my balls, and I wasn't sure just how long I could resist the urge to let go.

I also wondered how it would feel to have the boy's hard dick slide into my ass, and have him enjoy his first real fuck. And that thought did little to dampen my excitement. Being first to receive a youngster's cock is almost as good as being first to plug his tight little ass and fuck him to his initial prick-induced orgasm.

Freddy must have realized the effect his oral efforts were having on me, and he was not about to miss the load of cum I had waiting for him. Larry wouldn't let him take it all, of

course, but he could at least get the first delicious spurt before releasing it for the cameras.

Pulling his tongue out of my butt, he licked his way over my balls, up the ventral ridge, teased the head with a few flicks, then fitted his lips over the head of my cock and tried his best to swallow it.

He gagged when the big knob slipped between his tonsils, and he drew back just long enough to gather courage and take it deep again. I grunted with the pleasure of that engulfment, for his tongue was pressing my cock up against his palate, creating a tight channel, and his head began bobbing to fuck my prick with that torrid grip.

Each time he raised his head, pulling his lips up the shaft, he sucked it, a hot vacuuming that sent a pulse of sheer ecstasy through my belly, tightening my balls as they readied themselves to propel their fuckjuice into Freddy's nursing mouth. I helped by shoving my hips upward, making sure Freddy got the full length of my swollen prick.

Larry would have liked that shot to last a lot longer, and so would I, for the feel of that wet, young mouth was almost painfully good. That was the trouble. The pleasure was too much to resist, and I could feel the first delightful ripples of ecstasy that precede the gut-wrenching thrills of orgasm.

Freddy sensed it, for my cock was jerking as it slid in and out between those nibbling lips, and he knew from his admitted bouts of masturbation that we were approaching the grand finale. So, the youngster sucked harder and faster, his tongue lashing and flicking the head of my cock at every opportunity.

My hips arched, and I gasped at the incredible delight of that first powerful spurt of cum that raced up through my prick and splattered against Freddy's palate and tongue.

With a snort, the boy pulled his mouth up and off of my cock, letting the second volley splash against his parted lips and chin, his tongue reaching out to gather the slippery cream even as the next jet sprayed his neck.

He waited then, licking his lips and watching the cum spill from the tiny slit, the last few surges oozing out to roll down the jerking shaft, while the hand-held cameras zoomed in to catch every shiny drop.

Freddy could resist no longer. With a little groan, he opened

his mouth and claimed my prick again, milking it with lips and tongue, moaning with satisfaction as he swallowed the residue of tart cum. It was a scene Larry loved, and he remained silent behind the lights as the youngster released my dick to lick up the few tiny puddles that had splashed onto my belly.

My cock was still hard, and Freddy was hotter than ever. Tasting my ejaculate had only heightened the boy's desire for more of that male juice, and he was ready now for the invasion of his virgin ass.

Gripping his flaming hair, I pulled his mouth off of my cock, and urged him over onto his back in the hay, his own dick sticking up and jerking with anticipation. He pulled his knees up as I mounted his slender body, and I hooked them with both arms, draping his ankles over my shoulders.

His eyes stared up at me, glittering with a mixture of excitement and fear. He was about to be fucked for the first time, and it was quite natural that he should be a little apprehensive.

He licked his already wet lips, making them shine even more, as he whispered, just loudly enough for the microphones to pick it up, "Fuck me!"

Supporting my weight on knees and my right arm, I used the left hand to guide my prick until I felt the torrid circle of his anus against the tip. Freddy felt the pressure and he closed his eyes, lips drawing back across his clenched teeth as he braced himself for my entry.

I felt one of the cameramen brush against my foot as he crawled closer, getting a closeup view of my cock, just touching the boy's pink little asshole. I deliberately shifted my legs farther apart, giving him more room.

"Oh, God!" was Freddy's hoarse cry as I forced the head of my prick into him, pausing as the head stretched his sphincteral ring and poised, the flared rim of the glans just ready to snap through. "No, please, no!"

"Just a little more." I paused until I felt his muscles relax a little. We had talked before about how he could relax his sphincter, and he was trying to do just what I had told him.

His eyes blinked open, and he stared up into my face with an expression I hoped the cameras would record. It was the acceptance of the realization that the passage from innocent

adolescence to manhood was about to occur. Sucking my dick was but a prelude to what was about to happen, and Freddy's eyes told me that he both welcomed and feared it.

"Take it, Freddy!" I said thickly, and pushed my hips forward.

"Yeah!" he cried, for my prick pushed through that protesting ring and filled his colon with its torrid throbbing, stretching the tender tissues and rubbing the delicate nerve endings of that expanded anus. "Ram that big cock in there!"

The boy's ass was chewing and sucking on my cock, and he had freed one hand to pump his own dick while I reamed his ass with mine.

The cry was one of pain, acceptance, anticipation – and a new and unique pleasure. The pain would slowly dissipate, and the pleasure would grow. Freddy sensed this, and his hands gripped my arms as I pushed my cock deeper into his slowly yielding asshole.

Larry's suppository had made the channel slippery, and relaxed the muscles enough to permit my dick to slide through with only a little pressure. But, after each fractional increase in penetration, I paused, giving the youngster's anal tissues time to relax and adjust to their pulsating intruder. I wanted the full length of my throbbing prick inside Freddy's ass before I began fucking him.

The boy's hips squirmed, whether in an effort to escape, or to feel my cock more keenly, I could not tell. However, the effect was to screw his asshole farther onto my prick, the tissues clinging to the throbbing shaft and massaging it with every slight movement.

Once I had my dick securely lodged in his butt, I placed both hands on those firm thighs, levering his young body toward me as I pushed deeper into his colon. His features were contorted with strain, and he gasped each time I drove another fraction of an inch up that clenching passageway.

Freddy's own cock reared over his belly and chest, its tiny slit oozing the clear seminal fluid that betrayed his arousal more than his groans of mixed pleasure and pain.

I felt a slight resistance as the head of my cock reached the curve of his intestine, and he grunted as he felt the shift of his gut. His asshole was packed with all the dick it could possibly

hold, and I was buried to the balls.

He almost screamed when I tugged the big prick outward, its heavily veined shaft rubbing that sensitive anus and the tender walls of his colon. I felt the delightful grip of his sphincter, and I held it there, letting the involuntary contractions work their magic.

Then, slowly and carefully, I slid it back into him, not pausing until all of my cock was in him. His hips worked in a grinding circle, a combination of adjustment and the attempt to adjust to the complete filling of his young tail.

In and out, slowly, but with gathering speed, I drove my throbbing prick, and Freddy's soft cries became moans of unprecedented pleasure of having his dream finally realized.

He had wanted a big dick, and I was giving him all he could possibly handle, plunging deep in his belly with every stroke. It was the boy's first fuck, and I had made it easy for him, beginning slowly, and waiting for his own pleasure to build. Now, with his asshole loosened a little, I could screw him the way I wanted to, and the way audiences liked to see a youngster take a really big cock.

It was getting better each time I rammed into him, and I was now enjoying one of the many fringe benefits of anal intercourse.

With each retreat, his asshole tried to hold my cock prisoner, resulting in a sensation very much like the one created by a good blowjob.

It was as if his young tail was a hungry mouth, sucking and chewing on my prick as I fucked him, harder and faster, the pleasure more intense with every stroke.

"Cut!" yelled Larry, and I had to suppress a curse as I yanked my about-to-explode cock from Freddy's incredible ass.

"I want to use the cut-out," Larry explained, stepping forward into the lighted area. "The kid's about to shoot, and I want a close-up of it."

The cutout was a specially built platform about three feet high, with a square foot opening over which the actors knelt, knees on either side of the hole. The cameraman aimed up through the opening, and captured a closeup view of the two cocks, one swinging free, the other driving and thrusting.

Sometimes we used a glass partition, and let the cum splatter down onto it when the boy being fucked shot his wad, while a second camera covered the dominant partner as he spilled his seed onto the kid's arched back.

The edges of the opening were padded, so there was no discomfort involved for knees or hips. I had used the device in several films, but it was new to Freddy. While the crew rearranged the lighting, I explained its purpose.

"I don't care how we do it," he whispered back. "I just want you to come in my ass!"

I leaned closer, his red hair tickling my nose and my lips almost touching one ear. "I can shoot a load in there," I told the boy, "if you don't give me away."

His green eyes questioned me. "Then what about the cum shot Larry wants?"

"Just relax, kid," I said. "I can get another one ready in just a few minutes. I'll hose you down with that one."

"Jesus!" he exclaimed, a half-frown on his pretty face. "It feels so good when you do it! I was about to come!"

"That's what Larry wants. Just let it go, Freddy."

Larry waved us forward with his well-chewed cigar. "Get back just like you were," he ordered. "Give me about a minute of that, then get on your side - you know right where, Pete - and go at it. That'll give us three angles."

He looked at Freddy. "Can you come with Pete fucking you? I mean, without touching your own cock?"

The youngster nodded. "Yes, sir. I nearly did."

"Okay, let's do it!"

I guided Freddy into position over the opening, which the crew had edged with hay so the side shots would look natural, and he pulled his knees up, just as before. My cock had wilted a little, but it was stiff enough to slide back into his ass. Once in there, it swelled and hardened almost immediately, and the boy grunted his appreciation. I eased it in and out a few times, matching, as far as possible, the movements of the preceding shot. Then I eased my prick out and urged Freddy onto his side, facing away from me, one leg lifted to give me access to that inviting ass.

His lower leg and waist supported his body, and his dick was sticking out over the platform's hole. On my side, behind him,

I steered my cock into him slowly, letting the camera see its striated rim fold inward as my prick forced its way in. I took it easy, making him feel every inch as my cock spread those tender walls, and he gasped his delight at the renewed pleasure.

I began fucking him again, driving in and out with full length strokes, and again I felt that hot suction as his tight colon tried to hold my dick captive with each withdrawal.

Still hunching, I leaned over him, and Freddy twisted his upper body about to where our mouths could meet, tongues dueling and twisting while my prick rode in and out of his slippery tail.

I didn't have to look to know that he was about ready to dump his load. His asshole was puckering, and I could feel the slight swell of his prostate through the intestinal wall. I fucked him harder and faster.

"Oh, God!" he cried over and over, and his body jerked, his intestine shuddering and convulsing about my prick as his own cock spurted its cream across the opening, and down onto the camera below.

The guy behind the lens, Jimmy Willis, had fluffed me several times during long shoots and I knew how much he loved cum. I knew that he was trying to capture some of that cum in his panting mouth, while keeping the camera trained on Freddy's jetting dick.

The wide-angle camera was getting a view that made us appear to be still in the hay, and the portable camera behind me was capturing each thrust of my cock into the boy's tail.

But I wasn't thinking about any of that. I was letting the sheer ecstasy of screwing the boy who had eluded me for so long claim my thoughts and body.

I suspected Larry knew what was happening, but he didn't let on, and I pumped my load into Freddy with little groans, still thrusting deep and occasionally licking that delicious mouth and his extended tongue.

My cock was riding through a coating of its own semen, and the boy's ass seemed even hotter and tighter as he panted and gasped at the repeated fillings. He was a novice, but already he was learning to tighten those rectal muscles as I pulled my cock outward, and relax them when I drove in again. And, to my

delight, he was building toward a second orgasm of his own, his dick jerking with each thrust of mine.

I stopped worrying about camera angles and cum shots, and settled down to plain old fucking, riding the kid's ass with savage hunches, hammering my prick in and out of his juicy bottom as the goodness began growing again.

Freddy felt it too, and he began trying to work his hips to increase the friction. My hard belly pounded his firm buttocks, and my cock made a wet, sucking sound as it stroked in and out of his cum-filled butt.

"I'm gonna come again!" he panted, his legs jerking and quivering. "Oh, God!"

It was like a trigger to my own pending release. I managed four delightful thrusts before I tipped over the edge, and knew that I could not hold back.

Wrenching my prick from the boy's ass, I rolled him onto his back and thrust my hips forward until the head of my cock was almost touching his. Like two synchronized fountains, we came, the white spurts arcing onto Freddy's heaving belly and chest.

Then, even as my prick was still spilling its cum, I dipped my finger into one mingled puddle, carrying it up to the boy's eager lips. With a soft cry, he opened his mouth and sucked the semen from my finger, his tongue playing about the tip.

Without hesitation, I moved upward to insert my still oozing cock between those parted lips, letting Freddy suck the last few drops of cum from the pulsating head.

I barely heard Larry's cry when he signaled an end to the scene, for I was now thrusting my dick deep into the lad's throat, fucking his hungry mouth just as I had screwed his tight little asshole.

Reluctantly, we drew apart, and I let Freddy gave the head of my prick a last loving lick, his eyes telling me that he wanted more. I smiled watching his cute, no longer virginal ass wiggle as he walked off toward the showers.

I spotted Mark helping one of the men move a heavy flat and stepped over to him. "Well, did I fuck Freddy or what?"

Mark reached down and stroked my semi-flaccid cock. "Not enough. There's still life there."

I smiled. "Let me take a shower, then I'll show you just how

much."

I padded into the shower room Larry had built for a sequence in one of his films and continued to use. He had doubled the size of the original bathroom and installed a glass-enclosed stall with four shower heads and plenty of space for cameras.

Freddy was still under the spray, his slender body twisting as he rinsed off the soapy residue. He gave me a big smile as he gazed at my cock bobbing between my thighs.

"I want some more of that, Pete," he said, his own dick swelling and rising from a nest of soapy curls. "I didn't know how good it was gonna be."

I applied soap to my chest, under my arms, then my crotch. I was getting hard just thinking about fucking Freddy again.

"Call Claude and tell him not to bother coming in to get you. You're spending the night with Mark and me."

"Okay," he sighed, reaching over and stroking my cock.

"Now kiss it goodbye again, but just for a little while, okay Freddy?"

He obediently dropped to his knees on the tile and began sucking.

"I said, just kiss it, Freddy." I pulled my cock from his over-eager mouth and began beating his face with it. It grew harder with each slap. "You've gotta learn how to take direction."

In the Buick, Freddy sat between us, his hand on my thigh, while Mark's fingers fondled the bulge at the boy's crotch, squeezing and kneading until Freddy was whimpering with excitement.

"When did you first know you were gay?" I asked.

"I guess I've always known it," Freddy said. "When other guys would talk about girls, I was always wondering how they looked when their dicks got hard."

"How come you never tried fucking before?" Mark asked.

"I was scared," the lad admitted. "What if I just thought I was like that? I mean, I've heard of boys getting some man all hot and everything, and then backing out. Sometimes, the guy would get real sore and beat them up."

"What changed your mind?"

"Seeing Claude and the guys at the farm," he said. "I realized how much fun they were having. Then when you and

me did that bit at the barn, I got so hot I couldn't stand it."

"Why didn't you make it with one of the boys?" Mark asked.

Freddy shook his head. "I wanted Pete to be first," he said, his hand finding my outlined prick and giving it a tantalizing squeeze. "You know, start with the biggest! Is that a little crazy?"

"I don't think so," Mark said, his own hand busy between the youngster's thighs. "He breaks 'em in right. He was my first, and Kyle's first. I'm glad he was the one to break me in."

Freddy was silent for a moment, then he said, "I wonder why I don't feel jealous right now when I think about you guys doing it with each other." He looked down at Mark's hand in his lap. "Here you're playing with me, and I'm playing with Pete, and it all seems right."

"We're talking about two different things, love and sex."

"Oh."

"If you love somebody, it's natural to want to have sex with them, but, you can want sex with somebody you don't love. I think a lot of trouble is caused by mixing them up."

"Yeah," Mark interjected. "Some guys go crazy if their lover even looks at another man."

"Right. What they don't realize is that their lover just wants sex. It's got nothing to do with love."

Freddy chewed his generous lower lip. "Then, it's okay with you if I make out with Mark?"

"Mark is my lover. But we share everything. We sorta made up the rules as we went along."

Freddy looked a Mark lovingly while his hand continued to squeeze my cock.

"You think you can take care of both of us at the same time?"

"I sure do want to try!" he answered.

We stopped at a steakhouse on Sunset and talked about life on Claude's farm. Finally I told Freddy that Claude was an able recruiter and we could probably use all the dick he found, provided they were as attractive as the present crop.

Thirty minutes later, Freddy was kneeling between Mark's

spread legs, sucking noisily on his throbbing cock, while I stood at the foot of the bed, feverishly driving my prick in and out of Freddy's perfectly shaped – and now well-fucked – bottom.

18

The next day, I left Freddy and Mark at the apartment and went to the studio for the filming of the first and final sequences. I hadn't met Bill, the actor who was playing the role of the uncle, but knew his reputation. He had been considered one of the major studs in heterosexual porn during the early '70s. He was secretive man and few knew that he rented his cock to both women and men. Larry said Bill told him he was comfortable topping males, but had never been offered a gay film. Larry saw the publicity advantages of Morrison's return to porn, especially in a gay epic, and had waited until the stud was free from his job as a graphic arts salesman to take the role. As scripted, Bill would end up fucking his nephew.

"Helluva way to make a comeback!" the stud said, adjusting his tie.

The years had treated Bill well. To me, he was the epitome of studliness. The bulk he had added over the years only heightened my enthusiasm. He appeared to have little enthusiasm for me, however. He was pleasant, but aloof. I pictured him playing any number of roles in future films, all authority figures. I pictured him as the cop on the beat, the cop on the motorcycle, the prison guard, or the teacher who keeps the student after class. The possibilities were endless. I stepped over to where Larry was preparing his own office as the set for the first meeting of the uncle and the detective. "He's perfect," I told Larry.

"Wait'll you see him do his thing. He's a pro."

Morrison's professionalism quickly became evident when he started reading his lines. The dialogue had him telling me that I had been recommended by a friend, one for whom I had done some work a few months earlier. He had not called the police about his nephew because he feared any scandal might cause the authorities to take the boy away from him and place him in a foster home. "I'm all the kid has," he told me. "Find him

and I'll pay you fifty grand."

"I'll need a retainer. After all, I may not find the boy."

"Half now," he said, nodding, "and another twenty-five when you do." He handed me a large brown envelope. "I want all of this kept quiet, understand? That's why I'm paying you in cash, and I don't want a receipt. I've got to trust you."

"You can."

The dialogue continued with Bill telling me had received a ransom note, slipped under the door of his penthouse, asking for one million dollars, and telling him that further instructions would be delivered by telephone.

"I'll put a tap on your phone. When they call back, we can trace it."

"Should I get the money ready?"

"No. Let me see what I can find out first."

"I'm sure you can find him. That's why I hired you. You know the scene here."

I nodded. "Sometimes too well."

Larry shouted "Cut!" and I breathed a sigh of relief. It had gone perfectly on the first take. Bill was a pro, making me reach to be a better actor than I thought I was capable of being.

I stepped over to Larry. "I want to change the ending."

"*What?*"

"Yeah. I wanna get fucked by Morrison."

"*What?*" He nearly dropped his cigar.

"That'll make it, won't it? The return of Bill Morrison, and Peter Hardee finally giving the fans what they've been waiting three years for."

"It'll make it all right! But I never thought I'd hear it outta your pretty mouth."

"I'm in for part of the action now, remember?"

Shaking his head, he laughed, "You can say that again!"

Larry took Bill aside. While he was explaining there had been a change in the script, that I would be the one to get fucked by him, Bill glanced about the room until he found me. His face revealed no emotion; he just stared at me, as if he was trying to understand why I would want to do such a thing. Finally, he nodded and we re-assembled in Larry's office for the final sequence. Morrison was sitting at the desk when I brought

Danny in. They embraced each other and Danny tearfully told his "uncle" he was sorry for all the trouble he'd caused. At this point, we went to the new script, which I suggested we just improvise, knowing Bill and Danny could carry it. Danny said it was all worth it because he got to meet me.

"Oh?" Bill said.

"You're big, but he's bigger," Danny said, with a huge grin.

"It's not the size of the wand, boy, it's how you wave it," Bill said, with barely a trace of a smile.

That was the cue for the music to swell and the three of us to begin. We embraced, and the cameras caught our kisses in close up.

Our undressing, which seemed to take forever, would be reduced to blurred, frenzied moments in the final print. Larry always saved the magic moment for last, the camera's caressing of the mound in my white Jockeys as my partner slowly let the monster loose.

Surprisingly enough, Bill was abashed by the sight of my erect dick. "Damn!" he grunted.

"I told you," Danny sighed, dropping to his knees in front of me.

Bill moved in next to me and Danny took both cocks in his hands and stroked them for the benefit of the camera. Then, gleefully, Danny moved from my cock to Bill's and back again, licking, sucking, nibbling. My cock was longer, but not by much, and it appeared to me that Bill's was actually thicker than mine. And he was uncut, the foreskin sliding back completely when the tool was erect. After several minutes of this, Larry had Danny kneel on the couch in his office, his shapely ass poised and ready. Larry's suppository had already done its work, and my cock slid into him with one easy push.

"Jesus!" he gasped, his forehead pressing his forearms on the back of the couch. I felt the muscles contract about my prick. Beside us, stony-faced Bill watched my tool slowly disappear into Danny's ass. Danny turned his head to stare at his movie uncle's face, his own features contorted with the strain and pleasure of anal acceptance. He licked his lips, tightening his asshole about my driving prick. Bill climbed over him and stuck his hefty prick in the kid's mouth.

My hips worked savagely, my eyes glued to the luscious sight of Danny gobbling up Bill's cock. Danny's adoration of Bill's cock was forcing me to fuck at my peak. In that moment, I was no longer playing a role in a porno film, I was just having an incredibly good time.

Larry didn't interfere, except, after ten minutes or so, to tell Bill it was now "time."

Yes, my "time" had come. This was it, and I intended to make the most of it. It would be perfect, I thought, to be fucked while fucking. When Bill's slickened cock flopped from Danny's mouth for the last time, it appeared to have grown a couple of inches. I began to sweat, fearing maybe I wouldn't be able to take it, even if I had prepared my ass well. But I shouldn't have worried. Bill's professionalism extended to the sexual arena as well. He got behind me and, pressing down on my back, rubbed his cock along my crack. Then he squatted down and began eating my ass. A cameraman quickly moved in. Bill was so adept at tongue-fucking, I didn't mind it a bit that he kept calling my ass a cunt. I grabbed Danny's shoulders and kept fucking him, even as Bill was teasing my puckering hole with his practiced tongue.

A few minutes went by, then the stud stood. A hush fell over the room. I hadn't been fucked since Mark did it shortly after we met, and that was only about the fourth or fifth time in my life. I had wanted Kevin but that was not to be. Now it appeared I was going to get the fuck of my life and be paid for it besides.

Sweat dripped from my forehead onto Danny's smooth, tanned back; my well-prepared ass was drooling Bill's saliva over the back of my balls. Suddenly Bill became amorous, or at least as amorous as he was likely to get. He began to lick and suck on the back of my neck, causing me to automatically arch my back, pushing my ass against his pulsating dick. Mercilessly, and with a purposeful grunt, he easily popped his big knob into my ass. The entry was incredibly easy. The next part was the hardest. Inch after inch went into me and soon the only sound came from his hips slapping against my butt and his big balls hitting mine. He groaned deeply into my ear as he nuzzled my neck. My cock remained lodged deep in Danny's ass and I began to move rhythmically, taking my cue from Bill's

proficient humping. In a way I was fucking Danny with Bill's massive rod as well as my own. Danny was ecstatic, whimpering uncontrollably while he jerked his own cock.

The cameraman moved under us to get the penetrations in one shot. At that point, I moaned as the cum began to stir in my swollen balls. Bill grabbed my hips firmly and increased the intensity of his fucking. It was as if I was being gorged by the mighty cock, yet it was relatively painless, so sure were his strokes. After about ten minutes, just when I was beginning to think I couldn't take anymore, his great body stiffened and he gave a harsh cry, his huge cock throbbing, and pulled out. I reached behind around and grabbed the bloated prick, squeezing it twice, then heard Bill gasp. The cameraman caught his heavy load splashing on my back. I held off for a moment, waiting until Larry shouted at me, then pulled out of Danny, my balls erupting their cream onto his back.

We collapsed onto Larry's couch, with Danny in the middle. Our dicks had softened and were laying like thick fat sausages against our cum-streaked thighs, occasionally oozing a bit of cum. We both fondled Danny, hefting his balls, fingering his moist ass, sucking on his nipples, as if he were a sexual pet we'd adopted. We did everything in unison, tonguing each hairy armpit together, going for a nipple each, nibbling on his throbbing erection. We jerked him off, our free hands wandering intimately all over each other's bodies. I suddenly rammed a finger up Danny's sopping asshole to send him over the edge. He came in a long, tortuous, glorious orgasm that ended the film.

As we showered together, Danny couldn't tear his eyes away from Bill's swinging cock.

I finally said, "I'm sorry we switched on you at the last minute, Danny. When it comes to waving a wand, Bill just can't be beat."

"I could feel it, though, every single thrust."

Bill turned his back on us.

I took my cock in my hand and stroked it. "But Bill only plays for pay, Danny."

"That true, Bill?" Danny asked.

Bill turned slightly, switched off the shower. "Yep." He ran his bony fingers through his stringy blond hair and started

moving towards the door. His semi-flaccid cock bobbed enticingly before him. Danny smacked his lips.

I sighed. "Don't worry, Danny, he'll be wavin' it again for us very soon, and you're first in line."

Bill stopped before he closed the door and stuck his head back in. "Don't count on it, sport."

Danny frowned. "What the fuck got into him?"

"Maybe that's the problem. Nothing has *ever* gotten into him."

"Shit, you mean he's cherry?"

"You *know* he's cherry." I grinned. "Hey, there's the next Davis and Hardee production: Bill Morrison loses his cherry after all these years!"

"Yeah, the same scene that we just did except – "

"Now you're talkin'!" I took him in my arms and hugged him to me, our cocks dueling. "Just thinkin' about it gets me hard."

"HMMMM," he groaned, squeezing our erections together. "I'm ready."

19

"I got your present."

It was Sugar Daddy. It had been two months at least. He'd been traveling: Tokyo, Rome, then London. Returning to L.A., he went up to the cabin, found the tape of Mark and Kenny and my little note.

"Welcome back," I said.

"It appears you've been having a lot of fun up in the mountains."

"I've tried to keep the place clean."

He chuckled. "I've missed you."

"I've been really busy. I've got so much to tell you."

We arranged to spend Friday night at the Beverly Hills Hotel. I had told Mark I had business to take care of and to keep busy with Freddy. He started to question me, but I said, "Please, Mark, just do as I say."

Sugar Daddy kept a bungalow at the hotel where he put up visitors from all over the world. He had dinner delivered by room service and it was waiting when I arrived. Over rare prime rib and twice-baked potatoes, I told him about my new venture.

"I'm very proud of you," he said finally. "You have made the most of your assets and you continue to do so."

"I'll never forget the help you've given me."

Although I'm sure many suspected, no one really knew the details of my private life. I met my Sugar Daddy at a party shortly after I made my first movie. He was the kindest, most generous man I'd ever known. There was nothing he wouldn't do for me, provided I came across for him. It was a business arrangement, but I enjoyed it too. He never asked for much, and got what he wanted and more. I got the use of the cabin, my apartment in one of the buildings he owned, and he paid off my Buick. He made me promise I would not become a porn stud escort. I was his exclusively. The contract was open-ended.

"I've got a confession to make," he said, finishing his wine.

"Oh?"

"I've never enjoyed a boy as much as I've enjoyed you, Pete. And you've never asked for anything."

"I've never had to. You always gave it to me before I had a chance to ask for it."

He grinned. His dark eyes flashing, he pushed himself away from the table and came over to me. Standing behind me, he began massaging my back. "I don't want this end, Pete."

"It won't." I reached under the napkin on my lap and unzipped my pants. I began pulling my cock out.

"Oh, but I can see it now. You'll become very successful in the production end of the business and – "

I dropped my head back. "You worry too much. Shut up and come get your dessert." I yanked the napkin off my lap, exposing my throbbing erection.

His eyes bulged as they always did. He said nothing more, simply bent over and kissed my cock.

We moved to the bedroom. I got naked and lay back on the bed, my legs parted. He undressed and joined me, getting on his knees between my legs. As he began kissing my cock, I ran my fingers through his silvery hair. I knew the adoration of my cock would continue for about a half an hour before he actually got around to sucking it in earnest. It was always incredible to me how much he worshipped my cock. Sucking one of the biggest cocks in porn was the greatest aphrodisiac he could imagine, I realized, and I played my role to the hilt, regaling him with stories about my latest co-stars and how they enjoyed it when I fucked them. I began by telling him about meeting Mark.

He gazed at my cock fondly, drooling a bit, palming its full length, and on the downstroke moving under the balls to give them a few gentle squeezes. Finally his jaws were stretching to take the big one down his throat, and for a moment I was startled to realize he really had it all the way in.

From time to time he lifted my balls to kiss the underside, then tongued and kissed the lightly-furred sac before sucking my testicles in his mouth. While he gummed them, he moaned ecstatically. His eager tongue and mouth had my cock up as hard as it ever gets, and vibrating for him.

As I continued telling him about Mark and how we got involved with Kenny, I watched him closely. He wasn't a bad-looking guy for fifty. His body was lean, and his cock was a respectable six inches. He jerked off while he sucked me. He had never asked me to touch him. It was as if he was ashamed of his cock. "In the presence of such greatness, I am puny beyond measure," he said once. I left it at that; if that's what he wanted to believe, so be it. I knew from magazine articles that he was married and had some kids, but we never talked about them. We never talked about his business either, only my business. He was a voyeur, fascinated by the sordid gossip of a world alien to him.

I went on to describe in lurid detail everything I had done with Kenny and Mark. His tongue stabbed my slit and swirled over the massive purple head, diving under the ridge and moving along its perimeter, then flattening so it could lick its way down one side and up the other. When I got to telling him all about Mark and Freddy and the incredible night we had spent together, I began shuddering. My first orgasm of the night. He was delighted. He took my avalanche of cum in his mouth and swallowed it. Even after he let my cock plop from his mouth, he kept licking it, waiting for me to harden again.

"Peter, Peter, Peter," he chanted. "You're a cocksucker's dream come true."

20

The next day I took Mark and Freddy to Disneyland. They liked Space Mountain the best so we had to ride it twice. By six we had Freddy back at the farm and we were looking forward to a long evening together, just the two of us. Along the way I picked up a supply of Jack Daniels, and a couple of bottles of wine that Mark said looked good. He was becoming quite a connoisseur – in many ways.

Suddenly, Mark shuddered. I asked him what was wrong.

"I was talkin' to Freddy about his life and, well, if it hadn't been for you – "

"You'd be at the farm, too?'

"Or worse. Much worse."

"Well, I'm glad it worked out for both of us."

After fucking nearly all night, we slept late and spent a rainy Sunday afternoon watching old movies on TV. Mark made sandwiches, and we took a long nap, not even considering sex, but holding each other and reveling in the extraordinary closeness we had found.

I next morning, bursting with energy, I decided to clean the apartment. Mark was still asleep, so I started in the living room. It was then that I found the roaches under the cushions of the sofa. I was shattered. I had stopped smoking marijuana after I met Sugar Daddy. He had taken me places, showed me things I had never imagined. I began to enjoy the taste of Jack Daniels and California Chardonnay. When Sugar Daddy wasn't around, I grew bored with ending too many nights lying on somebody's living-room rug, staring at the ceiling and saying, "Oh, wow!" Besides, I'd seen too many kids get fucked up on drugs. Grass was fine, but it often led to heavier stuff. Working for Larry taught me that to give a good performance, you couldn't be high. I saw what drugs did to my performances off the set and knew he was right. If Larry ever caught anybody with drugs on the set, they were banished forever.

Now I was confronted with the prospect of banishing Mark

from my life. The kid had never said anything about dope so I presumed it was Freddy who had been the instigator. I poured another cup of coffee and sat quietly in the living room sipping it. I began to blame myself: I had gone off and left them, tending to business. While it was a business that many people would not approve of, it was *my* business; I mean, what else can you do when you're "a cocksucker's dream come true?"

I was, for better or for worse, always someone's dream lover. In real life, I was now Mark's dream lover. The difference this time was, he was my dream lover as well. He was someone I could take under my wing, the way Sugar Daddy and Larry did me, and help him develop to his full potential.

As I contemplated all this, I saw that for me to come crashing down on him as his parents did and force him to give up whatever it was that pleased him would drive him away. "Self-righteousness," Sugar Daddy once told me, "is inappropriate for those of us with a less sterling record of resisting temptation."

Finishing my coffee, I made up my mind: Mark would have to make his own choices. He'd done well so far, and I was determined to cut him as much slack as he needed.

21

Over the next week, Larry involved me in the editing process and we were able to get a rough cut assembled in record time.

"I want to preview this," he said finally, caressing the tin of film as if it was a baby's bottom.

"Preview?"

"Yeah, like they do the big movies."

"Where would we do it?"

"At the Tomkat. They'll let us have the place on a Monday night. No big deal, especially since they've already signed to get the opening."

"I'm all for it."

"Good, 'cause you'll have to pay for it."

After leaving the studio, I hung a left on Santa Monica Boulevard and when I had to stop for a light, I looked to my right to see a familiar face in the yellow Mustang idling next to me. It was Morrison. I stared but he continued to look straight ahead. When the light changed, he gunned it and raced ahead of me. Feeling adventurous, I followed him to Sweetzer Avenue, where he turned right. I kept on, climbing up the steep incline. I slowed when I saw him turning into the garage under the apartment building on the corner. I parked on the street and raced into the garage. My heart was pounding. I went to the elevator and pressed the button. The door opened and there he stood. "Yeah?" he said. His frown creased his forehead.

"Hi," I said.

The door shut behind me and the elevator started moving up. The bulge in his jeans was breathtaking. I didn't ask for permission, I simply reached out slowly and put my hand on his leg, halfway between his knee and his crotch. I felt his muscles tense instinctively. My hand wandered upward...

Moments later, we were just inside the door to his apartment. I had his fly open and my fingers were inside his pants. He wasn't wearing underwear. I pulled his cock free of

his jeans and opened the top button to part them as wide as I could. I bent down and ran my tongue lightly through his pungent bush. I lifted the soft root of his cock and drew back the foreskin. As the bright pink head slowly emerged, I licked it. I held the cock in my hand, overwhelmed at the heft of it. I began to slither the tip of my tongue up and down the outrageous length of it as it hardened. It was, I decided then and there, undoubtedly the most beautiful cock I had ever seen.

I got on my knees, opened my mouth, took it in. His cock filled my throat when it was fully erect, but I pushed myself to the limit, having all I could do to keep from gagging each time I took it all the way down.

He held my head and his legs stiffened; he was gasping hard, his breath catching in his throat. His strong fingers dug into my hair and squeezed my skull, pressing my face still deeper into his crotch. Soon he began battering my throat.

When he came, his hands pushed all the way down on the top of my head and held me there. I helplessly swallowed blast after blast of his jism. I gagged on the fullness of his load and felt it backing up into my mouth, but his hands kept me on his cock until the very last tremor had subsided.

Wiping drops of his cum from my lips, I stood. His breath was still ragged and he remained leaning against the wall, his eyes closed. "Well..." I started.

He said nothing.

I shrugged and opened the door. After I stepped out into the hallway, I turned back to see the door gently click shut.

22

The entire cast and crew were invited to our preview, plus some columnists from gay magazines and newspapers. Morrison, Larry said, had sent his regrets.

Mark and I dressed in matching three-piece white suits, black shirts, and Cuban heels. When Larry saw me, he said he thought John Travolta had wandered into the theater by mistake.

One of the columnists standing with him joked, "Oh, no mistake, Larry. Travolta *is* here - in the john sucking Paul off!" Paul Baressi, a hustler who had once worked for Larry and was one of the stars of "L. A. Tool & Die," was rumored have been the Oscar-nominated movie star's lover. It was a prospect that tantalized everyone I knew.

Tantalizing to me was the young blond Claude had brought with him. The boy had his back to us, talking with Freddy and the others, and the way his ass filled out his jeans immediately caused a stir in my Jockeys. I left Mark with the columnist and pursued the new arrival. I stood behind him, my eyes on Claude. Claude looked up and said, "Peter, I've brought you someone."

When the kid turned around, my jaw dropped. "Chris! It can't be!"

Four years before, I had lived alone for awhile in Nashville, struggling to make a living as a model, and the Gulas family, all six of them, had the apartment next to mine. Nick, the father, owned a clothing store, and three of his sons worked there. Chris, the youngest, at fourteen, was home alone a lot of the time. He was obviously gay and developed a crush on me that I found difficult to ignore. He was beautiful beyond words, with dark curly hair, a pair of full, sensuous lips, and an ass that begged for a hard cock. But I decided he was too damn young. It was one of those memories you have that make you wonder if you'd do the same thing again. It was the closest I had come to accepting the offering of a minor, although it was

not the only time it had happened. Once some boys discover that you're a porn stud, they want to sample the cock they saw on the screen or the tube.

Chris was surprised to see me. It was as if he was struck dumb. He mouthed my real name as if it was caught in his throat.

"How are you, Chris?" I asked, taking his hand.

He mumbled something and I took him by the arm. I calmly led him over to the punch bowl Larry had set up in the lobby. He was shaking so hard he could barely bring the cup to his lips.

"There, better?"

He nodded. "It's just a shock. I mean, I never expected – "

"Me neither. So, how are you?"

"Now I'm fine," he said, "Claude and the guys saved me."

"What happened? What made you leave Nashville?"

"It's a long story," he said.

Just then, Larry came over to me. "Let's get this show on the road."

I nodded, and turned to Chris. "I'll catch up with you after the show and we'll have a long talk."

"Promise?"

"Promise."

The lights dimmed, the music began flowing over us, the screen lit up. I took the seat on the aisle next to Mark that he had been saving for me. He put his hand in mine and I squeezed it.

"I love you," he whispered.

I brought his hand to my crotch. "I love you, too," I said, and just then the titles started to roll.

PETER HARDEE
BILL MORRISON
A DAVIS AND HARDEE PRODUCTION
"RANSOMED TAIL"
Featuring DANNY MURPHY
And Introducing MARK STARR

I grinned. I couldn't help it.

"Mark *Starr*?" my lover asked.

"That's you, dummy. I wanted you to be a star in your first film. Now, you'll always be a star. No matter what.'

"No matter what," he said, chuckling.

As the film played, I realized Larry was right, it was a damn good little fuck flick. More "artsy-fartsy" than I would have preferred, but exciting, and different enough to create a stir in the theaters. After that, it had to be converted to video tape as quickly as possible.

Mark was thrilled to see himself on screen. He stroked my cock all through our scene, the precum staining my pants.

As the lights went up, there was polite applause, followed by embraces, handshakes, backslapping, and even a little groping.

Larry and I got separated twice but finally found each other again. Over the heads of the crowd, he waved his unlit cigar at me, and his chubby face registered a look of profound relief.

"We've got ourselves a hit!" he said when we managed to connect by the punch bowl. I told Larry about Chris.

"I told you Claude would work out," he said.

"I don't know if the kid's game to get into the business, but at least I can, you know, feel him out."

"Nobody can feel 'em out the way you do, Pete. Well, take your time. I've got to get some new cameras and a lot of other stuff. Goin' to video ain't gonna be easy."

"But you're sure that's the way to go?"

"Damn sure."

"We'll get together next Monday, partner," I told him.

"I wish - " He stopped himself, drained his glass of punch.

"Wish what?"

"Oh, nothin'." He stared at his empty glass.

If he thought his gayness was a secret, he was mistaken, but I wasn't about to destroy his false sense of security. While it was undoubtedly good business to hire me to appear in his films, I knew there must be more to it than that, but he kept saying he was a "professional" and there was no "casting couch" in his office. For that, I was profoundly grateful.

I circulated, accepting congratulations and handing them out. Several guys asked me when the next film would start. "You'll have to ask my partner," I said.

Claude caught up with me while I was talking with Kenny, luscious in full drag. "Chris says you're going to take him home with you."

"Oh." I blinked. "Yeah, I guess. Yeah. We've got years of catching up to do." Chris hadn't changed, he was still pushing.

Claude gave my crotch a quick grope. "Well, stud, don't wear it out."

"I'll save some for you."

"That's a date."

23

When I slid into the front seat of the Buick beside Chris, he unhesitatingly wrapped his arms about my neck, his pretty face tilted upward and those dark eyes searched mine. His appearance was little changed. The hair was still that cap of black curls, and the features would have let him pass as a pre-teen. His lips, full, moist and parted, offered themselves without hesitation.

"Don't mind me," Mark chuckled as he slid in next to him. "Go on and kiss him."

The permission wasn't necessary, but the cue brought our lips together, and that delicious young tongue wriggled between my teeth and filled my mouth with its sweetness. The years seemed to drop away, and I was back in Nashville, surrendering to the allure of the youngster who vainly pleaded with me to "teach me how to kiss."

The lips were soft and yielding, responding to my kiss with an avidity that promised an even greater delight when used for more erotic pursuits. When we parted, I suggested some dinner.

His hand became fastened on my thigh, as if reassuring himself that I was there, and he shook his head. "I'm too excited to eat."

"You know," Mark chuckled, "I do believe this boy's horny!"

"Then we'd better eat so I can build up my strength. It's going to be a long night."

We stopped at a diner on Santa Monica famous for their burgers and shakes. As we dug in, Mark had an opportunity to flaunt his new knowledge of filmmaking, explaining how the various scenes were shot, and Chris listened attentively.

"I can't imagine getting paid for doing that," Chris said finally. "I know some guys sell it on the street, but this is different."

"You bet it's different," Mark said, waving his shake for

emphasis. "All I know is that I get paid for enjoying myself."

"It helps to be an exhibitionist," I said.

Mark didn't know what that was, but Chris did and explained it to him. "It's like being proud enough of what you got to want to show it off."

"Gosh," Mark said, at his most disarming, "I never knew what I really was till now!"

I left the waitress a tip that made her eyes widen, and we hit the road again, arriving at the apartment just a few minutes past ten.

I gave Chris a quick tour. He peeked into the bedroom, then into Mark's room, which the boy seldom used.

I started to mix drinks because I could see Mark had other ideas. "Want to take a shower with me, Chris?"

Chris turned to me for guidance.

"Go on," I nodded. "I want you two to get acquainted. Just don't get carried away."

"I won't rape him," Mark laughed. "I'll leave that to the master."

I built three tall drinks while the boys were in the shower, then shed my John Travolta outfit and slipped on the blue robe.

A half an hour later, Mark and Chris came back into the living room with towels wrapped about their hips, but there was no hiding their erections.

"We washed each other," Chris said, blushing. "I've never done that with another boy."

"Like it?" I asked, handing them their drinks.

"Yeah. I guess I wanted to do a lot more, but Mark said we had to wait."

"How nice."

"I warned him, Pete," Mark chimed in. "You're gonna really stretch his tail."

"Fuck, I don't care," Chris insisted. "I've waited *years* for it."

"You're really still a virgin?"

"Oh, yeah, at least that way."

"You better give Chris one of Larry's suppositories," I told Mark.

"He did. He even put it in for me."

Mark imitated Larry with his cigar in an unconscious mimicry of Groucho Marx. "I used my finger, but I really wanted to push it in another way."

Chris's cheeks reddened. "It seems so strange talking about it like this, without being ashamed and everything." He took a sip of his drink. "Why do people think it's wrong, Pete?"

"Not everyone does, Chris. Just the narrow-minded ones who think they have the right to set the rules for everybody, everywhere."

"Like my folks," Mark interjected.

Just then the door chimes rang out, and Mark set his drink down. "I'll get it," a well-trained Mark said.

"Find out who it is before you open the door," I said, the stick up still fresh in my mind.

Mark peered through the tiny viewer, and called back over his shoulder, "It's Kitty!"

Chris stared at the new arrival. "I didn't know you liked girls?" he whispered.

"Oh, Kitty is very much a boy, except for his tits, of course. He owes it all to hormones and surgery, he says."

"Christ! I've heard of that, but I've never seen it."

"First time for everything," I muttered.

After Mark fixed Kenny a drink, he said, "I think I'll take Kitty to my room – "

"Yeah, c'mon, stud, that movie made me horny as hell," Kitty laughed, leading the way, and Mark closed the door behind them.

Chris immediately put his arms about my neck. Our drinks were on the table, ignored now, as we feasted on each other's mouths.

I waited until we were in the bedroom before I gently removed the towel from about his hips. His cock, eight magnificent inches of throbbing, vein-laced hardness, thrust out invitingly.

When I shed my robe, he gasped seeing my cock in the flesh. "Oh, god It looks even bigger than in the movie!"

I stroked it for him.

"Oh, man, I wanna suck it!"

"Okay." I lay down on the bed and spread my legs, ready to make up for lost time.

"It's all yours, Chris. Any way you want it."

"Ummmm!" he breathed, dropping to his knees between my thighs and bending over. His warm fingers curled about my prick and cupped my balls. His lips parted, and his tongue tasted the tip, licking and caressing. Then, with a sigh of satisfaction, he took the head of cock fully in his mouth.

After a few moments of Chris' spirited sucking, I couldn't take it any longer. "I want that ass! Straddle my hips and take that prick!"

His lips slid up my dick, and he stared into my eyes. He licked the tip of my cock and then cried, "I'll try! God, I'll try!"

His slender legs spread, knees pressing on either side of my waist, his fingers gripping and guiding the throbbing shaft of my cock, he adjusted himself over me. His hips moved down, slowly, taking it in. I felt the hot circle of his anus press the tip. His face contorted with strain, teeth clenched and his head thrown back, eyes closed, as he forced his asshole down onto my prick, the torrid wetness gripping me with spasms that made my hips jerk with pleasure.

Only when his balls were jammed against my pubic hair, and he was completely impaled did his eyes open to stare down into mine with an adoring gleam.

"This is what you wanted?" His chest heaved as his asshole was flexing about my cock.

"Yeah!" I groaned.

He began riding me, his hips rising and falling to slide that slippery channel up and down my prick. He let out little cries of ecstacy as, thrusting out over my belly, his own cock jerked and swelled, its cum arcing in silvery spurts onto my chest, each one echoed by a loving contraction of his colon about my prick.

I closed my eyes, savoring the feel of his tight ass as it chewed and sucked my hardness, my own orgasm building. To me, he like Mark, the epitome of virginal sexuality: hungry, eager and uninhibited.

As my cum shot deep into Chris's clenching asshole, he cried out, delirious with happiness. I held him close, coming down gradually from my high, my prick softening inside him.

After a few minutes, he was begging me, "I want you to come again in my mouth!"

I pulled back, drawing my prick out of his ass, straddled his waist and knee-walked up to where I could steer my throbbing cock into his hungry mouth. Just before the head slipped between his warm, succulent lips, he sighed, "Oh, yeah, Pete, I want it all!"

When I awoke the next morning, I was in bed alone. The red numerals on the digital clock said it was nearly noon. I relieved myself in the bathroom, splashed some cold water on my face and went to look for Chris. As I left the bedroom, I noticed the door to the second bedroom was closed and stepped over to it. My ear to the door, I could hear deep moans, groans and the unmistakable high-pitched ecstatic cries of Kenny in the throes of yet another of his incomparable orgasms.

Yes, I decided, Chris was going to fit in just fine.

I moved on to the kitchen. Mark had prepared the coffee and I poured myself a cup. I took it back to my bedroom and sipped it between showering, shaving and dressing. I left the empty cup on the counter in the kitchen under a note I scribbled to Mark: "Whatever happens, remember, you're my lover." Then I hurried downstairs to the garage.

In less than an hour, I was leaving the freeway using the same exit I did that day I saw Mark trudging along. Today, however, there were no hitchhikers. I sighed. At last I would have a day or two at the cabin alone.

As I passed the convenience store, I remembered Mark sitting in the car that first day, taking off his boots while I shopped. I got an erection just thinking about the sight of the bulge of his crotch when I returned to the car. And now he was back at the apartment – with Chris. I thought about Chris, how much I had enjoyed fucking him. I was not expected to choose between them, I was supposed to want them both, fuck them both. And I was expected to want a change of air occasionally. A Kenny or a Claude and even the big, beautiful cock of a Bill Morrison if I wanted.

Climbing higher and higher into the forest, I began to wonder what Mark and Chris were doing. I suddenly missed them both. My hand dropped to my crotch and I began rubbing my erection. It was useless. I slowed the car, made a sharp U-turn, and sped back down the mountain.

"Love is a spark,
Lost in the dark,
Too soon,
Too soon.

We're late,
Darling, we're late.
The curtain descends,
Everything ends
Too soon,
Too soon."

— From "Speak Low,"
Lyrics by Ogden Nash,
Music by Kurt Weill

The Boys of Paradise

A Novella by
HARRISON CHALFONT

STARbooks Press
Sarasota, FL

*"A Paradise on earth: the climate can be marvellous,
the scenery is lovely and the boys are so beautiful."*
- Christopher Isherwood, August 1976

1

Jimmy had planned his sailing trip carefully. He'd spent hours pouring over maps and charts, read as much as he could get his hands on about native flora and fauna, and day-dreamed. He had put away as much cash as he could and then had taken a year's leave of absence from his business. Perhaps that was a foolish move but he had committed himself and it was too late now. He wanted a whole year in order to do something he had dreamed of ever since he was a kid. He was thirty-four now, and wanted to take his big adventure while he was still young enough to enjoy its pleasures. He had thought about it long enough and now it was time to act. Perhaps a year was a long time for a holiday. Perhaps so, but he thought it would be barely enough to accomplish his goal.

He intended to buy a boat in the South Pacific, someplace like Timor, then sail at a leisurely pace though Indonesian islands on his way to Singapore. Once there he would sell the boat then fly back home. If he sailed direct from Timor to Singapore it would hardly take a year, of course, but he intended to explore, visit, and experience as much as he could of the natural and aesthetic wonders: beautiful seas, mountains, and glittering beaches on innumerable islands – the inhabitants. He was very specific in his wants. His taste had been formed early, and silky-smooth Asians was it.

He started to get interested in stuff when he was ten or eleven – he forgot which but it didn't matter – but he hadn't actually made out until he got to the 9th grade. Like other kids he fooled around, but his first real piece had been Billy Ching, a cute little guy who always hung around him in the shower after gym, sneaking looks at what he had. Guys had whispered stories about Billy. At fifteen Jimmy already had gotten tired of his fist and had been roaring to go. Until then his mind had been focused rather vaguely on feeling Sylvia Wilson's big tits again as she jerked him off, but when Billy Ching got up enough nerve to offer him his round little butt he didn't hesitate and went home with him at once.

They were so hot they could barely wait until they got in the door, then did it right away, standing up in the back hall with Billy's pants dropped to his knees. The stories must have been true because Billy sure knew how to wiggle on a dick. Jimmy marvelled at how good it felt up inside a hot body, while Billy gasped, then moaned, then went "Ooo! Ooo!" at every thrust. After a Coke they did it again on the kitchen floor. After another Coke Billy took him to his bedroom where they threw their clothes off to do it a third time naked.

Billy told him he was finally getting what he had dreamed of, so they did it every afternoon after that. Jimmy found the hot kid intensely satisfying. The more he had him the more he wanted, and for the next two years Billy had been eager to oblige. Then the kid's parents moved away, taking Billy with them, leaving Jimmy unable to be satisfied by anything else.

His desire was now an obsession. There weren't many Asians around where he lived, but like every town in North America, his had a Chinese restaurant. Many times he'd tried to force down yet another plate of Cantonese food as he gazed longingly at Joey Wong sitting at a back table dutifully doing his homework. At first he'd hoped that Joey would take Billy's place, but the kid was oblivious to his need and deaf to his hints. Fortune-cookies promised nothing.

He left home and first began serious hunting at the tender age of eighteen. He found lots of guys interested in him once they found out what he had, but none were as good as Billy Ching. In order to get the hairless type he wanted he chased boys for a while, but the price of that was a desperate furtiveness he didn't like, not to speak of the fear of getting caught. He hated that, but stayed with it for a while because nobody hairy could provoke the kind of volcanic eruption he'd experienced with Billy. Not until he was twenty, that is, when Mike Takamatsu caught his eye at the beach.

Mike had been even better than Billy: twenty-four and, if possible, even hotter to get it. Mike had been around a lot but nobody had satisfied him before he met Jimmy because Jimmy really buggered his butt off. Like Billy, little Mike had hardly a hair on him, which Jimmy liked a lot, and wanted to get it all the time, which he liked even more. He was crazy about Mike's

smooth little body and hadn't had such big orgasms since Billy. Mike liked it when Jimmy slept on him like a mattress, and a wonderful mattress he was too, with the neat little buns tucked snugly into his groin.

Even though Mike was two years older he was spoiled and had to be pampered like a baby. And that's what he was, too, Jimmy's butt-baby. True-love hit him in the form of Mike's bouncing bottom. He'd never been so excited for such a long period, even with Billy, and could barely wait through the day until he could get home. Then one day he came back to find Mike and his stuff gone. Not even a note. He drove along miles of streets trying to spot him but he never did see him again.

Now that he had actually arrived in Indonesia he knew that this trip would be entirely different from his other holidays, even from the holiday spent in Brazil. From all reports, the situation in the South Seas was distinct from anything he had experienced before, with countless stuff. There were millions of them in this part of the world. If he screwed a different one each waking hour of every day he still couldn't get through them all. By the time he'd finished the last one then the ones who had been born and grown old enough in the meanwhile would be at the end of the line, waiting. He grinned to himself. He wished he had that kind of stamina, but regrettably he was only an ordinary man.

Well, perhaps he wasn't exactly ordinary. He was well enough endowed so that the small type of Asian like Billy and Mike really had to stretch to take him, which they had dearly enjoyed. He discovered with pleasure that the peoples of the southern seas were equally interested. In the boy-brothel he visited on Timor, all the kids ooed and ahed and had to feel it, and most wanted to sit on it to see what something that big felt like, and they wouldn't charge him anything, either. He could have laid back and boys would be bouncing on him still if that was all he wanted. It was what he wanted, but not all. It was too easy. Another thing he had discovered about himself since Mike fourteen years ago was that he didn't want little queens any more, no matter cute. Instead he wanted the impossible. His dream now was to have someone as highly-sexed as Mike but more masculine, and virgin; he wanted a smooth kid under

him, squealing bloody murder as he forced himself very slowly into a hairless virgin butt. The thought of that, among other little dreams, had brought him to Southeast Asia in the first place.

In most parts of the world, as he had discovered to his infinite regret, virgin boys willing to roll over for him were very difficult to find. They might be attracted well enough at first, but got scared when they saw what he wanted them to take. In southeast Asia, on the other hand, he had been told by those who should know, that hot bodies were a dime a dozen; sometimes less, though few of them were virgin. In fact, if he got desperate enough to try kids again, there were tales that child slavery was alive and well. It was illegal, of course, but still widespread.

During his holiday in Brazil he'd learned first-hand how extreme poverty caused families to send their boys out onto the street, though they pretended that the money they brought home resulted from shining shoes or something equally absurd. He'd had his shoes shined a lot while in Rio. He'd liked kids' smoothness but never found them really satisfying. In southeast Asia, if the tales were to be believed, apparently there was no pretence of anything as silly as shining shoes and they were sold outright. If he couldn't find a willing virgin then he might buy one for his very own and take him, willing or not.

While he was in the brothel he spoke to the owner, trying to get information concerning the source for his boys. Like most, the man was Chinese, thrifty, solely commercial, and entirely without scruple but with a fine sense of the value of his merchandise. By his speech he seemed educated far above his present station in life, which Jimmy found curious.

"Please, just tell me your requirement and I'll get for you," he sighed impatiently after Jimmy had beaten around the bush for several minutes.

Jimmy explained, leaving out a few parts.

"A little fellow, then," the man said. "I can manage that. What age do you prefer?"

Jimmy explained that it didn't really matter, but he had to be hairless and virgin. The Chinese didn't bat an eye.

"That's not so easy, but I can find one. Do you desire a fuck-

boy?" he asked rather baldly, "One to give you his ass whenever you wish? Or would you prefer a slave? Whores are a simple matter, as you may deduce from this establishment. Many boys are available, and for a reasonable price. But slaves are not so simple. It's difficult now to find a papa willing to sell his child for that purpose. They want considerably more money."

"Slave," Jimmy managed to croak.

"There are two kinds," the man told him, holding up two redundant fingers covered with rings. "One is expensive, the other almost ruinous," he said, as if the matter in hand was the characteristics of differing straw mats. "How well endowed are you, then?" the man asked.

When Jimmy told him eight inches the guy pursed his lips and frowned.

"That's far too much for a virgin," he said disapprovingly. "You would hurt a boy badly and papas do not like that. You must have a slave-boy, then." The man gave him a close look. "I estimate that is what you desire, huh? Very expensive, old chap. The papa of a boy like that would throw up his hands and complain loudly that his boy would get hurt badly by a man so large; very greedy fellows."

"How much?" Jimmy asked, his throat dry.

"One hundred dollars for one week," the man said, "providing you are careful not to rip his anus or mark him. But for five-thousand dollars, old chap... Well, for five thousand dollars the boy is yours to do with as you like. For that kind of money papa dries his tears and runs home to make more boys."

Jimmy swallowed hard. That's what he wanted, but he didn't have five thousand dollars to spend that way, not unless he gave up buying a boat and went home. If he went home then he certainly couldn't take a boy like that along. Asian slave-boys were not on Customs' list of approved imports. The man knew the price was too high for him. He shrugged.

"Some years ago, when times were much worse, virgin lads were very cheap," he lamented. "Now that life has gotten better, they cost a great deal."

Jimmy nodded. He paid the fellow the consultation fee he demanded, then staggered out. He grabbed two boys and went

back upstairs. They were well-trained and agile, but they were too well-used to make him really explode.

That was the dream. The reality was different, as reality has a habit of being. Even then it was pleasurable enough so that he really had no right to complain if he were a sane man. He wasn't, but unlike most he was fortunate enough to know it. He was fortunate in practical ways as well. He couldn't believe his luck in finding exactly the right boat, an ancient but sturdy Dutchman, a ketch with bluff bows and very solidly built throughout of mahogany and teak. Whoever had owned it previously must have loved it dearly because it was in a remarkable state of preservation even though now incredibly filthy. He went over it in close detail, haggled sharply and at length over numerous small cups of tea, then laid down cash to a startled Chinese who plainly thought this round-eye was mad.

He had it put up for an inspection of the hull, a thorough cleaning, and as good a refit as he could afford. In addition to a rebuilding of the old engine he had some small additions made which he hoped he would never need but would regret not having if he did. He wouldn't have bothered if he wasn't going through the South China Sea, but out there one man alone in a small boat would be fair game. The rocket-launcher cost him more than he thought, but he got an M-16 quite reasonably. There were so many floating around that they were cheap.

After much bureaucratic red tape and the associated bribes he got his papers all in order, swallowed hard, and rubbed his crotch for luck. To him the refitted craft was a thing of beauty and just barely small enough for one man to handle if he was a careful sailor and didn't run into anything really nasty. He set sail toward the fabled islands where rumor said most slave-boys originated, or at least used to.

2

Like most dreams, Jimmy's remained unfulfilled. Oh, he had guys regularly without any trouble, but not virgins. Hundreds of villages on these coasts sent out fishing craft which would stay at sea sometimes for months on end, crewed by every able-bodied man in the village and by every boy over ten. As he understood it, the men fucked the boys over fifteen; adolescents fifteen and under fucked the little boys; and the little ones waited impatiently until they reached puberty so they could do the same. A common sight, when passing such a vessel at dawn, was that of bare brown behinds hung over the side, relieving themselves of the blessings they had received the night before.

Once he had watched a travelogue on television narrated by what could only have been an innocent and very dense young man, who commented adversely on the quality of diet that made bowels so loose on these ships. Jimmy had nearly died laughing. It was obviously so necessary an expedient with an all-male crew at sea for months on-end that no one thought anything about it except westerners. The fact that villagers like these had been screwing butt continuously at least since the Stone Age, and seemed no worse off for it, always infuriated the righteous. Jimmy grinned.

So then, getting sex was simple. All he really had to do whenever he was in harbor was to piss over the side when small boats were passing. Usually he would have a smooth brown body in his bunk a few minutes later, sometimes more than one. They wouldn't be virgins, however, they couldn't take anything his size and the wise ones knew it. Some older and more experienced ones could, however, and with a little effort did, though with much theatrical straining. He had lots of sex but not what he really wanted, and especially not what he desired most of all.

He was never physically frustrated but his emotional frustration grew, particularly because he saw so much of almost

exactly what he desired. He would stare hotly and get friendly waves in return, but that was all. The wide grins and teasing wiggles from those who understood exactly what he was after were the most annoying. Worse than that, as the Chinese whoremaster had told him, slave-boys were difficult to find. So difficult, in fact, that he found none. He inquired at a few places in a round-about way but got either hostile looks at once or stares of incomprehension. The papas here were no different from papas anywhere, protective of their progeny. Screwing of their seemingly numberless older sons was a different matter and that was all right. One needn't ask papa then because big boys were fair game. Virgins, on the other hand, were quite a different matter. He moaned and cursed a lot.

One extraordinary incident almost caused him to give up his plan. He had put in to a small Indonesian port to buy some items he needed. In the morning he found that a trader had put in close alongside during the night. The crew was the usual mixture of ages and races but the owner was Chinese, a wiry middle-aged man who winked and grinned widely the moment he saw him, then rubbed his crotch every time Jimmy went up on deck. It was almost funny. He would have ignored him but the man had some marine supplies on board and his prices were low, so he saved one trip ashore at least. The Chinese was a sharp trader, like most, but was affable enough, especially since he was interested. Blond westerners turned him on.

"Ver nice ass," he said with a grin, almost licking his lips. Jimmy grinned back and shook his head. Taking dick up his butt wasn't what he had in mind at all.

After dark that night the Chinese captain's boat was quiet, with just a few crewmen sitting around smoking and talking in the semi-dark, speaking a mixture of languages but mostly pidgin. He could distinguish the captain when he came on deck because of his cap, and he was leading what looked like an ape by a chain around its neck. It was too dark to tell exactly. There was a murmur from the men on deck and two more crew wandered up from below as well. There was some movement and he watched the men line up. He was confused for a moment as to what was happening, but then it became clear. Whatever it was the captain had brought on deck, it was lying

on its belly and the crew was in the process of humping it. There were six and the creature took them all, one right after the other, making little squeaky noises. When the crew had been satisfied then their ship went quiet.

When he went back on deck in the morning he was greeted by a bizarre sight. The captain was lying naked on the "ape's" back as the creature made those little squeaking noises he had heard the night before. In the morning light he could see that it wasn't an ape at all, but a naked small boy with long hair, his behind raised to take what was being rammed into him. The crack of the man's belly against the kid's buns was sharp and loud and he didn't see how anything so small could possibly stand it. The captain saw Jimmy gaping at him and grinned.

"Hot-ass!" he shouted. "Ver good! You watch me fuck, huh?" Instead of finishing, however, he pulled out and stood to show himself off with a laugh. "Nice, huh? You want?" Jimmy grinned and shook his head. "Fuck monkey-boy then?"

"Sure, why not," Jimmy said, horny enough now to screw anything and curious to find out what the creature actually was.

He jumped to the other rail and saw that the small creature wasn't a little boy, but a short, thin young man. He pulled his pants down and pushed himself in between the small wet cheeks, then almost jumped in surprise. "Holy shit!" he exclaimed, and the captain laughed loudly at his reaction. The little body under him was so loose it felt as though he had stuck himself in a bowl of warm Jello. He'd never felt anything like it.

"Nice and easy, huh?" the man laughed.

Monkey-boy must have liked his size because he squeaked loudly, pushed his behind up, and wiggled hard. When Jimmy finished and pulled his pants back up the captain pulled the naked figure by a light chain attached to a collar around his neck. When he stood, Monkey-boy was no more than five feet tall and had the slim, delicate build of a Cambodian. Shaggy long hair hung down to cover most of his face, and his eyes had an odd blank look. The moment he stood there was a liquid noise as he dripped onto the deck. He seemed unaware of it.

The captain watched Jimmy's face with interest then turned the guy around to show that his back, legs, and behind were

covered with scars from old beatings. The captain pushed him to bend over. Although he wasn't really surprised, the visual effect made Jimmy gasp even louder.

"Nice, huh?" the captain said with a grin.

What would have been a brown button between the small hairless cheeks of a normal boy looked more like a mare's cunt.

"Many year fuck," the captain explained. "Can take anybody."

He got the story out of the captain as they had tea, monkey-boy squatting naked. As he suspected, the small young man was a slave. The captain had gotten him ten years ago, when he was about fifteen, from a Burmese ship whose owner had bought him as a ten-year-old virgin to keep his crew satisfied on long voyages. Other than sex he had no duties. When he was ten the boy might have had some problems coping with grown men, but he had been so savagely broken-in that now, as the captain said, he could take anything and could be fucked for hours with no observable ill effect.

"Burma man ver nasty. Liked to hurt boys," the captain said with a frown. "I don't hurt, only fuck." He smiled. "Monkey good, huh?"

"Very good," Jimmy agreed.

He felt envious. This Chinese trader had almost exactly what he desired himself, except that he wanted a virgin, not a kid with an ass like a sewer and beaten into animal stupidity by some Burmese sadist.

The captain was in port three more days and Jimmy stayed as well, the three of them frequently piled together.

"You ver' pretty man," the captain told him. The fellow was so interested in him that he tried to convince Jimmy to put his boat up and sail with him and the monkey-boy from port to port. "You fuck monkey-boy all you want, and I fuck you," he said with a grin.

In one way, at least, it was a tempting proposition, especially when he had the boy wiggling under him, but he declined with regret. His own goal was slightly but significantly different. He parted from them to continue his journey.

3

Jimmy's trip was idyllic, really. If he hadn't been obsessed it would have been the perfect travel-poster vacation. Volcanos smoked on the horizon from time to time, forests swept up from shorelines to blue mist-covered mountain tops, and he was fortunate in most of the weather he encountered. There were a few days which made him regret ever having put to sea, and one so bad he was certain that even his sturdy little craft wouldn't make it through another hour. Somehow it did, and he offered up thanks to whatever god of fools was protecting him.

There were great expanses of open passage, even in a sea crammed with islands, and he would sail for hours without seeing anything else on Earth at all. Then suddenly there would be a freighter or two or a dozen sails here and there on the horizon, then nothing again. Whenever he got seriously horny, which happened frequently, he would regret having left the captain and his boy. To relieve himself he'd spend a week on the next island. He always managed to find a lad willing to roll over for a well-hung and handsome westerner, and he'd fuck him until the lad couldn't stand any more before setting sail once again.

Twice he saw distant sails turn about to change course toward him when he was seen, and twice they sailed away again when he was spotted with an automatic rifle in his arms. There were friendly waves and big smiles but he wasn't fooled by that and simply waved back with a smile of his own. Once he gave passage to two young men who wanted to go from the island where he had stayed a week to another. They chattered continuously all day, then ooo'd and ahh'd over his size when he stripped to wash. They rolled together half the night, and after that as often as any of them could get hard. They were tight, hot, and wanted to experience a dick the size of a large banana. Most islanders boasted ones the size of a dill-pickle if they were lucky, which not all of them were. In return he almost sucked their pickles off, something they enjoyed with

many giggles and moans. They weren't virgins but they had a wonderful time.

He was two hundred miles off the coast of Vietnam when it actually happened. So far he had spent only six months of his year-long holiday. No matter how he dragged it out there didn't seem to be anything more to do or anywhere else to go. He'd humped numberless brown bodies but his dream of having a virgin slave-boy all his own began slowly to evaporate. The voyage had been so uneventful, except for a great deal of sex and some sight-seeing, that he was even beginning to look forward to its coming to an end. Crowded and noisy Singapore was only a few days' sail away. Merchantmen appeared on the horizon more frequently now, and a sail or two from native craft. One was closer than he liked, coming toward him on a course which would bring it within less than a mile, but then a sudden squall swept between them and a wall of blinding water and sharp winds took all his attention.

It was a very close thing. The squall passed just as quickly as it had appeared and the small sailing ship he had seen a mile away now was close upon him, bearing down fast. He could hear the rumble of a diesel more powerful than the maneuvering motor normal to a fishing vessel. They had changed course, covered by the squall, and he stared for a second, unable to move.

He shook himself and gave it a quick glance through his sea-glass. His fear was confirmed. Almost certainly Vietnamese pirates, the kind that for some years had been robbing then slaughtering refugees referred to in the West as the boat-people. If the victims were lucky, that is. If they weren't lucky then the pirates would kill the men in humorous ways then gang-fuck the boys and younger women until they ruptured and bled, after which they would throw them overboard. The blood attracted sharks at once, which the pirates found vastly amusing. In this part of the world as well as in too many others perhaps, life was very cheap. Altogether, they were not exactly sweet and lovable.

There weren't more than a half-dozen aboard the approaching vessel but that was more than enough to take a

single man in a ketch. Gone were the days of brandished swords and blood-curdling screams. These men had automatic rifles of their own and made no attempt to cover them up.

Jimmy shook himself and fell into the routine he had rehearsed many times but never really expected to have to use. He dropped down behind the quarter-inch armor plate he'd had installed around his wheelhouse just as some tentative shots popped overhead. He dug out the rocket-launcher and went through the drill, then sat waiting, taking quick looks though the peep-hole in front of his eyes. Some bullets whanged off the metal but since he had disappeared from sight the men weren't firing at him much, just enough to keep his head down until they could get alongside. He didn't give them that opportunity. Just at the moment when they were turning to come broadside to him, he rose, took quick aim, then fired the launcher. He ducked back down at once to reload, then heard a roar as he made a hit. He jumped up and fired again, then ducked back just as quickly.

With extraordinary luck, he had blown a hole in their bow at the water-line with the first shot. The speed of their vessel made rapid flooding almost instantaneous and they went heavily down by the bow and slowed dramatically almost at once. All his second shot managed to do was make some cordage fly around. The third one, however, was the luckiest of all and saved his life. He didn't know what he hit but the ship went up at once, the blast throwing him back hard enough almost to knock him out. It didn't, which was his second piece of luck that day in as many minutes. There were a few screams and a lot of gabble from across the water and he looked out carefully.

The vessel was missing a large part of its stern and afire, but going down faster than it could burn. The surviving men sprang into the water at once, swimming toward him. Jimmy knew that there was but one thing to do and he did it. They couldn't swim and shoot at him at the same time, but he certainly could shoot at them and did. He wasn't going to play humanitarian to men like these and then have his throat cut after they had climbed aboard and played ping-pong with his balls.

The M-16 burped and took them out, one after another, and

he made sure not to miss. There was one left, staring up at him in wide-eyed panic. Jimmy saw the small heart-shaped face and somehow knew, suddenly, that at long last he had what he'd been looking for.

He threw out a line and the boy took it, hauling himself in quickly until he reached the side, then he grabbed the gunwale and pulled himself aboard. As he came over the side Jimmy whacked him on the head with butt of the M-16 and he fell. He hadn't hit him very hard, so he took the precaution of tying him up, but not before he had pulled a pair of ragged pants and a wicked-looking knife off him. He threw both over the side. The combat-high wore off quickly, leaving him exhausted.

Behind him there was now no trace of the ship itself, just some rubbish and some bodies floating. On previous days, perhaps, they had sailed back to their coastal village, richer than they had been before they set out, then they would have patted their children and embraced their wives as if murder on the seas was just another job. To them perhaps it had been, but no more. Children would go unpatted that night and wives unscrewed.

He poured himself a stiff drink and threw it down. It helped steady him, then he saw to his boat. There were bullet-holes here and there, mostly through the sails, but nothing serious. The attackers had been terrible shots, as men were who relied entirely on automatic weapons. He patted his thin but adequate armor plate affectionately. Good Bessie.

4

He had a look at his naked captive. Beautifully-shaped round butt. Very nice. Though definitely young, he couldn't tell how old he really was from his back so he rolled him over with his foot. The face wasn't bad-looking and terrified wide-eyes looked up at him. The guy was conscious, breathing light and fast, but was petrified and careful not to move and made no sound. Jimmy looked down at his crotch to see a small cock shrivelled with fear to nothing more than a wrinkled nub. Around it was a nest of fine black hairs. He looked very young because he was small, even for a Vietnamese, but more likely he was nineteen or twenty. Jimmy felt a thrill and smiled. Perfect. Undoubtedly a bloodthirsty little bastard or he wouldn't have been aboard that ship. If Jimmy were lying there on the deck and the boy was standing over him he wouldn't take any bets on his lasting more than a minute. Unless the boy felt playful, of course, then he might last some time before he died.

As it was, he was on top and the boy was secured. The boy wouldn't die. No, no, Jimmy would keep him very much alive. He had dreamed of this for years. Now he had his own satin-skinned slave-boy. No one knew he had him, and no one was going to find out. The young pirate's friends were dead, after a few days his little wife would write him off to a storm or gunboat patrol, and his probable half-dozen brats would forget him in a week. Perfect. He checked his charts carefully, took some bearings, then put about. He wouldn't be going to Singapore after all. He had a slave-boy and six more months.

There was a steady westerly on his stern quarter and it promised to hold. Weather reports over the radio suggested no change and all looked well for the next day, probably for the next several days if the forecast was to be believed. He pulled up his deck-cushion and sat down to examine his prize. Being a mainlander and not from the Indonesian islands, even at twenty this one might even be a virgin. Jimmy was going to wait before he looked to find out because he relished

anticipating that he was. He hadn't had anything this attractive since Mike and wanted to savor his delight. It had to be savored well first because afterward he would be a virgin no longer. That was a fruit which could be enjoyed many times but could be picked only once.

The boy's body was one usual to young Vietnamese peasants, as he knew from years of poring over magazine pictures of South-East Asians. He used to run his fingertips over the photographs, imagining the texture of their smooth warm flesh as he jerked off slowly. God bless the National Geographic Society! Like most, this one was small-boned and slim almost to the point of being scrawny. He must have been eating better than the ones usually shown in the pictures, however, because he wasn't stringy. Like many Southeast Asians he looked more fragile than he really was.

His physical delicacy was quite elegant, and even though he had a bush of hair in his crotch he didn't otherwise look much different from a western pubescent. The eyes were large and dark with curiously heavy brows for an Asian. They gave him what probably would have been a fierce expression if he weren't so frightened. Jimmy didn't want to look at his ass yet. Not yet. He felt him, however, stroking the smooth flesh, feeling his legs and arms. While thin, he was firm with muscle. He tried to shrink back, too, but could only move an inch or so. Perhaps he thought that this round-eye devil was going to cut him up and eat him. Jimmy had no intention of cutting him up, although he had every intention of eating him. Often, but not yet.

He had tied the guy's hands behind his back, which made his control of him easier. He wanted to leave him freedom of movement yet at the same time be careful of his own security. He went below to rummage about until he found his Toy-Box, then returned with the halter of fine piano-wire he had made up then carried around with him for months for just such a hoped-for eventuality. He fastened one loop of the wire to a stanchion and snapped the small padlock attached to it, then went to the boy, paying out several feet. He took a small foot and put the other loop around the boy's ankle, making it snug enough so that he couldn't slip the foot back out of it, but not too tight, then snapped the second padlock.

The fineness of the wire made an excellent control device. The boy would discover quickly that trying to unfasten the locks just broke his fingernails, and pulling on the wire with bare fingers would only cut him without result. If he tried to move farther than Jimmy intended then he would hurt himself severely. Jimmy thought that the kid would understand that, but he made sure that he did with patience and many gestures, exaggerating a little. He told the boy that the wire would take his foot right off and he'd bleed to death in a minute. When he was satisfied by the kid's horrified look he cut loose the other fastenings. Except for the wire, his pirate-prisoner was now free.

Perfect. He indicated to the kid that he should stand up and move around. It took a few kicks to get him to do it, but then he was up, taking in exactly how he was secured and understanding in a moment just how much freedom he had, which seemed a lot but was really almost nil. Unless he was determined to rip his foot off he was a captive, and there was nothing within the area the boy could reach for him to use as a weapon to dispute that fact. There was nothing he could do at all except exactly as he was told. Even without the wire Jimmy was much stronger than this small creature anyway and would have been able to handle him without any other restraint than his fist. Still, he liked having him secured and didn't want to take the slightest chance.

After a few minutes of looking around and down at the method by which he was fastened, the kid saw that and squatted. Jimmy kicked him again until he stood up. He wasn't to make a move unless given permission. Jimmy didn't know any Vietnamese and the boy didn't know any English, but for the relationship he was going to have with his captive, cultural interchange and philosophical discussion wouldn't be required.

He went below to fix supper. When he came back later the boy was still standing where he had left him. The kid was quick. Very good. He nodded in approval and gave him a plate filled with food, gesturing that he could squat the way eastern peoples always did. He sat on the cushion with his own plate then nodded to the boy that it was all right to start eating. The kid hadn't touched anything until Jimmy did that. He indeed

was very quick. The boy started shovelling food into his mouth with his fingers at once, then Jimmy ate his supper as well.

When both plates were empty and the boy's licked clean he took them below for washing. When he came back up he sat, lit a cigarette, and admired his prize once again. The boy had moved from where he had been left and there was a thin bright-red line across one hand. He had tested the wire and found it to be exactly as Jimmy knew it was. Now he remained squatting quietly. Jimmy could almost read the thoughts going through the savage mind: if round-eye intended to kill him right away then he wouldn't have secured him so carefully and certainly wouldn't have fed him. Therefore it was likely he would live another day at least. The boy had been trembling every few minutes but now he stopped.

Jimmy didn't give the kid his cigarette but reached over and put it to his lips for a puff. He took one quickly before it was pulled away again. Jimmy smiled. Certainly the boy was wondering what these inscrutable round-eyes were like that they should do such things. As the boy exhaled slowly, in a quick gesture Jimmy touched the glowing coal to the boy's arm. It was so quick that he didn't have time to react until he was already burned. The dark eyes widened in fear again as the kid looked at the small red mark the coal had left on him. His mouth dropped open and he backed away. Jimmy followed him, enjoying the look on his face.

He had no love for pirates, and wondered how many refugee women and kids this young man had helped to murder in his short career. Anticipation is the joy or terror of most things and he let the boy wonder for a moment before he touched the cigarette to him again. He tried to dodge but Jimmy was too quick, touching him on the belly this time. The boy gasped and almost tried to jump away. Luckily for them both he remembered the wire around his foot just in time. He got as far away as he could then stood shaking. Jimmy didn't burn him again. He took a drag himself, turned the cigarette around, then offered him a puff. The kid stared then slowly realized that it was a signal that it was over. It wasn't over. There was lots of time.

He had planned to wait to sample his prize in the morning but after watching his naked little body a while he decided he

wanted to do so now. Not all at once, but some. He had the boy stand and washed him thoroughly first, but not the cleft between those round cheeks. He wanted to discover that tomorrow. He hoped to God that it wouldn't be anything like monkey-boy's terrible gash. Once satisfied that he was clean he began tasting him. The kid shrank away at first until he remembered that there was nowhere for him to shrink to and then stood still.

Jimmy went over him thoroughly, enjoying every square inch. It took a while to get a reaction from him. In spite of his fears the boy couldn't help but be stimulated eventually, and his small dick snapped up. Jimmy sucked it a few minutes then roved upward again. He made that tour several times, working slowly and enjoying the boy's warmth and silky skin. The kid was trying hard not to quiver at the sensations he felt but without much success. The stimulation got to him after a few minutes. He sucked his breath in sharply then gave Jimmy several spurts of come. Very nice! He pushed the kid down to a squat then took his aching dick out. The boy's eyes widened. Later the boy would learn to suck him but right now he had to come off at once and didn't want to take time to force him. He held him by the hair with one hand and jerked off with the other until he shot on him.

He had enjoyed that. The boy didn't dare wipe himself and Jimmy watched come drip slowly down his face. Since the tropic night was close upon them, he let the kid wash himself and piss over the side then gave him a mat to sleep on and a light cloth to cover himself when it got chill later. The stars were bright. He lashed the wheel then crawled into his sleeping bag.

5

When he opened his eyes in the morning he was relieved to find the weather unchanged. There were signs of a squall on the horizon but not headed in their direction. His boy was awake, his lovely behind hung over the side as he relieved himself. Jimmy did the same then went below to get them some breakfast. He didn't have any rice so the kid would have to eat what was given him.

Later he would have him fish, although he would have to teach him how because fishermen used nets, not fishing poles. He watched the boy wash himself.

In the morning light his captive looked delicious. As they ate, he thrilled once more to the fact that the little body was his to do with exactly as he liked. It would take both of them a while to get used to that. The kid was wild enough so that he wouldn't accept that fundamental fact right away and may even fight back or think of, or even attempt, some kind of escape. He would accept the truth eventually, that his old life had stopped the moment he had wriggled over the side. It would take a while for him to understand what his new life as Jimmy's toy was going to be like. But, on the other hand, he seemed bright and may learn more quickly than that. Jimmy would do everything he could to help his very own slave-boy understand. When they had finished eating he took the plates below.

When he returned he gestured for him to stand up. He caressed and felt him slowly, enjoying the silky and unblemished skin. He kissed the two little burn marks which were already scabbed over. The boy was young and healed quickly. Then he slapped him hard across the face, getting a yelp of surprise. He wasn't a crazy Burmese and didn't intend to beat him, he just slapped him around for a few minutes to illustrate the fact that he could do nothing except take it. The kid put his arms up to try to fend off the slaps, but then Jimmy punched him and pulled them back down again. He had to do that twice more before he got the message, then he stood with his arms down and his eyes closed, wincing as the slaps hit

him. Jimmy turned him around and slapped the nice round cheeks, watching them quiver. He wanted that cute ass very badly and had to struggle to leave it alone. When he really couldn't stand it anymore then he would fuck it. But not quite yet.

After that he gave the little body the licking and sucking treatment again, taking it slowly until the kid whimpered and came. When he had tasted all he wanted he pushed him down, took his aching cock out, and pushed it against the guy's lips. He understood what he wanted him to do, all right, but he wouldn't open his mouth until Jimmy had slapped him around some more. He sucked very badly, cooperating only as much as he was made to do and doing that not at all well. Watching himself in the small mouth excited Jimmy anyway, and he came quickly. The kid choked at once but Jimmy held his head on it. He started to gag but Jimmy pinched his nostrils closed so he was forced to swallow it instead of trying to spit it out. There was a quick convulsion as he tried to throw up but Jimmy kept pressed tight. When he felt him swallow he let go his nostrils. He would learn. Slowly, perhaps, but he would learn. His come was in this end today. Tomorrow he would give it to him in the other end as well. He let the kid alone for the rest of the day. At suppertime he fixed a big meal and the boy ate everything on his plate.

When he woke in the morning he stretched luxuriously. This was what he had been anticipating: de-flowering day. At least he hoped that's what it would be. He was almost sure of the guy's virginity. He went to his Toy-Box and got out the lube, then he fixed some breakfast. When he first saw the kid he thought he was okay looking, but after getting more intimate with him he seemed to be more attractive. He went over him again, as slowly and thoroughly as before. His prisoner knew what to anticipate now, and what pleasure he could expect from it, and was hard. Jimmy was excited too but was going to wait.

Before any more playing around he got out the charts. The wind held steady and the weather remained excellent. He couldn't just sail around in circles, however. There were enough supplies in the lockers to last a while yet, even taking the ever-

hungry kid into account. Still, much of his attention had to remain on the boat itself rather than his prisoner. He got out the sextant and shot the sun at midday then laid out the course.

He had spent a lot of money for detailed charts precisely because he was going to so many out of the way places, and now he was looking for one very much out of the way: a bump of an island somewhere, too small to support any inhabitants yet large enough to have a lagoon and not too distant. Trees and water would be a bonus.

After searching carefully he thought he found exactly what he wanted. Even on the small-scale chart it wasn't much more than a dot in a ring indicating a coral atoll, and didn't even have a name. The ring looked like an anchorage. Well, he would find out. At about a week's sail it was the closest one of the right size, and another day's sail beyond it lay an island large enough to be populated, where more stores probably could be obtained when needed. The dot wouldn't have any water on it, he was certain, but a ground-sheet laid out during the frequent squalls should provide that without any problems. Satisfied, he laid out the course, checked the bearings, and set the wheel.

Through all this the boy had been watching him, curious but silent. Being a seafarer he probably had a general idea of where they were even though many miles lay between their present position and the spot where his ship had been sunk. That was all he was going to get, too. It was highly unlikely that he could read charts, if he could read anything at all, and the marks on the paper would mean nothing to him.

Once those necessary things were done he got some lunch for them, and when that was finished he washed him thoroughly. The kid kept himself clean enough for all practical purposes, but not quite clean enough to chew on, so Jimmy did that. Later he could clean himself but right now he enjoyed scrubbing down the sleek little body. Now Jimmy was going to wash his ass for the first time and discover what lay between those nice round cheeks. He had to kick him some more to do it, but he got the boy to lie face down and spread his legs. Jimmy held his breath in hope, then spread the cheeks apart.

Bingo! A small, tight, dark-brown button stared back at him from the almost hairless cleft. It was possible that he wasn't

actually virgin but there was no evidence that he had ever been bounced on the way the island boys were. Small island boys had small buttons, to be sure, but not as small as virgins. In the last six months Jimmy had seen a lot of them and considered himself as expert on brown bottoms as any westerner was likely to get. Small Asian cocks don't stretch small holes much, but the island boys loosened quickly once they were gotten into. Monkey-boy, of course, was in a class by himself. This one didn't look like that at all. It would take a lot of forcing to get into that little thing and he could hardly wait.

He washed the behind carefully with soap and water. The cheeks felt perfect, still young enough to be plump with a layer of boy-fat, yet firm with the muscle of an active life. He lay down behind him and between his legs, separated the cheeks again, then put his face between them to sample him. There was a sharp exclamation of surprise and the kid tried to look back over his shoulder to see what was going on. Jimmy would have laughed if he hadn't been so busy.

This was one of the things he had been waiting for, the eating for the first time of his own boy who had never had it done before. The island kids had loved having it done to them, of course, but it wasn't the same at all. He pulled the boy's hips up to get at him better. After a minute or two the boy sighed and raised himself higher. Jimmy started pushing in the tip of his tongue and the kid opened up for him as much as a virgin could, which wasn't much at all. By now he heard some gasps of pleasure. Slave-boy relaxed fully and pushed back to take more. Jimmy felt between his legs and found him hard.

He worked on him a little bit more then reached for the lube. He spread some around between the cheeks, lubricated his finger, then pushed it into the hot little body. The guy jumped and gasped in surprise. It certainly stung the tender flesh and he tried to pull away. Jimmy kept pushing until he was in him up to the knuckle, then he wiggled it. The boy gasped again, probably never having felt anything that strange in his life. Jimmy doubted if it hurt him much. Even if it did he didn't care because the boy had a considerably larger surprise waiting. He pulled his finger out, added more lube, then pushed it back in again. A few minutes more had him thoroughly lubricated.

By this time Jimmy was very excited. He put lots of lube on

himself and a dab more between the boy's cheeks, then he moved up. He looked enormous next to the boy's narrow hips but he was going in him anyway. The kid looked back over his shoulder again to see what the pause meant. When he saw Jimmy's greased erection and the obvious target he cried out and started to struggle. Jimmy held him down firmly, placed himself at the right spot, then clasped him tight. He pushed and the boy gasped to catch a breath, clenching very tight to keep him out. He pushed again and kept pushing, steadily and firmly without actually jabbing. He wanted to fuck him, not rip him. If he did that then he wouldn't be able to have him again for some time until it healed for fear of infection. He knew he wouldn't be able to wait for that so he was determined to be careful from the beginning.

It was very difficult and extremely slow. All his being demanded that he ram himself right in, just as this little guy and his nasty friends probably had done to the women and boys on the ships they plundered. Unlike them, Jimmy was thinking of tomorrow instead of just today, and he certainly wasn't going throw his new slave-boy to any sharks. Not on your life. It was a strain for him but obviously getting agonizing for the kid, who started to pant with pain and with the effort of keeping clenched. There is no way that a really hard dick can be kept out of a well-greased butt, however, no matter how determined the possessor of it to avoid being possessed. Jimmy stayed very excited, getting hotter by the minute, and kept pushing. The muscles of the kid's sphincter weakened, then they got tired, then the skin started to stretch, as it had to, as it was made to. If virgins like this really were as tiny as they looked and couldn't be stretched then they wouldn't even be able to shit.

It took him almost an hour of unrelenting pressure. The kid began to yell as Jimmy finally forced a bit into him. The boy was so hot and so tight that he almost came but he strained to hold himself back. The kid yelled even louder then started gasping for breath, wiggling violently trying to get away from the thing that was spreading him open and going into him, but Jimmy held him in a death-grip. He wanted to have a virgin and that's what he intended to get. He could feel him stretching. Nobody before had been this tight and this

wonderful.

He had only a third of it in him but suddenly he couldn't hold back any longer and throbbed over and over again, shaking like a malaria victim. Just as he did so the kid's body gave up trying to keep him out and to his surprise he slipped in the rest of the way until he lay flat on the quivering back, buried deep. That was truly a surprise. Asians rarely could take more than half before it hit bottom.

The boy gasped, got a look on his face of utter astonishment, then twitched all over as he came in one sharp pulse after another. Jimmy was equally surprised, and lay there, unable to thrust one more time. His victim was so tight that it felt as though he had a very strong hand around it, squeezing it as hard as possible. He felt continual spasms inside as the little body tried to eject what had entered it so forcibly. It had the reverse affect. The sphincter's tight grasp prevented him from going soft and the constant spasms inside kept it hard.

The boy yelled and begged, trying to get him to pull it out. He struggled violently, trying to get from underneath Jimmy's heavier body. There was to be none of that, however. He was staying hard and he remained with his belly glued tight to the kid's butt. Scream as he might, this little pirate was going to get truly fucked.

As soon as he got his breath back that's what he did. The kid had been forced to take him and take him he had. He also had taken all of it, too, very deep for such a little body and Jimmy couldn't get over it. He must have filled the small rectum at once, then without feeling any barrier had gone through the second sphincter as well, right up into the kid's gut. As soon as that had happened then the boy had arched in repeated orgasm, and that had been the best surprise of all. His slave-boy turned out to be a genuine anal-sensitive, something the kid probably hadn't realized before. He could take it all, and it made him come. There was no question about it, this boy was made to be fucked!

He began a slow and careful screwing. It was so wonderful that he knew he'd come again soon if he tried anything faster, and the kid would be rubbed raw as well. The boy alternated more yells with some odd sounds, partly beggings, partly curses, Jimmy suspected. He moved steadily in him. His

6

After coming twice Jimmy did soften, and hard contractions forced him out immediately, followed by a sharp spurt out of the kid. Jimmy got up the minute he pulled free and moved well out of the boy's reach. He didn't want his eyes clawed out while he rested. His dick felt raw but wonderful and he lay back with a sigh. The boy just lay where he left him, sobbing and moaning, partly in pain and probably partly in shock at his own intense reaction. Those had been two of the biggest and most intense orgasms Jimmy had ever experienced. He had lain on his virgin boy's round behind, forced himself in against strong resistance, and felt marvellous. Even Mike hadn't been this good, and even Mike hadn't come without touching himself when he was fucked.

Jimmy had enjoyed Mike very much, but this brown savage was truly his ideal. All he had dreamed about for years was something just like this. When a slave-boy had dropped into his lap as a gift from the gods, so to speak, who was he to reject it: and especially one with a hyper-sensitive ass who could take it all. He didn't feel the need to justify himself. He could just as easily have shot him in the water and he'd be several days dead. Also, he had just given back a little of what he probably had helped to dish out as a youthful pirate. Served him right. Jimmy laughed out loud at himself. He actually tingled and felt wonderful.

He sat up and looked at the kid and the boy squatted, looked back at him, trying hard to look blank and unconcerned that he had just been raped. He probably stung like fire, too, but that wasn't as bad as the humiliation he probably felt. Undoubtedly he was thinking of all the wonderful slow ways to kill him if he got the chance. That chance would never come. Too bad, Jimmy thought. The guy didn't know it yet, but there would be a lot more for him to take. Even as small as he was, he was wiry and strong, but if he could possibly have overcome him he would have done so. He hadn't been able to, no matter how much he struggled. All Jimmy needed to be cautious of now

was surprise. A foot in his balls would feel nasty. Suddenly there was a splurt and liquid shot out of the boy onto the deck. He had never seen an oriental blush before, and for a fleeting moment he almost liked him, a well-fucked kid rather than a murderous savage. He grinned and the boy looked away, crying in double-humiliation. He'd been raped and it had turned him on!

Jimmy still felt euphoric at suppertime, sexually and emotionally satisfied, and perfectly content. When he handed the boy his plate he accepted it at once with no theatrical western-type gesture like throwing it in his face. Asians were eminently practical. Food was food. Anyway, Jimmy would have slapped him silly if he had done anything like that and the kid probably knew it. Perhaps the boy hadn't realized before how much stronger Jimmy was and probably hadn't even thought about it. He knew now, though, and knew as well that if Jimmy wanted him again right then he could have done it. If he could have gotten hard again he would have, too, but he was fully satisfied. For today, anyway.

He took their plates below and brought back a tube of ointment. He showed it to him, put a little on his finger, then rubbed it on the back of the kid's hand so he could feel that it was cool and smooth. He put more on his finger and reached between the kid's legs to rub it on his undoubtedly sore butt. The kid realized what he was doing and didn't protest. The little opening was clenched tighter now than it had been before, however, as if the boy feared he would stick a finger into him again. He didn't. Another time, but not right now. He wasn't being humanitarian, he was being careful. He rubbed the ointment in well.

He rode his prisoner the next morning right after breakfast. The minute he greased himself the kid knew what he was going to get and shook his head and started gabbling. Jimmy gestured for him to lie down then encouraged him with a hard slap. He had to encourage him some more by grabbing him and throwing him down heavily. The boy gasped what must be the Vietnamese equivalent of no-no-no and wriggled desperately to keep from going underneath him but Jimmy pinned him, panting yes-yes-yes. He searched between the kid's cheeks then

he pushed.

It took almost as long to get in him this time as it had before. The boy seemed determined not to yell again but he couldn't help it as he was penetrated. Since Jimmy knew from last time that he was built to take all of it, he went into him very slowly but completely. Because he was aware of what was happening this time he could feel himself go through the second sphincter until his belly was tight against the firm butt. The moment he got there then the boy groaned and pulsed in sharp orgasm.

Jimmy rested a minute to let him get as used to it as he could and tremble less, then he rode him slowly and deliciously. The little ass was just as tight and hot as before. Having been invaded once it adapted slightly better, too, although it obviously still hurt the boy to be stretched so much because he yelled a lot. Jimmy was in heaven and stayed as he was, moving slowly as he floated on a cloud for some time. Eventually the kid gasped and came a second time, and when he did then Jimmy couldn't hold himself any longer. He gave a few sharp thrusts then did likewise. He lay panting on the boy's back, trying to recover his breath.

They ate then Jimmy took a noon sight and checked the charts again. They were running briskly now before a freshening wind and making good knots, enough to make that island landfall in the time he had allowed. He thought about that for a while, then made a decision. He trimmed sail and changed course. The objective was going to be the same, but by the time he got there he knew he wanted his slave-boy to be thoroughly broken in, then there would be fewer problems. In the confines of the boat it was simple to manage him. On an island, who could tell.

The next several days were even better, almost a dream. He ate him all over. The kid liked that well enough, but when he greased up then the boy started to shake and cry. He had to hold him down, struggling and yelling, then he forced himself up into the wonderfully tight behind. It was going to take a lot more than a few days to loosen this kid, and he continued to yell and cry as Jimmy continued to hurt him. It was rape, plain and simple. Hurt or not, though, the boy was so anal-sensitive that taking it made him come hard, sometimes twice, and

As a navigator Jimmy was fairly good, but this time he was perfect. Late in the afternoon two days after Surrender Day an imperfection appeared on the horizon on the port quarter, which the glass showed to be palm trees on a flat little atoll barely clear of the sea. With the good breeze they were enjoying they would make it before dark.

The boy shouted to get his attention then chattered something which Jimmy didn't understand, pointing to the horizon astern. He looked and could just barely make out a rim of dark cloud. The glass didn't help much but the kid seemed to think it meant something. If it came quickly and was bad then they would have to run before it, island or no island.

The extra few knots the freshening breeze gave them made all the difference and their landfall became distinct, a tiny atoll indeed. The thick dark rim on the horizon astern had expanded and now covered much of the western sky. Jimmy didn't think it would threaten them before he could make the lagoon, assuming he could get into it. The boy was getting increasingly nervous, however, feeling the wire around his foot and pacing quickly back and forth.

Jimmy made one circuit of the reef in order to find a passage but could see nothing from the wheel except surf. He was going to need help, especially with the threat of those clouds and the approaching storm. He looked at the boy and the boy looked at him. Well, they needed each other now. He got the key and unfastened the padlocks quickly, then pointed to the mast then at the surf. The boy understood him at once and quickly shinnied up the mast. On their second circuit the kid chattered excitedly and pointed. Jimmy could see nothing but the kid obviously had. Jimmy lashed the wheel and beckoned him back down to help lower sail. Western rigging was strange to him, of course, but a boat is a boat and he figured enough of it out quickly to be of help.

Jimmy started the engine then got the lead out of the locker. A new boat would have bottom sonar but he hadn't been able

to afford that so this one had to be managed as ships had been handled for a thousand years. The boy knew what it was and took it at once, his small naked body hanging precariously over the starboard bow as Jimmy engaged the engine.

From the wheel he followed the boy's gestures closely. The breeze had died suddenly to an ominous calm that he didn't like at all. They had to get into the lagoon quickly or else turn about and run before the wind, which was sure to rise fast. The kid started heaving the lead. He had sense enough not to sing out numbers which Jimmy wouldn't understand but instead held up fingers. Then he saw the narrow gap in the reef that the boy's sharp eyes had spotted earlier. He hoped it would be deep enough for them to clear. Going dead-slow with just enough way to keep control, he sent the bow into it, keeping his fingers crossed. The slack jib flapped noisily. Wash from the surf to either side buffeted them about a little but he managed to center it with a little luck and a prayer, then on the next surge they rushed through to quiet water.

The boy also had experience enough to stay on the lead, signalling the lagoon depth at frequent intervals. Jimmy breathed a sigh of relief as it deepened suddenly. There would be sea-room after all, and he cut the engine. He and the boy dropped anchors fore and aft, lashed all sail, and began securing everything else securable. If the wind was too strong and the anchors dragged too much then the boat was lost, either bashing itself against the reef or being thrown on shore. But with luck the reef would take the brunt and the lagoon would be a refuge rather than a trap.

Jimmy opened some cans and fixed them a quick meal, then they sat to watch and wait. He didn't have time to think that this dangerous kid was loose, and perhaps the boy didn't have time to worry about the round-eye devil, either. They were just a man and a boy waiting together for what looked like a bad storm. The wind picked up quickly, hot, muggy, and almost unbreathable. Jimmy made a quick last check, then secured the hatch to below. There was nothing else to be done.

Except one thing, and he cursed himself for being stupid. He ripped open the hatch quickly, whistled to the boy to help, and dashed below, the both of them coming back up a minute later with the canvas bag containing the inflatable dingy. The boy

had no idea what it was but did what he could. Jimmy opened it, pulled the folded rubber out, then dashed below again to start the engine. The damn foot pump would take time and there was little of that left. He ran up an air-hose and inflated the dingy quickly. He gestured to the boy, who then understood what was happening, and he went below to secure the engine while the kid started tying down the dingy with quick and efficient movements.

When Jimmy returned and secured the hatch again the job was done. Just in time. The wind now shrieked through the rigging and the palms on the little island were dancing hard. The roar of the surf got louder, then much louder. The boy nudged him and handed him the end of a rope. Jimmy saw that the other end was secured to the mast, something else he forgot. He nodded in approval and tied it around his waist. It seemed unlikely that there would be waves in the lagoon high enough to wash them over, but with the high winds which threatened they might be doing a lot of dancing about on a slick deck before they were through. The boy fastened himself as well.

Then it hit. Rain like a solid wall swept over them until they were streaming and gasping for breath. The rigging sang like a demented choir until the roar of the surf against the reef drowned it and everything else out. It lasted many hours.

It wasn't as bad a typhoon as they would get when the season really hit. If it had been then they would have lost the boat and might be dead. As it was they dragged anchor perilously close to the reef and Jimmy was almost ready to cut the lines securing the dingy so that they might have some chance to survive. It took all night to blow itself out. By that time he was thoroughly exhausted and had been frightened out of his wits. During the worst of it the boy had turned white then had clutched him tight, which is exactly what Jimmy needed – to be forced to be protective rather than getting terrified about himself. During the night the ceaselessly heavy rain had turned chill and they shivered against each other. The boy's nakedness felt cold so Jimmy held him tight and kept rubbing him.

They must have slept. Sunlight woke him as the clouds

disappeared to the east to give some other poor devils trouble. The boy was wrapped in his arms. He found that pleasant and held him like that for a while until his bladder was about to burst. He shook the kid a little to wake him up, then the boy unwrapped and they stood side by side and pissed into the lagoon. Jimmy pulled off his wet clothes and threw them over the boom then took the boy below with him to help get breakfast. There was a lot of sloshing in the bilges and some water underfoot but they really had shipped very little, considering. The boy hadn't seen a western-style galley before and was fascinated, opening tins and smelling everything he could get his nose into. The pepper-tin cured him of that. On board the kind of ship he was used to there would be an open fire on a bed of banked earth on the afterdeck, tended continuously by the cook. The blue flame of bottled gas was beyond his comprehension, although he could tell that it was fire of some kind, probably cursed. Jimmy was starving and assumed the boy was too so he dug deep into his stores. They went back on deck and sat to eat. This time he was as greedy as the boy, though he didn't lick his plate.

It was then that he noticed the end of the piano wire, still attached to the stanchion. He went to his drying pants, dug out the key, and unlocked the other end of it as the kid watched him closely, then he threw it overboard and the key with it. The boy had surrendered and he wouldn't have made it through that storm without his help, either. The kid had earned something better than slave-boy. When he turned back he saw the kid was looking at him, then the boy nodded as Jimmy had nodded to him earlier, in approval. He dug out the waterproof cigarette packet and gravely handed one to the boy then took one for himself. They smoked quietly. When he was done he looked at the butt deliberately, looked at the boy, then flipped it into the lagoon. That business was ended. He held his arm out toward the kid. The boy looked at him, then touched the coal to his arm once, so quickly that Jimmy hardly noticed, then that cigarette followed, making another hiss in the water. Peace was declared.

It was already past mid-day and there was lots to do. Jimmy went below and kicked the engine to life, then engaged the

pump to clear the bilges while the boy washed their plates. While the pump was doing its job the boy helped him unlash the dingy, then they went ashore to see what their tiny kingdom was like. There were a few palms down and ripped-off fronds were scattered all over, but the storm hadn't been severe enough to do really ruinous damage. They walked across it in half an hour, finding the tree-cover thin and not a great deal of shrubbery, although the island was longer than they thought. There were acres enough to sustain several families had there been enough soil, but that was as thin as the trees, with numerous coral outcrops. The storm had left a number of fresh-water pools. Knowing they would evaporate fairly quickly, they brought plastic jugs ashore and topped up their supply of drinking water.

A coral atoll was essentially strange to Jimmy, though he had visited many, but the boy appeared to feel entirely at home, poking here and there, seeking anything useful. Fishermen visited the place frequently, as Jimmy saw, because the kid pointed out old mats, some broken bottles, and remains of what had been temporary huts. The quick tour told them as much as they wanted to know. As he had suspected from the beginning there was no fresh water except what rains might bring, and if anyone had to live on this place who didn't like an exclusive diet of fish then he would be in a bad way.

The thought of fish took them back to the boat where Jimmy dug out his tackle. The boy had no idea what the sticks and strings were until Jimmy hauled up something large and very brightly colored that he couldn't identify. The boy did, though, and clapped his hands, smiling broadly and licking his lips. At last, something real to eat instead of tasteless Western canned food. Jimmy got a knife for him without hesitation and continued to fish as the boy gutted their catch neatly and quickly. They took their fish ashore so that they could build a fire to cook it the way the boy wanted. They both ate a great deal and he thought the kid would burst. It did taste very good.

He had brought a bottle ashore too, and ceremoniously poured a little whisky for each of them. The boy smelled it curiously. It wasn't palm or rice wine and made his nose wrinkle. He watched Jimmy closely, and when he tossed it

down then the boy did the same. Jimmy thought the kid would explode right before his eyes. His eyes watered and he coughed and gasped then sat stunned for a moment, feeling his stomach. Jimmy knew that he was feeling the fire spread. Plainly he had never tried anything as strong as a good single-malt. After a second one a while later, Jimmy knew that the kid had enough. More than enough, actually. Whatever really went through the boy's mind that night he had no way of knowing. What he did know, however, was that the kid lay down on his belly, gave him a look, then wiggled his behind for him, wanting it. He accepted the offer before the boy sobered enough to change his mind. He didn't have any lube but he used lots of saliva.

He was very slow and careful and the boy was just drunk and relaxed enough so that he got in him with only one shriek and a few muffled gasps. He had never had sex quite like it before. The kid was every bit as hot and tight as he had been, though the liquor made him able to take it much more easily. The gesture of acceptance Jimmy had made by throwing that wire overboard and taking the burn was now being returned. He was careful but he wasn't quick. The kid squealed when he came, then shortly after Jimmy did likewise, with a bang. He sighed with regret when a spasm forced him out, but he kept his arms around him and the boy made no attempt to pull away.

As pleasant as the night, the embers, and the wonderfully satisfying sex all were, he didn't want to sleep on the beach all night to be nibbled by curious or even hungry crabs. The boy was no help at all returning in the dingy. Halfway back he moved fast to hang his bottom over the side, then spurt sharply into the water. He giggled helplessly all the rest of the way. Jimmy had to goose him hard to get him over the side onto the deck, where he promptly threw up, then he took him below. Since he didn't have to stay by the wheel he could sleep for once in his bunk. He tumbled the boy into the one opposite then crawled into his own. He stretched and yawned. The kid was already snoring lightly.

He smiled to himself. The surrender to assault was one thing, but the fact that the Asian boy had wiggled his ass for him still surprised him. It was a lovely, satisfying fuck, too. This was

turning out differently than he had planned. He was awakened briefly sometime later when a small warm body crept into his bunk with him. In large families or on ship the kids never slept alone but always huddled together like a pack of dogs. He held the boy to him, listening to the soft slap of water against the hull, then he slept again.

They pissed together over the side in the morning, then washed. The boy started cleaning himself but Jimmy took the soap from him and did it instead. He liked feeling the warm slippery skin under his hands. The kid enjoyed the attention to his body, especially when Jimmy washed between his legs. Then they had breakfast.

There were a few chores Jimmy wanted to do, like patching the bullet-holes in the sails before they frayed any more, and touching up where paint had been worn and chipped, but he felt lazy and just lay on deck instead, much preferring to watch the kid fish. He dozed a little, then found the boy was squatting close to him, looking him up and down. The examination proceeded more intimately as the small warm hands started to feel and investigate. The boy seemed determined to find out what this pale-skinned yellow-haired round-eye was made of, all over. He didn't miss a thing, either.

Jimmy had no idea how the boy felt about what his exploration had discovered, but when he lay down again he took Jimmy's dick firmly in his hands and began jerking him off. When he knew Jimmy was going to come, the boy put his mouth over the end as Jimmy shot with a sharp gasp. When the kid had it all he pulled back, gave Jimmy a deliberate look to make sure he was watching, then swallowed. There was some reflex gagging and he almost brought it back up, but with tears in his eyes he swallowed hard again to keep it. Then he raised his eyebrows in query. Jimmy smiled and nodded, then the boy grinned and nodded back.

Language lessons began the same day. At first Jimmy would give an English word, then wait for the Vietnamese equivalent. The boy shook his head and frowned at that. He wasn't interested in his past, just his future. Jimmy liked that. He drilled him over and over with words indicating direction, size,

shape, hot and cold, until the boy parroted them well enough, then he would point, waiting for him to repeat. He got most of them after a few days of drill, frowning with the mental effort. Following that, they went on to the really important things.

"Jimmy," Jimmy said later, pointing to himself.

"Chimmy," the boy repeated, solemnly, "Chimmy."

"Tommy," Jimmy said, then pointed to the boy, giving him a western name.

"Tomeh," the boy said, pointing to himself, then he giggled. "Tomeh, Chimmy," and he pointed to each of them. Jimmy nodded.

"Cock," he said, touch both his own and the boy's.

"Cock," the kid replied, having no trouble with that one.

"Balls," was next.

"Bawsss."

He reached between the boy's cheeks and named what he touched.

"Asshoe," Tommy echoed.

There was much more as Jimmy continued the lessons, speaking slowly and pointing at everything referred to. There were demonstrations as well, of every activity they had engaged in for the last several weeks, until Tommy finally had words to describe what they had been doing together. He lay back, his lips moving slowly as he recounted for himself the new words he had learned. After a while he looked at him. "Jimmy big bawsss, big cock. Tomeh small." he said with a worried frown.

"Small, but mmmmmmmm," Jimmy reassured him, licking his lips, and the boy grinned.

He decided that Tommy was of unusual, even exceptional, rational mind. His thoughts seemed to be turning over all the time, weighing his situation and his prospects. Jimmy tried to think those same thoughts and came up with what probably was the same answers. He was far from home and by now had no idea where. His comrades were dead, and if he did get back to his village he could only scrape the barest kind of living. The round-eye Chimmy hadn't killed him or even hurt him, except a little. The cigarette-burns had hurt less than coral scrapes, and he had been slapped around enough as a child by older boys to have learned to shrug it off. There couldn't be a greater

excitement than the one he felt when Jimmy ate him, and so often, too. Taking the round-eye in him still hurt but it made him come like a fountain and he was proud that he could do it. Besides, it didn't hurt as much now as it did the first time. If he treated the round-eye well then he was sure he would get treated well in return. Today was good, tomorrow seemed secure, and next week was a distant future beyond his ken.

Before they went to sleep each night Tommy rolled over and Jimmy took him slowly and luxuriously. When Jimmy wanted sucking then all he had to do was wave it and the boy would grin and trot over to him at once. At first he was just doing his duty, like taking it up his butt every night. After a while there was a noticeable change in interest and Jimmy didn't have to wave it any more. Tommy would stare at him, particularly when he was moving around and he flopped from side to side. Tommy would snap up, then he would come over to feel it. "Big," he would say, then kneel to take it soft, working it up in his mouth as he played with himself, and not letting him go until they both had come. It seemed that Tommy was beginning to like it, a change Jimmy heartily approved of. More often than not they ended lying down together. When Tommy was fully sensitized he'd push bits of himself between Jimmy's lips for nibbles.

As much as he enjoyed playing with his little Asian, Jimmy's true release came when he lay on the hot round behind. Feeling that furnace-like little body grip all of him so tightly was so intense a pleasure that he couldn't describe it. When he came he felt as he'd never stop, and he'd feel Tommy trembling beneath him as the boy had his own orgasm. Each night Tommy crawled into his bunk with him and the little warm body lay close. That was very nice. Very nice indeed.

By the end of a week their supplies were getting low, even with the addition of a considerable amount of fish. It was time to go to that larger island and see what could be gotten. There would be fuel for the motors of fishing boats, he was certain, and other essentials as well, but he wanted to have enough freedom so that if they were short or lacked something then he could move on quickly to the next landfall to find what they

needed. He got out the charts and had Tommy sit with him as he explained what they were. The boy wrinkled his brow for some time, concentrating hard, then slowly the form of the chart and its purpose was understood and he grinned and clapped his hands.

"We are here," Jimmy pointed out, "and we are going to go there tomorrow," and he pointed to the next island.

"Big place, eh?" the boy said. His vocabulary increased daily. "Now I can fuck!" which was something which hadn't crossed Jimmy's mind.

With all the sex and with his intense love-affair with the boy's hot little body he had neglected to consider that Tommy might want to do the same. He felt jealous then immediately felt guilty about that.

"Probably," he said with a smile. "We'll have to wear clothes."

Then he remembered that the boy didn't have any. He'd cut down a pair of dungarees in the morning for him.

"Hate clothes," Tommy complained, but wore them anyway.

The hundred or so inhabitants of the larger island turned out to be farmers and lagoon fishers, not high-seas fishermen. There was a village and a wharf, and luckily he was able to buy just enough of what they needed in the way of supplies at the trading-shack, although he had to pay more for fuel than he wanted. There was no bottled gas, however, so they would be forced to make fires on shore all the time instead. That was no real hardship and the boy was used to it anyway. He bought rice and Tommy stuffed himself greedily with expressions of great satisfaction. The place lay on a well-travelled inter-island shipping lane so they weren't exactly curiosities, although a small Vietnamese was strange to them.

Tommy nudged Jimmy when he saw a likely looking girl. Jimmy was surprised a second, then not. Tommy's curse (Jimmy would call it a blessing) was to be extraordinarily anal-sensitive, having a persistent itch no girl would ever be able to scratch satisfactorily. Aside from that his urges would be unexceptional. The kid made some gestures meant to attract but which really were grossly obscene. He got lots of giggles but one girl fluttered her eyelashes at him. Tommy grinned and

disappeared for a while, returning later with a smile on his face.

"Fuck two time," he said with satisfaction. "Velly good." Back on board for the night, Tommy felt and caressed him. "That girl nice but not make me come like you. Fuck me now, huh?" and Jimmy did. The return trip was uneventful but pleasant.

Several days later when Jimmy was down below he heard a sharp shout from Tommy above. He went up quickly and the boy pointed to a sail on the horizon. Jimmy thought it unlikely that there would be any pirates in these parts but it paid to be cautious and careful. He started the engine and they raised anchor to move to a position exactly opposite the narrow entrance through the reef, then anchored again. Anyone attempting to enter the lagoon would have to come right at them and get raked. He got out the M-16 and handed it to the boy. Tommy stripped and checked it expertly, then loaded a magazine and laid others close by. Jimmy got out the grenade-launcher and placed some rounds where he could reach them easily, then they got a quick lunch and waited. It would be a while yet before the sailing vessel could spot their bare mast against the palm trees.

It was two hours before the ship got close enough to be examined in detail through the glass. Jimmy passed it to Tommy so he could give a more expert opinion than his own. The boy turned and grinned.

"Fish-boat," he said, handing him the glass. Jimmy took another look and saw that they had taken so long to come up because they had nets and swimmers out with a crowd of boys in the water. Typical of such ships, there were at least two hundred on board, all working hard. Tommy sighed. "Much fuck tonight," he said, and grinned widely.

It wasn't precisely like that but close enough so as not to matter much. The fishing boat anchored in deep water for the night. He and Tommy got out the dingy and went out for a visit. The fishermen made them welcome enough and were obviously inoffensive islanders of the kind Jimmy had gotten used to at the beginning of his voyage. He could even understand some of their dialect and they were pleased that a

westerner could speak with them. Tommy couldn't understand anything but Jimmy kept a running translation. The kid would screw almost anything that would lie still long enough. His grinning interest in the ship's large crop of boys got a lot of giggles and stares, and when Jimmy rose after a while to piss over the side he got a lot of interest as well.

The fishermen were simple and unsophisticated folk and the more elaborate things that he and Tommy went through now and enjoyed so much were outside these men's experience. They fucked but they didn't suck and weren't interested. When it started to get dark the men and boys went to their mats to huddle together, then Jimmy and Tommy made their way back to their own boat, both worn out.

"Velly nice," Tommy sighed as he crawled into Jimmy's bunk and lay close. The water lapped against the side of the boat. "Those boy any good?" he asked, snuggling tight.

"You're better," he replied. "Much, much better."

"Damn right," the boy said.

8

"We can't stay here," Jimmy said after a few more weeks. It had been ideal but they had been very lucky with the weather.

"Why not?" Tommy asked. "Lots fish." He rubbed against him. "Lots Tommy. You like lots Tommy."

"Yes," Jimmy agreed, "and very nice, too, but more storms will be coming soon. Sooner or later we'll get a bad typhoon here." He had been listening to weather reports on a daily basis and it was obvious that the season would soon be on them.

"No typhoon now," Tommy said, groping him.

He looked down to watch it harden then pulled him to the deck. It was hot and nice, but afterward Jimmy insisted that he look at the chart with him and stop fooling around.

"If we get a really bad storm the boat will be wrecked," he said, "and not a palm tree will be left on the island." Tommy nodded reluctantly in agreement. "The lagoon simply isn't big

enough to be safe. We've been lucky so far."

And they had. Only once had they had to put out to sea to run before a bad wind that otherwise might have done them damage. Fortunately it had blown itself out almost as quickly as it had appeared on the horizon. As a matter of routine they had kept a storm watch, but Jimmy was thinking mainly now of night when they might be surprised by something they couldn't handle. The typhoon season hadn't actually started but it would be on them soon.

"Where we go, then?" the boy asked.

"There's nowhere absolutely safe, as you know," Jimmy said. "But at least we can join a settlement for a while so that if anything happens we'll be able to have help around us. Supplies, too."

They had been back and forth to the larger island every ten days or so, mostly for supplies but partly for a little social life for them both. Tommy would search out his island girl and Jimmy found a nicely built young man who usually had a girl-wife close by him but whose eyes kept dropping to his crotch. When the fellow was looking one time and no one else was, Jimmy contrived to give him a peek. The young man tried to pretend he hadn't seen it, but that night he left his little wife long enough to find him in the dark. He gasped sharply at first but then moaned happily as Jimmy bounced on him for an hour. The guy wasn't the heaving, gasping, wiggling and totally inspirational hot juicy fuck that Tommy was rapidly growing to be, but he surely wanted it and Jimmy surely gave it to him.

Before Jimmy had pulled him from the sea, Tommy had always been integrated tightly into the usual family and village unit like one dog in a pack. Not having that kind of interdependent support around him now, Jimmy took its place, and because he was only one instead of many the association had to be tighter. Whenever he looked up the boy was never more than a few arm-lengths away. Jimmy hadn't experienced that kind of closeness and absolute intimacy before, except for a few hours at a time in bed, and had to learn. He felt at first as though he was sharing a prison-cell twenty four hours a day, his fellow inmate aware of every fart, scratch, and blemish. It had its moments of raw irritation at first but he forced himself

The boy fished for three meals a day, although Jimmy never could get used to fish for breakfast and fixed his own instead. There were weather reports to check on the radio, then several hours were spent on English lessons and trying to teach the boy to read. Finally, after considerably pressure and sensible talk, Tommy sighed and agreed that they would have to go somewhere less precarious than their tiny atoll. He would not agree to go very far, however.

"This our place," he said as then were leaning together after supper. "I know all lagoon, want us close, to come back whenever we want. Even fish know me."

"You've dripped so much in that water that they're beginning to taste funny," Jimmy said. "Even the beach stinks. I bet you can smell this place miles out to sea."

"Good name. Come Island, then," Tommy said with a giggle, and pulled him back. "Eat Tomeh," he whispered into his ear. Jimmy did, until the boy got so sensitive he started to yell.

Within a week they had moved and reestablished themselves within walking distance of the village yet not too close. Unlike Come Island, the larger one had a few high rocky outcrops which made for a little variety in scenery, and fresh water as well. With some help from villagers they got the mast of the boat unstepped, then Jimmy had the hull winched out of the water and moved far up the beach for safety. He drained the engine and the fuel tank then transferred everything they wanted to a temporary shelter until they could build a better one.

They reorganized their life for the season. Tommy moaned and complained about wearing clothes but the villagers all did so they had to do so as well. Jimmy liked it even less because one of his pleasures was watching the slim naked body move, especially when the boy was unaware. It was his imagination, he suspected, but the boy's buns seemed to ripen daily, the cheeks to get fuller, practically glowing with independent life, demanding caresses and kisses. He was desperately and overwhelmingly in love with this boy's infinitely fuckable and deliciously edible behind. He wondered if Tommy understood what it did to him. Perhaps he did. He certainly understood

well enough Jimmy's addiction to the rest of his body, rubbing it against him all the time with a look of deep satisfaction.

One precaution Jimmy insisted upon was removal of the radio to a place as high up in the rocks as they could get, then a careful waterproofing of it and the emergency batteries. He thought it unlikely that such precautions would prove necessary but wanted to take no chances. Now that they were on more solid ground there was no need for daily reports anyway. What would come, would come.

They had occasional visitors. Jimmy's young man's little wife became obviously pregnant, but he came over at least once a week anyway. He liked giving it to the young man, mainly because it made him appreciate Tommy even more. Tommy's girl hadn't been able to wait until he showed up so she had seduced others and was getting what she wanted regularly from them. In spite of that she came over once in a while, probably because Tommy was much better.

9

The typhoon season came shortly after, and with a vengeance. There were two bad ones, like the Florida hurricanes Jimmy had experienced a few years ago, and they caused a lot of superficial damage. The frame buildings in the village weren't hurt much but a lot of huts went down, their own included. They were simple to rebuild, however, and such damage was a part of life here.

It was the next one, a month later, which was worse than anything Jimmy had ever experienced and terrified everyone into screaming fits. Tommy screamed too, almost without stopping, and clutched him so tightly he could hardly breathe. The rain was devastating and the wind unbelievable. Every hut was flattened and half the palms went down. The solidly built trading shack and the village school both lost their roofs, and Jimmy's boat was thrown off its chocks onto its beam-ends and almost wrecked. Four villagers were killed by flying debris and many injured.

Jimmy had grabbed Tommy at once the moment he sensed

it was going to be very bad, and went up to the higher rocks away from trees and wind-borne missiles. He held the boy tight against him in a cleft he had found weeks before and had noted in his mind. They got soaked to the bone and it seemed they would drown in the quantity of rain. It was like trying to breathe normally while in a combination shower and steambath. It took two days to blow itself out, leaving them and everyone else so exhausted that when it was over everyone collapsed into a drugged sleep and no one moved for a long time.

At the moment they finally realized that the danger had passed, Jimmy found the boy staring at him, his eyes very wide. Even as worn out as he was, the kid called upon some reserve of energy right then to kiss him all over as if to reassure himself that he was still in one piece. It wasn't sexual but it was completely demanding and then Jimmy understood that now Tommy felt as strongly about him as he did about Tommy. It wasn't western sentimental romance at all. Far from it. It was possession.

It had been an education for him to learn how other peoples devoid of western sentiment felt. He came to understand family interdependence and complete and unquestioning personal surrender. Now, with Tommy in his arms, clinging to him like a mad thing, he knew that whatever barrier might still have lain between them, however slight, was gone. Whatever terrors and mental wounds they suffered from the storm simply melted away. They had each other, which they discovered was everything that was really important to either of them. It was then that Jimmy finally understood deep in his gut that his former life was over, too. Finished. He could never leave this wonderful boy. Never.

After a quick trip to the village to see about the boat and find out what help they could be, Jimmy unpacked the radio and managed to contact the mainland. The radio in the trading shack had been ruined when the roof went off. There was a great deal of damage over a wide area and no one could say when or even if help could be sent. He gave them as full a report as he could. There were some medicines in the trading

shack that hadn't been ruined, and Jimmy was able to add a little from his own small store. Broken arms and legs were mended but one woman was too badly smashed up to live more than a few days.

It was a week before a government motor launch came in, making a round of the islands that had been hurt most badly. They told him that it had been the worst storm in thirty years but didn't have much to offer except condolences, and didn't do much except make an assessment for some report or other. It was two more weeks before a trading vessel got to them with needed supplies. In the meanwhile they ate fish. When Jimmy finally was able to buy some coffee and make himself a pot he said with a deep sigh that life could hold nothing better and all else was illusion.

"Even me?" Tommy asked.

"Especially you," Jimmy replied. "You're delightful, but not coffee. That is heaven." The boy shrieked and jumped on him.

After rebuilding their hut then helping in the village where they were needed, the next order of business was the boat, lying on its side with ripped-off palm fronds scattered over it. Jimmy went over the exterior of the hull carefully, and miraculously found nothing sprung or split. Below-deck was a jumble of soaked wreckage but with proper drying and sorting-out most was salvageable. By the end of the week they had it floating again in the lagoon, re-caulked where needed, and the mast stepped. After the canvas was refitted Tommy insisted they go to their island to see if there was anything left. Jimmy warned him not to expect much but he had to see for himself.

The first thing Tommy did after they left the lagoon was take his clothes off, then prance around in relief. Jimmy grinned then did the same. The day's sail was uneventful on a sea like a green mirror, which is just as well, because they spent nearly all the time chewing on each other.

Even with careful shooting and calculation Jimmy almost missed Come Island. If it weren't for Tommy's sharp eyes spotting the surf breaking on the reef he would have sailed right by. The island was only a few feet above sea-level anyway, and with every palm ripped off it was almost invisible. They made it into the lagoon without any trouble and

anchored.

When they got to shore it was an even sadder sight. Most of what little soil there had been was gone as well, leaving mainly bare coral. The heavy seas had scoured it from end to end. Tommy knew what to expect but Jimmy felt the boy's hand take his own and grip it tightly anyway.

"It will all come back one day," he told him.

"Not for long time," the boy said, then sighed sadly. "This was our place."

"It still is," Jimmy said. "Just close your eyes and remember."

Except for memories, this chapter of their past was now closed. Tommy fished for their supper while Jimmy built a fire on the remains of the beach.

When the sun set there were more stars than Jimmy had ever seen before in the newly cleansed sky. The boy sat close between his knees and they watched the fire die to embers, then they went back to the boat in a peaceful but very subdued mood. Sex was quiet and subdued as well, but nice. There was nothing at all to keep them there anymore so they sailed back the next day. Their hut actually looked good when they saw it. By the next morning

Tommy had recovered his high spirits and Jimmy understood that memories of the time spent so gloriously on their island were now stored away but not forgotten.

By the end of another week the fallen palms had been cut up and cleared and the school and trading shack had been reroofed with tin sheets brought in by trader. Jimmy tried to point out the dangers of those. When picked up by typhoon winds, the metal sheets became axe-blades, cutting anything in their path. There was no substitute except palm-fronds, however, and the villagers were too modernized to revert to that. Besides, he was still an outsider and a western one at that. He was thanked for his warning but it was waved aside. One who hadn't seen the island before wouldn't have guessed that it had been damaged at all. Jimmy and Tommy knew, however. It had been an extension of their own island, a temporary refuge during storm-season, and to stay there would remind them of that and little else. This time it didn't take any persuasion for Tommy to agree

to seek out an alternative, a permanent home, perhaps not theirs exclusively in this crowded part of the world, but as close as they could manage.

10

Jimmy thought that it was time for planning and time for a talk as well. At least time for him to talk, to think of their future, and to explain things as best he could, perhaps for his own sake more than for the boy's. Tommy listened attentively, trying to understand. Jimmy had a trading shack (business) across the Pacific which had done well enough for him to take a year off to look for Tommy, who he knew was out there somewhere. Now that he had found him he wasn't going back. He would have to arrange for the shack (factory) to be sold and the money sent to him because the money he had brought with him would only last a little longer. There would be no fuel for the boat, no engine repairs, no new sails when they were needed, and no single-malt for them to sip slowly in front of a fire. The money from the sale, then, was needed. If they were careful it would last them a long time. What they had to do right away was get to a city where there were banks and communications. He could cable instructions for sale, then they would have to wait for the results. Between times they could search for a new home.

To Jimmy, the wonderful thing about going through even those sketchy details was that Tommy kept nodding in agreement, taking what he said quite for granted. They were indivisible now and the possibility of Jimmy's leaving him to go back across the sea simply had never entered the boy's head. The matter of money was one he understood in his mind, but emotionally it was beyond him. No one starved in this part of the world, not fishermen with a boat anyway. He understood very well the necessity of keeping the boat operational but that really was as far as it went. Jimmy, fish, and the boat, in that order, was all that was really required in his life. Whatever else was needed to do he would do it, if he could, and if he couldn't

than Jimmy could. His feeling of security was firm and his faith in Jimmy absolute. It was completely naive and touchingly innocent, and Jimmy was going to say nothing more about it.

In any other part of the world, even to attempt a relationship of such intensity with a boy so primitive would have proved either a disaster or a soap-bubble of fantasy. Here and now, however, it seemed entirely possible that he might continue to live as he had been living, poor but enriched, continually excited and just as continually satisfied. He had his own boy truly captive now, in bonds much stronger than any wire could possibly have provided, and Tommy had him captive as well. Utterly.

He pulled the lithe little body to him to inhale its odors, feel its textures, then dine on it, very slowly. Tommy knew how completely he was desired and the intensity of it always made him weak. He surrendered himself with closed eyes and a beatific smile on his face. After supper it was Jimmy's turn. The boy raised his behind to accept him, and Jimmy stayed in him for a long time, hardly moving, so that they could remained joined together like one being as long as possible. Tommy kept pressed tightly against his groin to get every fraction of an inch as Jimmy caressed his body.

Then Jimmy sensed that something had changed from one moment to the next. He didn't try to analyze it but simply reacted to it. He started thrusting more strongly, then bounced wildly on the little butt, riding him harder than he had ever done as Tommy wiggled and gasped under him. The sharp smack of his belly hitting Tommy's buns echoed so loudly that he thought the whole world must know he was fucking his boy, who had the prettiest and hottest ass God ever made. Beneath him Tommy grunted hard, pushing up, wanting it all and taking it.

This was the magic moment. They had done it just enough so that for the first time the boy was able really to open up for him and he seemed almost to suck Jimmy into him. They had screwed a great deal but never like this. Jimmy understood from Tommy's reaction that the days of having to be careful were over. He rode him in the bunk, then out of it, on the deck and on the table, everywhere and in every position, screwing

his little round behind harder than he had ever taken anything. At first Tommy was a willing moaning limp rag in his arms, then an eager panting wildcat, then a maniac, screeching, scratching and clawing and pulling him in. On the deck, finally, as the boy moaned with an intense gargling sound and had his fifth orgasm, Jimmyshouted, then came again so violently and intensely that it was actually painful. He thought his balls were coming out of the head of his cock.

"Ooooh Chimmy!" the boy croaked, trembling hard, then fainted his arms. They were drenched with sweat. He held the little body tight and passed out.

When he came awake later they were still in each other's arms and the boy was snoring lightly against him. Jimmy was lost in wonder for a moment, then somehow he found the strength to pick him up and carry him to the bunk. In sleep, Tommy's arms came around him again and he slept as well.

Jimmy woke late in the morning, still partly stunned. He just lay holding his boy for a while, then woke him.

"Holy goddamn!" Tommy complained, touching his behind very carefully. "What happened last night?"

"All of a sudden I knew you were ready. I guess it drove me nuts."

"You didn't tell me it could be like that," the boy said, his deep black eyes wide.

"I never knew," Jimmy said in amazement.

He wondered what it was that he had ever seen in virgins.

It took another whole day before they recovered. By that time everything was aboard the boat again and they were on their way. Pandang in the Celebes was several days' sail distant. There was a little bad weather but after experiencing that typhoon little could bother them that didn't seem actually deadly.

They spent two days at sea before Tommy was ready to give himself again the way he had so suddenly and so marvellously. Jimmy was careful not to push him. That kind of sex required such a complete submersion that Tommy had to recognize in himself if and when he wanted it like that, to be set off like a skyrocket.

A few days later they lay together quietly, moving slowly,

enjoying their union with caresses. After an hour Tommy became increasingly sensitized and began to pant, then Jimmy recognized the sign. Without any other signal the boy began to open up and grasp him, there was no other word for it. From being a wonderful, eager but essentially passive fuck, Tommy began to toss and sweat, then started to grunt like an animal, holding him tight. Jimmy could feel fingernails in his back. The boy began to wiggle and rock, meeting his thrusts, then the balloon went up and he remembered little after that.

Orgasm seemed only a portion of a total experience which continued to grow. He barely remembered throwing the boy's body everywhere. If it had been physically possible he would have crawled into the kid on his hands and knees. It seemed he tried, or at least Tommy begged him to, or that's what he thought he heard the boy scream to him across waves of pounding blood.

"Chimmy! Chimmy!" the boy shrieked in one orgasm after another.

Then he felt what seemed like molten lead being sucked out of his cock. When there was no more left then he simply fell over. They lay in a pool of sweat and come and the boy was insensible in his arms.

The sea was calm that night and there was only a mild breeze. If there had been anything more dangerous then neither of them could have done anything to help themselves. It was late before either of them could stir, and separating from the sticky boy was like peeling free from glue. Somehow he got on his feet to make coffee. While it was perking he stuck his head out of the hatch and recognized numbly that all was well, or more accurately that they hadn't sunk during the night. He poured two mugs then sat on the bunk, handing one to Tommy. Only after several refreshing sips could he even speak.

"If we were trying to fuck ourselves to death, we almost made it," he croaked, then took another sip. "How's your ass?"

"What ass," the boy moaned.

They finished their coffee in silence. Jimmy put the mugs on the deck then simply fell in next to Tommy. They wrapped together and then slept some more.

It was the scraping and rattling of the mugs as they slid back and forth on the deck that woke him later. With an effort he got Tommy up and they staggered topside to drop the mainsail, leaving only the jib. They washed each other off carefully as the bow ploughed into a choppy sea, then Tommy took the wheel while Jimmy went below again to get them something to eat and more coffee. It wasn't easy to handle the boat, eat, and hold each other tightly at the same time, but somehow they managed.

11

Finally they reached Pandang, where Jimmy dug out some clothes that weren't too badly wrinkled or stained with seawater. Tommy stayed with the boat, since he had no papers, while Jimmy went to open an account at the local branch of a Japanese bank and then make some phone calls. It took forever to get through and then there were some surprised noises at the other end but he finally convinced his partner that he was serious. After that he sent a confirming cable to make it legal.

They remained in harbor for two days until the return cable came in with the balance of Jimmy's bank account at home plus a draft for the agreed-upon sale amount. They sat together for several hours to work out as best they could the supplies and equipment they might need. The boy could read now, although very slowly, which was a help. Orders were placed with suppliers at the docks, then there was nothing more to do except decide where they should start looking. They laid out the charts one by one.

"Here is one possibility," Jimmy said, pointing to a spot off Celebes, and he explained that he had spent a week in the area exploring as well as sampling the delights of the local village. "A day's sail north of Pandang. A small dead volcano, lush soil but too rugged for farming. Lots of coves but only a couple of good anchorages. One village of fishermen who didn't seem to bring back many fish, probably because they were too busy screwing."

"Boys good?" Tommy asked with a smile.

"Not compared with you," Jimmy said, "but there were a lot of them." He licked the tip of the boy's nose. "You can fuck yourself blind if you want to, though. Then there's this place," he added, pointing out a group of small islands. "Two villages on this one, one at either end, with some hills in between. Rice farmers mainly. Less rugged and spectacular but more highly developed. Two days' sail south of Pandang, three days east of Bali, yet off the shipping lanes."

Tommy wrinkled his nose at that one. Rice farmers were a pretty dull lot, in his estimation. It was agreed that they would try the one-volcano one-village island first as more likely to have an uninhabited stretch of beach for them. It wasn't a coral atoll and therefore would have no lagoon, so they would have to wait and see what the catch would be like.

"Volcano island is closest," Tommy said. "We can have our place sooner." His hand slipped down to Jimmy's crotch.

"You drive me crazy," Jimmy said with a groan.

"I know," Tommy replied with a grin. "Lie down. Tommy's going to send you out of your big beautiful blond mind." He did.

Three days later, with a heavy cargo of stores and supplies aboard, they sailed north. Just after dawn the morning after that, a blue-green mountain rose out of the water ahead. A few hours later they were coasting slowly along a shore where heavy foliage came down steeply to rocks right at the water's edge. The island had none of the appearance associated with atolls and coral reefs, and even looked forbidding. Just as Jimmy had remembered, there were numerous coves, and in these they saw bits of sandy beach. None was good enough for an anchorage, however, so they didn't stop. An occasional stream could be seen as well. There would be no lack of water here.

Then, suddenly, the wall of trees ended as they rounded a headland, and a small bowl-shaped bay lay before them, a narrow rocky entrance providing protection. Tommy had been standing by the lines so the sail came down quickly and Jimmy started the engine. As he had before at Come Island, Tommy took soundings as they entered and found that the lead didn't touch bottom until they were within a stone's throw of the

shore, when it shelved up quickly to a shallow beach. Jimmy cut the engine and they dropped anchor. He went forward to join Tommy in the bow. Deeper in the trees there was a lot of racket from birds but right by the shore it was quiet.

"What do you think?" he asked.

The boy pointed out several things to him.

"Trees cut, see?" and he pointed to several places where the foliage seemed thinner than elsewhere. "Not recent, though. Lots of birds, no smoke." He pointed to starboard. "Old wharf, tumbled down now. People lived here, all right, but not for four, five years, maybe."

They got out the dingy and paddled to shore. An hour's exploration showed them that Tommy's deduction was correct. There was a good-sized clearing a few hundred yards from the water's edge, with broken remains of a few huts, a couple of families' worth at most. The remains were old, too, and low foliage of new growth was already thick between the trees. A small rock-filled creek bubbled.

"I like it," Jimmy said.

"Let me check the bay first," Tommy said, not convinced. "No lagoon, maybe no fish, either."

They got back in the dingy and paddled out. Tommy slipped over the side with hardly a splash and was down a couple of minutes. The first time he had done that, back at Come Island, Jimmy's heart had nearly stopped, but the boy was a superb swimmer. Then suddenly his head broke water and he flipped wet black hair out of his eyes.

"Some, but not much," he said. "No coral and too deep." Then he swam back and climbed in.

He referred to the elaborate food chain that a coral reef could support, from plankton up to edible fish. Without that chain of progressively larger fish the pickings would be much slimmer for a fisherman, which explained the lack of inhabitants even though the bay was a secure one.

"Enough, do you think?" Jimmy asked the expert.

"It means fishing longer," Tommy replied as they started to paddle back to the boat, "but the ones I saw were bigger, too. Want to try it a few days?"

"Let's," Jimmy said. "I want to sit with you by a fire on that beach tonight."

"And get a poor boy drunk, too, I bet," Tommy said with a giggle. "How far away is that village?" he asked as they climbed aboard.

"About two hours' sail," Jimmy said. "Poor little boy indeed! You're the richest boy I've ever met."

"Rich?"

"You have treasure beyond price," Jimmy said, with a smile, but he meant it. "You have beauty and strength; you have the loveliest ass certainly in the South Pacific if not the world; and you have me. What else could any boy want?"

"That last thing most important," Tommy said softly, and drew him down.

They stayed at what Jimmy insisted calling Tommy Bay for three days, living on the boat but exploring much of the time. The more they saw then the more they liked it. Tommy was right about the fish, it did take longer to catch anything, and what they caught lacked the sweetness of lagoon fish but was firmer and more filling. The boy thought that was a fair enough exchange. On the fourth day they raised sail again and went down the coast to where Jimmy remembered the fishing village was located.

They were welcomed at the village, where visitors were few. All they saw were older men, women of all ages, and crowds of children. The old headman remembered him. Jimmy had hardly turned around to shake the man's hand before Tommy had vanished in hot pursuit of a giggling girl. Jimmy knew he wouldn't see him for a while, so he squatted and talked pidgin.

He took out the little flask he had brought with him and poured a single-malt, gravely offering it to the headman who sniffed it appreciatively then drank. To his credit only a few tears came to his eyes. Jimmy had one as well then offered him a cigarette which was just as gravely accepted. He asked about Tommy Bay, local health, how the men of the village were since he saw them a year ago, and a few names he remembered. The headman told him that while not exactly prosperous, the village had been fortunate. Not too many had died and many of those who had been born had lived. The last fishing voyage had been reasonable. A good year. No, there was no claim on Tommy Bay because no fish. No fish anywhere around here, which is

why the village boat stayed out nine months instead of the usual six. Jimmy explained that he and his boy would be living at Tommy Bay now, if the headman gave his permission, and that they would visit from time to time to share news, a sip of whisky, and a cigarette. He had some plans which he would like the headman to consider one day, when he was not too busy. The headman nodded graciously.

By that time Tommy had wandered back, looking a little dishevelled but with a self-satisfied smirk on his face. They squatted with the headman's family and ate freshly boiled rice with bits of smoked fish, which for Tommy was a real treat, then small-talked for a while to show their thanks at the courtesy. They left in time to get back to Tommy Bay before dark and were hardly on board before Tommy burst.

"Fucked three!" he hissed in a suppressed shriek. "Not one was a virgin," he said in amazement. "They wouldn't let me loose!" Jimmy visualized a pack of rapacious scowling adolescent girls surrounding a fearful and trembling Tommy until he agreed to mount them all. It broke him up.

"This is some village, let me tell you," Tommy said, "if fourteen-year-old girls are used to taking it."

"Probably by excessively horny twenty-one-year-old sex-fiends," Jimmy said wryly. They had celebrated the boy's birthday a month ago.

"Excessively?" Tommy asked, raising his eyebrows and coming close.

"Wonderfully," Jimmy amended with a grin.

"Are they as bad as thirty-five-year-old sex-fiends who wear a boy out?" and he rubbed against him.

"No, the older ones are even worse, everybody knows that," Jimmy confessed solemnly, "and some boys never wear out, thank God."

"Sex is a curse," Tommy moaned as Jimmy nibbled and felt him.

"It's a blessing and you know it," Jimmy disagreed.

"Is a finger all I get?" the boy complained.

Jimmy pushed him down as the boy sighed.

"You're going to stick it in me again, I bet."

"You guessed it," Jimmy said.

Tommy groaned happily and pulled him in.

12

One evening after supper, as they sat in front of the fire, Jimmy introduced the idea that had come to him.

"We have some money coming in," he told him, "and we don't spend much anyway, but there will be a problem next year."

"Like what?" Tommy asked.

"The boat is a good one but it's old. Next year it will have to have a major refit if not be mostly rebuilt. There goes our money. But I have an idea."

"We can always sell fish," the boy said.

"It's going to cost more fish than we could catch," Jimmy said.

"Sell my ass, then," the boy giggled.

"Not on your life," Jimmy said with a dark frown, and smacked his bottom.

"Ouch! I dare you to do that again!"

Jimmy grinned and gave him a couple of spanks as the boy shrieked. This was a game they played frequently. Sometimes Jimmy wondered whether the boy wanted more than a few spanks but he never pursued it.

"Shut up and listen, now," he said, pulling the slim body to him and giving it a bite. "Tourists. Back home there are always ads in special papers for all-male tours to exotic places. We could advertise in them too, and offer a lot more than cocktails and a little moonlight. Think of the effect just this one village would have on a couple of repressed and horny young executives who don't find more than one hot boy a month, for example."

"You mean bring in western men for sex? Then get paid for it?"

"Something like that," Jimmy said. "Send them back tanned, full of fish, and very tired. Word would get around so fast we'd have them lined up, panting. We'd charge a reasonable fee, something guys like that can afford after flying all the way out here. The amount wouldn't be much for them

but it would keep us in style in a place like this." As he developed his idea he got more enthusiastic. "There are hundred big cities on the Pacific-rim and each must have at least a dozen guys — maybe a hundred — who'd pay a lot for a full week of non-stop screwing. And not just westerners, either. Japanese, Hong Kong and Singapore hot-shots, too. Hundreds. No, thousands. Plane-loads, boat-loads!" He laughed and Tommy grinned in excitement. "We pick them up at Pandang, run them in and dump them at the village for their week's sex-fest, then run back and bring in two more." The boy's jaw dropped. "Not all the time," he hastened to explain, "only three months a year, when the fishermen are home. The men spend part of their time making more babies, as usual, then they screw our guests or let their boys get screwed. They'd love it."

That was a lot for the boy to think about and they had to discuss it again to see if they could discover any problems they hadn't thought of. They would have to spend a lot of time at sea, running customers back and forth, but that wouldn't be entirely disagreeable. The boy was reluctant about the name Jimmy wanted, but he was insistent. "Tommy Tours" was founded over a glass of single-malt, licks and kisses, then they hunched over the table to work out their ad. A lot of drafts were added to the pile of discards on the floor, but finally Jimmy had something he thought straightforward enough to do the job — a kind of reverse-advertising. It would for him, anyway.

"How about this?" he asked, then read it aloud.

Tommy Bay, Celebes
No pool, no sauna, no gourmet restaurant, no disco, no plumbing, no television, no tennis, no golf. To be frank, no nothing — except grass-huts and horny males. You better like fish. If you don't then bring your own food.
110 native men 18-and-up, hot enough to jump you twice daily. Bring lots of condoms. Tell us where to send your ravaged body. 97 hot juicy boys for you to jump. Admire their natural grace or fuck yourself stupid. No replacement parts supplied. Sorry, no virgins for 500 miles. Not any over 10, anyway.
Romance? Oh yes. Private huts for honeymooners. Unspoiled

beach. A million stars. Telex Tommytour.

They had to consult the villagers since they were crucial to the success of the plan. The proposal met with shouts, smiles, and clapped hands. The young men in particular, flushed with the ripeness of their virility, were charmed by the picture painted for them by Jimmy of numberless eager round-eye butts, and several swore to screw them all.

It was all pie-in-the-sky, of course, but remarkably enough that was exactly how it turned out. Jimmy discovered that the fee for Tommy Tours didn't have to be reasonable, either. The ad worked like a charm. From enthusiastic replies received there seemed to be an unlimited supply of well-off men with a passion to take on a whole village of horny fishermen, while others wanted to sample native boys. They went to Pandang to get some better and appropriate clothes so that they looked more like sailors and businessmen instead of beach-bums. In a tank-top and a pair of brief white shorts, Tommy looked so spectacular and radiated his intense sexuality so strongly that Jimmy sucked in his breath. The boy was enough to stop traffic. Even the salesman paled.

Once their guests actually started arriving the only problem Jimmy had with some was keeping their hot paws off Tommy, at least part of the time. The others wanted him instead, or both. A few times they obliged but usually not. There was one especially nice pair of New Zealanders, one quiet, tall, and handsome and the other vivacious, short, and pretty, who made charming company. Peter, the short and pretty one, completely dominated George, his bigger friend, which Jimmy thought amusing. They were content to swim, talk, eat fish, and drink quantities of scotch. They couldn't keep their hands off each other. In addition to being pretty, Peter was hung and George couldn't seem to get enough of it. Little vivacious Peter lusted so much for George's behind that he seemed always to be on him. Tommy enjoyed watching them, then would want Jimmy to do the same to him as they lay a few feet away.

Although interested mainly in each other, both of the young men admired them and teased them shamelessly.

"A beautiful ideal couple," Peter said. "Wherever did you

find this wonderful boy?"

"Fished him out of the sea one day," Jimmy said casually.

"Any more where he came from?"

"No," Jimmy said, catching Tommy's eye. "He's the only one in the world."

The boy turned pink and gave him a little smile. The inevitable happened and the four of them ended in a wild tangle of arms and legs.

"This boy's ass almost makes me believe in God," Peter sighed.

"Amen, brother," Jimmy agreed.

13

During the three-month season the handsomest and best-built of the local fishermen increased their annual incomes ten times from generous tips, although they had to hump their balls off for it. The boys got exceedingly well plugged by big westerners, and the grown men wore themselves out trying to satiate the insatiable. All tips went into the communal pot and so all got something. The villagers were so grateful for the unexpected wealth that one day they all showed up to build Jimmy and Tommy a proper house instead of a palm shack, then everyone got roaring drunk and had a marvellous dancing, shouting, singing, screwing time.

By the end of the first season Jimmy and Tommy realized that while they weren't going to get rich they would be very well off. They could easily run a half-dozen such boats if they wanted to, hitting one fishing village after another until all the men for a hundred miles around were employed, but decided not. A full-time business of catering to butt-humping was not what they wanted, no matter how much money was in it. Even three months was a strain, in spite of its exciting moments. The fishermen had done so well that they didn't need to go to sea for the usual nine months. Not all the men and boys needed to go out and then six months was enough to provide the little additional income the village needed. Jimmy and Tommy kept

the extra villagers busy making more guest huts at Tommy Bay, then helped them improve the village itself. While the villagers were doing that Jimmy and Tommy moved to Pandang for several months while the boat got its needed refit, new sails and a new engine. They returned to Tommy Bay with sighs of relief for six months of peace and each other.

While Tommy was fishing one afternoon, Jimmy sat on deck, watching him, as he did frequently, but this time he noted with surprise how much the boy had matured in the last two years. At twenty-two, Tommy had visibly changed. His lovely butt had become like a beautiful ripe peach begging to be caressed. The button hidden between the full cheeks had grown to something much more substantial. Tommy was still sufficiently young that his body and skin were fully elastic, and because of that it looked only slightly larger than normal. It wasn't normal, however, and would grasp him like a hungry mouth.

The changes in Tommy were so gradual that Jimmy had to make an attempt to remember what his boy had once been like when he first saw him. Obviously their relationship fulfilled him the same way it did Jimmy. He had gotten so used to taking Jimmy in him twice a day that, like a drug, he had to have it. Jimmy felt the same about the boy's beautiful small body. All Tommy had to was to touch him a certain way or look at him from under lowered lashes and he throbbed. It was the "eat me all over until I die" look that got him the most. Jimmy had only one look in reply, "come here," but that seemed enough.

There were trips to the village to be made on a regular basis so that Tommy could play around with the village girls. None of them had gotten before the kind of wiggling and acrobatic screwing that Tommy provided for them and they were suitably impressed. Jimmy wasn't so possessive that he couldn't recognize what these exercises really were. Tommy needed to keep from feeling no more than some man's bit of stuff, no matter how well beloved. Although they had developed some versatility, Tommy really preferred their sex-life to remain as it had always had been, which was fine with Jimmy. The boy was fully masculine in manner and never thought of himself as

solely a man's piece of stuff anyway, and their relationship was the richer for it.

Tommy grew fluent in idiomatic English, so much so that it seemed he had forgotten his native tongue entirely. Yet, in intensely passionate moments, he would still moan "Chimmy!" Their tourist guests mistook him for an American-born Vietnamese, which pleased him considerably. His reading ability improved, and Jimmy started buying what English-language books he could find for him on each trip to Pandang, teaching him what he knew but letting him discover things for himself as well.

Tommy was highly intelligent and one of Jimmy's fears was that his mind and interests would grow so much that he would be attracted to town life and get bored with their small and private world. The possibility that he might grow sufficiently to drift away was a part of that fear. He suppressed it as best he could and took him on frequent sailing trips to help ease what boredom he thought the boy might feel. He began to sense a restlessness hard to put his finger on, which bothered him even more, until one day Tommy resolved it all as they sailed back into the bay to drop anchor after a long trip to Bali.

"We spend too much time away from home," the boy said flatly.

He pulled off all his fancy clothes, flexed his trim body to enjoy its freedom, and that was that. Jimmy felt a load lift from his shoulders. He picked the naked boy up, threw him over his shoulder, and carried him giggling and screaming into the house where he threw him on the bed. And that's where they stayed until they got so hungry they had to get up.

"Mmmmmmm, you're wonderful," the boy sighed with a luxurious and fully satisfied stretch.

"I know. I don't know how you stand it," Jimmy said with a grin.

Tommy hit him with the pillow then pulled him back down.

"Me too, huh?" the boy asked.

"One side of a coin doesn't have to ask the other side how much it's worth," Jimmy said, then he licked his nose and kissed him.

"A coin, huh? Well, you can make a fortune betting with

me," the boy giggled. "No matter how you throw me up I always come down tails."

Then Jimmy grabbed him and rolled laughing with him all over the bed.

One thing Jimmy had forgotten briefly was that Tommy remained basically what he was at first, a Vietnamese village boy. He was considerably more knowledgeable now, but his basic needs had been formed before he wriggled over the side of Jimmy's boat. They were not isolated at Tommy Bay. The tourist business and their connection with the native inhabitants gave the boy in fact a much greater social outlet than he ever would have had in his home village. Tourists, in particular, and the society they represented, almost overloaded his mind. Other boys might have gotten glib and superficially urbanized by that pressure alone, but Tommy knew that it wasn't for him. He didn't reject it as much as he simply ignored it. What didn't serve the two of them together didn't have any worthwhile purpose for him.

Not all the time the boy spent in the village was spent chasing girls. Much of it was spent simply reacquainting himself with a way of life similar to his own roots. He even learned the local dialect. The fact that Jimmy was able to bend with his needs also helped, something which Tommy slowly became aware of, recognized as unusual, and was grateful for. The balance that was struck satisfied them both. Jimmy didn't "go native" so much as he went Tommy. The boy was flexible but there were distinct limits which Jimmy had recognized early and never tried to exceed. When he had accepted the boy's surrender that time on the boat he knew then that he was taking on a responsibility and commitment greater than a sexual partnership. He had never regretted it. Nor had Tommy regretted surrendering.

The youth sulked moodily from time to time, as boys will, and they had their arguments like any two people anywhere. Jimmy was not immune either. In spite of momentary irritations, the one thing which helped to carry them through any difficult spot was the unspoken but mutually understood necessity never to say no. Jimmy was available wherever and whenever the boy wanted anything from him, and Tommy was the same. If the mood of one or the other was negative to start

then it changed at once the moment they went into each other's arms. Whatever the little storms on the surface, their trust in each other was absolute.

14

Generally, they were fortunate in the kinds of tourists they attracted. The trip to their island was a long and expensive one even from places relatively close, like Singapore. As a result, guests tended not to be frivolous one-nighters out for a good time for the weekend at the local beach, although there were many who were sex-mad and made no bones about it. Two hundred available village men and boys was a challenge for some, and they did their utmost to get through them all before dragging their ravaged bodies back to their homes.

While the village and the attractions of its inhabitants remained the principal drawing card, Tommy Bay and its isolated peace attracted others. They had seen to it that the guest huts were constructed away from the main house to provide exactly that peace, both for guests and themselves. During the first season only half were occupied, but after that Jimmy had to set up a waiting-list. The more distant huts were taken by new lovers or sometimes men who simply liked the atmosphere of the place even though they had to live primitively. Even the primitiveness itself was a restorative to others, being a far-cry from the hustle and bustle of their usual lives. Only once was there an annoying problem: an obstinate and obsessive man insisted on trying to treat Tommy like a whore even though he knew better. Insisted, that is, until Jimmy put a hand around his neck and pinned him to the wall until he turned blue. He left the next day.

One event they thought might develop into something serious turned into a farce instead. Off-season they were relatively alone. Relatively, because villagers were always around in their twos and threes, or sometimes more. One afternoon someone called out and Jimmy went out of the house to see a small government motor-patrol come into Tommy Bay. It turned out to be from Pandang on a routine mission around the coastal villages and Celebes islands. There were so many that it took them months to make the complete circuit and this

was the first time they knew anyone was living in Tommy Bay again.

A slim, very formal and stiffly starched young officer came ashore with a quiet stocky sailor. He asked a number of unnecessary questions just to show his authority and found fault with everything. Jimmy had taken care to get a licence for his tourist operation but even that was examined with suspicion. In spite of the man's manner, Jimmy was perfectly civil, even to the point of insisting that they both have dinner with them and stay the night in comfortable beds. The sailor seemed willing but it was for his superior to decide. The young man took the offer as his due and they stayed. The dinner was very informal, but even then it passed a little stiffly as the pair slowly became aware of the relationship they had stumbled upon. The sailor seemed to take it in his stride but the officer was nervous and red-faced by the time they retired.

Jimmy's revenge was modest: he arranged for a surprise. He sent one of the village lads back to gather reinforcements, and by the time the two visitors were ready to crawl into their separate beds they found themselves suddenly smothered in boys. The house was solid but it wasn't sound-proof. Jimmy and Tommy sat on their bed holding each other and laughing as they heard grunts of surprise from the sailor, then outraged shouts from the officer and giggling shrieks from the boys, all followed by the scampering of bare feet, gasps, more shouts, though not as loud, then sighs and groans. It went on for some time.

Jimmy's instructions had been specific. As much as two grown young men could be held down by young lads, they were. Jimmy had made a shrewd guess then crossed his fingers, hoping he was right. The stocky masculine sailor was to be sat on by a half-dozen of the more wiggly boys. They weren't to stop until there was nothing hard to sit on any more. The high-strung young officer, on the other hand, was to be thoroughly and lengthily buggered by older lads. Before the assault-teams ran back to the village they reported in with grins, the sailor group holding up four fingers, the officer group five.

A tired, shifty-eyed, and very disconcerted young officer joined them for breakfast, suddenly all elbows and feet and not

knowing how to act after having been mounted so unexpectedly by so many. The muscular young sailor, on the other hand, couldn't stop grinning in satisfaction. Just before they left, the officer blushingly suggested that this part of the coast probably would require more careful observation in the future, then he looked alternately at the horizon and his polished shoes. Jimmy smiled and replied that close observation probably was exactly what was needed, since the local boys really were getting out of hand. The sailor nearly choked and the officer turned pink. Behind the man's back, Tommy managed to make a quick gesture to the sailor to indicate what had happened to him to make him act so strangely. The sailor's mouth dropped open then he snapped it shut again. The pair returned to their boat and sailed out of Tommy Bay without even a wave. Jimmy suspected they were both in shock and didn't blame them.

They did in fact run into the pair at Pandang later and became friends. It turned out that both had been interested in each other from the beginning but the difference in rank had inhibited any familiarity. After their adventure at Tommy Bay the tension between them grew until they could barely stand it, the sailor growling and the officer snapping.

Then one night the sailor came back drunk, determined now to get what he had wanted from the beginning. He knocked his young officer to the deck, yanked his pants down, then jumped on him. He bit the back of his neck, whispering how much he had always wanted him, then rammed himself into him hard and fast as the officer moaned half-hearted protests under him. Even after coming the sailor was still so hot for his victim that he stripped him naked and beat him. That made the shocked officer shriek, then to both their surprises it made him come like a fountain. Having his strong young sailor rape him then work him over so roughly turned out to be exactly what the young officer had been waiting for.

After that violent explosion their roles were redefined and they were perfectly happy. They visited Tommy Bay again, but this time it was the sailor who ordered his officer around. Like some other arrogant men Jimmy had met, the slim officer really had been waiting for someone to slap him down. Now that he had found the one to do it he loved it and wasn't embarrassed in the slightest. In the privacy of Tommy Bay his favorite

position was at his sailor's feet with his head in his lap, being petted. It was a classic sado-masochistic relationship, but it seemed to suit them both perfectly. Each night they would go off to their private hut, make quite a bit of noise, then reappear in the morning exhausted but content, the officer proudly displaying fresh bruises. It was extremely odd, Jimmy and Tommy agreed, but charming.

"They're almost as lucky as we are," Tommy said.

"Almost, but not quite," Jimmy replied, then kissed him.

Slowly the inevitable happened and the character of Tommy Bay changed. From one season to the next this couple or that would stay longer than usual. Some guest huts were rebuilt into permanent houses. A few who returned each season stayed longer and longer, then remained permanently. Before anyone was really aware of it Tommy Bay had grown into a fixed settlement. Trading ships began to call on a regular basis. Advertising had ceased to be necessary and word-of-mouth had taken its place. During the season it was much like the old days, but after that a village-like atmosphere prevailed. The change progressed slowly enough so that they got used to it then came to prefer it that way. While for the most part bare-bones primitiveness evaporated, simplicity remained. Jimmy's fear that Tommy would drift away because of the appeal of the wider world evaporated as well because the wider world came to the island, though in miniature and in a limited fashion.

Tommy continued to grow and change as well. By twenty-six he had a voracious appetite and what seemed like an inexhaustible capacity. His innocent love of sexual play changed. Jimmy tried to keep him satisfied in the usual ways but Tommy developed an intense desire for girls. Jimmy tried not to be jealous and almost succeeded.

The attitudes of the villagers changed slowly. The first several seasons were simply fun. That glow wore off slowly and restlessness was apparent. The village no longer had to depend on month after month of hard work combing distant seas, yet there still wasn't enough resource for the fishermen to do anything else. It occurred to one, then others, that even though they were enjoying themselves all they really had was half a fisherman's life and half that of an island whorehouse.

The permanent residents of Tommy Bay recognized that almost as soon as the villagers did and decided to do something about it. Their contributions, plus discussions with local government and banks, raised sufficient capital to buy the villagers a pair of modern fishing craft, modest in size yet sufficient for their needs. That changed matters entirely and they became exporters with a renewed sense of self-respect and importance. Had not their fisherman bonding been so ancient a tradition the new life might have changed sexual attitudes as well. In fact little actually changed. The girls Tommy used to play with grew to women with proper husbands and families of their own. The little boys had grown-up as well, proud of their virility and eager to display it to tourists.

Since relatively few were needed to man the modern fishing craft, the men and boys found themselves missing the communal sex-barge more than they had thought. That was relieved by encouraging them to use the shelters at Tommy Bay. As a consequence the sexual atmosphere remained noticeably strong.

At thirty, Tommy had ripened into a man so sexually magnetic that he made heads turn wherever he went. When dressed, he was attractive enough, but when naked he took the breath away. His body would always remain that of a slim Vietnamese, but what dangled between his legs would have done credit to a decently-hung westerner and seemed very large on his small frame. Behind, Jimmy's persistent efforts had truly opened him up. He never got as large as monkey-boy, but it was so much bigger than average that there was no pleasure they couldn't attempt and it couldn't appreciate.

Tommy was vain enough to relish the impression he made on others, although his stability of character enabled him to enjoy it all yet not forget the things which long ago he had decided were truly critical in his life: Jimmy, fish, and the boat. As for Jimmy, he could take fish or leave it, enjoy the boat or forget it, but Tommy was the foundation on which his life now rested.

On their tenth anniversary, Jimmy took him back to Come Island, now regrown, and they sat on the beach together at dusk before a fire, eating fish from the lagoon and drinking

single-malt.

"You taught me everything," the boy - now quite the man - told him, poking the fire with a stick.

"And you taught me everything, too."

"I never talked about love, though," Tommy said softly. "I kept meaning to."

"You never had to," Jimmy sighed. "I've always known."

They lay in each other's arms and watched the stars.

...And so we dress, undress ourselves,
make love and share our flesh
in the semblance of gods –
hoping that our passion
will exceed all human rules;
hoping that our fever
will be tempered by no storm;
hoping that our own legend
will be made tonight;
and that tomorrow
some god
somewhere
(perhaps the one
we now hold in our arms)
will remember us forever.

- *From "Immortality Comes"*
by Ed SantaVicca

CONTRIBUTORS
(Other Than the Editor, John Patrick)

"Someone Bought the House on the Island"
Ken Anderson
The author lives in Georgia and is a frequent contributor to *Iris*, the gay literary magazine. The story herein is an excerpt from Ken's forthcoming novel.

"What God Likes to Watch"
Antler
The poet, from Milwaukee, makes his living solely from giving readings from his books, including *Factory*, published by City Lights, and *Last Words*, published by Ballantine.

Winner of the Walt Whitman Award from the Walt Whitman Society of Camden, New Jersey, and the Wittner Bynner prize from the American Academy and Institute of Arts & Letters in New York, his poetry has appeared in many anthologies, including *Gay Roots* and *Men of Our Time*.

"The Paperboy"
Edward Bangor
The author, an Englishman, is a frequent contributor to the anthologies of Acolyte Press. Under the name of Headbanger, he contributed a piece for the fourth issue of the American gay comic book *Cherubino*. Several of his stories are slated to appear in upcoming STARbooks' anthologies.

"Ethan's Apology"
David Patrick Beavers
The author's first novel, *Jackal in the Dark*, about Los Angeles in the '70s, was recently published by Millivres Books, London. The sequel has recently been published. David lives in Los Angeles.

"Virgin Youth"
Lawrence Benjamin
The author lives in Philadelphia where, when not dodging hostilities, he is at work on a novel. Several of his short tales have appeared in STARbooks' anthologies.

"Breaking and Entering"
Greg Bowden
The author, who lives in California, has contributed many stories to magazines such as *Advocate Men, Honcho, Stallion,* and *Guys.* This the first of many of his stories slated to appear in STARbooks' anthologies.

"Does This Mean I'm Gay?"
Leo Cardini
Former Mineshaft employee Leo is the author of the best-selling *Mineshaft Nights.* His theater-related articles have appeared in a variety of publications, he is co-author of a musical currently being capitalized for a Broadway production, and his fiction has appeared in previous STARbooks publications, as well as in *Freshmen, Firsthand, Guys* and *Manscape.*

"Where There's A Hill..."
Sherwin Carlquist
The author is an accomplished photographer, hailed by critics as "the Ansel Adams" of the male nude. His book of photographs, *Natural Man,* is an international sensation, and he is currently shooting stills for a sequel as well as preparing two books of his writing. Sherwin lives in California.

"The Boys of Paradise"
Harrison Chalfont
This novella originally appeared under another title in *The Gay Review,* Vol. I, No. 3; used with permission of the author.

"My First Cop"
William Cozad
The author is a regular contributor to gay magazines and a new novel in the form of a memoir will be included in *Lover*

Boys, to be published soon by STARbooks Press.

"Slender Forms"
Patrick Dome

Patrick lives in San Francisco where we works as a graphic designer and part time author. Other stories and articles have appeared in *In Touch, San Francisco Sentinel*, and the *Western Producer* in Canada. He is originally from Massachusetts but prefers the winters on the west coast.

"The Young and the Flawless"
John C. Douglas

The author has an enviable track record, having some thirty novels published, and more than twenty screenplays produced. A former Alabamian, now living in Florida, Douglas has a number of works in progress. "Most of the time," he admits, "I don't have a firm plot in mind. I prefer to create the characters and let them do whatever they like. Sometimes, they surprise even me!"

"Sheriff's Posse"
Dirk Hannam

A California-based writer, Dirk's work has appeared in many gay publications, including *In Touch* and *Guys*. He can attest to the fact that the fields and backwoods of America are amply populated with gays, "they are just more reclusive than city folk. There are few gay pride parades on country back roads."

"Keyboard Stud"
Thomas C. Humphrey

The author, who resides in Florida, is working on his first novel, *All the Difference*, and has contributed stories to First Hand publications.

"Burning Bridges"
David Laurents

The author is a regular contributor to such publications as *Honcho, Overload*, and *The Journal of Erotica* (UK) and has had stories included in the best-selling anthologies *Bizarre Dreams* and *Meltdown!* from BadBoy and *Wired Hard, Of Princes and*

Beauties, and *The Beast Within* from Circlet Press. He lives in New York City.

"Chained"
Bert McKenzie
A free lance writer and drama critic, the Kansan writes a column for a major midwestern newspaper and has contributed erotic fiction to magazines such as *Torso, Mandate,* and *Playguy.* He is a frequent contributor to STARbooks' anthologies and will soon have an anthology of his work published by Badboy.

"Boys In Search of Something To Do"
Thom Nickels
The Cliffs of Aries, the author's first novel, was published in 1988 by Aegina Press. His second book, *Two Novellas: Walking Water & After All This,* was published in 1989 by Banned Books and was a Lambda Literary Award finalist in 1990 in the Science Fiction/Fantasy category. A regular columnist for an alternative weekly in Philadelphia, Thom has contributed feature articles, book reviews and celebrity interviews to several gay publications. A collection of his best writing was published by STARbooks Press under the title, *The Boy on the Bicycle;* the book contains the complete novel, *Sizeable Quantities.*

"Night Out" and "Boy"
Edmund Miller
Edmund Miller, the author of the legendary poetry book *Fucking Animals* (recently reprinted by STARBooks Press), is the chairman of the English Department at a large university in the New York area. The story "Night Out" is reprinted from *Playguy* magazine where it was given the title "Real Men Suck Cock" by the editors, ruining the O. Henry ending. The poem "Boy" appears in *Fucking Animals.*

"The Boy Trap"
Peter Z. Pan
A first-generation American of Cuban descent, this twentysomething author calls himself a "quintessential jack-of-all-trades: multimedia writer, theatrical director, and sometime actor-singer." Peter says he resides in Miami,

"physically anyway." Spiritually, he says he will always live where Lost Boys forever frolic: "...second star to the right, and straight on till morning."

"First Porn"
Peter Reardon
A former camp counselor and trailer park resident, the author is an artist, photographer and writer whose work has appeared in many national and regional publications. He resides in Southwest Florida where he is working on an exhaustive historical study of sexual depravity. A musician, Peter plays many instruments and, in his spare time, especially enjoys playing the organ.

"A Family Affair"
Andrew Richardson
An Englishman, the author recently completed a degree in American Studies at university,concentrating his work mainly on the exploration of the gay movement in the U.S.A. He will soon begin studies to earn a Masters degree in sexual politics and "keep up the battle for people to have a brilliantly queer future – world-wide."

He says he combines flights of fancy and real experiences to inspire his writing.

OUT OF PRINT BOOKS NOW AVAILABLE AS SPECIALLY BOUND EDITIONS

The beautiful Tracy, playing with his cum after an orgasm, was one of John Patrick's unforgettable lovers and was one of the "Insatiable/Unforgettable" anthology coverboys. Tracy was the inspiration for John's classic "Angel" series.

Because of the great interest in our out-of-print collections, we can now offer a limited number as spiral bound printers' galley editions. Included in the selection are:

SEDUCED
COUNTRY BOYS, CITY BOYS
INSATIABLE/UNFORGETTABLE

Each book is $19.95 from STARbooks Press, P. O. Box 2737, Sarasota FL 34230-2737. Postpaid in U.S.A.; overseas shipments billed on credit card; please specify air or surface posting.

FEVER! IS NOW AVAILABLE

One of the hottest anthologies in recent times, *Fever!*, is now available at $14.95 at bookstores everywhere or from STARbooks Press, P. O. Box 2737, Sarasota FL 34230-2737. Postpaid in U.S.A.; overseas shipments billed on credit card; please specify air or surface posting.

ACKNOWLEDGEMENTS
AND SOURCES

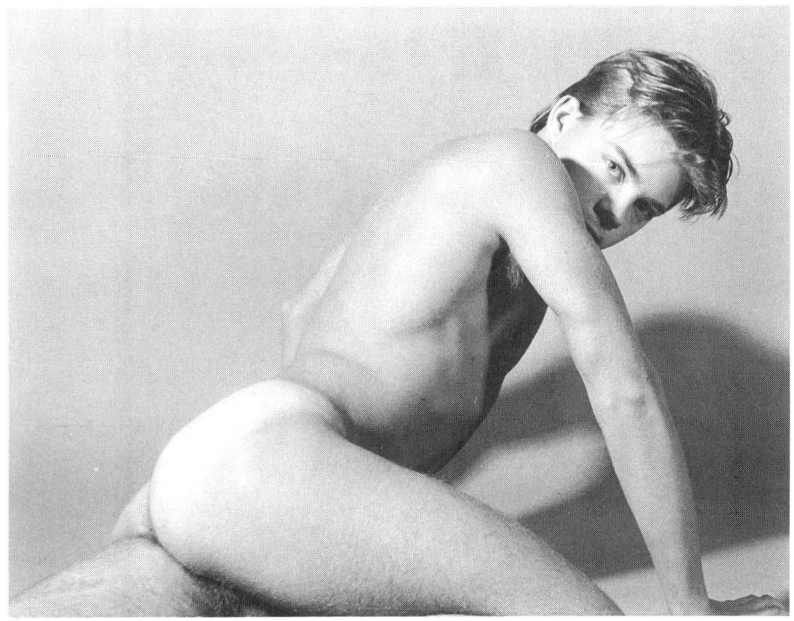

Our cover model Graham Reynolds was featured on the cover of Euroboy magazine's 1995 calendar and was fully exposed in Euroboy No. 10. Graham appears through the courtesy of the celebrated English photographer David Butt.

Mr. Butt's photographs may be purchased through Suntown, Post Office Box 151, Danbury, Oxfordshire, OX16 8GN, United Kingdom. Ask for a full catalogue.

ABOUT THE EDITOR

John Patrick is a prolific, prize-winning author of fiction and non-fiction. One of his short stories, "The Well," was honored by PEN American Center as one of the best of 1987. The author's acclaimed romans a´ clef, including "Angel: The Complete Quintet" and "Billy & David: A Deadly Minuet," have now been collected into a single volume. His novels as well as his non-fiction works, including "Legends," "Tarnished Angels," and "The Best of the Superstars" series, continue to gain him new fans every day. John is currently at work on the anthologies "Country Boys, City Boys," "My Three Boys," and "Boy Trouble."

A divorced father of two, the author is a longtime member of the American Booksellers Association, the Florida Publishers' Association, American Civil Liberties Union, and the Adult Video Association. He resides in Florida.